COLLAPSE

AFTER THE LAST DAY, BOOK ONE

BY

DON HAYWARD

This book is a work of fiction. Any resemblance to actual events or persons, living or dead, is entirely coincidental.

This book is a work of fiction. Any resemblance to actual events or persons, living or dead, is entirely coincidental.
Cover photo courtesy of jills at Pixabay.com

Also by Don Hayward

Under Shadows
After the Last day, Book Two
ISBN 978-1-7752459-4-0 (Soft cover)

The End of Shadows
After the Last Day, Book Three
ISBN 978-1-7752459-5-7 (Soft cover)

The Seventh Path
Follow on story to The End of Shadows
ISBN 978-1-62137-949-2 (Soft cover)

Journey's End
Sequel to The Seventh Path
ISBN: 978-1-7752459-3-3 (Soft cover)

Return
Science fiction sequel to Spielberg's Taken series
ISBN 978-1-7752459-7-1 (Soft cover)

Murder on the Goderich Local
ISBN 978-1-62137-993-5 (Soft cover)

Sherwood Green
ISBN 978-1-7752459-0-2 (Soft cover)

Echo of the Whip-poor-Will
ISBN 978-1-7752459-1-9 (Soft cover)

v

Contact Don with comments or to order paper books,

haywardon@gmail.com

https://www.danddhayward.ca/

I dedicate this book to my children and grandchildren as they enter an uncertain future.

Acknowledgement: To Alex, who read the manuscript and made suggestions for improvement.

To my wife Diane who patiently attempted to discover all of my technical errors, confusing text and provided many helpful suggestions.

All errors are the author's own.

Chapter One

Cold dampness seeped from the ground, penetrating deeply into Bill's body. The steel of his rifle drew heat from his hands. Prone on wet leaves saturated with the watery leavings of a harsh winter, he squinted through the naked brush where the odd, stubborn, twisted, brown leaf still clung to a branch. Details of a small clearing solidified in the early blue light of an April dawn.

Rivulets of grey smoke from a nearly dead fire rose into the calm morning air. A rough lean-to of poles and a blue tarp sheltered two adults. Another huddled beneath rude blankets near the fire. The sleepers had not bothered to post a sentry, and their ragtag appearance suggested this bunch was not likely skilled at fighting.

Matt Long and Stevie Hunter, the town constable, had tracked these butchers from Quinn's place where Matt had discovered the bodies. His description of the brutal deaths of Steve and Gail Quinn and their three kids cut deeply. Bill knew he looked at cold-blooded murderers undeserving of mercy.

The innocence of the sleeping forms did not reduce Bill's anger, but he did not want to feel any emotion. This job required deliberate action, and he dared not risk clouding it with hatred.

To his left, George Harvey, Stevie Hunter and Matt Long lay on the ground, clutching their rifles. Bob Spencer and Bill Simpson knelt to his right, alert, weapons ready; beyond them were the two Smith brothers and Willard Dick. Each group of three would take one suspect. Bill's group targeted the man by the fire.

Bill hoped they would subdue them quickly with no injuries. Anything serious might exceed the community's limited medical capabilities. An injury beyond a cut or scrape meant a painful recovery and probably disability. The community could not afford the loss of workers or the burden of supporting non-productive mouths. These realities had caused a heated debate last night. Some advocated killing these murderers outright. The lust for vigilantism almost defeated those, including Bill, who supported the rule-of-law.

Matt tapped his shoulder. Bill passed the signal down the line. As one, the nine men rose and rushed their targets. Surprise would make for an easier job.

"Oh," Bill gasped as a sapling struck his face.

"Shhh," Bob Spencer snarled.

Someone's foot broke a dead twig, and the loud report stirred the sleepers. The man by the fire rolled onto his right shoulder, just as the trio of deputies reached him. Spencer's boot heel struck the other shoulder, snapping the man back to his face down position. The man expelled a gasp as Simpson slammed a hardwood board across his legs and dropped hard on his knees, pinning the legs. Spencer's knees dropped onto the target's head and neck. Bill shouldered his rifle and held open handcuffs ready. Once they had immobilized the man, Bill tore the ragged blanket away, snapped the cuffs firmly onto one wrist and then yanked the arm behind. The man had some fight left and Bill struggled briefly to bring the other wrist into the clasp, but soon they had their target bound and helpless with firm coils of rope around his ankles.

"You bastards," the victim cried, muffled through the rotting leaf litter covering his mouth. Screams and curses from the tent drowned out his protest.

"Get off me," they had dragged the woman out and slammed her harshly to the ground. She kicked harmlessly before they tightened the rope.

"Oh," Willard cried as the second man's fist struck his stomach. His heavier body had resisted and given him time for one good swing. One of the Smith boys drove his rifle butt onto the man's head. He went limp, and moaned.

"I hope you didn't kill him," Stevie controlled his anger as he snapped cuffs onto the now helpless man. The Smiths found violence too easy.

"You bastards," the woman screamed, her shrill cries mingled with the loud curses of the prisoner by the fire and the moans of Smith's victim.

"How yah doing, Will?"

Bill placed his hand on the deputy's shoulder.

"I'll be okay. The damned jerk got me good. I could use a cup of Maud's tea," Willard gasped as he sat in damp leaves, his back against a tree.

"Take a minute, we all need a break. I was freezing to the ground. I'll stir up this fire until we're ready to go."

"Anyone want a cigarette? They got some tailor-made," Bob Spencer sang out.

"Leave my stuff alone!" The woman shrilled.

"Shut up, bitch! You're lucky you didn't get shot and burned right here like this cig." Spencer flicked ash into the woman's face, emphasized by a stiff nudge from his boot. She fell silent.

While the posse warmed around the fire, Stevie Hunter, a former Ontario Provincial Police officer, searched through the rude camp and found the knives that must have been the murder weapons. He wrapped evidence in an old blanket. Some things looked like loot from the Quinn house. Old watches, coins, and other items perhaps came from elsewhere. He kept a meticulous list of each item, and with photographs not an option, marked where he had found it on a rough drawing of the camp. Stevie knew if they followed anything resembling the old judicial process, there would be a lengthy examination of his evidence in court. He would hold everything pending a trial, if they could get a judge and Crown Attorney from the Province, although small communities could appoint judges and prosecutors if needed.

To complicate it all, Centerville did not have any legal standing. These were the first local murders since the initial flurry of murder-suicides and had created a mess to sort out.

Either way, Stevie reflected *it's becoming a big pain in the ass.*

The morning had completely broken. The posse adjusted the prisoners' foot bonds to allow a halting gait. Bound to a rope line and spaced about ten feet apart, each culprit had a backpack carrying Stevie's valuable evidence, food and some clothing.

These wretches are destitute, Bill thought, *but that's no excuse. Everyone's suffering these days.*

They began the hard climb to the concession road, lost in their thoughts. Two of the posse were ex-police, two others had helped law enforcement before. It was the first time for Bill, and he hoped it would be his last.

"Pretty rough, eh?" Stevie seemed to read his mind.

"Yeah," Bill gasped as he cleared a fallen log. "I hope I never have to do this again."

"Things are getting worse," Stevie continued. "We've been lucky up here so far… guess we had little worth taking until now. People are getting desperate."

"I heard it's bad down the Grand around Waterloo," George spat. "A bunch of hungry folks thought they could take it all, wanted more than the black hats just helpin' them. "It seems the black hats had some fight though. A couple died each way last fall. Them Amish ended up with new field hands, and I hear bigger congregations at the Friday meetings. Talk to them Koch folks that trade the veggies. Daddy Dave is a nice guy… likes to talk." George ran out of breath, but he had repeated what the rumour mill had embellished.

Bill often talked with Dave Koch who told the actual story. The Mennonites had not fought but fed the town folk and allowed the desperate refugees to live in abandoned houses in the old commuter village of Dorking. They worked for the Mennonites in return for housing and food.

The people remaining in Centerville were not as generous as the Mennonites. Koch's stories were part of the reason the town had put more focus on security. These murders drove it home. Desperate people wandered further than ever.

"The worst thing about this, it'll bring attention to us from the government folks." Stevie puffed on his third cigarette, his opinion rooted in his bitterness after the police force fired him.

"I wish I had a pipe of Cherry Blend," Bill had not found good tobacco for a year. "Shaved dandelion root just doesn't cut it."

Stevie patted him on the shoulder and blew his smoke the other way.

"We should take care of things ourselves and keep the Toronto ticians out of it." Bob Spencer supported the vigilante faction. The Smith brothers murmured in support.

"We'll take it to council." Bill Simpson sat on the council. "We got to decide quick… too much to do to waste our time on this crud."
Bill looked closely at everyone. They had become tired and depressed. The scared prisoners listened to the chatter. Their hobbled feet stumbled on rough ground.

"We didn't do nothing," the female shrilled.

"Yeah, we found them already dead," the older man cried in defiance, "Still warm and we heard a truck out on the road."

"Shut up, you bastards," the older Smith shouted, "You lying scum!" He slapped the prisoner, making his lip bleed.

"Cut that out," Stevie yelled. "Whatever they did, we will not knock 'em around."

"He got what he deserved," Spencer always supported the Smiths.

"You folk best shut up." Stevie ignored Spencer and put on his cop look. "I'll take your statements at the lock-up."

With the warming sun dappling through the budding trees, Bill knew it would be a beautiful day. That would be a treat in this cold, damp April, but almost mocking after the terrible crime leading to this morning's work. The force and speed Smith had dealt with the prisoner upset Bill. The violence became another thing to make him uneasy.

Perhaps things are getting worse, Bill thought. *People are becoming less forgiving.*

The village had split into two camps. One seemed willing to use intimidation and force to achieve things. This bunch, led by Roger Smith, the father of the two boys in the posse, wanted to take over the town. That made Bill and his wife, Sharon, uneasy.

Sharon and I need to talk this out.

Bill's thoughts drifted to the events that had led his world to this. He remembered the last day of the way it was.

Chapter Two

In an unusually hot September afternoon, the 25th Bill remembered, he had slipped out the side door of R.G. Wilson Inc. in Brampton. The company produced computer software for the popular video gambling slot machines that revenue-starved governments had allowed in all variety stores and universities. Casinos had sprung up everywhere. The moral implications never concerned Bill Shadly, although his neighbour, Warren Dunne had pointed out the folly of a government raising revenue from gambling, instead of real economic activity.

Bill gladly headed home on that stifling Tuesday afternoon. It did not surprise him that he remembered that day so clearly, even the day of the week. Many now saw September 25th as the last day of the old way. They counted the next day, over two and a half hard years ago, as "Day One", after the last day.

Bill had a good view of the 407 toll-road but seldom noticed the traffic's drone drifting across the open field. Toll roads now seemed remote, even the existence of a busy highway faded into memory. He considered using highways as part of his entitlement as a college graduate and management candidate. It started out as a typical ride home.

"It's sure a warm day," Jack Sloan eased along the passenger side of the truck.

"September was my favourite month," Bill opened the driver's door and automatically unlocked the opposite one. His shiny red pickup truck, nicely sized for comfort reflected his high-income status. "Now it's October, this hot, stinky summer won't end… global warming at work!"

"You believe that crap?" Jack snapped his seatbelt closed.

"Nope, but they brainwashed my kids at school." Bill turned the ignition switch and immediately put the A/C on full blast. Bill believed climate change was real and humans caused it, but to say so to Jack would lead to a long, useless rant turning the hour-long ride into a tedious ordeal. Sloan did not want to hear facts.

The stereo sparked to life. Bill usually listened to the all-music radio, but on the drive to and from home, he wanted traffic reports and compromised with the light rock station. A song finished, and an excited DJ broke in.

"There's panic on Bay Street. The market closed early, way down and investors have panicked."

"Holy crap," Sloan exclaimed. The truck jerked to a stop halfway onto the side street.

"What does this mean for our pensions?" Bill looked at Jack, an accountant who knew the financial stuff.

"If Wilson's stock dropped, we took a big hit." Sloan looked serious.

"Maybe putting our pensions into company stock wasn't a good idea. It's in a trust fund, isn't it?" Bill tried to remember details on the paper he had casually signed at the company meeting.

"Yes, it's a self-directed money purchase plan." Jack extracted papers from his briefcase. Phone in hand, he surveyed the internet. "Wilson's stock has gone over the cliff."

"Tomorrow, I'll put what's left into GICs until this blows over." Bill tried to remember other options. He had not realized the real implications of the news. Tomorrow, in the traditional sense, would never come.

"Just leave them in stock until the value recovers," Sloan muttered. "I don't plan to do anything. We don't want to panic."

He seemed satisfied by the figures on his pension report. Sloan had been concerned about the stock market for the past month and converted his holdings into the cash equivalent of GICs. Bob Wilson had agreed with him and sold off as much of his company stock holdings the law would allow. They had not shared their misgivings with their employees.

Bill decided to go ahead with his plan. He had less faith in a recovery than his co-worker. Honking brought Bill back to reality. He launched the pickup into the street and drove faster than he should have towards the 410. The radio reverted to its standard of old pop tunes.

"Can't we get any actual news?" Jack felt a growing unease. Bill tuned in the CBC, cursing as he searched for the unfamiliar setting. The announcer finished a smug rant. This crisis did not affect her as she only used public transit and rode a bike. The host gave way to the traffic reporter. Big Jim skimmed over a few fender benders and then launched into a detailed list of gasoline stations selling the cheapest gas, highlighted by a breathless reporter at a gas station tearfully reporting the two dollars and five cent price per litre of regular gasoline. This report seemed useful. Bill would soon realise that none of them had understood the calamity.

Reports of stations out of fuel, fistfights, and a shooting at a gas bar in Toronto would not start until the evening. The wisecracking media in the USA talked about murders per gallon.

The traffic report gave the radio producers time to line up an expert, a professor at the Rottweiler School of Business. The man launched into a monotone lecture, detailing the events that had led to the crisis.

"Hey, I met that guy!" Jack was excited he knew a celebrity. "I took a course with him."

The guest said the economy had stalled some years earlier, with high unemployment and futile government stimulus. Several events had combined, to cause this disaster. The Asian stock markets had gone into a panic when China raised interest rates to crush rampant speculation and stock market swindles. Over the summer, China had made enormous investments in Russian energy, selling their hoard of US bonds to raise the cash.

A dissident Chinese blogger claimed China quietly sold US dollars for months and received as little as fifty cents on the dollar. The American dollar had gradually strengthened over the previous year and spiked higher in the morning as investors rushed to safety. Once the blogger's claim circulated, the greenback value plunged and still fell when markets closed.

"Yeah, scared people bought US dollars and treasuries." Sloan talked over the expert, "but others got into the market." Bill sighed and strained to listen to the radio as he manoeuvred through heavy traffic.

The Rottweiler man went on. "Drought in the US central plains has made wheat and corn futures skyrocket. Fear has captured the Chicago commodity exchange."

"Will that affect food prices?" The announcer asked.

"It may raise flour prices and sweeteners, your burger bun could become more expensive than the meat," the expert laughed, "but it will soon hit the livestock industry hard. Feed corn and barley will be expensive and rationed. In the short term, meat prices might fall as ranchers sell off herds they can't feed."

"Great," said the announcer, "my steak is thirty dollars a kilo."

"Not so fast," Rottweiler chuckled. "Once the herds decline, meat will be in short supply and prices will skyrocket. Your bun will then be worth less than the burger once again, except the whole thing will cost a lot more."

"Will we be able to afford food?" The CBC interviewer sounded alarmed. "Will there be any food?"

Bill could not see the Rottweiler's shrug of uncertainty and would have to wait for the next newscast to discover the full scope of the day's events.

In the early hours of the morning, Middle East Time, Israel had bombed Iranian nuclear facilities, including the partly completed Ahvaz nuclear generating plant. The radio had referred to that on the way to work. It did not seem too important. Iran counter-attacked by bombarding Saudi oil facilities and sank a couple of tankers to block the entrance to the Persian Gulf, sparking the spike in oil prices. Iran had not attacked American ships or bases, and it had not attacked Israel, other than the downing of several airplanes in the initial attack. They paraded a captured Israeli pilot through the streets of Tehran. There was no current fighting. Iran played the victim.

These political events had caused the chaos in world markets. The European markets had fallen apart, and when the North American exchanges opened, they quickly reached "limit down". By noon, two Texas refineries had announced they would shut down in six weeks due to lack of affordable crude. The price of gasoline soared. Bids on benchmark Saudi heavy crude hit one hundred and eighty dollars. It was only a year since Mexico announced it was no longer exporting crude oil because of rising domestic demand and falling production. Worldwide commodity prices doubled in response to the collapse of the American dollar. Australia imposed an additional tax on coal and iron ore exports. China, Australia's biggest customer, had made their displeasure known, and had sent a delegation to Canberra to "negotiate".

Later in the morning, the merger of the two largest telecom providers collapsed. No one underwrote the fifty billion dollars of joint debt. A rumour circulated that both companies would declare bankruptcy, looking for a government handout.

The host turned the commentary over to a bank expert.

"It's only a minor correction. The USA released crude oil from its strategic reserve and calling on OPEC to increase shipments."

Bill thought the designated expert ignored the fact that this would be impossible with the Persian Gulf closed to shipments from key Saudi terminals.

"The European Union has made hundreds of millions of Euros available to the banks and cutting interest rates," the banker continued. "The USA followed suit." He seemed enthusiastic about this, while not bothering to mention that interest rates in the USA and Canada had been effectively zero for years.

"I must admit that bond interest rates are rising in a worrying way, but all will be well," the banker parroted other commentators. "We have a liquidity crisis, and when we fix that, everything will be normal."

Much later they realized they faced a solvency crisis. Most governments were bankrupt. Several European and South American countries had announced total default on their national debts. More nations would follow over the coming weeks. Unable to find more experts, reporters interviewed other reporters in a wave of uninformed speculation.

Quietly, the US Navy website announced the Mediterranean based Sixth Fleet had steamed towards the Suez Canal to guarantee Israeli oil supplies in anticipation of an Iranian counterattack.

The Fifth Fleet, with its three carrier groups and six marine expeditionary units, guarded the Indian Ocean. The tanker sinking trapped two of the carriers inside the Persian Gulf, with the third outside the straits near southern Iran. Iran not attacking directly confused the Americans and delayed response. Last, the carrier group centred on the USS Ronald Reagan received twelve-hour notice to sail from Norfolk for the southern Caribbean Sea off Venezuela. The media noticed the military implications later in the day.

Public interest built slowly, with only the cable news-networks and all-news radio giving full-time coverage. Initially, only the financial community, politicians, and that unique daytime audience of the Canadian Broadcasting Corporation paid much attention. The commercial media, especially television, had not interrupted their regular schedule. Police had caught singer Lulu Barry driving drunk again, and the media focused on that.

"Damn it," Bill exclaimed to Sloan, "as if global weirding wasn't enough, look at that lineup." Jack twisted to look out the passenger window, as the pickup sailed past a filling station. "They're out to the street waiting for gas. What was the price?" Bill braked to avoid a driver changing lanes without signalling.

"Couldn't tell; they blanked out the price sign."

"I'll stop for gas at the first one with no line-up."

Bill sailed onto the 410 and gunned the truck to highway speed. Vehicles jammed every station along the way. A car making a U-turn into the Petro Canada cut Bill off. In desperation, he would wait in a line for half an hour on Highway 10 to fill his tank, unaware of the trouble this full tank of gas would cause.

As he blasted past the slower idiots in their little cars, he still felt a sense of power and control even though panic nibbled at him. He was not a stupid man, but he had paid little attention to events outside his daily life.

"I'll see you tomorrow." Sloan slid out of the truck onto the driveway of his Orangeville home. "Can we go in earlier?" Jack leaned on the door frame. "Wilson will want extra help first thing."

"I'll be here at seven." Bill headed towards Weyburne.

***

The posse reached the town-line road and faced a twenty-minute walk to the old highway. The sun felt warm. It would have been a snap in his pickup truck.

Ah, the pickup truck, Bill remembered. He last saw the vehicle as it swerved around the end of his street onto Highway 10 with Bill running in pursuit down the middle of the road. Sharon enjoyed telling the story of his housecoat flapping in the wind. Someone stole the truck the spring after the economic crash. Losing the vehicle had not been the worst trouble the thing had caused him. In hindsight, he realized how self-centred he had been. Back then, the truck was his pride and joy. Bill had felt smug rolling home with a full tank of gas.

***

The small group, now well down the gravel concession road, sweated in the warm sun. They chatted about getting onto the land and the chances of buying diesel for the tractors. Bob's project for this year was to plant a bean crop and converting a tractor to run on pure vegetable oil. If it worked out, they would allow him to grow fuel for the farm equipment. Not that diesel or gasoline was unavailable. The Smiths sold it but charged a lot. Where they got the fuel was a mystery, but no one dared ask. None of the old filling stations had survived that first year. A good-natured argument developed when George claimed they could do more with horses, insisting hay and oats were cheaper to grow.

"Did you notice that decent maple bush?" Matt inquired. "I'll put it on the committee's list for a sugar camp."

The group groaned. The project list already overflowed with critical needs. They did not have enough labour to do everything. Maple sugar was a cheap substitute for cane sugar; both were a luxury. There was no longer a tourist market to subsidize production.

"You can take that effing list and shove it up yur arse." Bill smiled at George's outburst. The man was religious, part of a growing trend, with a complicated system of deciding on acceptable curse words. Everyone laughed, and that helped ease the sorrow and fatigue of their sad task.

***

Bill remembered the night of the last day. He and Sharon sat glued to the television; every channel covered the crisis. They munched a dinner of frozen pizza and pop. The kids thought it was great and did not understand why their parents were so upset.

Pizza and pop were a foreign concept in the third year of the crisis.

"Bill, we need a plan." Sharon had recovered from the shock.

"I'll go online and put my pension into something guaranteed." Bill kept his earlier priorities.

"Better do that now," Sharon headed to the door. "I think the banks aren't stable. I'll take cash out and grab some things at the Foodland."

Sharon would do many similar insightful things in response to the crisis.

Bill climbed the stairs to the second-floor office, and he was worried. The worry soon turned into fear. He logged into his retirement account. Faithful Financial had frozen all transactions. Bill could check his holdings, but not make changes. They dated the balances the 24th. Business and news sites gave a rehash of the television news. Deflated, Bill retreated to the living room.

"Honey, I'm home!" Sharon struggled through the doorway, her hands full of bags, chuckling at her reference to an old movie. She returned with a few weeks' worth of staples and five hundred dollars cash.

"There's more in the van."

"Can you get Jeff to grab it?" The American president held Bill's attention.

"Jeff! Jeff! JEFF!" Sharon always had to shout.

"Yeah, Mom?"

"Please get the bags from the van."

"Ok Mom, soon as I'm done this." Jeff never lost focus on the electronic game he played.

"What's the news?" Sharon slumped into a soft chair.

"I couldn't do anything with the RSP. There's a short-term screw-up. The Yank president is talking the usual bull crap and confirmed the military stuff. He says American forces won't attack except to defend themselves, but if Iran attacks Israel, it will be the same as attacking the USA. Nothing to worry about; he says their navy is ready."

"Jeff, please get the stuff in!" Sharon's mind functioned on many levels.

"Okay, Mom," he was about to reach thirty thousand on Alien Death Raiders.

"Prime Minister Harridan is going to be on all channels. Oops, the Yanks have just declared a bank holiday until Monday."

"JEFF!"

"Yeah?"

"NOW!" Sharon's exasperation flared. Her conversations with the kids had been like this lately.

"OK!" Jeff's voice was a combination of frustration and defiance. The fifteen-year-old stomped out the front door and struggled back in with a half-dozen bags.

"Any good stuff here, Mom?" Jeff rifled in the bags.

"Milk, bread and eggs" Sharon exacted revenge.

"Aw, Mom, anything GOOD?"

"A Crispy-Crunch… an Aero for Brandy… pop in the fridge... enjoy!" Providing the goodies irritated Sharon. Although she thought all effort deserved a reward, Sharon had not yet convinced the kids, or Bill, the reward for helping should simply be dinner.

"Harridan has declared the same bank holiday for Canada," Bill exclaimed. "No surprise there, he always mimics Washington."

The phone rang out an old Sly and the Family Stone tune and displayed Bill's office number.

"Hi, Bill, Bob Wilson here," the familiar voice sounded somehow strange. Bill frowned. Wilson never called employees at home. "Bill, we have a minor problem. I'm asking everyone to take tomorrow off."

"What's up?" Bill tried to sound nonchalant.

"The bank called." Bob's voice had a catch in it. "They froze all lines of credit until they clarify things. We can't process the payroll. I'm only bringing in accounting to work on the problem, push receivables, etc., and I can't fairly let others come in. I'll call when we clear things up. They tell me a day or two. We have solid cash receivables, so there won't be a problem. Enjoy the day. Bye."

"Who was that?" Sharon saw Bill's concern.

"Wilson, I have tomorrow off. He sounded depressed. They froze his credit line, and he can't run payroll until it's fixed. He says it'll be a day or two."

"Good grief! We only have a few hundred in the chequing account!" Sharon had thought of taking it all out. She wished she had.

"It will only be a day or two. We'll all get a bonus after this, knowing Wilson." Bill tried to sound upbeat, but Wilson's voice made him uneasy. Fear stirred. Sharon went to put the groceries away. Bill couldn't absorb any more bad news and killed the TV.

"Hello, Jack," Bill called Sloan. "Wilson called and told me to stay home… yes, the line of credit, have a good day. Get it sorted out soon, hotshot!" Bill smiled at the phone. "Let me know what's going on when you get back." The line went dead. Jack had not sounded happy.

Bill grabbed a beer and went out to the deck into a clear, mild night. He slumped into a plastic recliner. The dew was heavy, soaking through his pants, but he barely noticed. A deep swallow of cold beer reassured. Bill leant back, looking at the brighter stars struggling through the town's glow. He closed his eyes, resting his mind, remembering those nights long ago at camp, lying on the dock, under a carpet of stars, having no worries.

Bill stumbled on a rock the frost had forced to the surface of the road, returning him to reality. No one had graded the gravel roads in three years. He looked around from his position near the front of the line, noticing the Smith boys chatting quietly together. Deep in the back of his mind, warning signals clanged. He did not like the Smith family. Everything they did drew suspicion. The violence a few minutes ago strengthened that feeling.

The Smiths were an old local family of contractors with a company started by the brothers' grandfather, now run by Roger Smith. They came as close to elite as you could get locally, along with old farming families, who mainly produce milk and potatoes. The disaster had not hurt the Smiths. The family company worked for the rich folks in the hills east of town. Some of those had collapsed in bankruptcy and left the County, but many wealthy people had fled the city to live in their country homes. Considering the urban chaos, this was not a surprise. Smith built gates, fences, low towers, berms and bunkhouses for the rich. Bill had not seen it for himself but Smith's local labourers gossiped in Maud's café. Some of these new buildings Smith had constructed housed fit looking, uniformed young men, occasionally seen in town. The wealthy folks brought supplies up from the city.

There had been some conflict with Smith when he tried to bully the council into things only for his benefit. People resented his lack of concern for the residents. Smith had supporters since he employed many locals and paid wages in Canadian dollars instead of the local barter script. Despite shortages and inflation, dollars could buy things not produced locally.

The Smith brothers were not among Stevie's original selection of deputies. Roger had demanded Stevie bring his sons. Bill wondered why.

***

Bill finished his beer and followed Sharon to bed. He slept well, only to be jolted awake by the angry buzzing of his alarm. His interrupted dream seemed about gassing up the pickup. He leapt out of bed and headed for the shower before he remembered he did not need to go to work. Cursing silently, he smiled at how habits dictated life. Bill had set the alarm automatically. He stayed up, still worried over last night's shocks.

The morning news had nothing encouraging. An American flotilla had left Norfolk, its purpose and destination unknown. Reports came in that most NATO naval units prepared to put to sea along with news of other military activity. Gloom hung over the world and the early morning business news had an air of panic. With all banks and markets closed, there was little actual information to report.

Coffee in hand, still in his housecoat, Bill wandered out to the back deck. It promised to be another glorious day. Sitting on the damp lounge chair, feeling the cool morning air around his legs, he almost felt content and planned how he would spend his free day. Cold weather would arrive soon; he needed to ready the yard. There saw little to do but put the badminton net away, mulch shrubs, and maybe cut grass. It would be a relaxing day. The patio door opened.

"What a gorgeous day." Sharon smiled over her steaming mug, looking delightful in her pink housecoat and sleep-tousled hair.

"I have a bit to do in the yard before winter. I'll get on that today; now I have time." Bill drew another lounge chair close and Sharon eased into it. They said nothing more for a few minutes. Finally, she broke the silence.

"I didn't sleep well, worrying about how we'll meet our payments. How will we pay for food?"

"It spooked you! It won't come to that. There's too much at stake. The government and the banks will fix it." Bill's words were braver than his feelings, but he believed things would recover quickly. He had to think that. They had too much at stake. Wilson told him yesterday he had approved Bill's promotion to management.

"Spooked or not, this crisis has been building for a long time. Warren Dunne warned everyone about this."

"That nut?" Bill's disdain for Dunne surfaced.

Warren Dunne a retiree had talked for years about the end of, "Life, as we know it." Bill considered Dunne a crackpot; however, he was a decent gardener, friendly, well-spoken and shared an excellent fruit wine. He owned the property that backed onto theirs. Bill and Warren often talked over the fence. Bill did not buy into the message of doom in some videos Dunne had shown. He tuned out when Warren started talking details about oil, gas and resource stuff, and the pyramid scheme of the world financial system. Bill laughingly called him 'Warren Doom' when gossiping with neighbours.

After all, Bill thought, *some well-paid economists and politicos knew what they were doing. They would never let things collapse.*

Bill's training had instilled a deep-seated belief in technical solutions to every problem Sharon ignored this implied criticism of her intelligence. Bill could condescend, but he would listen and think about things, even if he questioned her arguments.

"Warren described yesterday almost exactly." She sipped her coffee, staring at the back-fence thinking, as she often did, that one could never know exactly what was just on the other side. Sharon was a bookkeeper with a bit of a poet in her. She took satisfaction in knowing she had passed this trait on to her daughter, Brandi.

"Humph!" Bill knew Sharon thought about global finances a lot. Perhaps, she did because she made the household work, taking care of all the details. Working from home had made that possible.

"What's bothering me is what Warren said about what will happen now."

"Like what?" Bill never paid much attention when Dunne discussed life after a collapse.

"The banks will close, as they already have. Then, they will re-open with withdrawal limits and suspended online banking, demanding payment of credit card debt and cancel lines of credit. Eventually, they will demand we pay our mortgages in full."

"Can they do that?"

"Yup, read our mortgage. They can demand payment in full of the outstanding amount. These mortgages are all recourse loans, so we can't default without them hounding us forever. They made that law about three federal budgets ago." She took another sip. "The law lets them control how much of our savings we can withdraw."

"Why would they do that?" Bill sounded exasperated; his tone revealed the anger he felt for never paying attention to these things. He stared into his empty mug.

"It's because they are broke. Banks loaned out many times their deposits. Even then, they don't have enough cash to cover deposits or pay off their own bonds and loans, especially if their loan-customers default."

She quoted Warren, but as a bookkeeper, she understood finance.

"The banks are broke and hoarding cash. That's why I grabbed the cash last night."

"I sure hope not." Bill sensed Sharon's fear and wanted to be the protecting man.

"It's worse," she sounded resigned. "The banks froze your company's line of credit. I bet they've cut off all lines of credit, including the town's bank-credit. No organization can function without a line of credit to meet payroll and other immediate expenses. Today, the school will be normal, and the town office will open, but what happens when the banks re-open, and people don't get paid?"

"There'll be a lot of unhappy campers," Bill shuddered.

"I think it's coming." Sharon looked at Bill and reached for his hand. "We have to be prepared for hard times."

Bill pulled her over to lie on top of him and kissed her deeply, hugging her tightly. They could work together.

"I love you, bookkeeper." They kissed again.

Chapter Three

"Ugh! Break it up, lovers!" Jeff startled them. The first day of the new world had begun.

"Dad, why are you still home?" Jeff asked an innocent question, but his tone seemed resentful. It tempted Bill to lessen the news, but he chose honesty.

"Not going in today. This worldwide financial mess has tied up Wilson's money. I'll be off until he figures out how to pay us. Probably be back there tomorrow."

"Great, I don't need to go to school!"

"Yes, you do, Buddy Boy!" Bill used Jeff's toddler name.

"Do I, Dada?" Father and son shared a genuine laugh.

Sharon went into the house to make breakfast. Normally, it was only her and the kids, hurried toast for them, then a lingering coffee for her after they left. She had a handful of clients and could finish their business in a few hours. Bill wandered in for more coffee.

Brandi appeared, towel drying her hair after her morning shower. She had her mother's quiet beauty and now, about to turn thirteen, was transforming into a woman.

Bill suddenly felt sad. Brandi's world might not be the one she had expected. He hoped the adage about good things coming from bad would work out for Brandi and Jeff. The kids had developed a good deal of maturity, likely because they had always had a stable home life, and Sharon and Bill had tried to be encouraging parents.

Both kids went through their morning routine and headed out with time to spare. They loved visiting and chatting with their friends before class. Brandi dashed back a moment later.

"Can I get the money for the trip? It's fifty." Sharon made out a cheque for Brandi. It was all a routine.

Bill and Sharon did not linger in the kitchen and dressed for the day. One of Sharon's clients called in a panic because they had a payroll to do and bills to pay. She could only assure the caller she would process the paperwork, but with the banks closed, people would have to wait for their money.

"I'll get right to it and try to find out what the score is," Sharon sounded like a reassuring parent.

Her morning turned into a zoo, with some clients showing up, wanting cheques processed, trying to get cash from the bank. The ATMs worked until they were empty of money. By mid-morning things quieted. Bill surveyed the yard, satisfied it was ready for winter.

Warren called him over to the fence. Bill listened intently. Warren wanted to get a neighbourhood cooperative organized, working on solutions and sharing resources. Bill resisted, saying they should allow a few days to see what would happen. In the end, he agreed to invite people to a block meeting to discuss the situation. Warren wanted Sharon to knock on doors and invite people to the Shadly's house. He wisely understood Sharon had more credibility with the neighbours.

Sharon visited the twelve houses on the short street. The unseasonably warm autumn breeze stirring red and golden maple leaves made it a pleasant walk. A light September haze rose in the warming sun as blue jays chased and played through the high trees.

Weyburne had languished as a quiet agriculture service centre for almost two centuries, only made important by the now abandoned railway. In recent decades, it had transformed into a commuter bedroom for the Toronto area complete with streets of poorly built suburban housing. The local councillors, all business people supported this explosive growth on the mostly unfulfilled belief that it would bring more business and put money into their pockets. The population had ballooned by several times, but most of the new residents remained focused on the south where they originated and where they still worked. Although the Shadlys lived in the old part of town, their street had evolved into a mixture of newcomers and locals. Bill Shadly fit the commuter profile. He and Sharon had fled Oakville when Jeff had been born, searching for an affordable house.

Many commuter types had stayed home that day. Sharon received a positive response. By the end of the day, Warren Dunne's reputation would improve, but that morning most considered him, "the oddball guy on Elm Street".

"Mom," Brandi burst into the kitchen at lunchtime, brandishing Sharon's cheque. It was unusual for Brandi to be home for lunch. She always took a sandwich and a juice so she could eat with her bus friends. "Can you give me fifty dollars cash? The school doesn't want cheques."

Sharon's temper flared, but then she remembered Brandi had little idea of the developing crisis.

"No, Sweetie, we need to keep the cash."

"But Mom, this is a big trip, to the museum, I want to sketch. They'll think I'm a loser."

"No, that's final. There's a big crisis right now. We might need the cash." Sharon tried to hug her daughter. Brandi twisted away.

"You're ruining my life," she shouted and tears appeared on her cheeks. She threw the cheque onto the table. "You don't care."

The door slammed as a sobbing Brandi disappeared.

Sharon picked up the cheque, called the school and confirmed the story. With the banks disrupted, the bus company wanted cash for fuel.

"Mom," Brandi reappeared shortly past three o'clock. "I'm sorry I freaked. The trip's off. Most of the other families don't even have cash."

Brandi gave her mom a long hug that reassured Sharon their strong bond could overcome these confrontations. She suspected the future would test their family strength many times.

At dinner, Jeff talked about his wasted school day. "Today was a bust," Jeff slowed his usual gulping of his food. "The teachers mostly talked about missing their pay deposit and worried about their pensions. We just chatted, played on our cells, or wandered around the halls. Mr Volk, the V-P didn't even yell at us. He only showed up to stop a fight between townies and bus kids. It was a great fight." Jeff smiled.

"I understand the teachers." Bill wondered how to let the kids know things were serious. "They froze my pension fund. I'm not sure when I'll return to work and things will be normal."

"What? You are going to be home all the time?" Jeff and Brandi exclaimed in harmony.

"Hey, is that so terrible?" Bill laughed.

"Sorry Dad didn't mean it like that," Jeff sounded confused. "What's the problem?"

"No line of credit for the payroll at Wilson's."

"What's a line of credit, Dad?" Brandi was never shy to admit she did not know something and did not fear appearing ignorant. This trait would be the foundation for the rest of her life.

"It's an open loan you can draw from like a credit card. The banks can cancel them or freeze them without notice. That's what they've done to most companies and people."

"Oh," Brandi appeared to be satisfied. A few minutes later, she asked, "Do we have a line of credit?"

Bill sighed, "Yes Baby, we do. I sure hope we can pay it off now."

***

At 6:45, Warren Dunne rang the doorbell. He looked ordinary, standing about five feet ten inches tall, 180 pounds with a medium build. His grey hair and closely cropped beard fit his 62-years. Sharon thought he was lonely. His wife had passed away eight years before. Warren had moved to town soon after, taking early retirement from his job as an arborist with the City of Toronto. He carried papers, a DVD and a delicious homemade carrot cake, his late wife's special recipe. Others arrived. All but one family brought some goodies. Sharon handed out drinks as people filed into their spacious living room. Most had never visited the Shadly's home. Everyone admired Sharon's beautiful prints of Canadian landscapes. By 7:15, half of the families on the street had arrived. Bill called for order.

"We should introduce ourselves." Bill had learned his meeting skills at corporate training sessions. Sharon knew everyone, but several met each other for the first time. Bob Durant piped up, interrupting Bill.

"I don't know what the fuss is about. This will sort out. It'll be business as usual. You are all panicking like Mr Doom here," he shot an angry glance towards Warren, "and those idiot teachers who wasted my kids' time today."

The Durant family had two teenage children in grades 11 and 12, both A students and ideal poster children. People admired their achievements in school and sports. Bob's pushiness revealed what lay behind those accomplishments. He was an ambitious, middle-level manager at an automobile company. Success was his only measure of worth.

"Well Bob," Warren kept a level tone, applying the skills he learned during fractious meetings at the City of Toronto, "the events yesterday are alarming and not surprising."

"You say!" exclaimed Durant. "It's bozos like you causing this problem. If you would all shut up, everything would go on fine, you and those other oddballs and commies on the CBC. You people destroyed the economy buying Jap cars and junk from China."

"I'm sorry you feel that way," Warren softly replied. "Talking about being prepared is not dragging down the economy. Who do you think listens to people like me? The pyramid scheme economy collapsed on its own. We've mistaken debt for wealth and have now run out of lenders."

"If you look into it," Bill defended Warren, "you'll see it's the corporations taking the jobs offshore for profits. Don't blame us, or Chinese peasants."

"I've had my say. I'll leave it to all you whiners. Don't screw it up more!" Durant's tone menaced as if he scolded underlings. "My kid has a hockey practice tonight." Durant left. His wife, looking a little apologetic, trailed behind.

"Don't worry about him," someone piped up. "You should hear him blowing off at the arena… only cares about his kid becoming a superstar in the NHL."

"Yeah, he's a legend in his own mind," another chuckled. "He only thinks he's rich, He's probably mortgaged to the eyeballs like the rest of us. No rich guy would live on our street."

"Maybe Bob's right," another suggested, "perhaps this will blow over."

"You could be right," Sharon joined in, "but shouldn't we discuss doing something just in case?"

"I think we should form a co-operative," Warren suggested. "We could bring all of our resources together and help each other out."

"What good would that do? What about the rest of the town?" Several voices rose in hopeful doubt.

"One step at a time," said Warren, "I agree the whole town should be involved, but we need to start somewhere. We should start local and recruit as many as we can as soon as we can."

"That seems hopeless. I don't see how to convince others, especially since this has just happened." Sharon's friend Jean Bennett spoke up. Jean was timid and undecided about many things; however, she was honest and a hard worker helping at the school and her church. Jean was in her 50s but looked older with her mousy brown hair tied up in a tight bun. Sharon believed Jean's controlling husband caused her timidity.

The discussion proved Jean right. After an hour, the majority felt things might sort out, and organizing should wait. Warren tried to get them to watch the video he had about community solutions, but most wanted to get home. Only Bill, Sharon and Warren remained, along with Jean.

"I didn't mean to be negative," Jean said, "but I think people are hanging onto hope. I still have trouble thinking this is it."

"Don't worry Jean. At least we got people to meet, and it helped. We can't count on the Durants. I'm nervous about them." They all agreed with Warren.

Warren ran a hand through his greying hair. "I've studied the whole thing for years; climate change; peak oil; the economic turmoil. I wasn't ready myself and still have a little doubt." The other three listened intently to Warren's honesty.

"I don't believe there will be any recovery this time. Resource growth has stalled. Debt can't survive without that growth. Debt is what the world has been running on," Warren paused, pondering the facts. "Going back to the bank crisis of 07 and the following stagnation, our society hit the ceiling. Growth ceased. It's now clear conventional oil production hit a plateau between' 05 and' 09 and only held steady by expensive efforts." Warren's ability to detail things off the top of his head kept everyone's attention.

"This year has seen a remarkable drop in oil production, about six percent year on year. Saudi Arabia claimed it was cutting production to support price, but their oil was selling at about $100 US dollars per barrel before yesterday. They are hiding a decline, just like what happened to the Mexican and the North Sea fields."

"But the pump price wasn't too bad," Bill interjected, "It hit a $1.90 per litre but had dropped a bit until yesterday."

"Yes," agreed Warren. "Unemployment has been high and rising throughout the industrial world. Demand has dropped a lot, especially for transportation, but the price has stayed high. The supply crunch explains it, and speculators exploited it."

"James and I don't drive," said Jean. "We never paid attention to the price of gas."

"The way it will play out," Warren carried on, "if the economy is collapsing the price of oil will collapse, but that doesn't mean the pump price for fuel will decline much. Every filling station has fuel at the old high price, and so do the refineries. I would guess they won't want to cut prices, at least until they receive new, dirt cheap crude stock."

"Won't they want to attract customers?" Sharon thought Warren had it wrong. "If we're out of work, we won't be able to pay much."

"People who need fuel will pay whatever it costs to get it. The rest of us will go without. Only the rich will drive. Eventually the price will drop, but our ability to pay will diminish too, so it will look like high prices."

"Geez, I am glad I filled up yesterday!" Bill said.

"Don't use it too quickly," Warren advised. "There might not be much more you can afford. If the companies can't get cash or credit, we might not have any for some time at any price. I'll believe it for sure if credit remains frozen for more than this week. I think it will. It will be the conclusive proof. If it's true, things will get chaotic quickly. Most people live on plastic credit. What will people do, and whom will they blame? I hope governments will still be able to pay for police."

Warren then added, "I don't want to talk about security and politics now, but they will be our greatest worry. What will governments do? What kind of government will we end up with?" Warren finally finished, leaving the others thinking about the implications.

"What do we do now?" Bill broke the silence, torn between wanting to act and hoping it would all blow over.

"We should inventory what we have available. Let's assume the stores will run low, at least for a bit, and things will be hard to get." Warren had worked it out long before this day.

Sharon replied, "Let's count our food, fuel, skills and tools and see where we are. At least we can work out a system before more people become involved."

The bookkeeper loved organization.

"Can we make a list of what we think we might need?" Jean liked planning action.

"One other thing," Sharon worried, "we need to think about the banks calling all our loans. It probably won't happen for months, but we should be ready."

The visitors departed into the September night. Bill and Sharon watched from the front stoop as Warren and Jean walked away, still chatting. Halfway down the block, a street light went out. Bill laughed at the symbolism. The power company had struggled for years to fix that light; they might never do it now. The light flickered back on, the way it always had.

***

Bill and Sharon spent the rest of the week worrying and acting. Sharon soothed her nervous clients at least once a day. They saw their bookkeeper as a source of assurance.

Sharon listed all the food and other items on hand. They were short of essentials. Shopping together, they bought bulk rolled oats, flour, sugar, and baking needs. Sharon scrounged free plastic storage pails from the Foodland. They would be glad they had not waited.

The lack of electronic cash, debit and credit cards prevented a rush on the stores; however, people did not realize the consequences of Tuesday's events. Innate human optimism made people think there was no real problem, or someone would solve it. Warren had gotten this detail wrong when he had predicted an immediate stampede to the stores.

Shadly's cash in hand declined to a few hundred dollars, and prices were up. The local paper had its usual fliers, but the stores posted signs to void the advertised discount prices, and police escorted irate customers from stores. The price of gasoline rose to four dollars a litre, cash only, on Thursday, with none available in town by Friday night. Many people had spent their cash on gasoline instead of food. Warren had been right on that one. Bill patted his red pickup truck and smiled.

Thursday was a quiet day until Warren appeared. "We should talk to the mayor."

"Ted Johnson? Do you know him?" Bill had only seen the mayor on Canada Day and in the Festival Parade.

"Ted and I argued before, but maybe now he'll listen."

They walked the five blocks to the town hall. There were few vehicles. Bill had observed Wednesday morning's rush was a lot lighter. A mini return rush hour developed about noon that day. Commuters had arrived at work only to return home. The flow of parents dropping kids off at school was greater on Wednesday. It would be much less by Friday. There were many empty on-street parking spaces downtown. Bill did not know if it was normal for a weekday. He had always been out of town during business hours.

"See anything strange?" Warren asked.

Bill realized, only the coffee shop, the variety store and the pharmacy were open. All other storefronts were dark.

"Most of them sell non-essential crap or services like insurance, mortgages and pool maintenance. I don't think people are looking for any of that this week."

The town hall was open, and the lights were on.

"Hi, Evy, is Ted in?" Evy smiled and winked. She knew Warren. Evy enjoyed eavesdropping on Warren Dunne's arguments with Ted.

"I'll see if he's available. If you're here to rock his boat, it's already swamped," Evy chuckled. Bill noticed a fleeting worried look crossing her face. Evy made a call.

"Give him five. Are you Sharon's husband?" She asked Bill. Sharon did the bookkeeping for Evy's husband's renovation business. Sharon was much better known than Bill. Sharon's friendships and connections had already proved to be a big help. Ted invited them in.

"Ted, have you met Bill Shadly?" Johnson gripped Bill's hand in a firm handshake as if claiming his vote with a salesman's grip. Johnson was both a politician and a salesman, short, middle-aged, and carried a few extra pounds. Ted sported light slacks topped by a herringbone jacket over a white shirt. He wore his tie, bearing the town logo with an immaculate Edwardian knot. No matter the occasion, Ted never dressed casually. He ran a car dealership and was always out to make a sale.

"It's busy here, boys. I always have time for citizens, but no time for BS today, Warren. What's on your mind?"

"How is the town doing during this crisis?" Warren had learned not to beat around the bush with Ted.

"It's damned hard today. We missed the payroll because of the bank fiasco. The guys and gals are troopers, but I feel sorry for them. I gave money to a few from my pocket."

"We've gotten a few people together on our street to see if we can help." Warren used his best upbeat voice. "How about calling a town meeting to get people together?"

"Ah, you're panicking, as usual, Warren, no need for that. This will blow over next week. The big deal in' 08 turned out to be nothing. Besides, I need a special council meeting to work out new procedures so that we can pay for things. We need a by-law, but the crisis trapped two councillors out of town. Lorna and George were at a conference, low on gas and having trouble finding some, especially since they have no cash. I'll have to send someone to get them, but they are way the hell down towards Windsor."

"We're hoping you're right," Bill interjected, "but we should prepare for the worst. I don't see how the town can last long if this keeps up. Almost no one commuted to work today. Many people have that cash problem your two councillors have right now."

"I was just on the phone with Fred over at the Sovereign Bank," Ted backed his words with a broad, reassuring smile. "He says the town's credit's fine; there's nothing to worry about. The banks need to make some adjustments and will be open for business Monday, same as usual. He says we'll get our pay processed, no problem." Ted felt confident in what he had heard, and he put a positive, political spin on everything.

"Ted?" Warren was trying to salvage something from the visit. "Would you call a meeting if things don't change?"

"Look, Warren," the mayor sounded exasperated, trying to hide his stress. "I'm not giving you a platform to spout this nonsense. We are the ELECTED council and will do what's right."

for ourselves, Bill silently completed Ted's sentence.

"Play it your way, Ted. We'll keep doing what we can, getting as many to work together as possible."

"Don't go causing trouble or sticking your nose in where it doesn't belong, Warren. And don't go riling people up." Ted always feared some group would organize in the community and pressure him, or even unseat him. Politicians feared upset voters.

"Don't worry Ted; I don't want your job. You have done a decent enough one. By the way, how are things over at the lot?" Warren wanted to leave on a friendly note.

"It's damned tough!" Ted paused, and his face clouded, as he remembered other problems. "I won't sell a thing unless people get credit. Fred says credit will come back, but a lot tighter. We're getting that new electric car next month. She's a beauty. Come and look; it fits nicely into your tree hugging."

"Sounds good to me," Warren ignored the implied insult and resisted lecturing about the uselessness of the electric car in fighting climate change. It was too little, too late and just added to industrial destruction. "All the best, Ted, I hope you get Lorna and George back."

Bill and Warren walked home in silence, Bill tried to deal with this new disappointment. Warren seemed to think things over. When they reached Shadly's house, they contemplated the street. It wore the bright colours of early autumn.

"Bill," Warren chose his words carefully, "there's a chance we'll get blamed for causing this, like Durant last night. Johnson is more or less sincere, but he'll look for a scapegoat. Are you prepared to be attacked and ridiculed?"

"I never considered it." Bill said. "Do you think it'll come to that?"

"Perhaps, and it worries me. I hope we get enough folks together to make it hard for people to gang up on us."

Warren walked off deep in thought, kicking at a few dried maple leaves.

Bill watched him go, his own thoughts heavy. He turned up his walkway, hungry and needing a hug.

Warren fell into his usual introspection. *I don't think I handled that very well. Why can't I be a better leader? I should have gotten Ted to listen.*

He paused at the corner to watch an overloaded SUV heading south with a gigantic pile of something on top, covered with a tarpaulin. A couple occupied the front seats with two little faces glued to the windows in the back. This family, Warren realized, marked the first wave of people fleeing to the city hoping to replace lost jobs.

I wonder what kind of life those little ones will face? His thoughts became gloomy. Warren disliked thinking about the future, a future with real people in it at any rate. It was too painful to contemplate the hardships that those two kids in the SUV would endure. He turned into his street.

I hope I didn't upset Shadly. Damn it, we need a proper leader.

Warren could not always see his strengths and often dwelt on his weaknesses. He entered his cramped, gloomy entrance hall and glanced at the small, framed picture sitting on a crocheted doily centred on a dark-wooden table. The doily was Susan's work; the table was a keepsake made by his father.

Susan's smile shone from the past, filling him with a warm feeling. She stood on a natural rock bridge, their favourite spot on the Bruce Trail. Eight years ago, when she lay dying, fighting the pain, she made him promise to cast her ashes from the bridge.

When you see the ferns and moss growing, it will be me.

The photo was the only sign of Susan on display.

"Don't make any shrines to me," she had insisted. "Remember me, but live your life. My love will always be with you."

Susan had died that night.

Memories trailed Warren into the kitchen. He missed her deeply. The grief had left him, but love remained. No one could take her place in his heart.

***

Ted Johnson stared at his office door. The two visitors had reinforced the apprehension he had been feeling all day. In fact, a sense of dread had gripped him since the bad news hit on Tuesday. Ted turned over the paper he had been reading when his visitors arrived, a fax from the automotive company that supplied his dealership. The message contained two bits of upsetting news. They were closing all factories for a two-week period to resolve payroll and parts issues. The company would not deliver existing orders, and would not accept new orders until they put a new schedule in place. More disquieting, the credit arm of the manufacturer would no longer issue loans to purchasers. The memo attached no time limit to that distressing news. Johnson left the office, fumbling for his wallet.

"Evy, I'm sending Phil down to retrieve Lorna and George. He'll be here in about half an hour. Here's some cash for him to buy gas. Tell him to fill a can of fuel in the yard and take it with him; they might be out."

He handed Evy two $100-dollar bills and noticed her frown as she looked at the cash. "How are you fixed?" Ted reached for his wallet once more.

"I hate to ask," Evy looked about to burst into tears. "We have little food; our cash is all gone."

"Take this." Johnson extracted several 20s. "Hank can come over and paint the waiting room at the dealership sometime this winter. Put it against what he'll charge." Ever the politician, Ted knew most people did not like receiving charity, so this would make it business and smooth over embarrassment. Ted headed to the door.

"I'm off to a business meeting at the Legion, see you in the morning." He disappeared down the steps. Evy carefully placed the 20s into her wallet, dialled Phil's mobile number, and reached the Works' boss trying to solve the latest crisis at the water tower.

Ted Johnson walked the three blocks to the Legion. Usually, he would drive his flashy dealer's car. The artwork spray painted over the vehicle was an eye-catching advertisement, but the financial crisis had changed his habits. With gasoline expensive and becoming scarce, Ted walked most places. With little chance of sales soon, advertising seemed pointless.

"Hello, Ted," one of his business friends called out as Ted sauntered into the members' lounge. He joined the usual crowd of Weyburne's local business elite. Most represented families who had been in the county for many generations. Less generous denizens of the lounge had dubbed this clique, "The Moving Van Gang" since they were the movers and shakers of Weyburne.

"Where's Powers?" Ted noticed the empty chair.

"He isn't coming out." Roger Smith, the wealthiest contractor in town, frowned at the Mayor. "He lost most of his money in the market crash and is hiding at home licking his wounds." There was disdain in the man's voice.

"We're all hurting right now." Johnson ignored Smith's judgment of their unlucky friend. The mayor knew Smith had most of his money tied up in land and equipment with a significant amount of credit mortgaging the lot. All of them could suffer the fate of the Powers family.

"I have some good deals in the works," Smith seemed smug. "The estates up in the hills have asked me to quote on some large projects. They want to make their places secure because of the crisis. I think it sets me up."

"How can we profit from this crisis?" Frank, the funeral director, glanced around the table. "There must be an angle we can play. I lost a bunch in stocks too." The man was the newcomer to the group, having bought the funeral home from its local owners a few years before. The mortgaged operation required a steady cash flow.

"There's always an angle." Another businessman waived towards the waiter for a second pitcher of beer. "Disaster is always an opportunity."

"You seem confident." Johnson's smile hid his doubt. The speaker was a borderline alcoholic and already tipsy.

"Property is going to be cheap." The man replied, slurring his words. "Lots of desperate folks will be selling. There's bound to be foreclosures."

"I'm watching some properties," Will Kirk, the real-estate broker, sipped a wine and frowned as he gazed over Smith's shoulder, studying the night's sparse menu on a chalkboard above the serving counter.

"About a dozen folks came in today, desperate to sell. They all plan to leave town. I figure some of them will just default. They'll be easy pickings if we can buy them out before the banks foreclose." Kirk called the waiter over and ordered the hot beef sandwich with French fries, the only choice on the menu. The rest of the group followed suit.

"We have to find the cash." Frank seemed interested.

"You would be stupid to use your own cash." Kirk puffed. "You borrow money and write it off on taxes."

"That could be a problem short term." Smith scowled. "My bank called me in to discuss my line of credit and overdraft. They're worried about being paid. I don't think they'll be lending soon."

"All that will go away." Johnson tried to be positive. "Our bank told me things will be back to normal quickly." The others nodded. Collapse of the business world seemed impossible, and they did not realise they might have bigger things to worry about than income tax.

"One slight problem might get in the way." Ted Johnson had news. "I had a visit today from people who are organizing a group to help everyone survive this. These guys think we'll never recover from this crisis."

"Who are these idiots?" Will Kirk could only conceive of business as usual. He shot an angry look towards a table of noisy, hard-drinking, peacekeeping veterans.

"It was Warren Dunne, and a guy named Shadly." Johnson tried to sound disdainful. The politician in him made it impossible, too used to pretending to like everyone.

"Dunne's a crackpot!" Several exclaimed at once.

"Yeah, remember that meeting he called at the library last year?" the drunk slurred. "My son went. Dunne brought in a nut case who believes our oil supply has peaked. The speaker got into an argument when that old vet, Charlie, lit into him and told him a good stint in the army would have knocked all the bull out of him. Charlie called the guy outside, but he was too chicken. Charlie was so worked up he would have had a heart attack. I thought we wouldn't hear any more from them."

"Dunne had to pay the speaker out of his own pocket. Only six showed up, and no one was going to donate anything for that crap. There was a woman there named Shadly, that small-time bookkeeper, an out-of-town newbie."

For decades, the established families of Weyburne had looked down on new residents. Commuter residents' spending was the only real injection of cash into the town, other than the old age home and schools, yet, the descendants of original settlers looked on newcomers with disdain.

"He's dangerous." Johnson joined the Dunne bashing. "They have a street full of folks riled up and looking for more support. If this drags on, they'll get stronger and screw it up for us." Ted feared to lose his job as mayor.

"They could keep their property." Will was afraid of losing his windfall.

"We got to cover that self-help angle, just in case." Ferguson owned a small strip mall and a gasoline station. "We should form our own group. We're rich and respected; people will join us first. We can give them just enough help to keep them needing us. Then, we can encourage them to sell out cheap and move, or let them rent. These troublemakers don't stand a chance."

Everyone nodded, but no one seemed enthusiastic. The idea of easy money had faded. The businessmen would have to work harder to implement their scheme.

"So where do we start?" Smith looked at the Mayor. "Ted, you're the people organizer here."

"We need people to do the work." Ted had been mayor and a boss too long and depended on his staff. "I'll ask Evy to coordinate things through the town office, and I'll send my young salesman, Matt Long, over to help. He has nothing to do at the moment." Ted looked despondent. None of his employees had anything to do, and he would have to lay them off until the economy improved.

"I have a sales rep I can spare." Will had several part-time and one full-time agent in his brokerage business. "Walt Lefevre will be a big help. He was a hotshot salesman in Toronto but wanted a quiet life up here. Walt knows his stuff, and people like him. He's honest. No one will question his motives."

"Will they do the job?" Roger Smith believed employees were lazy, stupid and a costly necessity.

"As long as we pay them," Will pushed his half-eaten meal away and took a long sip of wine. "God this food is crap. I'll have a word with the manager. They had better do better than this." The other men did not complain, but the realtor Kirk preferred lobster and steak.

"We should be able to pay once the banks reopen next week." Ted believed the banks would fix things. "If not, I'll have to lay everyone off including the town staff."

"I'll send my oldest boy over to help." Smith eyed Will's half-eaten meal, wondering if he should order a second helping. The others frowned at the mention of Smith's son. No one had much regard for Smith's sons. Both had attitudes and drinking problems. Ted decided Roger wanted a spy inside their organization.

"Well, they won't need to do much." Frank laughed. He did little else at the funeral home than count the money. His son and staff did the undertaking work. "I'll send Sheila over to help. So, what'll they do?"

"We want them to hand out enough charity to keep people hopeful." Will was the one who hoped to gain the most from this misfortune. "Let them come to us if they need food or whatever. Maybe we can hand out a few dollars in loans."

"I'll put out a decree saying the town has teamed up with our businesses to help." Ted sketched out a proclamation.

"What will the people need?" Frank asked.

"Who knows, and who cares?" Smith had finally ordered a large piece of apple pie. Contrary to Will's opinion, he liked the Legion food. "We can gather food to give out."

"One other thing," Johnson had completed his draft announcement. "The service clubs, including the Legion, the food bank and the churches, will try to help people. We should ask them for the names of the most desperate."

"Great," Kirk exclaimed, "Walt could go around and drop off the help and a real-estate brochure. We'll only help those with mortgages." Will imagined his profits.

"What about this bunch Dunne is putting together?" Johnson wanted to wrap up loose ends.

"Keep telling jokes about the crackpot and no one will join him. Things will be back to normal soon. We'll have some cheap property in our pockets." Will was planning to market these bargains to a fresh wave of buyers from the city. The group broke up, leaving their drunken friend as an easy mark to buy the moochers free beer.

Chapter Four

Bob Wilson did not call. Bill was nervous but waited it out. He did not want to annoy Wilson and lose his promotion and believed things would return to normal. Announcements from the governments in Ottawa and Toronto fed everyone's hopes. Politicians appeared on TV, claiming that things would be fine and they were taking steps.

Ted Johnson's story seemed to be correct as well. Late on Friday, the banks announced they would re-open on Monday and that calmed things down. The media went back to programming talent shows, sports events and gossip. That weekend, they discussed Lulu Barry's alcohol problem at great length. Bill took a walk downtown on Saturday. Stores had opened and allowed credit to trusted customers.

Monday was a day of surprises. The banks re-opened, but not as advertised. There was no electronic or phone banking, no ATMs operated, and they cancelled all overdrafts. They limited withdrawals to fifty dollars per day. The constraints were meaningless to many customers who were below water. With overdrafts and lines of credit gone, they had no access to cash and became desperate. Despite the restrictions, bank branches quickly ran out of cash and organized special armoured car deliveries for later in the week.

Sharon went to the bank each day, patiently enduring the long delays, and took out the maximum until she drained their account. It was a matter of time until the Shadly mortgage payment, and other automatic withdrawals bounced. No one at the bank could answer any of her questions. Dorothy Kim, the branch manager whom Sharon had met several times in business meetings, avoided her. Once, when Sharon had finished with the teller, she spotted Dorothy standing near the customer service counter. When she approached, making eye contact, the manager retreated into her office.

The banks announced they would contact all clients to discuss amounts owed through credit cards, lines of credit and mortgages. Governments reduced interest rates to zero and said they would buy all defaulted retail assets from the banks and take on the role of debt collector. With the banks freezing lending, it seemed meaningless. It surprised Sharon that the bank had not seized their cash to put against their line of credit. In fact, the banks themselves were in turmoil and were unsure, with the additional government measures, that they had the right to take cash before scheduled due dates.

In frustration, Sharon phoned an old accounting professor. She and the woman had spent many hours in the campus pub, discussing men and the state of world finance. Sharon knew the woman had a steel-trap mind about the financiers and Revenue Canada.

"If you want a loan," her teacher friend began, "I'm wondering if you have twenty bucks." The laughter brought back the smell of beer and the sound of awful music.

"Come live here instead," Sharon was serious. "I really want to know what is happening with the banks and will it fix things."

"The sleazy bastards," the woman no longer laughed. "They're making taxpayers cover all the banks' losses, at least in public loans."

"So the banks won't come at us directly for what we owe?" Sharon asked.

"No," the woman had calmed, "but the feds might, although it will delay that for months or years, short-term politics at its best."

"So the banks won't grab our deposits?"

"Deposits are a liability to the banks," she laughed. "You must have slept through my lecture."

"The government isn't directly touching banks' liabilities, they owe us that money, but the federal cash to the banks should cover it since they are only paying it out at a small amount per day."

"So we are okay then for now," Sharon was relieved.

"For now, if you have cash deposits," the professor hesitated, "but the banks can't cover inter-bank loans and bonds. Likely the government won't help them there. All hell is going to break loose in banking, and that will lead to bad things for us all."

"What are you going to do, Jan?" Sharon wanted to digest this mixed news and worried about her friend in her Forest Hill house.

"We have a winterized cottage at Rosseau," Jen said. "Josh is moving all our personal stuff and stocking food there this week. We will keep working but have a go-bag packed and can get out of town on an hour's notice. The kids and their families know to go there if they need to."

"Be safe," Sharon whispered.

"You too," Jen rang off.

Stock markets re-opened, but went 'limit down' almost immediately and closed, destroying investors including the investment arms of the major banks. Later Monday, the government imposed a stock market holiday of two weeks. All the major banks announced they were severing off and selling their investment operations. Commentators noted these severed businesses were worth only pennies on the dollar. Once again, cheerleading business media claimed, 'there are bargains to be had'. No one could name potential buyers for these new ventures.

The regular Monday garbage pickup took place with its diesel fumes and grinding of the compactor. The power of hydraulics and diesel engines was impressive. Warren Dunne had always referred to these as energy slaves.

Jeff and Brandi left for school feeling their parents' worry, but still eager. They were home by 9:15. The teachers' pay had not gone into their accounts. Most were refusing to teach despite the school boards' pleading. Some teachers had no cash at all. Jeff said he felt unsafe in the school.

The principal cancelled all classes. Buses arrived to return the kids home, and there were stories of vandalism and violence on the vehicles. Drivers dumped younger children at their homes with no one to look after them. Fortunately, none of the little ones had suffered. Recriminations would persist for some time, but events quickly overwhelmed people with more serious issues.

Bill and Sharon recruited Jeff and Brandi to help organize the basement. They complained up front but seemed glad to help and being included in the work and conversations made them feel mature.

"I looked over the accounts last night." Sharon was shifting a large plastic container. "Without an overdraft or credit, we need cash before the middle of the month."

"Do you think we should throw anything out?" Bill was looking at a pile of truck magazines, not listening.

"Don't worry, dear. You can keep all your junk. We might need to burn it for heat." Sharon chuckled. "What we need is space for storage. We should empty water-proof bins to use for food and get more buckets."

"If our cash situation is that dire, why bother? We'll lose the house anyway." Bill sounded matter of fact, but fear tore him up inside.

"We owe a lot of money. Those cards and the mortgage add up to a couple of hundred thousand, not to mention your red rocket."

"Don't get on my case!" Bill had a flash of anger at Sharon mentioning the truck. She opposed buying the expensive vehicle. "What about your fitness club, and golf with the girls all the time? You have your mini-van."

"I don't do poker nights with the boys and not get home. You blow a lot of money." Sharon rushed upstairs sobbing. Brandi and Jeff stared at their father until he put his arms around them.

"What's wrong with Mom?" Brandi was sobbing. She could not remember her Mom and Dad ever arguing.

"Things are dire." Bill decided not to mince words. "We'll sit down as a family and go through it. I'll go up and see your mother now. Take a break and grab a pop out of the beer fridge."

The permission did not make them feel any better. Dad had always warned them about touching the beer fridge. Things must be serious for him to okay it. The youngsters retrieved their drinks, relishing the feeling when they opened the fridge they did not feel sneaky.

Bill found Sharon slumped over the table. He hugged her tightly and stayed quiet, letting her sobs subside. She trembled with little, irregular spasms. Sharon was not a rock. They had to give each other strength.

"I'm sorry, sweetie," Bill finally spoke. "I'm spooked by this and can't think right."

"Damn it, Bill, I figured I had it together." Sharon's sobs diminished.

"I'm scared. We're going to lose it all."

"I know," Bill was trying to find something comforting to say. "I'm scared too. The kids need us, and we need them and each other. That will always be true. This is a damned fine family. We'll fight together."

Bill kissed her lightly on the cheek, and Sharon relaxed against him. The moment of peace restored them. They did not see the youngsters standing on the stairs, watching and listening.

The family had a frank discussion over dinner. For once, the kids wanted to stay at the table instead of rushing off. The afternoon conflict had dug deep into them.

"Brandi and I have been talking." Jeff sounded mature past his years. "We're scared and don't know what's going on. The teachers were stupid. Some wished us good luck. They said we would need it, and it was the end of our 'smart-ass world'. Is it the end of the world?"

The teachers were unprofessional. Their actions showed just how upset and scared adults had become. Bill and Sharon exchanged glances instinctively wanting to protect the kids, but they were afraid and confused too. What should they tell the children? Bill looked at them, Brandi appearing small and vulnerable, his sweet little girl. He could almost feel her, as a newborn, sitting in the palm of his hand. Jeff no longer looked like a boy. His body had changed struggling to grow into a man showing earnest maturity across the table. It saddened Bill. The kids might have to grow up faster than anyone planned.

"We're hoping it will be okay," Bill started the conversation, looking to Sharon for encouragement. "There's a chance it will last for a bit. We must be ready for anything."

"How long… Dad?" Jeff needed answers.

"I don't know."

"Is it the end of our smart-ass world, Dad?"

"BRANDI!"

"Sorry Mom, but is it?" Brandi smiled, pleased at using an adult phrase in an adult conversation.

"To be honest," Sharon hoped she was always honest with the kids, "some think it's the end of the old system, and we are going into something new, something harder and poorer than before."

"What Mr Dunne is saying?" Brandi was wide-eyed.

"I don't know if I believe all that," Bill was still trying to come to terms with the possibility. "I expect Wilson to call anytime, and I'll be back to work. Just in case, we're trying to organize here with our neighbours."

"We plan to call Gran, Nan and Papa Maki, and your aunts and uncles this week, just to touch base, and see what can be done with the family if things get bad." Sharon had held off phoning to avoid worrying anyone. Now, they needed to know how everyone was doing.

"Just how bad can it get? Will we see them soon?" Brandi suddenly appeared fragile, looking to her Mom, Dad and back again, needing comfort.

"We don't know, Sweetie. We hope for the best, but we'll plan for the worst."

"Will we lose the internet and TV?" Brandi had priorities.

"What about the house? We heard you talking about the bank and stuff," Jeff was focusing on the essentials.

"Well, we have a bit of debt." Bill knew it was a lot more than a bit but did not want to alarm them.

"Could we go like that place down the street where the Flacks live now? Didn't the bank take that house from the Andersons?" The family had suddenly disappeared over Christmas, the previous year.

"If we don't have money coming in, we won't be able to pay it off. It will be grim if that happens, and we'll lose some services, maybe the house too. Everyone we know is in the same boat."

"The ship's sinking. Nobody is directing this movie," Jeff's wisecracking had gotten him into several scrapes at school. Brandi glared at Jeff and stuck her finger into her open mouth in the universal sign. They all laughed, washing away the tension, signalling an end to the conversation. The kids scattered. Bill and Sharon sat, silently thinking, hoping the stress would not tear their family apart.

Later that evening, Sharon called her Mom and Dad who lived in a large, comfortable house on a big lot in the western suburbs of Toronto, just north of the lake. Her father was an engineer for Hydro One. They were suffering from the same issues as everyone else, but so far, did not feel any danger. It had not occurred to them that the crisis had affected Sharon and Bill so quickly. Sharon arranged for them to come up for Thanksgiving Sunday. She talked to one of her brothers, extending the same invitation. He complained gasoline was tight, and cash too. In the end, Sharon's family would travel in one van. Brandi and Jeff were eager to see their families, especially the three cousins.

Bill talked to his Mom who was only concerned about the crisis disrupting her television shows. Sharon's parents neared retirement. Bill's Mom was in her 70s, and his Dad had been dead for several years. She had good pension income and other money from his Dad's estate and lived alone in a high-rise condominium in the city. Bill suggested his mother move in with his sister Joyce, who also lived in Toronto. She replied with laughter and a flat 'no'. He had the same reaction from his sister; however, she agreed to drive up for the Thanksgiving get together. Their Mom's car had a full tank of gas and needed a run. Bill and Joyce's husband had never gotten along, and his brother-in-law would not be coming.

Luckily, Joyce has no children, the thought crossed Bill's mind for the first time,

It exasperated Bill and Sharon that none of their families knew or cared about the dangerous possibilities. They would talk about it on Sunday. Sharon and Bill would have been equally uninformed if Warren had not been their neighbour. Worst of all, Sharon's older brother was an economist working for an investment house. Harry Maki would push his usual investment advice, telling them to buy some get rich quick stock. This time, Bill decided, he would no longer bite his tongue and ask Harry, if he was so smart, why was he not rich?

***

The schools did not open Tuesday and stayed shut the rest of the week. It created urgency in most people, panic for some. More neighbours attended the second meeting at the Shadly's house. The gathering encouraged everyone, and they agreed to share supplies.

"Two families over on Third Street won't join," a member said. "They bragged they have enough food to last and don't need spongers and think the whole thing's going to blow over."

"I head the committee to list skills and resources," Sharon explained to the newcomers. "We'll have a list of needs ready for the next meeting."

"I agree we should share," a more reluctant joiner said, "but I want to keep everyone's supplies separate while we do it."

Nodding heads confirmed they all wanted to follow that idea.

One step at a time, Sharon thought.

Betty Durant attended. She sat quietly but lingered to talk with Sharon.

"Sharon, I want to help, but Bob's against it. He's getting angrier every day." Something in her voice scared Sharon.

"Betty, he needs to work with others. It's the only way to be safe."

"He's a boss at the factory. Bob thinks they need him or they'll go bust. He can't follow anyone, hasn't for years. He hates his bosses but acts friendly to their faces. They're all two-faced like him. He has no friends, just useful people."

"Bill has a nice employer. It's a great place to work." Sharon talked as if Bill would be at work tomorrow.

"Lucky him and lucky you," Betty did not sound bitter, perhaps envious

"Betty, come over this week and have a coffee with me."

"I would like that."

"Is Bob still going to work?"

"Yes, so far the company has had no problems, at least none they're admitting. They postponed the last pay. It's hard. We have no cash."

"What do you need?"

"We have run out of coffee and milk."

"I can give you a bit of both, but powdered milk. Your family should join and contribute. We all need help."

"I'll try to talk to Bob, but he gets so angry." Betty left with a small bag. She found ten dollars in with the food.

Warren, Jean, Bill, and Sharon remained, planning the next moves. The others saw them as the group's leadership. Warren wanted to give others some responsibility. He knew there could be resentment towards any leaders whenever things did not go well. He often said, "There will be lots of chances for things to go wrong, and they will." Warren sometimes made Bill wish for politicians like Ted Johnson with his rosy spin.

Jeff and Brandi had sat on the stairs, listening to the proceedings. Bill suggested they include the two, and all members bring their older kids. Children had to grow up too soon. Sharon and Bill did not like it.

***

Bill woke to early morning light creeping into the bedroom. Birdsong came through the open window on the gentle breeze of the extended summer. A flight of Canada Geese passed with their honking and wing pounding fading away. A chipmunk chattered and then a hollow thump.

"Shhh," sounded through the window. Bill had never heard that bird before. Then what sounded like "shut up". Bill jumped out of bed. Two figures crouched beside his pickup. Bill let himself out the front door and stepped around into the driveway.

"What the hell are you doing?" Bill shouted.

"Screw off, old man!"

Two boys about 16-years-old, wearing hoodies, expensive looking blue jeans and high-end runners jumped to their feet, defiant, ready to fight, glaring at Bill.

"We're doing nothing, butt head." Bill struggled to control his temper. The boys had a gas can and a hose. He did not see any weapons, not even a screwdriver for the gas cover. The two were scrawny. A grey car sat on the street, idling and wasting fuel.

"Get the hell off my property!" Bill stepped forward.

Bill was not a big man, less than six feet, but solidly built with his 200 pounds spread evenly. The physical effort of the past week had toned him a bit. These two did not seem formidable. Bill moved towards the boys.

"Get lost, goof!" The smaller one had a big mouth. Bill advanced. They both stepped back.

"What do you need the gas for?" Bill thought he might calm them down.

"No gas and no cash to buy it," the bigger one said.

"Shut up, idiot!" the smaller one was the leader.

"Don't you guys have jobs?" Bill was still determined.

"Are you kidding? My mom used to be generous. Now she won't help me keep the wheels turning, the useless broad!" The small one forgot himself in his anger and fear.

Bill decided the spoiled ingrate was beyond hope. He closed in. The bigger one ran, shooting past at full speed. The mouthy one finally moved clenching his fist, cocking his arm for a running shot. Bill ducked sideways, avoiding the blow. He stuck his left foot out sending the boy sprawling full length onto the asphalt driveway. The trespasser jumped up, bloody scrapes on his face and arms, balling up his fists as if to fight back, cursing Bill with an impressive string of expletives. Thinking better of it, he retreated to the car's driver's seat. The other lad spat at Bill and flipped the finger as they sped off. The license number was easy: 'ROADRAT'.

They had failed to pry the truck's locking gas door open. A few scratches were no big deal. Bill knew there would never be a trade in for the thing. He went into the house too keyed up for sleeping, planning to call the cops right after breakfast. The coffee finished when the doorbell rang.

"You the owner of that pickup?"

A town cop was at the door; and not friendly. Another stood near the road. The constable seemed late middle-aged, but his backup looked like a kid. There were two types of police officers in town, young rookies, or those retired from the Toronto Metros. This chap's greying grandfather look contrasted his rudeness.

"Yes, it's mine. I was just about to call you. I'm Bill Shadly." Bill stuck out his hand. The cop ignored it. "A couple of punks were trying to steal my gas."

"We have a complaint you assaulted a minor with no reason. Friend, you can't go around beating on kids. We don't put up with that around here. Let's have your version."

His tone was condescending with authoritarian threat right out of the policing handbook. Bill inclined to cooperate with police and up to this point, trusted and supported law enforcement. This cop raised warnings. Bill became cautious. Trying to sound cooperative, Bill slightly glossed over the truth, saying when the boys ran away one tripped and fell on the driveway. He denied hitting him.

"They were trying to steal from me," Bill added. "You should charge them."

"Look, Shadly, be thankful I don't take your statement down at the office." The hostility persisted. "I'll run this by the Chief; don't you make more trouble in the meantime."

The constable strode across Bill's lawn and joined his partner in the cruiser. He gunned the motor and sped off.

What was that all about?

It puzzled Bill until Jeff told him the boys were from well-to-do families up in the estates. People called the older subdivision "The Estates" because of the expensive houses on large lots. Most of the homeowners were from old local families with money, the bulk of the local establishment. Several were councillors. They were not rich enough for the Hills but could be snobs towards lower income residents.

"The cops know who to suck up to," Jeff said.

This cliquish behaviour had not affected Bill before that morning. Warren pointed out the folks in the housing estates did not have any cash either.

"They are as in tough as the rest of us when their plastic cards don't work. These rich folks have another problem," Warren said. "Their kids have high expectations raised to get what they want… maybe we all were, but these folks will find the loss more painful. I think it will make them dangerous."

"Most young people might be hostile, especially if they blame us for stealing their futures. No one likes to have their dreams taken away."

Chapter Five

The week quickly passed as people organized lists and storage space, with ad hoc meetings of two or three people comparing notes and speculating about the future. Most hoped the crisis would pass.

A couple who worked at a local car parts plant dropped out. They reported for work after the company guaranteed their pay. The promise had been a lie by some local managers who believed that if they bluffed for a few days, everything would return to normal. A week later, the group welcomed the return of the contrite pair.

Bill heard nothing from the police, but a patrol car passed the house several times a day. Previously, police had rarely appeared on their street.

Shadlys had most of what they needed for a traditional Thanksgiving meal. They emptied the freezer as a guard against losing electricity. Sharon's trip to the Foodland added a bag of frozen cranberries, day-old bread, frozen juice, and soda water for a punch. She hated spending the cash, but the family was worth it.

The store owner had no employees but his family. He had received a shipment from the central warehouse; however, the truck driver demanded a cash bonus to cover his services. The grocer believed things would be back to normal soon. When Sharon revealed they had started a self-help group, the grocer showed her the announcement from the mayor's office. It referred to "a group of troublemakers led by Warren Dunn" and implied dealing with other groups would disqualify people from town help. Sharon returned in an angry mood, but organizing the family Thanksgiving cheered her.

On Sunday, the aroma of a roasting turkey filled the house. Sharon tuned the stereo to a light rock station playing oldies from the 1990s. Sharon and Bill feared their families might not be together again for some time, and Bill hoped to convince his mom to go to his sister's or come to live in Weyburne.

The kids loved family visits. Two of their cousins were coming making if fun. In the past week, they had spent boring time with their friends gossiping and playing video games.

Bill's sister and mom were the first to arrive with warm hugs and smiles. Joyce followed Sharon into the kitchen, delivering a box of cookies and a bottle of good local wine.

"Sorry I couldn't bring more," she seemed disappointed. "We don't have cash, and the cards aren't working."

"Don't worry Joyce; we have enough for today. It's cash only up here too. Just seeing you both is great and the kids love their favourite aunt. How's Sarah doing?" Sharon thought her mother-in-law looked frail.

"She's confused and scared; hell, we're all scared. Mom's used to everything running on its own, automatic payments and deposits. Her cable went out, and she can't get anyone to fix it. Her life is watching television, and it has hit her hard. I've had her over at our place to watch her shows. On the ride up, all she talked about was getting her TV fixed."

Sharon sympathized. "We have all the services but it would be difficult without television. The music channel distracts the kids although Jeff and Brandi watch the news too."

Harry's minivan pulled into the driveway. The cousins ran ahead into the house, and Brandi and Jeff greeted them enthusiastically, then they disappeared up the stairs. Sharon watched from the front entranceway. For the first time in a week, her kids seemed carefree. Her Mom and Dad came with warm hugs and a kiss on the cheek from her father. He pressed a large bottle of fine wine into her hand and set a well-stuffed bag on the kitchen floor. Peter showed a calm and strength Sharon always found reassuring.

"How's it going, Shadly?" Peter and Bill got along well, but Maki Sr. always referred to Bill by his last name, a male thing. Sharon did not like it.

"It's a disaster, haven't been to work since the 25th and have heard nothing for a week,"

"I wouldn't worry. Our office has been near normal. They promise to pay us on time. Most people have carried on. A few have carpooled because they have no gas. There's plenty for sale, but you need cash to buy it. Things will be fine. Did you see the last Argo game? What a mess this year!" They spoke no more of the crisis until after dinner.

Bill took Peter out back to chat in the warm October sun, sipping beer and talking football. Harry Maki came out later holding an imported brew.

Peter and Harry became involved in a heated conversation. Harry argued the NFL was real football, the CFL sucked. Bill had seen this before and wisely shut up. He disliked gridiron football, preferring the soccer he had played at school. Father and son agreed on one thing; soccer was a "pansy game". Bill sipped his beer, watching blue jays play tag in the now bare maple.

Upstairs, the kids were listening to the latest pop music, catching up on happenings since their last get together in August. Brandi and Jeff's cousins were envious. The Shadly kids had not gone to school for a week. The cousins went to a private school, which was still open. Their older sister had gone to New York City on a school outing and would be back Monday. Brandi and Jeff thought it scary to be away from home in this crisis.

"Hey, listen to this latest Barry one… what a hottie." Jeff's cousin was a typical 15-year-old boy. The girls just rolled their eyes, but they liked the song.

The women sat around the big, maple kitchen table renewing their friendships over a glass of wine. The mothers-in-law had grown closer after Sharon and Bill's wedding even though Cheryl Maki lived a much richer lifestyle. Sarah Shadly was older than Sharon's mom, the big sister Cheryl never had.

The older Makis accepted everyone as they were. Peter came from a working-class background. He had never become a snob despite being an engineer and manager. Sharon's oldest brother Harry had become arrogant. Sharon thought it came from the financial elite that employed him.

"The drive up scared me." Sarah Shadly seemed more frail than normal. "Lots of people hung about on the street, and we passed a big brawl."

The others added they had seen many idle folks about all week. The traffic seemed light, but they did not know what normal traffic would be like. Mary added she had not seen real trouble, although squeegee kids were aggressive when she did not give them money.

The afternoon gave way to dinner time. Peter claimed his position as patriarch and carved the turkey. Sharon set a festive table, with an earth tone tablecloth and a dried leaf centrepiece. As tradition demanded, Cheryl said grace. No one thought it out of place that none of them attended church services. The last time any of them had been in a church was at a wedding. None had any support network beyond family, a few friends, work or school. Only the small-town Shadlys had a stronger support-circle, which they had firmed up during the past week.

Humour and teasing filled the conversation. Bill and Sharon wanted to make the dinner positive and keep wonderful memories from the day. They still hoped for a return to normal, but deep down they suspected something worse. Mary photographed everyone hugging their parents and made a group shot on the self-timer. She promised to e-mail the pictures.

The men cleared away the remnants and placed coffee and wine refills on the table. Bill steered the conversation to the crisis. The children stayed. He outlined what they were doing, honestly stating their hopes and fears.

"I think you are way overboard, Shadly," Peter sounded fatherly. "The government and the banks will fix it."

"Hate to agree with you, Dad," Harry chimed in with his version of humour. "The government's injecting big wads of cash. The banks will start lending. I wish I had more cash on hand, but that's just an annoyance. No problem!"

"This local thing you have going," Peter had little to do with neighbours except those with a common fence, "is wasting your time. These people will take you for all you have. A few came to our place trying to get our neighbourhood together. I told them to move on." He paused. "I said I didn't believe in that co-op crap."

"Besides," Cheryl chimed in, "we are flying to the Yucatan for a week. Everything will be fine."

"Mom," Sharon exploded. "You can't be serious? It's way too dangerous in Mexico. Haven't you listened to the news? Since the oil thing, the violence has gotten worse. Even their cops are gangsters."

"Don't worry, little one," Sharon's father reassured. "We've been there a dozen times and saw nothing more dangerous than a shark."

Sharon would never persuade them. They had travelled there often. Maybe she was just overly cautious. Living so far from the rest of the family had made her nervous. She feared the crisis would leave them permanently separated.

"This is a great opportunity!" Harry interjected loudly, "We should look for investment opportunities." Bill was pondering the verbal "why aren't you richer" take out, but decided for the better. He did not want bad feelings on this family day. If he ever had Harry alone, he would say his piece. Sharon and Bill thought Harry and his family were living way beyond their means. If things did not improve, Harry would be his own worst enemy.

"We need to plan for the worst. Either way, we would have more security."

"That's a waste of time," Harry sneered, "you need to get on with life."

The other Makis nodded in agreement. Bill cursed himself for making a strategic error about his Mom's safety. With the Maki clan so optimistic, she was firmer in her desire to stay on her own. They resolved nothing and moved to the living room to spend a last hour reminiscing.

The day passed too quickly. No one wanted to be on the road at a late hour. By nine o'clock, they were putting on coats. Sharon hugged her family extra hard. Bill squeezed his Mom and asked her to consider moving in with Joyce or to Weyburne. She smiled and said she would be fine. Bill told her he loved her.

It was a clear October night. A north-west wind carried the touch of cold. Summer's heat and semi-drought had persisted into September. October had begun pleasantly warm, but the summery weather was ending. The year's first hard freeze would be tonight. Stubborn, dead leaves rattled in the big maple. A dust eddy wandered down the street as taillights flared red and disappeared around the corner. Sharon shivered. There was a tear in her eye. Bill hugged her. There was no sound but the wind.

***

The Tuesday after Thanksgiving, Bill could wait no longer. He called his boss, but the answering machine picked up. Bill punched in Wilson's extension and got his automated message. "Because of circumstances, we will not accept incoming calls". Bill left a brief message. He would try each day hoping to catch Wilson.

Warren dropped by to ask Bill to use his truck to fetch some food. Bob Spencer, a grower up the Fourth Line, had potatoes but no buyers. Dunne figured there could be hundreds of pounds for the families in the group. The trip turned into three, with two loads of potatoes and a load of carrots. Each family received several bushels. Bill found the use of volume measure novel. He had always bought by weight. It was an early hint of what happens when they had to simplify technology. Spencer asked for a written IOU stating if the recipients got the cash, they would pay the farmer. Warren signed the paper.

Schools stayed closed all week while the school board sorted out employees' pay. Government workers still had their money deposited into their banks. The post office, OPP, Hydro-One and other direct government agencies continued to function. The federal government put its employees on monthly rather than bi-weekly pay. A payroll date loomed, and transactions would freeze without the banks' cooperation.

The federal government publicly threatened the banks with new regulations to force federal and provincial cash flow. Even though the Feds could issue bank notes, they required payroll to move easily. The banks relented, but the feds could not apply the agreement to local governments, leaving them with no cash available. Local employees stayed at work on faith they would get their pay.

The banks did not restore business lines of credit and cancelled overdraft protection. At the private level, all credit remained frozen. In this frenzy of activity, governments announced massive layoffs of civil servants.

Sharon had Jeff and Brandi invite their friends for cookies and juice. Six kids arrived, and it amazed Sharon they thought about deeper issues.

"Have you been to the Cut-Rate?" asked one of Jeff's buddies. "I was in there yesterday, just looking, until mean, old-man Williams kicked me out. He cut the prices on his junk except for pop, chocolate bars, and stuff."

"All food is up in price," Sharon chipped in.

"Why is that, Mom?" Brandi had not shopped for a week.

"People with cash need to buy food, so the price is up. They don't need everything else, so no one is buying. Mr Williams wants to get something for the luxuries and has cut the price."

"Why are pop and candy high?"

"To some people, candy is food, and they will pay. Gas is expensive because people who need it will pay. Gas ran out two weeks ago," she explained to the group, "and now it's available at a high price. Demand is down, but the price reflects what it cost the service station."

"Why don't people need gas?" Jeff paid keen attention to his mother.

"Most commuters stayed home the past week or two and didn't need any. People are walking whenever they can."

Sharon invented a project for the kids. "Track the pump price down at the Petro over the next few weeks. See if it comes down. Ask Mr Banerjee what's going on." Sharon did not think prices would drop. The station had to make the most from each sale. Fuel remained costly until supplies finally ran out.

The kids loved the cookie party. Their friends told Jeff and Brandi their Mom was "cool and made good cookies". All of them took a few extra in their pockets and Sharon doubted they were eating well. The cookie party at the Shadly's grew to include about a dozen kids. Every time, Sharon became more impressed by their intelligence and understanding. This trait was not clear before the crash when hoodies covered heads, and texting on cells seemed to be their only concern. The kids still used cells, but while they were in Sharon's kitchen, the youngsters did not bother. Parents came by to thank her. She always invited them in for tea and cookies, recruiting more for the emergency group.

Thursday, after Thanksgiving, a group met at Warren's house to socialize and watch the television news. This gathering had become a common event. After declining for many years, tax revenue plunged after the September crisis. The federal and provincial governments issued bonds to cover their daily expenses and cash injections to the banks. The financial elite would refer to this day as the real collapse. The glum news anchor announced the failure of the Canadian bond sale. International governments had issued notes as well with no buyers. Investors did not trust government bonds.

The talking heads tried to spin something positive from the news, but none of these self-appointed experts mustered a smile. No financial industry spokespeople appeared on camera.

Before the bond fiasco, politicians had injected huge amounts of cash into the banks. Lending between banks had been difficult for years, and the situation grew worse in the summer before the crisis. Most banks had been hoarding cash to pay off their mutual liabilities. Insiders knew that every institution held massive amounts of worthless debt. Bankers and politicians around the world had lied about bank solvency and the disaster surprised the public. Government officials admitted uncertainty about a solution. Warren's group did not understand.

"What does all this mean?" one asked. "I'm no expert and am confused."

"It means the governments have no money and neither do the banks." Dunne said. "They don't trust each other and the bond buyers don't trust any of them."

"What does that mean to us in Weyburne?"

"Does anyone here have government bonds?" Sharon saw the implications. Several people owned Canada Savings Bonds.

"I don't think..." Sharon hesitated, "I don't think they will be worth anything by the time they mature."

"My God," people exclaimed. "All of my savings…"

"We'll know soon enough." Warren said. He owned government bonds. "I don't think any investment is worth anything, including stocks, mutual funds and even GICs."

It did not surprise Warren. He had been preparing for disaster abstractly. Now, it became a reality. Dunne glanced around his living room writing off his possessions including the house. His calm face masked hidden turmoil and sadness. He would try to lead by being calm and clear-headed.

The Canadian government quietly abandoned its bond campaign and suspended redemptions of maturing bonds. The rich hoarded their money, and few others earned any. By the week's end, the news viewing parties at Dunne's had become depressing affairs.

The USA became chaotic. Marines landed in Iran to open the straits from the Persian Gulf, but it turned into a bloody debacle. The US military underestimated their opponent. The horrific casualty figures remained unpublished along with the numbers of cruise missiles they had used. Spectacular video of exploding warheads gave way to scenes of distraught relatives of dead and missing soldiers.

Rioting broke out in many cities. Demonstrations demanding food turned into mob events of burning and looting. Soldiers' relatives began calling for the return of their loved ones. The United States government agreed. They wanted the troops home to help suppress the riots. The huge, ferocious crowds outmatched unprepared National Guard units, and the militarized police.

Europe saw some of the worst riots in years, and the UK turned into a bloody battle zone. Street fighting in Belfast was out of control, with the old religious, racist overtones rampant. Racism was one of the common themes in almost every country. Ethnic communities waged brutal battles against each other. This news made the Dunne organization uneasy. Black and Asian families had joined the group, and many more lived in the community.

In Ontario, things had taken an ugly turn. Toronto police guarded the stock exchange, city hall and the headquarters of banks and the upscale neighbourhoods represented in the Legislature by government members. The government left hospitals, universities and residential neighbourhoods to their luck. Massive demonstrations demanded food, cash and a guarantee that landlords could not evict for non-payment.

Local, middle-class people looted and firebombed several bank branches in wealthier neighbourhoods. The poorer parts of the city remained relatively calm. One journalist pointed out that poor people did things with cash, and the credit freeze had little impact. The reporter visited these places expecting to find looting and chaos but discovered a scary development. Local gangs were issuing cash to needy residents. These thugs used huge amounts of ready cash from their drug operations to buy support.

Prices in the poor neighbourhoods remained high, while formerly richer ones saw falling prices because of the lack of cash. Chains diverted what food they had to the higher priced stores in the formerly poorer but now cash-rich neighbourhoods. Shortages appeared in upscale places. The underprivileged areas might see chaos in the future, but for the time being, cash was king.

Bill's torture ended on the next Sunday evening. Sharon handed him the phone and mouthed the word, Wilson. She looked hopeful.

"Shadly," the voice was thin and choking, "Wilson here… I'm out of business. I can't get any money at all." Bill heard a noticeable sob. "I liked working with you, Bill. I'm sorry it has to end like this. There isn't any severance or back pay; I'm sorry. All the best to you and your family, goodbye." Sobbing came from the other end of the line, then silence. He would never hear Wilson's voice again.

Bill hung up the phone, turned and hugged Sharon. She did not need to ask.

The Friday after Thanksgiving, the school boards announced the schools would re-open on Monday. Many were relieved, and sceptics taunted Warren. Many of these waved Ted Johnson's decree in Warren's face. They said he was wrong again, just a wacko. He tried not to show it, but this hurt him deeply and made him depressed. Dunne did not want the schools to stay closed just to prove him right, but people's eager embrace of any positive news disheartened him. Bill cheered him with one of his remaining bottles of beer.

On Monday, the kids reported to class, but the schools did not operate as usual. Several teachers did not arrive. They had panicked when their pay was missing and went to find other jobs. The cafeteria staff and educational assistants did not cone to work. Principals assigned students to help handicapped kids. Custodians were the only non-teaching staff present.

The schools depended on bussing for most students. Everything was fine the first couple of days, but on Thursday some buses did not show up for the afternoon run. They had run out of fuel. The drivers used credit cards to fuel up the units, but plastic no longer worked. Cash was not an option since the banks had cancelled the bus company's line of credit. On Friday, several drivers tried to run their kids home and ran out of fuel on the way. Dozens of kids walked home in an icy drizzle. The last two buses to service the schools made their last runs on the following Monday. Abandoned buses languished in their parking lots and along the roads.

Some families tried to drive their kids to school, but few could afford the fuel. Most children stayed home, suffering in semi-isolation in hundreds of suburban-style houses spread thinly along the back roads.

Jeff and Brandi reported the schools were less than half-full, and many teachers did nothing. This situation with the schools lasted two weeks until the school board missed another payroll. Unannounced, the province had cut off transfers to the boards. The schools closed, never to reopen. There was no official announcement. Students and teachers showed up to find the doors locked and the buildings dark. Parents did not believe the story, and a large crowd of bewildered adults and students spent the morning milling about the front doors of the high school. Their world had changed with a final certainty.

Town staff had the message of change delivered harshly. For the second time, the town missed its payroll. The bank told the municipality they had no credit, refusing to process any transactions. Weyburne laid off all employees with no severance pay; just a thank you for their loyalty in a flowery letter over Ted Johnson's name.

Johnson, showing compassion, delivered each notice personally, with handshakes and a promise to find some money for them all. Ted was the mayor and their boss but he considered employees as friends. The police stayed on, sticking to their posts despite not being paid.

Word of mouth quickly spread the news. After Thanksgiving, the local paper stopped selling new advertising and laid the employees off without notice. The previous week's hope changed into gloom and fear.

Chapter Six

"Hello Betty," Sharon held her front door open wide. "It's so nice to see you." Sharon welcomed someone she hoped would become a friend.

"Sorry to bother you," Betty Durant was embarrassed, "but I wondered if you could help me again." She fidgeted uneasily. Betty wore a warm expensive powder-blue ski jacket but hugged herself and held her hands, in pink wool mittens, against her sides. Sharon at first thought her visitor was being defensive but then realized Betty felt cold from hunger.

"What do you need?" Sharon calculated what she could spare.

"I can't serve the kids any breakfast. Bob brought home a few things provided by his company, but it's gone. The kids are hungry and depressed. I'd like to get something hot into them." Betty dropped her arms to her sides; palms turned forward in a gesture of helplessness.

"I can give you some oatmeal, powdered milk and a little sugar to dress it up. Would that do?"

"It would be wonderful. The kids are used to their special sports diets, but they're hungry. I'm sure they'll eat that." She flashed a genuine smile, and Sharon felt a positive connection. As she organized the supplies, she planned how to get Betty more involved. The group decided right from the start charity and handouts would not lead to actual solutions. People had to work together. Warren wanted to build a network of people committed to mutual help.

"Why don't you come back soon," Sharon suggested, handing over a plastic bag containing enough material for several breakfasts. "I mix one part oatmeal with two water in a bowl and nuke it three minutes. Don't let it sit long before you add the milk; mix the powder up first. I've been stretching that out ten to one. The recommendation is six. Times are tough."

Sharon had explored how to use oatmeal once milk was gone. She tried frying oatmeal cakes instead of serving porridge. The kids and Bill seemed to enjoy the little pancakes. Bill called them "Scottish tortillas".

"Thank you so much," Betty sounded relieved.

Sharon stood in the chilly October morning watching Betty hurry towards her house. Within half an hour, the doorbell rang. A sobbing, distraught Betty Durant confronted Sharon.

"Sharon," she sobbed, "the kids were awful and refused to eat the oatmeal. They said it was pig food, and it disgusted them. They said I disgusted them." The woman slumped against the doorframe. "Bob has said that to me many times. The kids must have heard him."

Sharon drew Betty inside to the kitchen. The kettle steamed for morning tea. With Bill and the kids at Dunne's to organize his storage, Sharon had looked forward to a few minutes of peace. Betty's anguish concerned her.

"What happened?"

"I got home with the food and had everything ready. When I called the kids down they took one look at it and started attacking me." Betty sobbed, and Sharon found her a handkerchief. "Bob and the kids have become abusive. They shut me out of their world in the past few years. I never shared Robert's hockey ambition. It was Bob's baby." Betty paused and composed herself.

"Bob was an excellent hockey player before we met, maybe he could have made pro, but had an injury, and that ended it. He drove Robert hard to have the career he never had. They think winning is the only thing. Bob wanted to move to the city for Robert's career, but we can't afford it. He blamed me for that too."

Sharon poured the tea.

"Did you eat?" Sharon cut a large piece of carrot cake.

Betty devoured the delicacy.

"Thank you, Sharon. This cake is wonderful."

"This is Brandi's birthday cake. She's 13 today." Sharon had promised a little celebration at lunch, much different from the party she had been planning.

"I ate the oatmeal to show them it was good. It tasted wonderful, but the kids just yelled at me more." Betty took a mouthful of tea.

"Roberta has pushed away from me, taking her Dad's advice on everything. We used to be so close when she was in primary school, but now all she talks about is becoming a rich lawyer. They think I'm a stupid failure, a dumb stay at home Mom who never completed high school."

Sharon noted both the children's names came from their father. It was apparent who ruled in the Durant house. Her heart went out to Betty.

"Betty, I'm sure they love you." Sharon was not sure.

"It doesn't seem like it. Bob wrote me off a long time ago. I worked hard so that he could go to college, but as he got up in the company, he pushed me away. I thought it was because he was busy, but I guess he thinks I am a useless old broad." Betty sighed deeply.

It appeared to Sharon Betty had resolved these issues long ago, and she had come to terms with her life. The physical and emotional stress of this economic crisis had made her vulnerable. Sharon thought about the strength required for Betty to survive emotionally. She thought the catastrophe would tear the Durants apart and wondered why Betty had not left long ago.

Sharon smiled. "We can turn you into a useful old broad."

"I thought you might have enough of those."

"As Bill's fond of saying if we had a few more women working the men could just sit and drink beer."

"That's what they do best," Betty laughed, "and stand around giving orders to the real workers." The women giggled.

"Bill was going to become a manager. I told him he would have been the man in charge of the lucky sevens on the slot machines." Sharon almost snorted tea out her nose. The women laughed in unison. "Now, I call him the potato king. He calls me the carrot queen. We told the kids their names are Bud and Julienne, but they don't get it."

Tears streamed down Sharon's cheeks. The sad morning turned into some relief. Sharon had not realized how much stress she had bottled up. These silly jokes opened the relief valve.

"I love it that your family has so much fun." Betty leaned on her hand, contented. "Can I take some home in a bag?"

"No, you can't," Sharon replied, more seriously, "but you can come for a refill anytime."

The women's talk turned to practical things. They worked out a plan for Betty's role in the self-help group. Sharon needed someone to do the record keeping.

Sharon hugged Betty at the door when Bill and the kids arrived. Sharon had given Betty some bread, cheese and lard to make grilled cheese sandwiches. They were certain the spoiled brats would eat those.

"You two seem to be good friends," Bill looked pleased.

"Bill, she's a lonely woman. I don't know how she lasts in that family. Bob's abusing her, mentally at least. We will be good friends. Betty will help with record keeping. We had a good cry and a good laugh. I like her."

"Happy birthday, Brandi," Sharon gave her daughter a big hug and a kiss, "now I have two teenagers to deal with." Jeff pretended to give Brandi advice on bugging her parents. Bill produced a gift wrapped in Christmas paper.

"We couldn't find birthday paper, Sweetie. Don't tear it. We might have to use it for your Christmas present too."

Brandi opened the package and found a well-bound drawing book and a set of expensive pencil crayons, drawing pencils and water paints. She was an exceptional artist. They had bought the present in August in Toronto.

"Thank you so much. It's perfect!" Brandi hugged them all, giving Jeff an extra hug when he produced several reams of good computer printer paper as a gift. They all knew Brandi had artistic talent. Bill and Sharon hoped drawing would give her some happiness, not knowing it would come to fill her life.

Birthday lunch consisted of grilled cheese and tomato soup, using up the last of their cheese and some of the remaining ketchup. Brandi's birthday cake had two slices missing. She joked it had been pre-tasted. Their next meal would be oatmeal pancakes fried in chicken fat and Warren's pickled beets with water to drink.

"We've laid off all municipal staff." Ted Johnson glanced across the room to where Matt Long and Walt Lefevre were busy examining lists of the needy. "I let Matt go from the dealership. He's willing to work with us."

"Walt's hanging in too. He'll have a job when business improves." Will Kirk did not look up from his notebook.

"He'll make some money out of it too." Johnson had some guilt at exploiting the situation but justified it by believing someone would have the advantage. It might as well be him.

The mayor and the real estate broker sat at the head of the council table in the town office. Matt and Walt occupied a separate, smaller table beneath the window. The rest of the original group of schemers looked after their own concerns. The alcoholic had dropped out when it became clear he would only benefit if he did some of the work. All the other helpers disappeared as soon as their jobs went.

Unpaid wages led to hard feelings. Several town employees had left angry. Matt and Walt remained as the only remaining workers, while Evy the receptionist volunteered to help the mayor.

"All we have to do is to help these folks hang on until we get their properties." Will Kirk ignored the other two men in the room. He only considered people important if they had use to him. Will believed Matt and Walt shared his greed and would keep silent. "It'll be a month before we grab the properties. Many will sell to us for a promise to pay." Matt and Walt stopped to listen.

"There are a few dozen folks on the list we've been promising to help." Ted glanced at the list of names and addresses. He frowned. Several were his neighbours and friends. "We can't expect to get all of them, but we'll roll up at least half of the properties at a few cents on the dollar." Ted and Will imagined the expected profits.

"Our problem is getting them what they want." Ted frowned again. "Walt told me people expected processed stuff. Most of them don't want to do the work. We can only scrounge up potatoes, carrots and live chickens."

"We don't have enough people to do the work for them. These two aren't enough." Matt and Walt listened even more intently. "Smith got his potato farmer buddy, Bob Spencer to give us some produce as long as we cut him into the profits. Spencer sold some to Dunne for an IOU. Roger thinks we might squeeze Dunne with it if we need to. Maybe we can get the jerk to shut up. Spencer can't deliver the stuff. "

"I'll have these guys take my van and get what we can, probably only a few bushels for the few who will take it." Ted sipped his coffee.

"Hey, Matt, how many potatoes and stuff do we need?" Johnson walked over to check the men's figures.

"For a couple of weeks, we need four bushels of potatoes, two of carrots and about 48 chickens." Walt shuffled through his lists. "Can we get the butcher at the Foodland to cut some meat? We rounded up some lamb, beef and a goat, but need someone to butcher them."

"They let the butcher go. He farms south of town. I'll find him." Ted leant over Walt's shoulder. "Take the van from the dealership. You two go to Spencer's for the potatoes and carrots. We'll start with that."

"Spencer's on the Fourth Line near Fifteen Side Road. The big red potato shed on the east side."

The mayor returned to his seat in a sombre mood. Johnson realized the services everyone depended on were disappearing. The situation had gone out of control; their efforts seemed puny.

Matt and Walt left, wanting to get the food back to the town office before dark. They walked in silence for a few blocks. Finally, Walt spoke.

"What did you make of what we heard?" He looked unhappy.

"We're part of a get rich scheme they're running just to hook desperate people into being scammed."

"That's my reading of it." Walt tied his boot. Most of the leaves had fallen on the ground and covered the walkway. A mist had formed. It would be a classic, foggy fall night. "I don't like being used. They just want to keep people going and get rich off their misery." He was angry.

"I don't like it either. What can we do? We're helping people in the short term." Matt fumbled for the keys to the dealership.

Walt pulled Johnson's flyer from his pocket. He carried a few to give to people who needed help. "There's this other self-help group headed by that Dunne guy. If Johnson bothered to badmouth them, he sees them as rivals. I've heard Dunne isn't out for himself. Maybe he just wants to help people. We could throw in with them."

"We can at least find out about them." Matt had the door open and went to retrieve the van keys. When he returned, Walt grinned.

"What's so funny?" Matt led the way to the big one-tonne panel van with the flashy sales graphics. The advertising seemed hollow.

"I have an idea that'll help us decide, and we'll get revenge for being duped. Just go along with what I say to Spencer."

Matt sent the big van speeding up the highway. There would be no police speed traps. They arrived as Spencer left his storage shed.

"Hello, Mr Spencer," Matt said. "Ted Johnson sent us for some potatoes and carrots. He said Roger Smith had talked with you."

The farmer hated to backtrack and do work; however, Roger was an ally but dangerous. Spencer would do nothing to upset him or the movers and shakers who ran the county. He might need all the friends he could find. Bob owned his farm outright. He had mortgaged the rest of his business and needed cash to make payments.

"Okay, let's load you up. Back in through the big door." The lights revealed tonnes of potatoes in bins and overflowing wooden carrot cribs.

"What do you need?" Spencer offered heavy gloves to the visitors.

"Twenty-four bushels of potatoes and half of that in carrots," Walt jumped in. "A few more of each will probably take us to the end of the crisis." Walt winked at Matt.

"Do you have bags?" Lefevre pushed.

"I have lots of old grain bags," Spencer seemed unperturbed. "Fill the potatoes over there at that hopper. The chute's handy. We have to hand load the carrots."

The men worked for an hour, joined by Spencer's wife who had come looking for Bob at dinner time. They finished after dark. As Matt slammed the van doors, Bob produced a clipboard and noted the amounts.

"I'll need this signed for Roger to reckon up later." Spencer might have donated the stuff, but he had to follow business procedure with his wife present. The woman did not believe in giving anything away.

"No problem," Walt replied cheerfully. He signed Will Kirk's name. Spencer paid no attention to the signature. Walt's future lay elsewhere than in the real estate office. He felt liberated.

"What do we do with all this stuff?" Matt turned the overloaded vehicle towards Weyburne. "I'm mad at you for the extra work." It intrigued Matt Long more than upset him.

"Let's find Dunne and offer him the extra." Walt chuckled.

Matt joined in the laughter as he guided the load around potholes.

Warren Dunne's garage soon held 20 bags of potatoes and ten of carrots. Matt and Walt agreed to attend the group meetings. Walt Lefevre needed to provide for his family. Their explanation of their boss' plot cheered Warren. The personal attack in the flyer hurt him deeply. The truth helped. Matt and Walt delivered the rest to the town hall and resigned. Ted Johnson and Evy would dispense potatoes to grumpy citizens.

"I always enjoyed travelling in the States." The scenes of violence on the midday news mesmerized Evy. "Now it looks like Syria."

"It's war." Ted Johnson leant forward as a rooftop camera showed live images of police and militia units trying to capture a massive street barricade in Chicago. "Look at all the guns those rioters have." The television commentary characterized the citizen-army as rioters and criminals, reserving the word "insurgent" for foreigners fighting their own governments.

"I can't make much sense of this... Oh God, they just shot those people." Evy sank back into her chair away from the violence. "Every large American city's like this."

"This crisis is only a few weeks old and lots of violence already." As if Ted prompted the script, the channel cut away to Toronto coverage.

"We now have a live report from the Don Mills shopping complex. Here's Saachi Nairat on the corner of Don Mills Road and Lawrence Avenue East and remember you saw it first on PopNewsNet."

The scene changed to a jerky view of a grey wall, and then the camera panned to a street entrance to the maze of streets and shops. Thick black smoke and flames rose from deep in the complex. The sound of shouting and breaking glass accompanied wailing sirens. A young reporter clutched her microphone.

"This is an uncontrolled riot," Saachi gasped. "People tell me this began about ten this morning. Someone spread a rumour that the Foody-Doody supermarket had supplies and would open. The crowd gathered before daybreak and became violent when the store did not open. Most of the rioters are in their 20s and older."

Saachi ducked as the sound of gunfire erupted behind her. She disappeared for a moment while the camera recorded police rushing into the complex and a fire crew crouching against a building. Saachi reappeared just as several people rushed past the firefighters carrying looted electronics.

"The police have moved in and we hear gunshots. You can see looters escaping." She blinked and dabbed at her eyes with a sleeve. "I'm sorry, the tear gas is bad." The coverage continued for a half hour until a police constable shoved the news crew away as paramedics carried injured officers from the mall.

"Not as bad as the USA." Evy said. "At least it's Toronto and not here."
"Don't count on it." Ted had become more upset than Evy. "Things in Toronto usually bite Weyburne in the ass."

Ted and Evy spent most days at the town hall doing little but watching television news and fielding calls from angry residents.

"We should just record our message," Evy had said to the Mayor. "All we ever say is, there's nothing we can do at the moment; we'll get back to you. Would you like some potatoes?"
"We wouldn't have to put up with the abuse."

In the days after the Don Mills riot, there were hundreds of similar incidents. In reaction, the Province decreed they would control food and fuel distribution.

"The Province wants to sort it out, but they're off to a poor start." Evy sounded discouraged. "All they've done so far is screw things up. Looting and violence are increasing."

"My guys are getting a handle on it." Ted was a loyal member of the ruling provincial party. "These 100-dollar vouchers and the gas chits will settle things down. Everything will improve soon."

"I don't see what a 100 bucks will do." Evy had always demurred to the mayor on political ideas. The crisis had shaken her faith in politicians, including Ted.

"I can answer that, young lady." The local Member of Provincial Parliament pushed through the doorway. "It'll calm people down and buy us time. We froze all prices to what they were on the 25th. The people deserve the help."

Evy smiled. Maybe the MPP had news, but whenever Ted and Joe McCarty, whom she called "Malarkey", got together, it usually led to a lot of empty talk. Ted had lost to McCarty when Johnson made a try for the provincial nomination. The Premier had hand-picked party insider McCarty. Ted did not like the man.

"It looks good, Joe," Ted never revealed his true feelings. "The media say the help is too little and open to abuse. Stores are overcharging, and people are selling and trading their gas vouchers. Someone mugged one old lady right outside the office."

"There's lots of that going on. Security is sketchy with the riots and all. Selling the vouchers is free enterprise in action." McCarty sounded smug. "The media never liked us and always whine. The Premier doesn't care. He says these will be cheap votes. He's sorry about the killings at Queen's Park. When they hurt that cop, the police went nuts."

"The reporters say it looks like you're learning as you go." Ted nodded towards the television.

"More media distortion, our constituency offices are distribution points in our ridings. Everyone needs to know; it's our party helping them. Opposition ridings have to wait."

"When will we get help?" Ted's concern for his town trumped support for his political cronies. "Your office in Orangeville's a long hike for folks."

"Look, Ted, you're a politician. You know we take care of swing ridings first. You people up here have never voted in an opposition MPP. We don't worry about your loyalty. Your turn's coming." McCarty kept smiling.

Ted seethed inside. Johnson disliked McCarty as an outsider with no local roots. On the television, a mob surged down a wide street. The graphic said it was at Bathurst and Steeles in Toronto's north end.

"Damned uppity immigrants," McCarty scowled, "we let in too many. They're using drug money to get one over on us." 'Us' meant the wealthier white people who lived in government represented ridings. He forgot many of his supporters were wealthy immigrants who paid their way.

"We're making sure food and gas goes to our areas. These punks will get leftovers."

"We should have voted for the other guy once in a while." Ted needled McCarty.

"You guys are smarter than that and benefited when I got the highway re-paved. You'll get yours, eventually."

McCarty suddenly looked worried. "We have no hope of solving this if the Yanks and the rest of the world don't. We import most of our food and fuel. The local fruit and vegetables are rotting because the factories closed, and the grain is sitting in bins. The milk plants closed, and slaughterhouses aren't working. On the Q-T, our warehouses are almost empty. We won't be shipping outside the GTA for a bit. No, the Yanks have to save us."

The television showed a riot outside the port at Philadelphia. Many undelivered containers held food. McCarty's cell phone rang.

"I got to go," Joe picked up his coat. "There's trouble at my office in Orangeville. I'll be back. The Prem. wants us to tour and let everyone know the party's working on it."

Ted and Evy returned to the local news. The mob surrounded a supermarket on Bayview Avenue, smashing windows. Gunfire sounded from inside. An overturned ambulance lay in front of the Halloween display.

"You look terrible." Evy was alone in the town hall when Joe McCarty returned two days later. McCarty had a large welt on his eye and scrapes on his cheek.

"Had a little scrap at the Orangeville office, I won." He tried to smile. "Where's Johnson?"

"Ted's out meeting some business people to organize his aid effort. A lot has gone on since you were here."

"Yeah, I've been on the phone with The Park almost hourly. Did you see the cop on cop thing last night?"

"No, but the chief told me this morning, he was upset."

"They shouldn't have put it on TV." McCarty disliked the media even more. "Some cops went rogue and weren't following the plan. They let those welfare punks have food from that store on Yonge Street. It was supposed to be for our riding folks. They even arrested some of the good people for complaining."

The news had shown fistfights and an armed confrontation with the officers.

"That shootout started when we sent a squad to replace them with loyal cops." Most local television outlets had shown a vicious gunfight between the cops inside the store and other officers outside, but coverage suddenly stopped.

"The Mayor and Premier had their friends who own the cable systems block that crap." McCarty frowned. "They won't be mentioning it again."

"Once was enough," Evy agreed. "We haven't had a food shipment since last week."

"Doesn't look good short term," McCarty slumped into a chair. "Dishonest people are taking cash for what's in the stores and then running off. A lawyer in Oakville has organized a vigilante outfit. They are fighting the outsiders for their share, but the warehouses have little. Few trucks get there. Crooks hijack them, especially near London; other drivers sell to the highest bidder on the 401.
Where did you say Ted was?"

"He's over at the Legion."

McCarty headed out the door.

That evening Bob Durant swung his Escalade into a parking spot near the Rec. Centre main door. There was only one vehicle in the lot, unusual for a practice night.

"Where's everyone?" Bob paused at the manager's office. Robert dropped his equipment bag and slapped the blade of his new Easton onto the cork tile. Beyond the double glass doors to his left, the arena was dark.

"We're closed." The manager struggled out of the office. "All minor-hockey's cancelled." He glanced towards the darkened ice surface. "Haven't you seen the news?"

"Just got home from work; how come we didn't get a call?" Bob looked peeved.

"Not up to me, Dick's the convener. They postponed all pro sports indefinitely because of money. The NHL cancelled everything until December and will decide on the season in November; same for the NBA. They cancelled the CFL and NFL seasons until next year."

"That's not fair!" Durant flared. "What a bunch of sissies."

The manager shrugged and returned to his desk and the NHL's Top Ten Playoff Games running on TSN. Bob Durant and his son made their way into the gloomy night.

In the middle of the night, while the family slept, Bob Durant quietly went to the basement and unlocked his gun cabinet.

Chapter Seven

Bill stepped out his front door into the frosty morning air on the last Thursday in October. Brightly flashing lights of emergency vehicles at the big house on the corner caught his attention. Garish hues of red and mauve reflected from the houses and barren tree trunks. He had not heard sirens.

"Sharon! Come see this."

"Oh my god, Bill, it's Durant's! What's going on? I don't see smoke."

Sharon shivered in the cold air and squeezed Bill's arm. A paramedic came out of the front door, stumbled to the kerb, and threw up. They could hear him sobbing. Another medic followed and leant down to put a comforting arm around him. He too sobbed.

An OPP cruiser pulled up. Two officers hurried inside. A small crowd stood opposite the Durant house. Bill and Sharon headed down the street. Bill was soon helping Sharon home, her hard sobbing making her stagger.

Bob Durant had shot Betty and the two kids before killing himself. A fellow hockey parent had discovered the grizzly scene.

No one knew any details that morning but later learned Durant had lost his job at the car plant when it closed the week before. He had left the house every morning pretending to go to work. He had a foreclosure notice from his bank. The Durants had been in financial trouble for months before the crisis. The cancelled hockey pushed Bob Durant to murder and suicide, his big dream shattered. Grief and shock spread through the community. One paramedic and two town cops could no longer work. They all left town to be with family.

The tragedy left a big hole in Sharon's heart. Her friendship with Betty Durant had been growing. They had been getting together every day for tea and chat. Betty was a warm, caring woman with a sense of humour.

Bill and Sharon spent the morning comforting each other. They had never experienced such an event involving people they knew. Bill loved his wife and kids deeply. He could not understand how a man could kill his family. Shadlys thought they had suffered. Now, they genuinely understood sorrow.

Jeff and Brandi took the news with little reaction, worrying Sharon and Bill. It would have been better if the kids cried, but they did not know the Durant kids well. With school closed, there was nothing to make the tragedy real.

Sharon telephoned her parents. She needed the reassuring voices that had protected and nurtured her.

"Hello?" Her mother's voice soothed Sharon.

"Hello, Mom."

"I have some terrible news," her mother launched into her own concerns. "Our trip's cancelled. The airline is bankrupt. Peter says they've all gone under."

Cheryl acted like a hurt kitten.

"They won't give us our money back!"

Sharon had never heard her Mom sound this vulnerable. "Imagine them keeping our money! We haven't heard from PJ in days."

Sharon's younger brother, Peter Junior was an officer in the Canadian Forces and overseas somewhere. "No one at Trenton can tell us anything. They say everyone will get home. It's dreadful!"

After her mother had listed the beautiful things they would miss in Mexico, She finally let Sharon talk. Her mother was sympathetic but did not feel Sharon's grief. Sharon had renewed worry about her brother, but it relieved her that parents could not leave the country.

All domestic airlines closed stranding thousands of travellers. The federal government would send flights to retrieve those trapped abroad. It stunned group that anyone would have dared to leave the country in the past few weeks. Warren related something he read about the great depression of the 20th century. A quarter of the Canadian population had not noticed the depression. He guessed much of the country still lived in that delusion.

The day after the Durant killings, Sharon and Bill headed to Warren's house. They needed some action to take their minds away from their grief. Until the horror of the previous day, they had not appreciated the crisis, even with Warren's earlier warnings. They now understood the confusion and fear of people surprised by the crisis.

Sharon and Bill turned onto the main street, merging into a stream of people filling the street heading downtown. Everyone had grim expressions; a few were vocal. Homemade signs demanded help.

"Yes, we are marching on the town hall now," a woman said into a cell phone. "Join us, bring others."

"What's up?" Bill asked one man as he rushed past.

"We're fed up with this crap," he almost spat on Shadly. "Someone has to fix this. These useless politicians have to get our jobs back."

"And get my credit fixed," a marcher joined in, with a murmur of approval from others.

"How can they do that?" Sharon asked calmly, "The town can't take care of this problem."

"You on their side?" he glared. "We'll make 'em."

"I don't think there are sides. We need to get together and help ourselves." Bill defended Sharon. "We can't count on a saviour."

"Look, dick-head," the man glared, balling his fists, crowding in towards Bill. "Since I moved to this hick town, I've minded my business... let them do what they wanted. They screwed me, screwed all of us. I knew they were all like this. That's why I never voted, crooks, all of them! Join us or butt out, if you know what I mean."

"Do what you want," Bill stepped back, "but it won't get you anywhere." The man closed in on Bill once more, gave him a shove and hurried away, yelling at the crowd.

"Wow," Sharon gasped, "I thought you were going to get a bloody nose. They sure are angry. Too bad we can't get them to work with us instead of just blowing off."

"I think we should collect Warren and head downtown to see what this is all about," Bill recovered from the adrenalin rush. "I can't believe they're all as useless as that jerk. Warren was right. These people need someone to blame. They don't understand who the real culprits are, so local politicians will have to do. Anyone who disagrees with them is a target."

"I wouldn't write them off," Sharon was more forgiving. "They're scared and hungry. We need to know more."

Warren wanted to check out the excitement. Boredom mixed in with the work made anything unusual a pleasant diversion. "Besides," he said, "I think we'll get to meet some people to join us."

The trio reached Main Street and found a disorganized crowd in front of the town hall. Two of the larger town cops stood on the concrete steps at the front doors, arms crossed and grasping nightsticks. Face shields hid their grim expressions. Two uniformed figures peered through the front doors. The loudmouths stood at the front near the steps, perhaps leaders or just more outspoken alternated between yelling at the police and the crowd. The shouting at the front diminished towards the rear where less aggressive people had gathered.

The crowd reflected the town's population. The front echelon had a good number of young to middle-aged men and women sporting tattoos and piercing of various types, accompanied by several dogs. A man wearing a baseball cap and plaid bush jacket was one of the loudest agitators and held a chain leash, restraining a fierce-looking terrier.

"See the bunch with the dogs?" Sharon leant close to Bill's ear and whispered, "They're what I call the moochers. Most welfare recipients just need help for a bit and find work, but this pack has been living off us for years. I see them all the time, wandering around doing nothing or heading to the tattoo parlours. Some are disabled, but most could work if they wanted. I'm surprised they have the gumption to be here."

"When were the welfare payments due?" Bill asked.

"Ah, ha, yes," Sharon smiled, "they missed it last Friday. These guys have no money."

"Who are the rest?" Bill knew few locals.

"Most are strangers to me," Sharon surveyed the crowd. "I see people who used to work at the parts plants, a few teachers, local small business owners, a couple of my clients and two or three cops out of uniform."

"We want money. We want food," chanted the crowd.

"When do we want it?" the man with the dog cried.

"NOW, NOW, NOW!" the crowd responded. The newly unemployed and the welfare types had found unity.

"We want our share. We want our jobs back." Another self-appointed spokesman crowded out the first speaker. "We don't want charity. We want jobs." He threw a disdainful glare towards the welfare recipients.

"The politicians stole it all. They are keeping it from us," the man who had pushed Bill yelled. "Johnson is fat and happy." The man faced the crowd and jerked his thumb over his shoulder towards the hall. "He isn't hungry and still has a job, and his buddies do too."

His words resonated. "They aren't hungry… They have jobs…" rang out in a vigorous chant that lasted several minutes. Most of the angry crowd ignored the common knowledge the town had not paid its employees since

September and had laid them off. Evy and two others were unpaid volunteers.

"Where are they? They're scared to meet taxpayers." The belligerent ignored the fact he was in no position to pay tax. "Come out and face us. Come out and help us."

"Come out, come out, come out," the new chant rang from the crowd. Sounds of foot stomping and the clanging of spoons hitting metal cooking pots joined the shouts. The officers on the steps tensed, but there was no movement from the throng. They only repeated the loud chant. Ted Johnson did not appear.

"Split up and talk to folks," The mass of hostile strangers made Warren nervous. "Find out what they're thinking. Don't tell about us unless you're comfortable."

Warren headed along one edge of the crowd. Sharon spotted some people she knew and dove into the masses. Bill followed Warren's example and worked his way around the other side, at first listening but getting braver.

"We're hungry. We want food," the crowd chanted.

"How did this get started?" Bill asked a calmer onlooker on the edge of the crowd. The man wore a ski jacket, expensive boots and a toque from an upscale ski hill. A woman overheard the question and piped up.

"Word of mouth," she exclaimed. She was middle-aged and attractive, with blond hair in a ponytail, wearing a bright blue windbreaker with the ornate gold and red crest of the Canadian Legion. "See the guy with the dog? That bunch showed up at the Legion yesterday bumming beer and food, not that we have any to spare. I work at the Legion. He tried to mooch off me. We had a big argument, but then Jack came out and started talking to them. He decided we should come here today. The idea spread to the members and friends."

Many townsfolk frequented the Legion branch where they could pass the boring hours and vent. It seemed futile, with no leadership and no focus. The Legion was fulfilling its purpose, allowing people to unload their feelings onto others who could understand. For those traumatized by war, the organization had provided a venue for self-medication with alcohol and amateur psychotherapy. Vets would listen to others as they sipped beer with everyone being both client and amateur psychologist.

The present crisis drew the newer members into comradeship only sufferers could understand. Younger ones had never endured the boredom, futility, fear and horror of wars that had haunted the now dead veterans. The new members now shared a new, fearful reality.

"Today," she continued, "is only the first. We intend to get these bozos to fix things fast and will be back here every day until they get her done."

Bill moved on, shaking his head at the woman's mixing of a desire to confront reality with bumper sticker wit. He saw the magnitude of the change in thinking required before they could improve peoples' lives.

"How are you doing, Jim?" Sharon reached a group of acquaintances.

"Hi, Sharon," the young man wore the coverall and ball cap uniform of a contractor. "Things are tough. I think this is a waste of time though."

"Why do you say that?" Sharon had done the books for the man's small contracting business. Jim was hard-working, competent and ambitious.

"The mayor can't fix anything," Jim explained. "This isn't local. Outside stuff screwed Weyburne. Yelling is pointless. Johnson is helpless. We got to help ourselves."

"Why don't you come in with us?" Sharon had tried to draw Jim in a few weeks before, but it had been too soon. He had hope then. "Drop over to our house tonight."

"Can we bring our little girl? We can't afford a sitter." Sharon assured him Brandi would entertain little Kim.

Warren made the most meaningful connection. Al Wright, the United Church pastor, was on the fringe of the crowd, talking with a few others.

"Hello Al," Warren was not a church member but had chatted with Wright before. "What's going on?"

"Hello, Warren," Al smiled warmly. "We're wondering how to turn this energy to good use."

The Reverend spoke loudly above the din of the mob. Chants and vulgarities echoed between the ornate façade of the town hall complete with its unused bell tower and the blank wall of the furniture store across the street. The street served as a civic square, now overflowing with the desperate crowd.

"A few of us are trying the same thing." Dunne wondered why they had not approached the churches. "We have a small group working to help each other."

"We have been doing that too, in our congregations." Wright turned slightly towards another man and said, "Kevin, this is Warren Dunn; Warren, this is Kevin DeSantos. He's the pastor of the New Faith Vision. We work together on the pastors' council. Unfortunately," Al went on, "none of the other congregations want to work with us. They have too many old folks, too many who think they can go it alone. Maybe, when they get hungry, they'll change. Pastors are willing, but they can't get their congregations to follow."

"There's a dozen of us," Warren responded. "Not enough, but we're just getting started."

"We aren't large either," Wright followed along. "The town must work together. We tried to get Ted Johnson to help. He thinks the government will solve it."

"We asked Ted," added Warren. "I figured it was because it was me asking. That flyer from the town didn't help."

"He gave us the bum's rush, but wanted us to give them the names of those we were working with." Al Wright looked upset by the memory. "I saw their pamphlet, horrible. I didn't think Ted could be that vindictive. Every effort is helping. It isn't enough."

"I don't want to sound vengeful," Warren glanced past Al towards the town hall. "I've heard that Ted, Will Kirk, Roger Smith and few others plan to buy the properties of desperate people. They are trying to get the names of those losing their property and keep them going long enough to sell out."

"They've always been opportunistic," Wright agreed. "I like Ted, but he's out for himself."

"Can we work together?" Kevin steered them to action.

"That would be great." Warren said. He saw a chance to have more leaders. He would feel safer sharing the load with respected community members. "Can you, and your followers, come to our meeting at the Shadly house tonight?"

The men went their separate ways into the crowd. The three let another half-dozen people know there was an organization for self-help. Sharon, Bill and Warren finally met, pleased with their effort. The negative agitators failed to dampen their new hope. They headed off to prepare for tonight's get together. The mob was running out of steam, and people drifted away.

"I don't think they will do anything more than vent. A few days of this will get them to accept reality or make them violent. I don't want to predict."

As if to mock Warren, the crowd surged forward. The speaker with the fierce-looking dog lunged towards the police and encouraged his dog to attack. It lunged at an officer and grabbed his gloved hand. The other constable smashed his baton onto the dog's head, making a loud cracking sound and either stunned or killed the dog. The owner swung his fists towards the police. A cop swung his baton, connecting with a shoulder, and the man collapsed in pain and cursing loudly beside his silent dog. Several men and women who had surged forward quickly backed off. The two cops stepped forward and swung their clubs wildly, contacting the closest people, before they could retreat. One constable gave the dog a hard kick as if to ensure it was dead. Someone came forward and helped the injured man to his feet.

"We'll get your dog when these jerks back off," he muttered to the stunned victim.

"Don't bother, he's worthless now... couldn't feed him, anyway. I'll get another one soon as I'm on my feet," the suffering man gasped through his pain. "Those jerks can bury him. I know that cruddy cop. He's going to get his."

"Here, you take him." The rescuer rudely shoved his burden onto the closest bystander. "I'm not helping someone who doesn't give a damn about his dog."

The man strode off in self-righteous fury, taking his anger out on the police. "We will be back. Watch your back, buddy!"

The police directed obscenities at the group, slapping nightsticks into the palms of leather-gloved hands. The Chief of Police joined them with the Corporal snapping pictures on a digital camera.

The crowd dispersed, sullen and muttering, leaving the body of the dog at the feet of the constables. Someone kicked over a mailbox in front of Chellappah's variety store. Several broke branches off trees along the sidewalk. One angered citizen broke a toe kicking a steel sidewalk bench. That night, vengeful citizens smashed storefront windows with rocks. The variety store owned by Mr Chellappah came in for special attention, with the door smashed and racist graffiti smeared over the plate-glass window.

Chapter Eight

Tonight would be the last meeting at the Shadly's home. Three dozen families packed the living room. People spilt into the dining room and kitchen.

Warren grinned. *Finally,* he thought, *we are getting somewhere.*

Bill introduced the Dunne group.

"Everyone knows why we are here," Warren said. "To help each other and survive this crisis. We organized our group to do that, but it is obvious we are too small. We have too little food to make it through the winter." There was a gasp. Some had not thought it through to the point of possibly starving in the cold.

"We all know we can't make it on our own. When we met with Al and Kevin this afternoon, it seemed an opportunity to combine our efforts."

"We barely get along with each other. Can we work together to do this?" asked one of Wright's parishioners.

"It won't be easy," Al answered. "We have argued amongst ourselves. Let's put that behind us."

Bill jumped in, "We can put rules in place to help us resolve differences. All we need is for all of us to want to make it a success." *Good old Wilson and his team building* thought Bill. *I hope it wasn't all BS.*

"We need all the help we can get," someone said.

"Okay," Warren continued. "Can we agree we need one large organization? Our group isn't interested in running it. We want to share responsibility. We need a formal structure."

Al Wright and Kevin DeSantos agreed. Their followers were eager to get involved, and the congregations respected and trusted the two pastors.

"Are there questions?" Warren asked.

"Yes," Sharon's friend Jim Handley looked nervous. "We're short of food. Our little girl is suffering."

"Hi Jim," Sharon jumped into the conversation, "everyone this is Jim Handley and his wife... I am sorry I don't know your name."

"Sarah," Jim spoke up for his young, shy wife.

Sharon looked at the young couple and then to the crowd. "We need this organization. Jim, see me after the meeting. All of us are already hungry. We need to get moving quickly to find more food."

"I propose we form a group and call it the Emergency Aid Committee," Kevin DeSantos was a man of action. Experience had taught him not to leave a problem lying in front of people for too long.

Vacuums suck in the garbage, he thought.

"We need a chairperson and a small group to sort out issues and prioritize. We will bring anything big to a membership meeting." Al shared Kevin's experience and outlook. Overseeing a church congregation seemed like "cat herding," as Al was fond of saying.

"What if we have a big disagreement?" one woman asked. "What if we're too big to meet?"

"I hope we get that big," both Al and Warren spoke stirring up laughter. "Anyway," Al continued, "I remember some disciples worried about the size of the crowd once with Christ, and he just called the meeting on the side of a hill. We'll find a way."

The Sermon on the Mount fascinated Al Wright. He often made up new sayings related to it. He developed the habit of opening every meeting by saying, "Blessed are the bread makers for they shall receive thanks."

Bill Shadly became chairperson with Warren, Al, Kevin and Walt Lefevre forming a steering committee. When someone pointed out the committee was all men, Sharon said that she would just tell Bill what to do, anyway. Once the laughter had subsided, they agreed any contributing member of the EAC could call a general meeting.

"Lorna," Al Wright turned to the secretary of the United Church. "Please take minutes."

"Do you think it's a good idea to record names and dates?" Bill asked.

"We need to know who is doing what and when," Al replied. "There's no harm in that."

When Lorna asked if she could state a purpose for the committee, Al Wright simply said, "We aim to keep as many people as possible alive," driving home the danger facing them.

They directed anyone with an urgent need to come to the Shadly's house. People volunteered to find supplies to tide the needy over the next few days until they built a better system.

The crowd was not ready to leave. Bill and Sharon provided coffee and tea while more goodies appeared from the group.

"Does anyone have any bread or fish?" Al wandered about trying to lighten the mood.

Walt Lefevre's harmonica materialized. Fractured versions of old songs and some newer pop tunes sounded through the house.

Jeff and Brandi mingled with the crowd along with several other young people. Jim and Sarah's little girl Kim entertained everyone as she danced and munched on a big cookie Brandi gave her.

"What about that group we saw at the town hall today?" Warren chatted with Al and Kevin.

"I think we let them stew for a bit," Al said. "Let's get our plans in place and then we can give them something definite. They need to blow off steam. Some of that crowd avoid work, but many will pitch in. We need to be firm and focused. They have to learn to work for their supper."

"I've noticed," Al continued, "that a lot of the go-getters and hard workers have left town, probably headed to the city looking for work. I hope they find it, but I think we're better off staying put and trying to survive here."

Chapter Nine

Halloween was a big worry. The holiday had always had two sides. Violence, egg throwing, and teenage vandalism offset the fun of the little kids. It shaped up to be the worst year ever. Ted Johnson decreed there would be no door-to-door activities, abandoning the night to the teens. Organized night watches on many streets discouraged attacks, but unorganized areas suffered. The police cruisers endured the vandalism. With a shortage of eggs, vandals chose excrement as ammunition. On November 1st, the police vehicles sat covered in poop and paint. The night had provided a chance for angry residents to get revenge.

Sharon turned the weekly cookie party into a Halloween event. Her pumpkin flavoured cookies, with faces in orange and white icing and chocolate chip eyes were a hit, along with her jack-o'-lantern. Dressed in an old dress, straw hair, rouge covered face, and a homemade hat, Sharon was a convincing witch. Laughter filled her kitchen and raised spirits. The young people spread the word, and the EAC drafted Sharon to organize Christmas celebrations, even though she had never attended church.

Except for the Chief and the Corporal, the town cops packed up their families and headed south, lured by stories of paid security work in the city. Most of the ex-teachers and upper-level municipal staff, outsiders who had no family ties to the town joined the flight to better prospects. Some emigrants made a show of proclaiming no one appreciated them, and they would go where someone would pay their worth. Those remaining in town shrugged this off. Everyone had more to worry about than hurt feelings.

Weyburne kept the Mayor, Evy in the office, a lone man in the works yard, and one of the sewage plant operators. These four stayed to ensure essential town services functioned. They lived in town and benefited directly from their work and hoped for pay. Bill had one less worry. The officer who harassed him after the gas theft fled south.

The next trouble came in the second week of November. Jeff returned home at lunchtime sporting a bruise near his eye and rips in his jacket.

"What happened to you, baby?" Sharon asked.

"I ran into a gang of kids hanging about downtown, bad-mouthing people and making trouble." Jeff dabbed a cold rag on his eye. "They picked on Mrs Williams, you know, the older lady who lives over by the church, swearing and pushing her around. They wanted money and blamed her for their problems. Someone said it was older folks who stole all the money so the kids couldn't have any." Jeff grimaced in pain. "They knocked her down, and she begged them not to hurt her. I helped her up and told her to get going."

"She went into a store and then the gang turned on me, about 20 of them. Only two were doing the physical stuff, and they came at me. I got in a few good punches, but they knocked me down, kicked me and called me a mamma's boy."

"Where were the police?"

"Are you kidding, Mom? They've been hiding in the cop shop ever since Halloween, and now there are just two of them. They were always useless anyway. I think Mrs Williams went there after the goons left."

Sharon hurried downtown in search of Mrs Williams. The woman had disappeared along with her attackers. After fruitless inquiries at the few open stores, she headed home.

"Gimme it; I'm older." The little girl's voice interrupted Sharon's thoughts. "I want to take it to Mommy."

"I found it." A younger boy whined. "I want to."

A little girl about five and a boy, perhaps a year younger, were scuffling on the walkway of a side street. They wore dirt-stained, high-quality snowsuits. Their hoods hung down, revealing scraggly long, blond hair. They looked at her with brilliant, blue eyes.

"Hi there," Sharon tried to sound friendly. She had seen these two running about, but did not know them by name. "Can I help?"

"Missy wants to take my quarter." The little boy pleaded. "I found it all by myself."

"I'm bigger. I should carry it." The little girl pushed forward.

"Is the quarter yours?" Sharon knelt to make eye contact.

"I found it all by myself. My name is Kyle." The little boy showed a mixture of pride and defiance. He stepped back a pace, perhaps fearing that Sharon intended to take his coin. His right hand slipped into his snowsuit pocket.

"This seems a lot of fuss for a quarter." Sharon was trying to draw the little ones into a conversation.

"We don't got much money. We need money, Mom says. She will be happy to see it," the girl said, tugging at her brother's sleeve as he twisted away.

"I don't think it should matter who carries it home." Sharon smiled and tried to appear like a friend.

"Missy thinks Mommy will give her something if she brings it." The little guy stepped toward Sharon as if sensing an ally. "She would too, but I found it," he repeated. "She should give me something. I found it! Missy always gets the good stuff."

"Why don't you carry it together?" Sharon wondered if they had encouraged this rivalry at home, or it was ordinary sibling competition. She remembered her kids' tiffs. "I bet Mommy would give you both something then."

The two little ones looked at each other, trying to decide how much they trusted the other. The solution had not occurred to them.

"How can we do it?" The girl decided she liked the idea.

"Trust each other and want to share." Sharon hoped she was not lecturing. "Do you have a bag you can put it in and each hang onto it?"

"Nope," they responded in unison, looking desperate as if the new solution had disappeared.

"Remember I said you have to trust each other and want to share." The two silently nodded. "Missy, hold out your hand," Sharon took the girl's wrist and turned her hand palm upward. "Kyle, bring your hand and hold Missy's hand with the quarter in both your hands like this." Sharon drew his hand from the protective pocket and placed it into his sister's hand so that the quarter was flat between their palms. "Both of you hold on tight and take it straight home to Mommy," Sharon stood and smiled. Missy reached out and using her free hand brushed some sidewalk dust from Sharon's brown slacks. They smiled and turned down the street. Sharon watched them hurrying along, holding hands.

"Mommy!" she heard them both call out as they turned up a walkway to a nearby house. Sharon walked home, smiling, thinking about cooperation and of how the lowly quarter had become so valuable.

Later in the day of Jeff's attack, Sharon watched an unruly gang of young people swarm past Shadly's house towards the high school. Many were texting or talking on cells. In a violent afternoon, they trashed everything vulnerable around the school and park. They cracked some school windows, but the mob had not gotten inside.

That evening, they set fire to a portable classroom. The building burnt to the ground. There was no functioning fire department to deal with it. Several dozen adults converged on the scene and discovered the young people gathered near the fire, cheering and chanting anti-school and anti-adult vulgarities. The bright orange light from the flames reflected from youthful faces creating a macabre effect. Disembodied faces danced in the surrounding darkness. Lit screens of cells moved in the darkness giving the impression the youngsters carried blazing torches in some religious ritual.

"Get lost, losers!" the youngsters taunted the group of grownups. "We'll burn you too!"

"What started all this?" a man asked Bill Shadly.

"These punks have been running around hassling older people for a couple of days now," another bystander said. "I had to run for it earlier today. They said I stole their future."

"They beat up my kid today," Bill added, "when he tried to help an old woman they were assaulting."

"Oh! It was your boy," one man came over. "Thank him for me. That was my mother they were after." The man shook Bill's hand vigorously. "I hope he's okay."

"He has bruises, but he's fine. Do you think these kids started this fire?"

"I sure do," the other replied. "I think we should hang around and scare them off."

It proved to be a good plan. Once the blaze subsided, the young mob headed off chanting loudly and looking for other targets. They still taunted the adults but made no trouble. Bill noticed the butt of a shotgun sticking out from under one man's coat. Perhaps the kids had seen it too.

"I think we should follow them and make sure no one gets hurt." The man with the shotgun did not smile. The adults trailed the noisy youngsters as they smashed their way towards downtown.

They found a bizarre scene on Main Street. Weyburne had installed decorative lampposts and fixtures to make the town appear to be nostalgic and attractive to visitors. The brightness of the modern lamps in antique gas light globes cast a garish, yellow light over a scene of mayhem. Fires sputtered in street trash-bins. Someone tried to ignite the wooden cribbing of a planter box. Smoke drifted on the still November air. Bill thought it looked like a movie set. The mob had stopped in front of the variety store.

"Burn the Pakis!" Someone shouted. The mob chanted the call. Rocks hurled against the storefront, this time successfully smashing the plate glass and sending shards into the street. A primal roar rose from the mob as vandals surged into the darkened interior. Lights came on. From a safe distance across the street, Bill could make out hooded figures ransacking the store. Almost no stock remained. The looters carried out armfuls of adult magazines and old newspapers. Most of these went to feed the growing fire on the planter box.

"Here's that stupid sign," one boy waved a single piece of paper above his head, yelling as if he had just bagged a trophy. He laughed, dancing wildly about the burning planter. The paper was the handwritten sign, "In store only three students at time." taped to the store's door. "I guess we win that one," the boy shouted. With a flourish, he tossed the paper onto the burning pile. A roar rose from the nearest youngsters.

It was a mystery to Bill that the mob had not torched the store. Maybe the youngsters realized it would have destroyed half of the downtown. Someone spotted the cops standing at the door of the town hall. Perhaps that diversion saved the buildings. A shout rose. The rioters surged towards the despised police.

"Pigs! Pigs! Pigs!" The cry came from the youngsters.

"Kill the pigs!" an adult voice called for murder.

Several rioters held their cell phones high, videoing the scene. Bill was sure he would find these on Quiver or one of the other internet chatter sites.

Chanting degenerated into a confused mixture of threats and obscenities. They smashed into a nearby used furniture store, and piles of old furniture, clothing and anything combustible appeared in the street. At first, Bill thought the mob wanted a barricade between themselves and the police, but flames erupted from the pile, and a roar rose from the crowd. Acrid smoke mingled with smoke from the smaller fires. Lamplight streamed through the haze in yellow shafts. Bill retreated from the smoke as it washed against the town hall and flowed around the building into the darkness. The bonfire created its own weather. Convection sucked the smoke high into the darkened sky.

The success of the fire gave the mob courage. It chanted louder. Threats against the police and the mayor echoed through the night. Frenzy built until the throng pushed forward, surging towards the police.

The fire forced the mob to split into two streams around the blaze. As the leading edge of each arm turned towards them, the constables threw two tear gas canisters, one landing in front of each half of the crowd. The mob stopped short; the rear echelons surged over top of those in front. Many of the original leaders fell to the ground. Bill could hear screams of fear and pain cutting through the mayhem.

Confusion stopped the charge momentarily. Then someone grabbed one of the spouting canisters and tried to heave it through a window of the hall. The second followed although both missed their mark, bouncing harmlessly off the brick facade with the throwers nursing burnt hands to remind them of their folly but encouraging the kids. With new bravery, shouting wildly, the mob started a second charge.

To the policemen's credit, they did not seem to shoot to kill. It appeared to Bill, the first volley from their handguns went low intending to hit legs. Bullets found targets and several people collapsed in loud agony. The officers levelled their weapons directly at the front of the crowd.

The mob stopped and fell silent, suddenly comprehending this was real and the bullets had hit. Cries and whimpers from wounded teenagers sounded loudly in the street. The rest came to their senses. Within minutes, the crowd disappeared leaving three injured young people, a small cohort of watching adults, and the police.

The cops hurried to check out their victims. Bill and several others came to assist. Someone ran to find the nurse practitioner. The volley caused one shattered leg, a broken foot, and a girl's calf muscle shredded by a bullet. In normal circumstances, these would be repairable wounds. In this world, turned upside down only a few weeks before, no one thought these youngsters would fully recover.

Tammy rode with Ted Johnson in his dealership van, rushing the wounded to Orangeville, hoping the doctors there could help. When the vehicle departed, the police retreated into the building. The fires had burnt down to glowing embers, sending the odd bursts of sparks skywards. Bill and the others returned home.

In the middle of the night, someone smashed the windows of two police vehicles parked beside the station.

The next day, Bill, as representative of the EAC, went to the mayor's office with Al Wright to see if they could improve security. Although Ted Johnson was sympathetic, he refused to let the two remaining constables make patrols. He wanted them to defend the town hall.

"What do we do now?" Bill asked Al, as they made their way out of the building.

"Some folks organized neighbourhood watch groups during Halloween. We could do the same thing to discourage some of the vandalism and harassment. It would have to be round the clock."

They reworked the casual security squads from Halloween into patrols. A few confrontations occurred, but no violence. The shooting at the town hall had taken the fight out of the discontented. Many people were angry with the police shooting. Bill tried to describe the scene truthfully hoping to discourage rumours. He reminded many he had no love for the cops, but he could not fault them for defending themselves.

The onset of winter weather finally cleared the streets. The discontented youth gathered in abandoned houses, searching for liquor and sharing their misfortune. Snow and the threat of winter trapping them in town stirred many families to leave. Fewer kids remained to cause trouble. By the end of November, about one-third of the town had left.

"I'll be out of town for a while." Will Kirk sat opposite Ted at the mayor's big redwood desk. "I didn't want you to think I just took off like these other quitters." Kirk nodded his head disdainfully towards the window. Several heavily loaded vehicles had been heading past each day on their way to the cities.

"Where are you going, Will?" Johnson was in a gloomy mood. He barely glanced at his visitor.

"The wife's family is down in London. We're going there. I hope to find something to last until we can get our plan going here." Kirk rubbed his eyes. Dark bags and lines suggested sleepless nights. He looked hungry.

"It seems this thing is playing out longer than we thought." The mayor tried to smile and slid a sheet of paper towards the real estate broker. "It's getting worse."

"What's this?" Will read the paper and frowned.

"They will indefinitely shut the auto plants." Ted turned to look out the dirt-streaked window. Remnants of feces hurled on Halloween night smeared down one side.

"Yeah, well… I can't get any capital right now either." Kirk dismissively slid the paper across the desk. "It looks like our plan is dead. It was a gigantic waste of effort."

"Seems so," Ted responded listlessly. "Matt and Walt have joined up with Dunne."

"He won't ever work for me again!" Kirk flared. His anger aroused no response. Ted had decided the old way had gone. Who knew what the future might bring? Minor disputes and pettiness no longer mattered.

"Reverend Wright has joined with them. They seem to be honest, but naïve." Ted's tone showed it was no great matter. He regretted throwing in with Kirk in such a poorly thought out scheme.

Maybe I should join this EAC myself.

The mayor kept his thoughts to himself. He had been mayor and business owner too long to be a follower. The EAC already had leaders.

"When I get back with some cash, I'll make a killing," Will was still faithful to the dream. "Don't worry you will get your share." Kirk misinterpreted Ted's grimace as meaning the mayor only worried about his profit. Johnson thought his friend was delusional. Deep depression gripped the mayor.

"The mail is still running once or twice a week." Ted tried to be cheerful. "Keep in touch. I'll let the others know your news."

"Only Frank seems to be interested," Will stood preparing to leave. "Roger has those big jobs he bragged about and doesn't care anymore."

"I'm sure he'll be in tight with us if the money's there," Johnson was sarcastic.

"Goodbye, Ted. I hope we meet again soon."

Ted Johnson sat back and closed his eyes as Kirk disappeared through the doorway.

Chapter Ten

In the greater world, fighting erupted in the Middle East, with all-out war along the Lebanon-Israeli border. Iranian forces captured Kuwait and headed toward Riyadh after the US fleet fought its way, with heavy casualties, through the Straits of Hormuz. Their three aircraft carriers and their accompanying flotilla now floated in the Indian Ocean.

Europe seethed, and England had declared martial law. There were no other governments able to help. Every government in Europe was under siege. Britain rushed its forces home from everywhere. NATO finally abandoned the perpetual mission in Ukraine.

The American navy found a purpose, supporting the evacuation of American personnel from fragmenting nations. The Indian sub-continent erupted in turmoil. Pakistan lacked a functioning central government. In India, the upper classes desperately tried to put down riots by the poor, and no news came from China.

Sharon received one item of importance. Greece and Turkey had renewed their war. The Greek military dictatorship, in place since the national bankruptcy a few years before, wanted the population to hate someone other than their government. The Turkish dictator had a complex problem involving religious fundamentalists, ambitious military officers and Armenian and Kurdish separatists. War seemed an excellent diversion.

It all focused on Cyprus. The Shadlys feared the worst. Sharon's brother PJ last called home from Nicosia. He should have left long before, but no one knew. He told his father they had escaped the Lebanon/Israel border under fire before fighting destroyed the United Nations' outposts. Contrary to official reports, PJ had told his father there had been at least one nuclear explosion in southern Lebanon.

In Canada, the government collapsed. People demanded protection from eviction and asked for help. The Prime Minister made reassuring statements but did nothing. Opposition parties denounced the Prime Minister. They demanded the government inject money into the economy, but no one had a detailed plan. Prime Minister Harridan's government claimed they had no money and introduced a bill defaulting federal debt and raising the pension age to seventy, cutting off those already receiving payments. Bank deposit insurance increased to a quarter of a million dollars although most people had long since withdrawn all their money. Only the wealthy had savings, making it obvious whom the government cared about; however, no payments were possible. The motion failed when half of the government members revolted.

Pay deposits and paper cheques became impossible. The government had no way of paying its employees or anyone else. To keep some of the civil servants working, the Canadian Mint stepped up the printing of physical money. Special military flights began delivering the bank notes to Ottawa from the printing plant in Winnipeg. Armed guards took cash to every government building and dispensed it directly to the civil servants including Members of Parliament. No one had seen cash payroll in Canada for 50 years. Within a week, it caused price inflation in the Ottawa area, made worse by shortages of food and fuel. Printing money had little impact outside the capital, and remote government offices closed.

With the government's defeat on their money bill, and under immense pressure from opposition MPs who had formed a coalition, the Governor General asked the head of the next largest party to form a government. The patched-up government lasted two weeks. Before the end of November, the new cabinet announced Harridan had been right. They had no money since the bond sale failure in October.

It became impossible to conduct any business in the House of Commons. Fistfights forced the speaker to empty the chamber. The new Prime Minister resigned.

The Governor General made a fatal mistake. Harridan had appointed the man because he was a famous hockey and television personality. The Head of State represented the most recent of a long line of media darling appointees. He saw himself as part of the country's marketing machine, not having a critical political role. This unqualified individual did not understand what his decrees might mean. He dissolved Parliament and called an election.

With transportation and communication systems in chaos, Elections Canada could not conduct a vote and had no legal means to apply alternatives. The country entered a political vacuum. In the absence of Parliament, the weak government in Ottawa could only sit and fume. Self-serving opportunists would soon exploit the situation.

In the years before the crisis, all media had fired most real journalists and filled time by treating comments on social media as news. Serious, funny, stupid, silly, but especially viral comments on Quiver and YouYouMag sites, blaming everyone from the Russians to aliens for the problem, received endless attention on television.

The public demanded the government do whatever it took to fix the economy, and get pro-hockey going again. The producers jumped onto the National Hockey League bandwagon, ever mindful of the push for more viewers. It did not occur to media executives that things had changed forever. Higher ratings had no potential for paying sponsors. The government remained the only possible advertiser, and even they could only issue IOUs.

With the media dependent on the government, the pieces of a dark puzzle began falling into place.

The "shenanigans" in Ottawa were of little concern to the people of Weyburne. Federal and Provincial governments had done nothing to help. Most people were two months behind with no possibility of ever paying their mortgages. Foreclosure and eviction were the big worries, but the breakdown in infrastructure helped debtors much more than government action.

The collapse of the airlines substantially disrupted mail delivery. Government-owned, cash-starved passenger rail service could not help. The large central mail sorting factories shut down, and for a few weeks, the mail trucks stopped running into the hinterland, preventing delivery of payment demands, foreclosure notices, and other flotsam of the financial system.

***

"Hey Ted, the government's here to help!" The police chief appeared in Ted Johnson's doorway. "They have a bunch of vehicles up by the Legion."

"Let's go look." Ted grabbed his hat and warm jacket. This mid-November cold snap was a break from the strangely warm autumn.

The two men rounded the corner, approaching the Legion. A long line of identical, black SUVs stretched behind a large, black coach. The smaller vehicles had radio antennae protruding from their roofs and pulled enclosed trailers, painted black. The top of the coach supported a satellite dish and GPS dome. A small crowd of locals stood on the opposite side of the street from several strangers wearing scarlet insulated jackets over light blue jump suits. A large maple leaf decorated the jacket backs, and a shining white cross cut through the leaf.

"They don't look like any official government bunch," Ted commented as they neared the vehicles. Short-wave radio chatter filled the air. Ted caught the words, "Rendezvous at Whisky One, eleven hundred hours."

"Who's in charge here?" Ted used his authoritative voice.

"Who wants to know?" A large man stepped forward.

"I'm Ted Johnson, Mayor of Weyburne and this is Police Chief Thomas." The Chief tried to look menacing.

"It's nice meeting you brother." The man offered his hand but no name. "We are on our way to the place God has prepared. We're waiting for more of the brethren before we head on out."

Ted remembered that a group the locals called "religious wacko survivalists" had built a compound on the Grey County line. They had tried, with some success, to recruit locals into their group. Most of their message advocated building a bomb shelter to make it through the coming nuclear war. Roger Smith had done some site preparation, building a driveway and levelling about five acres on the gravel moraine and sold them a few dozen truckloads of sand. After that, the group brought in equipment and completed the rest of the work on its own.

The county issued a permit for a large house and outbuildings, but locals guessed they had built a lot more without permits. Truckloads of reinforcing steel and ready-mix cement had gone in. Bush hid the site. Nothing was visible from the road except a wind turbine. Five years later, most locals had forgotten about the place.

"You have quite a convoy." Ted surveyed the vehicles. The doors and the trailers bore the leaf logo with the four sections created by the cross bearing symbols for shelter, food, faith and security.

"How many are you?" The police chief asked.

"Enough," the man obviously did not want to reveal too much; however, he seemed to enjoy the attention. The chief noted the visitors had empty pistol holsters on their waists. Through the open door of an SUV, he could see a gun rack holding a large bore shotgun.

"You have a lot of vehicles here. I guess you have lots of food." Ted was eating less and never felt satisfied.

"Not just food," the stranger suddenly became more forthcoming. "Here, look."

He unlocked a trailer. Food, fuel and a motor generator filled the vehicle. The police chief noticed cases bearing the logo of a firearms manufacturer.

"Hello, hello, brothers," a middle-aged man descended from the motor coach. "I see Brother Mason has been entertaining you." The man directed a stern look at Mason. He hurriedly locked up the trailer and scuttled away. The newcomer wore a cream coloured, meticulously tailored jumpsuit. The cross and shield logo adorned his left breast. A well-trimmed beard partly concealed his face. Long, slightly greying, straight hair hung down, curling at his shoulders. Ted stared and barely suppressed a laugh. The leader mimicked the picture of Jesus adorning Al Wright's sanctuary.

"Welcome to Weyburne." Ted used his effusive, tourist board voice.

"We won't be staying." The leader offered the comment absently as if it were not important. "We'll be back in a year to help any survivors."

"What do you mean?" The Chief asked. "Things aren't that bad."

"I see only one result of this financial disaster," the man projected his message across the street to the gathering crowd. "In a few days or weeks, there'll be a nuclear war. It's in the scriptures. We've been preparing. The time has come for the glory of God to manifest on the earth and smite the sinners. The righteous will rule the land."

"Aren't you supposed to be raptured or something before the apocalypse?" Ted attended church as part of his political efforts and had heard some end time preaching. He was more familiar with the watered-down version in the United Church catechism.

"The Holy Book says the righteous will emerge to rule the earth. After a thousand years, the Father will take us to glory." The preacher patted his hip. A Christian Bible bound in red leather protruded from a holster.

"We have a shelter, so that the righteous will survive. We will emerge to claim our ordained place. Christ himself will descend to take command. We'll follow and obey."

A column of vehicles rounded the corner and stopped behind the convoy, interrupting the sermon. Ted counted 40 vehicle-trailer combinations. Many carried young couples and children. The preacher hurried off to greet the new arrivals. With no fanfare, the column roared off out of town, up Highway Ten at exactly 11 in the morning.

"Do you think there'll be a war?" The Chief looked concerned.

"There's nothing to suggest that on television," Ted looked skyward, "But there sure is a lot of fighting going on. Who knows? It might happen, but if it does even those guys will die."

The pair walked back to the town hall in cheerless silence. In the following weeks, local congregations saw their numbers swell. Church attendance had been growing from the beginning of the crisis. The prediction of the end times cast a pall of fear over many people. Some residents arranged their basements into bomb shelters.

Chapter Eleven

Dorothy Kim arrived at the HBRC bank branch before eight o'clock in the morning. She felt her hard work and willingness to contribute unpaid hours had led to her rise to branch manager. Dorothy was a good-looking woman, only 29-years-old with straight black hair, alert dark eyes and a friendly disarming smile. Her finely proportioned features told of her Korean ancestry. She struggled against her physical beauty, focusing on academic and business success.

Being a third generation Canadian, Dorothy did not have to overcome old family cultural values. Her father, a retired teacher, and put a lot of pressure on her to be successful. Her graduation cum laude in finance had been one of many prideful moments she had given him. Dorothy felt she was only as good in his eyes as her next success. Her brothers had already accumulated small fortunes.

Despite her advantages, Dorothy felt lonely in Weyburne. Head office in Toronto had sent her to run the branch. This was common practice. Successful appointees earned a promotion, to bigger branches or head office.

Dorothy tolerated her social isolation expecting her advancement would come. At least, promotion would have come if the economy had not betrayed her. Like most people in the financial system, she blamed the government, stupid consumers or speculators for the crisis while believing the financial wizards would soon fix it. Hope sustained her even though sometimes in the past two months she had despaired.

This morning, messages in Dorothy's e-mail inbox started a frustrating series of events. There was a long list of defaulted mortgages and collateralized lines of credit. She was to prepare a foreclosure notice for each of the defaulted loans. Normally head office mailed these out, but mail service was unreliable. She must deliver each of these by hand.

Only Kim and Fred the loan officer, another corporate employee were now at work. The bank had let other staff go with no compensation. By the week's end, Dorothy and Fred had created a pile of almost 1,000 notices to deliver in Weyburne and elsewhere in the county. With no fuel, they put out-of-town notices aside and made plans to walk around town, delivering each document. The number of defaults sickened Dorothy. They represented a disaster of unimaginable extent. Reluctant to do the unpleasant work, the pair put off the start until the following Monday.

The first morning of the fateful week was sunny and mild following the blast of winter weather in November. Dorothy Kim took this as a good sign.

"Fred, you take that pile for the south side, and I'll do the north-west." Dorothy had divided the papers into neat piles by the street with the closest ones on top. She took enough to fill two hours of walking and headed out. The first house was dark and looked abandoned. After several minutes of knocking, she left the notice stuck between the doors. At least half of her targets were unoccupied. Dorothy thought her job might be easy.

A defeated looking woman answered one knock and blankly stared as Dorothy explained they must either pay in full by December first or leave. In reality, if the courts were functioning, the process might take months. Dorothy did not know what would happen in present circumstances. The eighth call brought disaster.

"What do you want?" A big man in his 40s, unkempt, dirty and smelling of whisky answered Dorothy's knock. "I ain't buying nothin'."

"I am the manager of the HBRC bank." Dorothy kept her distance from the man, wondering how he got a mortgage with her bank. "You have a mortgage with us."

"Thought you would get here eventually," the man slurred his words licking spittle from the corner of his mouth. "I got no money, honey. Want to take it out in trade?" he leered. Dorothy stepped back, her heart racing.

"I am just here to give you this notice. Pay us by the first or vacate the house." She fought for control.

"Hey, you little Paki bitch," the man stepped towards the much smaller woman. He either could not or did not bother to differentiate between which racial minority he hated. "Who do you think you are ordering me about? I got rights. I'm a real Canadian and earned this house. It's not my fault they took my job from me. You foreigners, are to blame."

He took another step towards Dorothy and slapped her hard on the face. She stumbled and fell against a porch support post.

"Get off my property you Paki, get out!" He lunged at her. Dorothy benefited from his drunken clumsiness and ran down the steps, sobbing from pain and fear, dropping the foreclosure notice on the path. She winced as she felt her lip and found blood on her hand. Dorothy's relief getting back to the branch died when she saw Fred hunched over his desk in pain, his face bloodied.

"Two neighbours I delivered to jumped me. Beat me up pretty good." He coughed slightly.

"Are you hurt badly?"

"Don't think so, but we need protection," He winced and closed his eyes.

"I got slapped too," Dorothy was relieved no one had attacked her that hard. "I'm going to see the police."

Ted Johnson believed in law and order and wanted to be on good terms with the bank, even though the town did business with the rival Sovereign Bank. Ted Johnson asked the police to accompany Fred and Dorothy.

The two bankers and the cop spent a busy morning walking up and down the streets in the older part of town. Dorothy felt optimistic, and believed they would soon finish this distasteful job. Disaster cut the work short.

"Hey! This is my house," the cop exclaimed as they turned up a walkway.

"You're Robert Capper?" Dorothy wished she had asked the man's full name.

"That's me, lady," the cop lost all friendliness, "I'm not helping you evict my family. Give me that paper and get lost!"

Dorothy and Fred scurried back to the bank.

"What do we do now?" Fred sounded defeated.

"Fred, we think about this for a while, a long while."

Dorothy Kim had become angry, angry at being helpless, angry at her luck, angry at the world, and angry with her bosses for dumping this impossible task on her. She realized she had no future with the bank. The bank had no future. Her world had collapsed.

"Fred," she said slowly, "we won't deliver any. If head office calls, I'll talk to them. Let them think we distributed the notices. Who can check? They have no way to enforce them. Half the places are empty, anyway. I'll keep coming here until they fire me. You can do what you want. I'll cover for you. There's some cash in the vault."

"You're right, Dorothy. I'll keep showing until they tell me not to. I've nothing else."

After that day, the pair reported to the branch, replied to the odd e-mail and phone call and waited. They paid themselves out of the cash on hand, so the charade was not pointless. The local establishment people who were so friendly to her when they needed the bank had disappeared. Dorothy had no friends or existence outside the bank. Fred missed most days, and Dorothy languished alone. The world closed in with snowy hints of winter.

***

Signs of winter came between unseasonably warm stretches. Bill often telephoned his Mom. She worried about the possibility of losing everything, and she had received a foreclosure notice.

"Mom," Bill tried to calm her. "It's bad. Move in with Joyce."

"I can't," Sarah sobbed. "Joyce has an eviction notice too."

"Then both of you come up here," Bill was calm and forceful. "At least you won't be near the street fighting."

"But Dear," she cried harder now, "I can't give up this beautiful apartment."

"You don't have a choice, Mom!" Bill hoped he did not sound harsh. "It's gone, anyway. Call Joyce, I will too, and get her to pack up all her cash and as much food as she has and pick you up. You do the same. Bring little else. Make sure you have the mementoes, Dad's stuff and all that. Do it today." Bill had worked out this plan a few weeks before and hoped the foreclosures would get them moving. "I'll tell Joyce to pick a safe route."

"Oh Bill, I love you and Sharon, but I just can't."

"Mom, you have too," Bill was talking louder. "Our old world has gone and we need to do things differently."

"Bill, don't yell. I can't..." The line went dead.

"Mom, Mom, MOM!" Bill shouted into the phone.

He redialled trying for the third time before realizing he could not hear a dial tone. Bill stood staring at the cell phone and sobbed, tears trickled down his cheeks. He imagined his mother panicking at the other end of the line.

Sharon began a frantic search for a working phone. She had exhausted all leads but then discovered the town phone worked. In one of the few useful things that Queens Park had done, they had ordered the phone companies to continue government services.

"Hello, Mom." Sharon reclined in the town clerk's chair.

"Sharon? Thank God! We have been trying to call you all day. It says you are out of service. Didn't you pay the bill?" Sharon's Mom did not understand. "Your Father had a devil of a time getting ours working. Good thing Hydro One still has some pull."

"How are Harry, Mary and the kids doing, Mom?" Sharon had imagined many horrible scenarios.

"Your brother's gone nuts." Cheryl sounded miffed. "Mary and the children have been with us for two days. Harry has disappeared, gone looking for work. The investment house fired them all. Harry thinks the big boys took bags of cash and ran off."

"Don't you know where he is?" Sharon asked. Her brother was a loudmouth, but she loved the "big jerk".

"Not a word, Dear," her Mom's voice trailed off and whispered, "it's Sharon." The next voice was her Dad.

"Hey Baby, are you all right?" As usual, her father sounded in control. "How can we get in touch with you? Damn phone companies!"

"Try the town hall up here," Sharon gave him the number. "I am not sure how long it will take to get a message to us. This phone seems to work for now."

"Cut it short, Sharon," Ted Johnson's voice came through the open door. "I have to make a call."

"Got to go, Dad, any word on PJ?"

"We heard from him today. He made it to England, just ahead of the fighting in Cyprus. It's bad in the UK, worse in the Middle East. He's at an RAF base, looking for a flight home."

"That's great, Dad. We love you all, bye." She blew a silent kiss over his goodbye.

"Ted," Sharon poked her head into the mayor's office. "If anyone calls, can you get a message to us?"

"Could you come and check? We can't run all over town." Ted Johnson sounded frustrated.

"I can send the kids down every day. Hey, if you get busy maybe we could work out some runners using the kids. They need more to do."

Sharon put her mind in gear after her stressful worry about her family. "Ted, work with the EAC. You have lots to contribute."

"I have already contributed Matt," Johnson chuckled. "My place is here. Besides, most folks hate me now."

"That isn't true, Ted. Many would follow your lead, and that would be good. We need more people and most people need help."

"You don't know the story," Ted sighed. "Tammy and I barely made it back in one piece the night of the riot. It's worse in Orangeville. We left those injured kids there. I had to tell their folks. Those parents blame me for the shootings. They didn't want to hear about the call to kill the constables, and me. I think I was safer in Orangeville." Johnson fell silent, reliving that horrible night. "I'll think about it." He tried to sound encouraging. His face said "no." She started the short walk home.

Perhaps later, she thought. *How can we lure Ted?*

Main Street was gloomy in the failing light of late afternoon. Most windows were dark and some, like the looted variety store, boarded up. The town looked abandoned. There would be no Santa Claus parade this year. Sharon remembered Ted always played Santa at the Legion's Christmas party. She walked on, smiling and humming "Here Comes Santa Claus".

After Sharon arrived home with the news of a working telephone, Bill hurried to the town hall. His Mom did not answer. The company had disconnected Joyce's phone. It turned into a sorrowful evening.

***

By December, most people had lost their connections to the outside world. All digital services, cell phones, cable, satellite television, and the internet shut down. Television antennas suddenly became more popular. With the loss of the internet, young people could find little else to do but play electronic games. Rechargeable battery cells became a valuable commodity, the object of trade, theft and extortion. Losing television had not affected Warren Dunne who had only ever used an antenna. Warren's desire to avoid cable allowed the little evening group to watch one of the watershed episodes in the great decline. It occurred unannounced after a long December day. The core group, tired after helping the needy, socialized at Warren's house.

"Here are tonight's headlines," the announcer frowned nervously into the living room in contrast to his usually smooth presentation. "We have exclusive coverage of two major stories. First, the Provincial Government has disbanded the Legislature and is running the province by decree. Our second exclusive exposes the bribery and corruption involved in the legal fight for control of our banks. We have inside, confirmed information that they bribed justices destroying the court's neutrality."

The group in the living room had not been paying close attention, but Warren suddenly waved a hand for quiet. Newscasts had been bland for weeks. That night there promised to be some excitement.

"There's something important happening." Warren leaned forward from his old, comfortable chair.

"This broadcast is live to air." The announcer seemed nervous. "Last week, they forcibly ejected MPPs from the legislative chamber at Queen's Park. The Speaker used the pretext of rowdiness, but some MPPs have told our reporter the government staged it. One Informer called it the Fisticuffs Coup. Our reporter, Janet Silver, has the latest." The scene shifted to a pre-recorded report.

"Good evening, folks. I am in a secret location with one of our MPPs who had been a member of the governing party. He fears for his life and is now hiding somewhere in the city. Sir, what happened this week in the Legislature?"

"Janet, the Premier staged a coup." The man fidgeted and his dishevelled greying hair contrasted with the typical blow-dried conformity of most politicians. "They wanted emergency powers from the Legislature but failed. Members wanted to discuss the issue and put limits on their power. They broke many rules over the past few weeks. The debate would have lasted for a few days. The Premier objected, and he promised me a lot of cash and an important post if I supported the coup. I stuck it out until they asked us to stage a fight on the floor of the Legislature so they could close it down. They were quite honest in caucus and used the expression, take over. That is when I bolted. I have sucked up a lot of crap over the years, but people are suffering and dying now. These people want power. The big money people are behind it."

"Some will say you are just showing sour grapes because they passed you over for a cabinet job." The reporter did not avoid the hard questions. "Is that true?"

"I was upset after the last shuffle." The man looked directly into the camera. "I would have been a good minister, but I asked too many questions in the caucus meetings. It's not about me. They destroyed democracy." His forcefulness startled the reporter. "I implore everyone watching to oppose this. These people are massing police and some militia units to secure their power. Soon, they will be too strong to fight. It's probably too late to stop it with talk." His eyes were full of emotion. The viewers could see fear. "I am doing what I can," he concluded, "I'll likely be dead soon."

"There you have it." The camera turned to Janet. "I am on my way to interview the Premier. I hope to have that report shortly."

"Janet filed that report yesterday." The news anchor looked concerned. "We are broadcasting it today because Janet Silver disappeared after filing that story. No one has located her. Also missing is her camera operator, Jason Mark. We sent a team down to Queens Park today to follow up, but police stopped them well south of College Street. Police and other security forces have the area cordoned off. They saw heavy construction equipment moving into the area and trucks carrying shipping containers." The scene on the screen changed to some poorly focused video of large vehicles and a line of police across University Avenue. The film ended with jerky footage as the reporters fled.

"As you can see our team shot some footage secretly but had to run for safety. We are happy to report all our people returned safely. Perhaps you heard what sounds like gunfire on the tape. We will try to have more on this on the late edition and still hope for the safe return of Janet Silver and Jason Mark."

The next segment documented the hunger and suffering of many neighbourhoods. It contrasted the partially supplied upscale areas with the destitution and lack of food in the poorer communities. One scene showed paramilitary units in one of the poor neighbourhoods, organized by former drug gangs. Food now replaced drugs as the commodity to control. The video showed several people wearing police uniforms alongside roughly dressed gang members. It was unclear if these were former constables or people wearing contraband uniforms. Desperate police had sold items to get cash for food. This trade included weapons, radios, and operating patrol cars. The reporter tried to interview the mayor but found city hall locked and guarded.

"Now, we turn to our other big story," The anchor reappeared. "There are several significant lawsuits in the Superior Court right now. Court staff, including the judges, lost their jobs. Sources tell us litigants who have filed the lawsuits have funded the courts and paid judges to hear their case. The plaintiffs are bondholders who gave loans to the big banks. They are trying to have the courts declare the banks bankrupt and give them control."

The scene cut away to two nattily dressed men and a middle-aged woman in a business suit. These lawyers represented the Upper Canada Legal Defence Foundation. This group of lawyers had become an unofficial watchdog of the justice system, advocating for those wrongfully convicted and against abuses of power by the legal system.

"We have talked with lawyers involved in these suits. They tell us the fix is in." The woman summed up the presentation. "We don't support either side. The hearings are a travesty and mean the end of a neutral legal system in Ontario."

Suddenly, the scene shifted to the anchor desk.

"This newscast is being brought to you by a working group within this network." The anchor hurriedly read a statement. "Our bosses vetoed all the segments you have just seen. As journalists, we felt we must air them. We have taken over this studio, to tell the truth."

The man suddenly glanced away from the camera. A loud banging came from out of view, then a tremendous crash followed by shouts and the sounds of a scuffle.

"We won't be able to do this again." The man rushed. Despite the shouting, the viewers in Weyburne could hear his rapid breathing. "Keep on fighting for the truth. They are taking power, and we will all suffer!" He shouted the last words as two burly cops rushed into view and slammed the announcer to the floor behind the desk. A few vicious blows followed. The camera spun around to show several armed men charging out of the shadows.

"Did you get the control room?" A commanding voice demanded. The butt of a rifle drove into the camera lens. The scene went black. Sounds of screaming and blows sounded for a few seconds until they too ceased.

Everyone sat in stunned silence. The television remained black for a few moments and then leapt back to life with the rebroadcast of a nature documentary.

"I think," said Al Wright, "things will get bad, very bad."

In the following week, two radio stations especially critical of the government suddenly ceased operation leaving an AM station dedicated to the older generation. It had always been conservative and pro-government and became the unquestioning voice of regime policy with news identical to the one television channel. Both claimed to be the official source for information.

By the middle of December, it was apparent that all news was propaganda. There was little reason to pay attention to the broadcast media. Members of the EAC tuned in once a week to listen to official decrees.

Chapter Twelve

The front door reverberated to insistent banging. Wilf Simms looked past the display shelves to the smeared glass. From his pharmacy counter, he could not make out who was knocking. The bright morning light silhouetted a figure beyond the glass. Simms ambled towards the door. He did not bother hurrying. Anything new always turned out to be just another problem.

"Thank God you're here," a young man exclaimed as Wilf opened the door. "We have a resident with severe pneumonia." George Buck worked as a nurse at the old age home.

"Who is it?" Wilf enquired.

"It's Mrs Edwards, remember her? She used to live out on the Eighth Line."

"She was a regular customer until she went into care two years ago. She must be in her late 80s. I recall she has a bad thyroid, high BP and other things wrong with her."

"She's in terrible shape. Her meds ran out." George stepped into the store. Wilf carefully locked the door. People walking in demanding drugs had become a problem. He recently had physically ejected an obvious drug- abuser. Since then, he locked his door with a "please knock" sign.

"George," Wilf walked towards the pharmacy, "I don't think," he hesitated, "Mrs. Edwards is a top priority for meds. Too many need them. I have a short supply."

"You mean she isn't worth saving," George was bitter. "How can you decide?" He bonded to all in his care and wanted the best for all of them.

"It isn't a matter of worth, George," Wilf was quiet and unassertive. "We must decide where to use our resources."

"You can't decide on your own. Hell, the two of us have no right to decide." The nurse grieved.

"I know," Wilf responded quietly.

A woman's voice interrupted them, "Good morning."

"Hello, Tammy," Wilf brightened. "George, do you know Tammy Waldon? She's a nurse practitioner, used to work in Orangeville. Tammy, this is George Buck, from the county seniors' residence."

"I know George," the two shook hands. Tammy remained the closest thing to a doctor left in town. The General Practitioners and the other Nps disappeared, looking for paying work. Several had gone to the city where they felt the need was great. The woman had fled north when Orangeville became too dangerous. People needed her services everywhere. It did not matter which town she helped, and she had a key to the back door.

"Wilf says we need to pick whom to save and whom to let die." George sounded bitter.

Tammy poured a cup of weak tea from a thermos into a mug with a big yellow face and the word "Smile". She delayed, considering her response.

"I agree with Wilf," Tammy finally replied. "It's horrible we have reached this position. We don't have a choice."

"How can you say that?" George cried. "We're sworn to help everyone." Buck was younger, out of nursing school only a few years. He had the idealism of the young.

"It's never easy," Tammy replied softly, trying to help the nurse find the logic in the decision. "I spent several years working with an emergency response unit. Once, we flew out to help in a cholera outbreak in Nepal. We found many sick, and we had very little medicine. We had to decide who was too sick to save, and who would survive on the little we could do. It was the hardest thing I ever did in my life until now." Tammy had a tear in her eye. She had seen more die in the past month than in a typical year.

"What can we do for Mrs Edwards?" George asked.

"I'll triage your facility. We have to decide whom we can help."

"We have an additional problem. Disabled people live on the back roads. We have to get them to town. Some will not make it unless we get medical supplies., and they'll die sooner out there in the cold."

"Yes," Wilf responded. "I've been sorting my customer list into needs, and it discourages me. We are almost out of insulin. I have a few small cylinders of oxygen."

Tammy's face grew dark. She had many diabetic patients and a few with breathing problems and had made frantic calls to get supplies. Everyone had hoarded, including the local old age homes.

"I can't get more," Wilf stated flatly. "I owe suppliers. They wouldn't ship on credit in October. My last response, in early November, came from a wholesaler who had no stock because they shut the factories."

"Tell you what," Tammy had decided. "I'll go with George and start the process. Could you list those disabled folks and line up some transport into Weyburne?" Tammy handed a slip of paper to Simms. "Here is my list."

"Where the hell am I going to get a wheelchair vehicle?" Then Wilf thought of an answer. "Reverend Wright has a self-help group. I'll go see him."

Bill Shadly evaluated the visitor. Wilf Simms looked sincere and caring. Bill did not understand why Simms remained an outsider, considering he was born and raised in town.

Simms was in his 40s and the only child of a single mother who raised him on her own, struggling at poor paying restaurant jobs to put him through school. His father was the son of a local establishment family and had ignored the girl after she became pregnant. His mother had instilled bitterness in Wilf towards the town's elite. After university, he bought his business from a retiring druggist.

Simms had a generous heart and had helped many people over the years. During these first months of this ongoing crisis, he had dispensed medication for a modest fee, or free to those who had no money at all. Wilf had joined no service clubs or other establishment organizations, including the churches. Approaching a group with Al Wright in it required a hard, personal effort. He saw the Reverend as part of the establishment clique.

The handicapped dilemma had not occurred to the EAC.

"We need transport and a place to house these people." Bill wanted to get this resolved quickly. The priority was the shortage of food and uniting people.

"We have a wheelchair school bus, but it has no fuel." Walt Lefevre spoke up. He had been looking after transportation for the EAC. "I've talked to Bob Ferguson at the gas station. He has lots of fuel, but the price is terrible, four dollars a litre for everything. He said, he doesn't have that much and only a few still have cash."

"Who has cash?" Al wanted a solution without spending the money the EAC had scrounged.

"Ferguson's best customer is Roger Smith," Walt replied. "I don't know if he'll help. I saw his sign up as a hockey supporter at the arena. He was in cahoots with Johnson and Kirk in the real estate scheme."

"I'll go see him," Kevin DeSantos interjected, "I know him from the club." Kevin was a member of a local service club and had connections.

Bill drove Kevin in Sharon's mini-van out to the Smith work yard. They turned into the property, a desolate, barren landscape. A potholed roadway paved with large protruding stones led from the concession road past a scale house made from a hodgepodge of salvaged, multi-coloured siding topped by old, steel, barn roofing. The windows were dark. Conical piles of sand, crusted with traces of snow, lay to both sides of the mist-filled gap into the pit proper. Bill eased Sharon's beloved van through the passage, searching for Roger Smith. They found him helping to repair a front-end loader.

"Hello, Kevin, what brings you out to the boonies?"

"Hi Roger," Kevin returned the smile. "This is Bill Shadly. We're from the self-help group. We need a favour."

"I heard about you people," Smith's smile did not fade. "The club hasn't been able to do much, glad someone is trying. What do you need?" Both men knew of Smith's dishonesty but placed the disabled ahead of their feelings.

"We have to rescue disabled folks from the back roads. We have a wheelchair bus, but no diesel. Could you spot us fifty litres?"

"That's a sizeable chunk of cash." Smith's face finally clouded. He removed his toque and ran his hand through his greying hair. Smith was a big man. His calloused hands suggested he was not afraid of hard work. The pause gave him time to devise an inexpensive angle that would make him look good. He smiled. "Okay, get it at Ferguson's. I don't do business with the Paki at the Petro."

"Yup," Kevin replied and stifled his disgust. He would later pray for forgiveness for his un-Christian feelings.

"Tell Bob to fill it. It might as well be ready just in case."

"That'll be at least 400." Smith's generosity surprised Kevin.

"I just got a big contract with that guy Angel up in the hills and have no problem with cash. I'll add it onto their bill; it's time they contributed locally." Smith turned back to the loader and ended the meeting. Kevin and Bill left to get the bus.

"I thought you hated those troublemakers." The voice of Smith's mechanic came from beneath the machine.

"This makes me look good. People will hear I'm generous. Folks will blame Mayor Johnson for all their problems. Someone will replace him so why not me? You can profit from others' bad luck. Here, spray this on that stuck bastard." Smith placed a can of penetrating oil into the worker's grease-stained hand.

The struggle for winter survival consumed the Shadly's time, distracting them from their grief. They briefly talked to Sharon's family every week, but Bill could not get in touch with his mother or sister. Sharon made a point of hugging him as often as possible. Jeff and Brandi felt closer to their father.

Some people accepted one encouragement as a mysterious gift from God. The electricity and natural gas kept flowing. The Provincial Cabinet decreed electricity and gas suppliers could not cut off supply with no people evicted until spring.

Utility companies and mortgage holders registered mild protests, but it suited them. Suppliers would know how much each consumer had used. They would recover the money later. Threats from the increasingly ruthless provincial administration added the pressure of taking them over to keep natural gas suppliers in line. The province had expropriated Hydro One from its private owners and absorbed bankrupt municipal systems.

Dorothy Kim's experiences repeated everywhere. Banks lacked the means to evict defaulters and the dispute with their creditors distracted them. The bondholders' legal attempt to seize the major Canadian banks had its toll. The trust between bondholders, shareholders, and major borrowers had collapsed.

With the loss of export markets, Alberta companies sent gas east based on government promises to pay. They would need to formalize this arrangement, but for this first winter, it worked as a patch-up.

People in town felt comfortable, especially in the above-average number of warmer days. Anyone on truck delivered heating oil, or propane had no heat. This affected farmers and rural suburbanites, and many moved to town to live with friends or squat in abandoned houses. More fled south to the cities.

Desperate Weyburne residents sought the strength of the committee in that first dreary December. The EAC became the focus for those needing and wanting to help. Two ex-teachers fell into the second category. Brent and Samantha James were husband and wife who had taught math and English in the high school. They offered to set up a school for the kids who wandered about with little to do. The two did not ask for pay, but only food and necessities.

The committee functioned on emergency first aid with the principle of helping members before assisting the larger community and took care of the workers first. Few complained since anyone could join and volunteer; however, many residents remained outside the group, clinging to their past individual entitlements and hoping someone would restore them.

The school buildings were too big for a few students. The group selected space in the United Church for the school for sixty children. The emphasis was on primary school age and provided tutoring for the older ones. Brandi Shadly would complete grade eight.

Organizing the school for the James' led to a fortunate discovery when a work party, sent to the schools for desks and supplies discovered working phones. The committee set up shop in the high school office. The flow of natural gas had kept the heating system working, and nothing had frozen; however, it wasted heat. Al Wright convinced a grumpy old custodian named George to forget his self-pity and take part.

George drained and isolated most washrooms and pipes. He turned down the heat but found offensive graffiti on walls and desks. George took great pride in his school and removed or painted over the mess to meet his standards. Students had done much of the damage, but teachers had left the most objectionable notes in their lounge. The crisis brought out the worst.

By mid-December, one of the wheelchair people brought in from the country joined the committee. Shelly was in her 30s and had operated a retail sales business and web page design from home. She became office manager. George turned the teacher's lounge into an apartment for Shelly and her supportive mother.

Having the telephone allowed them to talk to Ted at the town hall without having to walk there. People walked everywhere in town and shortcuts developed between houses. The community made spontaneous decisions on right-of-passage and broke fences open for shortcuts. A despondent Ted Johnson refused to deal a few trespass complaints.

"Fred, what's up?"
Dorothy Kim had let herself in later than usual, and normally, she would be at her desk when Fred appeared. Fred had a bank box on his desk and had filled it with his personal effects.

"Check your e-mail," Fred seemed about to cry.

She read, "Dear Ms. Kim, please accept our thanks for your loyal service. Unfortunately…"

Dorothy sank into her chair; her dreams finally destroyed.

"Look who sent it." Fred said.

Dorothy read, "Mr. James Ribold II, Williams, Ribold and Company."

"The money fund guys… bond sharks."

"That's them, so we know how the court fight went." Fred carefully placed the framed photo of his wife and their two kids into his box and then lifted his coat from the chair.

"Amy and I are taking the kids to Mississauga. Maybe we'll find something there."

He zipped his coat and came to hug Dorothy.

"Good luck, babe," his favourite tease for her, "I hope we meet again. Amy likes you."

Dorothy, still in her coat, watched a swirl of snow came through the door as Fred left. She did not know how long she sat, staring and breathing shallowly.

At last, Dorothy took a sheet of printer paper and a marker and wrote,

"This branch is closed indefinitely. Thank you for your patronage, D. Kim, Manager."

She gazed at the paper for a minute and then scratched out the word manager, wrote "ex-manager" and

cello taped the paper to the front door.

She had little of personal value at work except her family picture that included her successful brothers; her framed degree and a portrait of her father, the man she loved and whose praise she longed for.

Dorothy stared at his image and tears ran down her cheeks.

I can never face him, she thought. He will say that *I am a failure.*

Dorothy trudged through the un-cleared snow to the lonely apartment she had called home for the long but hopeful exile in Weyburne. That hope had evaporated.

I should go home, and food is running out, but I can't face him. I'm a failure.

Dorothy wandered in the street as she had for the several days since her personal disaster had hit. *There is nothing left.*

Two days later, a neighbour found her body lying in the street, cold, in the drifted snow.

Chapter Thirteen

Christmas week became a strangely wonderful time. While much of the town resisted, many people had joined the EAC. The group focused their first efforts on survival regarding food and emotional care. The expanding James' school initiative signalled that scope, but it remained tentative. Beyond the physical issues, Sharon Shadly tried to bring some brighter emotional light into this flood of gloom, striving to make the holiday season more joyful. With electricity still available, they encouraged everyone to put up outside Christmas lights and other decorations.

Those who had been active in various environmental efforts objected. While the committee sympathized, it felt the positive psychological benefits exceeded the impacts of climate change.

"Besides," someone said, "allowing for the increase in building fires, especially in the USA, there's probably a lot less carbon dioxide being emitted now than in September."

"Ignoring the waste disposal," Warren added, "it uses the base load from the nukes, and we have already paid in environmental destruction."

A baking bee produced fifty pounds of Christmas cake covered in sugary icing and multicoloured sprinkles. Church congregations organized a choir. The singers went from street to street, singing a carol at every occupied house, knocking on each door and offering a bit of cake to the occupants, along with hot chocolate powder and powdered milk. This token gesture lifted many spirits. There was little possibility families could stage a decent Christmas at home. The EAC had a Christmas Eve concert and a Christmas Day carol service featuring hot meals, a sing-along and a bag of sugar cookies for each of the children. The troubadours invited everyone to the Christmas services and concert but also listed unoccupied properties. After the festivities, a task force from the committee would follow up this long, depressing list.

Church congregations had grown substantially. No sanctuary would handle the festivities. The high school auditorium hosted the event using the school's kitchen facilities.

Food appeared miraculously. One pastor mimicked Al Wright, and described the festivities as a modern, Sermon on the Mount. They offered turkeys roasted to a golden brown, sizzling hams and juicy beef and pork roasts. Vegetables were plentiful thanks to the committees' work. The bulk on each plate would be potatoes and carrots smothered in gravy. Unfortunately, with bread in short supply, they had no stuffing. The event required much effort and used food they might have saved for leaner times; however, the EAC members saw the signs of stress and breakdown, driven home by Dorothy Kim's death. People needed encouragement.

The committee members suffered stress. Being busy had not lessened their anxieties. Bill Shadly grieved his family. Fellowship and laughter were what the doctor would have ordered.

On Christmas Eve, people filled the auditorium, most smiling and chatting, some quiet and unsure. The large room held long tables in four spacious rows with white tablecloths, real china and flatware with spruce boughs and red ribbon centrepieces. Assorted festive knick-knacks and wall hangings decorated the room. Two long tables laden with food and large punch bowls stretched along each sidewall, where volunteers served the feast. A decorated spruce tree stood near the stage, lights blinking and piles of bagged goodies beneath. They had seating for about three hundred with lots of room to mingle. At the piano in front of the raised stage, the Anglican Church pianist played old favourite carols and popular, seasonal tunes. Music stands stood nearby; the waiting instruments promised more music to come.

Just after seven o'clock, four pastors mounted the stage and formed a formidable line of black polyester and stiff white collars. Reverend Wright, whose voice, even un-amplified, commanded respect, smiled benevolently down upon the throng and asked everyone to receive the blessing. The four church leaders joined their hands. The attendees hesitatingly followed suit.

"Dear Lord," Wright's voice boomed over the room but then dissolved into a quiet, penetrating power, "we are here tonight to celebrate your coming, bearing the promise of peace, love and life. You were born into a world of darkness, danger, death and doubt, into a world of uncertainty where a power that overwhelmed, a power that seemed unstoppable, oppressed your flock, offering no hope. Tonight, we find ourselves in that world. We reach back through the centuries to grasp that flame of hope you first ignited in a cold, bleak land. We thank you for that promise and hope of salvation. Thank you for this food and the many hands that prepared the feast. Most of all, thank you for the hands that will share this food, and for the opportunity to live your love. Amen."

There were teary eyes and a profound silence in the room. No one moved for a few seconds, pondering the words. While believers felt their Lord in the room, others felt human love and caring. Their lives still held hope. The pastors hugged and descended to sit among the guests. The meal happened in orderly chaos, but in the end, everyone had their fill.

Children scrambled about in carefree abandon. The clinking of cups and spoons and the loud buzz of conversation filled the auditorium. The lone piano struggled through the din. Many guests volunteered to clean up and wash dishes.

The programme was short on talk and long on entertainment. The pastors delivered messages focusing on the blessing's direction to hope and salvation. Then several musicians from the high school jazz band augmented the piano with the sounds of a cello, clarinet, two guitars, a violin and a trumpet. Once they played, magic filled the room. People sang with gusto and tenderness following song sheets diverted from the town's seasonal celebrations. Mr Chellappah and his wife, the young Sri Lankan couple who ran the variety store, sang a wonderful Hindu chant. The echo of their sweet voices filled the room. Sharon Shadly appeared dressed in red and green, an oversized elf. Ted Johnson played Santa, handing out the goodies to the children with a hearty "Ho, ho, ho".

"We need to do this regularly." Sharon leant over so Al Wright could hear her above the din. Al nodded his head.

"Looks like a scene out of Dickens in his brighter moments." Reverend Wright's face had a big grin.

Sharon felt happy that her plan to entice the mayor into the EAC had worked. Time flew, but no one wanted to leave. Finally, one pastor called an end to the night with a prayer. The trumpet player rose and began a soft solo, a sweet rendition of Silent Night. As the other musicians softly joined in, people made their way quietly to the doors. People who had never met before went off singing together into the cold December night.

On Christmas Day, most people from the evening before attended the morning service, as well as new faces and many new volunteers.

The room overflowed. Christmas lunch had the same menu as the night before but was self-serve. Little packages of sugar cookies and apples surrounded the Christmas tree. The warmth of the celebrations could not overcome the limitations in the community. No toys or other gifts had been possible. Like the previous night, everyone lingered to prolong the joy that contrasted so sharply with the mean existence most were enduring. The band played lively Christmas tunes, and people danced.

The crowd gradually dissolved, leaving those with clean-up duties supported by many spontaneous volunteers. The band jammed away, having a special time together.

Bill, Sharon, Jeff and Brandi headed home, arm in arm, singing a silly song about reindeer. The sun had set leaving a lingering green glow in the western sky. A bitter wind did not diminish the warmth in the Shadly hearts. The family agreed it was a wonderful Christmas, even without a pile of gifts and a lot less food. That night though, Sharon and Bill hugged and cried for their families who were so far away, some still lost.

The Christmas get-together lifted spirits. Unfortunately, the committee estimated they had only reached out to about a fifth of the people still in town. Half of the town's residents on September 25th had disappeared. The largest exodus was in November, after the first snowstorm. Many had fled towards the city. No one knew how many had moved into town from the rural areas.

On what would have been the Boxing Day shopping extravaganza, teams of volunteers checked the vacant houses. The results upset all. They found most places abandoned. Footloose teenagers had vandalized some empty homes.

Several properties left horrible nightmares for the investigators. They discovered two more cases of family murder and suicide. The scenes were a contrast. One showed signs of a bloody struggle and futile resistance, while in the other a family of three; mom, dad and a baby girl lay peacefully in their beds. Later, OPP officers thought the latter suffered accidental carbon monoxide poisoning. A car sat in the attached garage, empty of fuel with the ignition switch in the run position. Most members of the EAC believed it had been a deliberate act. Both families had recently arrived in town with no local friends.

Bill Shadly led two other men to the front door of a nondescript bungalow in what the locals called the "new" old part of town. These streets had welcomed mostly locals who had built these houses and moved into town for various reasons.

No one responded to the doorbell and loud banging remained unanswered. The door opened at a turn of the knob. Bill stepped into a cold house. A look at the thermostat in the hallway showed it set to just enough heat to keep the pipes from freezing. They went ahead, cautiously but confidently, expecting to find this place, like all the others, abandoned. The only difference here showed in that thermostat. The owner had obviously thought about the pipes and saving money before they abandoned the place. Perhaps they had planned to come back.

Bill turned down the hallway to the bedrooms as the others explored the kitchen and basement. He swung the door open to the master bedroom and a puff of even colder air hit him. He flicked the light switch. His second step had just touched the carpet, the only room in the house with broadloom when Bill stopped cold in his tracks. Two people lay on top of the bedspread, unmoving.

The old couple, appearing to be in their nineties, lay side by side. The man wore a fine brown suit, ordinary dark tie and leather dress-shoes. She rested in a simple, elegant dark dress, a set of pearls around her neck, understated make-up and neatly brushed hair. White short gloves covered her hands while low-heeled shoes completed her look. Both had their eyes closed with contended, half-smiles and their fingers intertwined. The old couple looked like they were ready to attend church, or a funeral.

"I knew these people," Bill's companion choked on the words. "Harry and Doris Filler, they had a farm out west of here, on the 10th Line, cow-calf I think. They retired and moved here about twenty... thirty years ago; damn useless son took the place and ran it into the ground, drank himself to death. Harry and Doris outlived all the family and their friends. Kept to themselves, and I used to see Harry at the senior hockey but haven't seen them out to anything in years, just like Harry to worry about the pipes and the gas bill."

"There's no food in the kitchen," the third man said, "looks like they ran out and lay here to die."

Bill stumbled back to the EAC office and called the OPP, then found a quiet spot in an abandoned hallway. Sharon located him an hour later, sitting on the cold terrazzo floor, his head on his knees, barely visible in weak light from the skylight and sobbing uncontrollably, muttering his mother's and sister's names.

"Bill," she gently touched him. He did not move. Sharon sat beside him and held his hand. She said nothing, waiting. His sobbing diminished along with the brief spasms.

"Shhh... Shhh... Sharon, they were so helpless. There... there was nobody for them," Bill struggled to control his breathing and speech. "It could be Mom or Sis."

"I know, sweetie," Sharon raised his hand to her lips and kissed it gently. "But we must try to have hope. We must believe they have found safety. We will hear soon."

Sharon articulated the hope she had been trying to believe for the months since their Thanksgiving get-together. She talked to her family regularly but feared they could disappear at any moment. The huge stress tore them both down.

"I am going to call Dad and see if he can find your Mom and Joyce. Come with me, Darling." Bill stood, leaning on Sharon. "Let's make the call and then go home."

After the grisly discoveries, the EAC stopped the effort to avoid trauma to the search teams. They asked the town to organize a bigger effort.

Warren Dunne and Reverend Wright caught up with Ted Johnson at the arena. With his spirits somewhat restored by the success of the Christmas services, Ted recruited an arena worker and had the place opened up. The sounds of skates and laughter greeted the leaders. Several dozen children and adults sped around the ice. Ted skated in fast circles around the rink, smiling, forgetting the town's grim reality.

"Ted," Reverend Wright leant through an open gate in the boards, "we need to talk. Our guys found some more dead families."

The smile faded from the mayor's face. He lost control in a defensive version of Bill's reaction.

"What the hell can I do?" his eyes flashed a helpless look. "I don't have anyone to help, no one. The town doesn't even exist. Nothing I can do," his voice trailed off. "Nothing I can do," he repeated, tears forming in his eyes.

"Ted, let's call that town meeting," Warren felt action might help, "and organize something. We cannot go on like this. You cannot go on like this, and the committee cannot handle it all. We can barely help each other."

"How can I do that?" Ted was helpless without a paid staff at his disposal.

"Will you, as Mayor, chair a meeting at the school auditorium if we call it in your name?" Wright could see that the mayor was suffering. Gone was the happy Santa of only a few days before. Ted nodded.

"Give us two days. It will be at two PM on Friday." Wright took charge. "Can we help you home?"

Johnson refused, heading back onto the ice and speeding around the circuit even faster as if trying to outrun the horror.

Warren and Reverend Wright watched unfamiliar faces stream into the auditorium on Friday afternoon. On this wintry day, snow-snakes drifted along the streets on a strong north-west wind.

The mayor arrived at about 1:40, and while some of the townsfolk came to say hello; others glared at Johnson. At two o'clock, Ted Johnson sat at a small table on stage. All other councillors had resigned, and Johnson felt alone, not understanding he had new allies.

"Can we come to order, please?" Ted did not raise his voice; few paid attention.

"COME TO ORDER," Reverend Wright's voice boomed through the crowd. Silence fell.

"Okay," Ted began timidly, "if you don't know why we're here, it's deciding what to do about running the town. We have no money, no credit, no paid staff and no elected officials but me."
"We are in deep then, aren't we?" a loud voice called out. Murmuring swept the room, and a few cursed Ted.

"Yeah, with that jerk up there... his fault... idiot... ass," the chatter went on.

"Now wait a minute," Wright's voice boomed once more. "Three months ago, none of us would have believed it could get like this. Let's be fair. Warren Dunne tried to warn us, but no one, including me, would listen."

"So, Dunne did it!" the play on words raised a laugh.

"Don't go blaming anyone else," Ted felt too much self-recrimination to catch the humour. "I was in charge. I didn't see it coming, turned a blind eye like everyone here." Ted took a drink of water and found some of his old political strength. "We don't have time to blame; we have to decide what to do."

"Isn't that what you're paid to do? Where the hell were you?"

"I haven't received a cent since this started," Ted retorted.

"Neither have I, and I want my money. You didn't give me a cent of severance, and you owe me wages you cheap creep." A former town employee glared at the Mayor.

"You owe me too," another jumped up, "I only want what's fair."

"I'll tell you what's fair," Bill Shadly jumped to his feet with fight in his eye. His grief, and the hardship he saw as head of the EAC, left him short-tempered with other's petty selfishness. "People have died, some are starving, others are working hard to help, and you only bitch about yourself?" Bill's grief and anger energized his speech. "Where've you two been when we needed help these three months? Who here got any severance or back pay, or anything, when we lost our jobs?"

"WHO?"

The audience broke into applause. A chorus of, "Shut up you two!" filled the hall. The duo sat.

Wright would seek the former town employees. He never gave up on anyone.

"So, what should we do, Ted?"

"Legally the town can't function. We've no council and no one in any of the positions defined by the Municipal Act. It's impossible to run an election." Ted had read up on the legalities, trying to figure out how to keep the town going. "The town is bankrupt."

"WE are bankrupt." Al Wright put it into perspective.

"Can we abandon the town and start over? Can we declare bankruptcy?" A murmur of support came from all sides.

"Yes, we can surrender the town's charter," Ted replied.

"Then do it!" The audience chanted.

"I'll send the papers tomorrow, but what do we do then? The point of this meeting is to set up something workable."

"Someone did some organizing for this meeting. How did that happen?" asked an EAC member.

It was a leading question, politics at its best. On cue, Reverend Wright bounded onto the stage. Al had arranged this little charade. It would be a good if EAC members ran things.

"Folks, most of you know me. Some of you have lasted through a few of my sermons." Laughter rose from the crowd. "But I will not preach. A few of you don't exactly share my beliefs," again laughter, "but we are all in the same fix. We have to survive together." The crowd agreed. "We want to make sure no one can blame Ted if the province gets its act together." Al's voice carried authority, and more than a few of his congregation believed Reverend Wright could guarantee their safe arrival in heaven.

"Ted, I think you should resign, effective noon Tuesday. This meeting should vote to accept your resignation." He addressed the Mayor. His voice carried to the audience.

Ted offered his resignation. A show of hands from the auditorium accepted. It was done. Johnson looked relieved but defeated.

"What replaces the town?" another question from an EAC member. "Do we form another town?"

Wright allowed ten minutes of free discussion before intervening.

"We can't legally create a town. Once we surrender the charter, the legal obligations go to Toronto, but we can elect a committee to run our affairs. Lorna is taking notes," he pointed to the woman writing furiously at a desk. "I propose we establish a committee, tell it what to do, and decide the length of its mandate."

"You're doing this all wrong!" An elderly man leapt to his feet, standing with his hands on his hips. "This isn't how we do it in the army." The man looked around the room, but he did not look for support. He seemed to expect unquestioning deference. Ted Johnson's eyes rolled with a look of disdain at his old enemy. Bernie had been an officer in the military, retired to one of the nearby townships and was a pain in the side of local politicians. He had attended county council meetings regularly. His letter writing to the local papers had been prolific, full of arrogant condescension and individualism.

"You should appoint a powerful man to run things like the army. We did things quick with no arguing."

"Yeah but you screwed up too, and lots of your buddies died for nothing." Ted shot back at his old tormentor.

"Right or wrong, the army was always good for a decision, not like your council." Bernie shot a sneering look towards the stage. "We need someone decisive and willing to take risks, issue orders and expect obedience."

"I suppose that someone is you." A disembodied voice rose from the crowd. Bernie had some admirers but had alienated almost everyone.

"If you want me, I'll gladly serve." Loud groans drowned out lacklustre applause.

"You couldn't even run the Legion." The disembodied voice cried. "You lasted three months in that job."

Bernie served a short stint as president of the local Legion, but he had isolated himself from other board members, and they ousted him. His confident opinions had led to his election, but people soon saw them as stubborn, self-absorbed individualism. He lacked any understanding of politics as a compromising mechanism. His downfall in the Legion had been over what he called, "the purity of the members", meaning that only individuals who had served could be a member. His idea would exclude most of the active members and kill the organization. The members had abruptly impeached him.

"Sit down and shut up, Bernie!" The current president of the Legion stood and glared at his former member. "We have a lot of work to do." There was general applause with the insult magnified as the man who dressed him down had only been a private soldier, not an officer. Bernie rushed to the exit.

"He's upset because he can't send letters to the editor anymore." Ted chuckled. Al hoped the comment meant a renewal of the former mayor's spirit.

The discussion went back and forth for over an hour. Resolutions came fast and furious, only slowed by the need for Lorna to write them down. When the dust settled an organization was in place to run the town and, as the wording went, "as far out of town as we can, if no other group challenges us". This last clause was an acknowledgement to a few local farmers. No one knew how they had heard of the meeting, but they wanted to join the town. With no other economic base, the town also needed an agricultural hinterland.

A considerable debate occurred over the town's name. They called it Centreville and the committee, the Centerville Administrative Council. Although it would have no authority under the law, the meeting gave the CAC the power to make all economic decisions affecting the area. Residents were to contribute hours of service. The CAC would define commitment needed. The service was no problem. Most people were staying at home, trying to survive and making lots of labour available.

Reverend Wright became the head of the CAC, with Warren Dunne as his deputy. There were no other defined positions. The Council would decide each member's role. The meeting elected one non-EAC member. Bill thought it a good thing and important to have an outside opinion .

The Council would use the town hall, leaving the high school in the hands of the EAC under the authority of Council. The meeting broke up, amid tremendous applause for the new group. When Warren tried to get a round of applause for the former mayor, he discovered Ted had left, quietly ending his political career.

Ted Johnson spent Saturday morning writing letters to the Provincial Government surrendering the town charter, and to all creditors and former employees announcing the bankruptcy. On Saturday afternoon, Evy took them to the post office, which remained open, with one employee paid by cash from Ottawa. Weekly mail service would last until late winter when Canada Post collapsed. Evy returned to the town hall. Ted hugged her.

"The town doesn't deserve you, Evelyn," his voice carried a touch of bitterness. "You've made it a pleasure to be here." One more hug and Ted slipped on his coat and disappeared into the gathering winter gloom.

On Wednesday, they found Edward Johnson, the loyal mayor and car dealer, hanging in his showroom, surrounded by unsold vehicles. After all the tragedy they had seen, the town still wept.

Chapter Fourteen

The weather turned nasty, hitting the town with a paralysing storm. Thirty centimetres of snow fell, and the icy wind on the back of the storm blocked huge drifts, all roads and isolated Centerville. People hunkered down for two days; however, January 3rd dawned with a brilliant sun and no wind. People cleared snow and chatted with neighbours. In the more densely populated parts of town, everyone shovelled the public walkways near their houses, and it became easier to get around. The newer sub-divisions did not have enough residents left to make paths.

Reverend Wright organized a funeral for Ted Johnson, and people packed the high school auditorium for the sombre affair, shaking off the storm-induced lethargy.

The remaining two town cops resigned. They were in legal limbo and feared recriminations once things returned to normal. Al's assurances things would never be normal again did not stop them. They headed south to find paying police jobs in the city. The new Council went to work.

"We should assess everyone's skills." Warren applied concepts he had thought about for a long time. "We can compensate them for how much they contribute. What do you think Reverend?"

"Are you a socialist, Warren?" Wright peered at Dunne over his wire-framed glasses. "That sounds like Marx' saying, from each to each."

"No, I don't like any ideology," Warren said. "but it's one concept of 20th century politics that's useful."

"Just asking," Al smiled. "How do we make it work?"

"I need helpers to run the water and sewage. I'm overwhelmed. This is a good way to get more hands." The works manager spoke up.

They asked people to register their skills and say how they would prefer to contribute. Evy took careful minutes. Nothing would be off the record. She would stay on in the town hall, struggling with her grief after Johnson's suicide.

"Evy," Al asked, "how would you like to be Chief Administrator? We'll give you the clerk's office and triple your pay." The laughter gave relief. Evy had received no pay as it was.

"I want a new car too, Reverend." Evy got into the spirit of the thing and smiled; however, the mention of the car brought the former mayor to mind and her face clouded. It would be a long time before she found a light heart.

"I know, Evy." The Reverend, sensitive to the visual cues of his flock patted her hand. "By the way everyone," Wright looked around the table, "my name is Allen, so call me Al. I'm Reverend on Sunday morning."

"I got your campaign slogan for the next election, Al," one wiseacre piped up. "All's Right with Al Wright!" It took a five-minute break to recover from their giddiness. Anyone who had been under long-term stress would recognize the hair-trigger emotions and the humour necessary for survival.

In the countryside, the big storm made things harder. The could plough, but no one wanted to waste the diesel. Branch electrical lines fell. The snowed-in roads kept the repair crews away and increased farm families' isolation and suffering. Technicians still operated the local Hydro One yard, but the crews could only wait.

The corporation had worked out a system of delivering cash and supplies from yard to yard, so that the workers stayed. The local yard had good people. Some yards' staff demanded bribes leading to anger, violence, and in some places, a breakdown in electricity supply.

In Ottawa, all activity had stalled. Trying to recover from his ill-conceived election call, the Governor General asked all political parties to meet and find a resolution. They spouted many positive phrases such as, "progress is being made", and "everyone is working hard", but they achieved nothing. The remnants of the civil service only reported on payday to pick up their cash.

One of the national banks declared bankruptcy and closed. It had no active customers, no cash, and worthless assets in defaulted mortgages and foreign loans. The lawsuits by bondholders had pushed it over the edge. Declaring bankruptcy reflected the high-level fighting between factions of the elite. No one believed any official version of things. There were almost no employees left at the time of the bank failure. The CEO, CFO, and the members of the Board of Directors disappeared. Several hid out in their estates east of Centreville.

All the banks soon ceased operations, but this did not end the machinations of the big money factions who took part in the deadly struggle for control of the Province of Ontario. Hidden from public knowledge, dark events unfolded.

All the television networks had disappeared except for one broadcast channel calling itself the CBC. None of the frivolous cable channels remained once satellite and cable distribution ceased.

Some radio stations originated in the USA. One was a wildly fundamentalist Christian outfit; another was the official channel of a military government in Washington. From what little passed for actual news, it seemed the USA had fragmented. Texas had decided to go it alone.

An admiral from Norfolk, claimed to be president and ran the central government in Washington. It appeared Washington still controlled the nuclear weapons and the military government occupied the states of Virginia and Delaware.

No one could separate truth from propaganda. They heard little official news of trouble in Canadian cities, but phone calls from families told of bloodshed.

The Government of Canada announced reorganization into a, "dispersed and laminated administrative matrix structure".

Warren said, "They are saying they have no control and no one to do the work, so we are on our own."

It signalled the unwinding of the Canadian federation. Many MPs drifted away from Ottawa during the winter. The administration that pretended to be the government lost all legitimacy.

By the end of January, the CAC had accomplished much. Evy had recruited youngsters to deliver messages. Everyone over the age of 13 registered their skills. Two thousand names appeared on the list, a fifth of the town's original population.

Workers cleared enough snow to allow food distribution, shovelling a one-metre path down the middle of each street. These paths served better than the sidewalks and proved a bonus when the winter thaw hit and opened most streets to allow vehicles to move.

The mild spell lifted spirits. The temperature hit ten degrees Celsius for three days with 40 millimetres of rain. All the snow, but the deepest drifts, disappeared. The committee sent out expeditions to check nearby farms.

Rationing had not prevented widespread hunger. With so many mouths to feed, it was imperative to find more food, especially protein and milk. Many needy lived on farms. Too many had adopted the suburban lifestyle without stores of produce, preserves or dry food. Desperate farm families moved into empty houses in town.

Some evacuated farms had healthy animals and well-stocked grain bins. The CAC devoted a considerable amount of fuel to truck in animals and tractors to bring in hay, straw, and grain. The teachers' parking lot filled with tractors, wagons and loaded grain carriers. They converted most of the high school to a farm.

Jim Handley replaced the gymnasium doors with wooden barn doors. He set up stalls in the gym for cows, sheep and goats. The gym office hosted laying hens.

Several Swiss-brown dairy cows, chosen for the higher, butterfat content provided milk. Their lower production made them less likely to have mastitis. New urban farmers quickly learned the skill of hand milking. Brandi Shadly remarked it differed from trimming a milk-bag.

Butchers gradually slaughtered any surviving Holsteins. Most dairy herds died once milk-trucks stopped running, but many heifers and bull calves survived and occupied one of the car washes. Un-butchered animals would have access to a town park for summer pasture. Beef and potato stew featured as a regular menu item for months to come. Accumulated food kept everyone alive, but they had to replace these stocks to survive the second winter.

They discovered more discoveries of family tragedies on the farms. The two Provincial Police officers preceded work parties, sparing others the trauma of seeing horror but stressing the constables to the breaking point.

Willard Dick and Stevie Hunter rolled up the Quinn driveway in a powerful police SUV as they checked occupied farms. Willard was an ex-OPP constable in his early 40s, injured on the job and retired on a disability pension and often hunted with Steve and Gail Quinn. Hunter was one of the remaining provincial constables. The Quinn's farm lay to the east of town near the hills, and Roger Smith kept their road open to connect his work yard with the big estates.

"Hello Willard," Steve Quinn called out from his back steps.

"I don't think it's hunting season." Everyone laughed. A large, whitetail buck hung behind the house with its head down in bleeding position.

"I see we're too late anyway," Willard grinned as he nodded towards the deer carcase. "That boy could be an eight-pointer."

"Got me red-handed," Quinn glanced towards Hunter.

"We aren't the MNR," Stevie replied. "If you aren't shooting people, I'm not interested."

"Most of the ones I would shoot all disappeared," Steve winked at Willard. "Come in and have some tea. Gail has rabbit stew and biscuits, if you're hungry."

As they reached the porch, they heard a truck on the side road, invisible from the house, hidden by a thick stand of cedars. It was a beautiful and private spot.

"The Committee thinks you should come into town." Willard finished the last of tasty shortcake covered in gravy. "We think it could get dangerous if people head up here from the city. You would be okay in town."

"We're doing fine," Gail Quinn laughed. "It's lonely here, and annoying listening to Steve's hunting stories for the tenth time. We're fine for food."

"The kids are stir-crazy," Steve added. "Come spring they'll be able to ride their bikes into town."

"You all should come in regularly," Willard missed his visits with Steve. Because of the crisis, they had not been hunting the past fall. "You missed the Christmas shindigs."

"We heard about that after it was all over," Gail sighed. "We'll get to town more often. I can ride a bike too."

"How are the animals fixed? What will you do about spring planting?" Hunter was not part of the committee, but he had heard enough to see problems.

"That'll be a challenge. There's not much fuel and no seed. We won't be able to plant grain. I guess just pasture what I can and slaughter a lot of them in the fall."

"We can provide some help I think." Willard had participated in the discussions about the coming growing season. "We'll let you know about the planning meeting. You should attend. Everyone needs each other right now."

Steve Quinn left to chore the animals. The visitors tagged along. The Quinns owned a cow-calf operation with about 30 cows and almost as many unsold calves.

"Normally, I would have shipped the calves as feeders last fall, but they're in the pole-barn." Steve Quinn looked at the large females quietly munching good green hay in the barnyard. They had bred the animals before the crisis hit and would deliver their calves in April.

"We won't give the girls grain until they are ready to freshen a few weeks before they drop the wee ones." Quinn sounded loving. He enjoyed the animals.

In a smaller barn, a hand full of sheep bleated a hungry greeting. There were a half-dozen ewes. A large ram contemplated the visitors with sleepy eyes. He had done his work months ago and was longing to return to the pastures of clover and grass. Steve spread a square bale of green alfalfa hay into the long, wooden manger.

"We'll have some nice lamb by summer's end." Steve shut the door. The crisp winter air was a relief from the pungent odours of the barn.

They retreated down the lane bearing a couple of bundles of venison. Stevie drove silently, remembering horrible experiences on farm visits.

Sometimes, he looked at the wrapped meat; *this job has its rewards.*

It froze hard after the thaw, but it did not snow for another week. When snow came, it did not overwhelm as it had in January. Except for a wild attack by the March Lion, the rest of the winter proved tolerable. Snowmobilers visited outlying occupied properties. Few remained in rural residential properties. Those who did were uncooperative, and the town left them to their own devices, live or die.

They found the roving gangs that had appeared after the thaw not so tolerable. Some people thought taking what they wanted was easier than working. Mobs swarmed several homes and looted. Some occupants resisted and in one case, someone fired a gun.

The CAC organized area security captains, establishing a network of runners to summon reinforcements if trouble developed. It soon proved its worth when a group of looters headed towards the high school. Word spread quickly and just after the gang entered the school, 25 armed patrollers arrived. The troublemakers were not hardened criminals, just desperate, lazy, self-centred people who surrendered without a struggle.

When the raiders had entered the building, Shelly the office manager greeted them. Perhaps her being in a wheelchair or her outgoing personality stopped the group. No one knew. She had sat quietly talking to the intruders until help arrived. The Committee inherited two more rifles and a shotgun. Jailing the group would have been more trouble than it was worth, so they took names before sending them home with a warning. The committee convinced several looters to join in the cooperative effort. The security problem would disappear when spring weather hit and most troublemakers left town.

Shelly's bravery became a legend.

In all this, good news came Bill's way. Sharon's Dad had located Bill's Mom and sister. Peter's access to the hydro personnel had finally led to word coming back that they had been at Joyce's house, trapped with no cash and running out of food. Using a borrowed corporation truck, Peter brought the two women to the Maki's house. Joyce's husband refused to come along.

Sharon tried once again to get the family to come north. They still refused. It was the same for many families in town. Relatives disappeared. Like the Shadly's parents, many did not want to move.

The Shadlys combined celebrating Bill's good news with Jeff's 16th birthday on the 31st of January. Their friends on the EAC high jacked the quiet family event. Someone scrounged up a cake with 16 candles liberated from the old dollar store. There were no presents, but the hour of fun with family and friends satisfied Jeff. Sharon and Bill watched their son mingle with the others. He had matured. They had a sense of pride that he had become part of the community.

"That was sure a big blow!" Steve Quinn slapped his wool toque against his thigh and found a chair. Willard Dick had brought Steve to the old high school on his snowmobile. "It took three days to get the path from the house to the cow barn cleared. That Case and the blower were tempting, but diesel is tight, need it for those damned round bales."

He talked about the big March storm. Steve found a chair, draped his parka over the backrest and smiled at the familiar fellow farmers.

A dozen people sat at the large square made up from schoolroom desks. Most were farmers with a representation of small gardeners. Warren Dunne represented the food committee of the Centerville Administrative Council. Warren realized building unity might be his biggest challenge. The feet under the table seemed to tell the tale. Some wore high-end designer winter boots. Then the footwear descended through various levels of status and quality to Co-op style, manure stained, insulated green rubber boots. It encouraged Dunne to see the mix. Murmuring washed over the table as people became acquainted.

"I don't need to tell you how grave things are," Warren set a sombre tone. "Let's introduce us."

Warren noted some key people had shown up. Quinn was a cow and calf operator, and the Munks from the north were potato growers. A family from the edge of town raised sheep and had a small market garden. Members of the largest market gardening family in the county flanked them. It disappointed him that the dairy goat operator had not shown, but they lived too far out to make it through the remnants of the March storm. Several people owned big acreage but rented out their property to industrial growers. Two organic gardeners from the town were present. Warren had bought most of his summer vegetables from one of them. A few local gardeners the organic growers dubbed "chemical Charlies" for their use of pesticides and synthetic fertilizers shared the table.

"We have two problems," Warren spoke up as soon as the introductions had finished. "We are going to run out of food reserves before the end of spring, and we need a plan to grow enough to last to the harvest in the fall."

"We have potatoes in storage, about fifty tonnes," the Munks said. "Maybe someone has carrots and turnips."

"Bob Spencer has carrots," another farmer spoke up. "Where's he?"

"Going it alone," Warren sighed. "He's trading potatoes and carrots using the Legion as his base."

"It's tempting," Dave Munk replied, "but we think working together is best."

"Bob's wife doesn't like to let a nickel slip through her fingers," one other piped up.

"Forget him." Steve Quinn added. "He might come around later. I have a few calves and cows that could go to slaughter. It'll be a struggle to feed my herd next year, and I'm not sure I can breed the cows. I suspect the artificial folks are out of business."

"There's a hungry bull across the road from me bellowing." A pair of green rubber boots stirred under the table. "He's a big Charolaise and only had one cow to do in that barn, haven't seen the cow all winter. I think them folks left or are dead. I'm afraid to go into the house."

Stevie Hunter would inspect the property and a horse trailer would move the bull. By the time discussion ended, it had appeared the bull would have several farms to visit. The group chuckled and nicknamed the beast, "Lucky".

The immediate food crisis resolved quickly as sheep, goats and even domesticated rabbits joined the list, with small quantities of other root vegetables from storage. They supplied these to the school's community kitchen. The fare did not encourage in its variety, but creative cooks applied imagination to the food.

"The next harvest is the big problem." Warren led the group forward. "We need seed, fuel, fertilizer and equipment. The first two are the most urgent."

"I have much land planted in winter wheat," Mr Singh, one of the larger landowners spoke quietly but firmly. "Mr. Jacob Myers has planted about 200 hectares of my land, and I cannot get in touch with him. I don't think the gentleman is coming back."

The East-Indian man had never had much to do with the local community, but the crisis had changed many things. He and many members of his extended family had fled Brampton in November and occupied the old farmhouses on their local holdings. Rumour had accused the man of unfairly evicting a local family to make room. In reality, they had offered to share the accommodation with their former tenant who had not paid rent for several months. This family had refused and squatted in an empty house in Weyburne. They spread the fiction of abuse to justify not wanting to live with people of another race. Unfortunately, others suffered unfair evictions giving credibility to the story.

"That crop should be ready for the combine in August." Singh went on. "We donate that crop, but are most desperate to find some goats, sheep and chickens to put in our large barn."

There were a few hostile glances towards the man, but the market gardener spoke up quickly.

"We have some chickens, all layers though, but you could have them now. Perhaps you could help us with spring planting in exchange."

The desperate families got some stock, and their land added to the list for planting along with several other plantings of winter wheat totalling five hundred hectares.

"We have the equipment, and can do the harvest, but where's the fuel?" said a commercial cropper and a landowner. "If I use my diesel for spraying, I won't have enough to combine anything."

"Do you have the herbicide?" Warren did not like the idea of spraying, but these people donated, and he did not want secondary arguments.

"No, I just get it from the aggro when it's time." The man looked shocked, and realised the implication. "I guess that means no spraying."

"It makes the fuel issue easier." One of the organic growers smiled but did not celebrate any victory. Before this new economic reality, the pair might have had a fight.

"Assuming we have the fuel," Warren said, "we must decide how to get a crop in and harvested for next winter. We need animal and human feed, likely grains mostly for this year and want to minimise fuel consumption."

"I don't see how to get a decent crop without fertiliser and pesticides." The cropper said.

"My granddad used to tell me about cropping without sprays way back when," an old timer stood courteously. "They used to plough in the fall and double harrow in the spring just before seeding. Sure, they got weed seed in the grain, but it was just for their use. We're in the same boat."

"Another thing," one of the organic guys stood, honouring the older speaker, "that fertilised land ought to have one more decent crop in it before it gives out, then we'll have to reduce acreage and spread manure."

An even louder discussion erupted, and Warren let it run its course. He could see some nods and smiles from some of the big farmers. Warren speculated the big operators would find their new freedom from the debt owed on their machinery offsetting the frustration of the lack of supplies. Warren brought them back to the task.

The winter wheat farmer spoke up, "My crops, and those of Singh here, are too far out of town to be replanted. My fields are nearly up to the county line. There's lots of good land closer. I say we take our wheat off this year, but plant on closer places."

"There are good places right out of town," Warren added, "Can we get them involved?"

"That place up the third was a play farm. They had pretty ponies and such," one of the old farmers was scornful. "Those folks ran in November. The others, I don't know."

Another spoke up, "There's lots of forage and feed in the barns. Bring the animals and feed closer to town to save fuel."

"I have to decide how many animals to keep," Quinn said. "It makes more sense to move animals nearer to the feed than moving the feed."

"Fortunately," Warren frowned, "so many people have left the food problem is much smaller than if they stayed." All faces reflected Warren's sadness about the human tragedy.

The group headed to the school café for a hot lunch. One of the farmer's sons had been taking the food course at the high school proudly served his father and his friends. The man bragged about his son, "the chef". Before the crisis, the boy and the father argued about what work a "real man" did. Views changed one attitude at a time.

Mr and Mrs Singh sat alone. Warren joined them.

"I am glad you came." Warren opened the conversation.

"To tell you the truth, Mr Dunne we need help," the man frowned.

"Warren, please call me Warren. What do you need?"

"There are many of us, and we are far out of town. We brought much food from the city, but it will not last, and we are fearful."

"We can get you food," Warren replied, misreading the man's fear.

"Yes, that would help," Singh replied, "but we fear for our lives. There is no one nearby. We fear many from the city will come." Warren glimpsed why the couple fled to the country.

"Was it hard getting up here?" He stared at his plate, not wanting to seem like an interrogator.

"We are peaceful people," Mrs Singh spoke, "and did not want to fight. We have lost most of our possessions."

"It was a choice of either joining the Sikh militia or leaving. As my dear wife says, we are peaceful people. Many believe in violence, but we do not. Our own people might have killed us, and certainly many other groups will kill their enemies. The hot heads in the militia wanted to attack the pacifists. Many wanted to attack the Hindu and the Muslims. The Christians are too busy fighting each other. Down there you die whether you fight. The television is hiding how bad it is. In the middle of the night, we ran away with our brothers and sisters." Warren knew the media hid the truth, and this shocking story did not surprise.

"We can move you into town, or you can have an abandoned farm to live on near town."

"We are not farmers really," Singh replied. "I had a business in India, and we have education. I bought the farm as an investment, but we work hard and have many hands to help. We can try the farm, and we will help Mr Sorrento on his vegetable planting too."

"I know it must be hard abandoning your place." Warren was trying to imagine the feeling.

"Yes, but we no longer own it. We have not paid the mortgage since October."

"The banks won't be able to do anything for a while." Dunne's smile masked the sadness he felt, remembering Dorothy Kim; however, he pondered how the Singh's sophisticated understanding of the overall situation could contribute.

The Singh clan would move as soon as weather permitted. Their plight led to a discussion of the safety of the outlying farmers. Only two families would move closer.

"We'll be fine," Steve Quinn was firm. "We're not too far out and have the big estates behind us. With all that activity, we should be safe."

Making the big decisions left hours of detailed work, with small groups looking after the details. Warren would run the seed group. He already planned a seed recovery operation in the summer. They left the problem of fuel to Al Wright. They needed to improve nutrition. For this first year, they had little choice but would soon have to consider health, not just fill stomachs with calories.

"You know, diesel will not last forever." One of the organic growers wanted to discuss work animals. "With horses, you can get out earlier and work wetter land."

"You're talking lots of extra work." The big growers scoffed.

"I'm not saying not to use tractors, but I think we should prepare, in case we need the horses."

A programme for using horses, donkeys and mules took shape. There was no one around who had any experience with oxen. They would use an abandoned farm on the edge of town to develop work animals. It had a flowing stream, a dug well and could function without electricity. They assigned a team to round up suitable animals.

"Don't go bothering with them Clydes and Perches," one old geezer advised. "They're just pretty looking, but we ain't gonna be pulling no beer kegs," he sipped his tea. "A couple of nice Belgian mares live out the Fourth, above Five Side Road. Them rich folks on the first east, down from the highway has some fine standard stallions. See if you can borrow one to breed the mares. We would get a nice small plough horse for sure."

"I don't think that'll work too well." Mark bred racehorses. He was an expert on genetics and breeding. "I'd rather keep the breeds pure and only slowly try hybrids. Those Belgians are Granger's bunch. If memory serves, there's a stallion down Laurel way. I think we go look for it."

"Aren't there some Canadian horses down towards Orangeville?" One of the younger people chimed in excitedly. She had hoped to ride in gymkhana events but merely wanted to work with horses.

"Didn't know that," the old farmer rejoined, "but they would do a fair day's work, I tell yah!"

Warren suppressed a giggle. The conversation seemed like an old cowboy movie. He saw knowledge and wisdom well mixed with the preconceived errors that came from the local farm tradition. Combining this practical knowledge with good scientific understanding could build a firm base. Ordinary people had impressed him often in the past six months; these people would get them through the first few years.

They found two good Percheron teams, half-starved, but salvageable, in the care of desperate owners. A family with healthy Clydesdales joined the group. The Belgian mares and the ever-useful Canadians grew the herd.

Amid the progress, the fear that external politics and human greed would overwhelm them constantly nagged Warren. The turmoil in the cities horrified him. Singh's story only deepened that feeling. He could not know that the danger to the community could come from closer to home.

Chapter Fifteen

Hunger dominated everything until the harvest in September and no one took food for granted. The need stimulated innovation and violations of food safety standards. Inspectors would not be visiting the community, and common-sense safety decisions replaced centralized control.

Empty houses provided only enough food to last a few weeks, and much had little nutritional value. It added variety, but would sustain no one. Functional kitchens in abandoned houses in the older part of town accommodated families from the country and unsustainable sub-divisions.

The central kitchen made for efficient use of resources. Single men and women, apprenticed in the kitchen, some had never learned to cook, and working from scratch fascinated many who had lived the fast-food lifestyle. As supplies gave out, families gravitated to the EAC cafeteria.

The farm roundup yielded an assortment of root crops, maple syrup and tonnes of raw oats, barley and wheat; however, they were running out of flour and rolled oats. The local feed mill, only certified for animal feed, processed the supplies of wheat and oats into animal feed plus coarse flour and rolled oats. In these were desperate times, the community kitchen produced edible, nutritious meals from these makeshift basics. Sourdough creations became popular; however, the pungent aroma of the yeast growing operation in one of the school laboratories became a daily reminder of the basic nature of the struggle. The variety and quality of food declined until early spring edibles became available. It was barely possible to produce enough calories to sustain the population. A large-scale exodus lightened the burden at the end of March reducing the local population to a quarter of what it had been in September.

This exodus in the first spring led to an unfortunate altercation involving Bill and his truck. On a sunny day in the first week of April, Bill and Jeff were in the driveway checking the pickup to prepare for the coming planting season.

"Hey Shadly, how's the truck running?" The aggressive voice belonged to Jean's husband. He had contributed little, in stark contrast to his wife's exceptional effort. James had eaten only because of the high regard everyone held for Jean.

"Hi, James," Bill did not like the man.

"I need a ride to Toronto."

"Sorry, no gas, can't do!"

"I know you have gas. You are going to do it," James stepped towards Bill, balling his fists and glaring.

"Where's Jean?"

"To hell with her," James shouted. "She wants to stay here and play the hero with you losers."

Bill spoke slowly, controlling his temper, "She's the hero, and you're the loser." Jeff stood open-jawed. He had never seen his father so angry.

"Let's go, Shadly," he opened the passenger door, "or do I drive myself?"

"Get out of here, NOW!" Bill stepped towards the man. James turned and took a swing at Bill, striking him on the shoulder. Bill gasped, but Jeff stepped quickly forward and grabbed James' arm as he tried to throw another blow, pulling the man's arm down hard, causing him to twist around, so they were eye to eye. James' look of hatred unsettled. Jeff had never played violent sports that would have prepared him for conflict. Bill recovered and grabbed his free arm before James could do any more damage. The two Shadly men pushed James down the driveway and into the street. Bennett silently hurried down the sidewalk. Bill looked at his son. In the depression and hard work of the past few months, he had not noticed that Jeff had become a man.

"Thank you, big guy," Bill hugged him hard, his eyes moist. Every father imagines the day his son will become his friend. He had not expected Jeff to be so young when it happened.

Later in the day, Jean knocked on the Shadly's front door.

"Have you seen Jim?"

"He came here demanding a ride to Toronto. He had a full backpack and attacked us. Jeff and I escorted him off the driveway."

"He talked about leaving, but I thought he would stay," Jean slumped to the steps, and the tears flowed.

Good thing he wasn't another Bob Durant. Bill thought.

He did not know how Sharon would have survived if Jean's husband had murdered her best friend. Sharon comforted Jean who eventually fell asleep on the Shadly's couch.

***

The beginning of April signalled the start of the frantic farming activity. Planting began with the last diesel from a local filling station augmenting supplies from farm tanks. Mr Banerjee had an extensive network of contacts and could negotiate a COD shipment. Centreville paid for it all. It required most of the cash reserves, but diesel fuel guaranteed a harvest. The third shipment made it through. The driver sold the first loads to higher bidders on the way, and it cost an additional ten percent when the driver and his heavily armed partner demanded the fee before unloading.

Most economic activities had evolved into a cash and consignment system. The diesel belonged to the truck driver who had paid cash for it at the refinery rack. Fresh supplies arrived under the same condition and brought by ship from an east coast refinery. They passed through the St. Lawrence Seaway, paying a fee in fuel at each lock. Extra bribes drove prices sky-high, and the men had paid several bribes along the way.

This shipment would supply Centreville's agricultural needs for a year. Armed guards protected the filling station. This transaction marked the end of Mr Banerjee's fuel business. Ferguson had already closed; neither had the cash to buy any more supplies. Banerjee turned over his station to the CAC and devoted his time to the community effort.

The Easter service attracted a large crowd. Sharon modelled it on the Christmas celebration, but with much less food. The only groups not taking part were the Mennonites and the small Jehovah-Witness congregation. They had been involved with all other aspects of the community relief effort during the winter, but not any of the social or religious events.

The Jehovah-Witness community suddenly disappeared in April, abandoning their homes and the meeting hall. They had moved a hundred kilometres to the south-west to a small enclave where several congregations worked to build their community.

Imitating the believers, during the pleasant weather of April, about a third of the remaining residents moved on. Some used vehicles to take them as far as fuel would allow. Many had no option and began a long walk. Some signed their vehicles and other property over to the CAC, handing in keys saying, "The bank owns it, anyway". A few emigrants joined to fuel a pickup truck.

"To me, this looks like a Mumbai municipal bus." Mr Banerjee smiled at his wife as a vehicle made its way past their filling station. The pickup truck almost scraped the ground, overloaded, with passengers standing and holding onto steel ladder racks.

About half of the remaining residents of the old age home had died during the winter. The constant sorrow stressed the staff to the breaking point. Volunteers went to help as nurse apprentices to George Buck and Tammy Weldon. Graduates from this effort would form the backbone of a medical system for the town.

The decrease in population meant fewer mouths to feed, but the extra work spared no one, from Al Wright down to the children. Even though the remaining dentist, nurse practitioner, pharmacist and an optician received special support, they contributed extra labour. This was a levelling of the social and class structure in Centreville.

***

The winter deaths led to an accumulation of corpses in various freezers around town. The council had to bury the victims before everyone became involved in the spring farm work, so Al Wright went to talk with the undertaker.

"Frank, the Council wants decent burials for these folks." Al rested comfortably in an overstuffed red leather chair.

"How many are there?" The mortician's eyes brightened, anticipating a windfall profit.

"Two hundred and fourteen," Al fought to suppress his grief. "A third of them are children."

"That would be mighty expensive." Frank mentally counted the fees.

"What?" Al exclaimed, startled at the mention of money.

"I don't work for free." The man looked stern. He had been upset since the swindle had collapsed and winter had been hard. Frank savoured this golden opportunity.

"We figured you would do it as a community service." Al smiled, trying to hide his anger. "We understand there would be no embalming or any of the regular funeral procedures, but we thought you'd help us do it right."

"I'll give you a break, ten thousand for the lot if you dig the holes." He pulled out a standard funeral contract as if there had never been a crisis.

"Are you crazy?" Al could not hide his upset.

"Look, Reverend, you and I have done a lot of funerals over the years." Frank sensed the deal slipping away. "I owe you something. Make it eleven thousand and keep one thousand for yourself?" He seemed to think the bribe was a standard business transaction.

"I don't think so." Al Wright stood. "You're not a Christian at all."

Al stormed through the silent lobby of the funeral parlour and outside, and his thoughts were not holy. He was not sure if he was angry with the greedy businessman or himself for taking on God's role, condemning the man. He stomped toward the town hall in furious silence.

"Evy," he growled at the smiling woman, "have someone find Kevin DeSantos and get him here."

The woman watched in amazement as the usually friendly and sensitive man strutted into the mayor's office. She still stared at the opening, immobilized by Al's brusque demeanour when he reappeared, smiling.

"I'm sorry, Evy. Frank just made me so angry I forgot to be human. Please have someone find Kevin. We'll have to plan some other burial arrangements for those folks on ice."

She brushed off his lack of courtesy with a smile of her own, but he was still upset. Ordinarily, the loving Reverend would not have referred to the deceased so callously.

The town pastors formed a burial committee and went about doing the work of the undertaker. Al Wright was not a vindictive man, but he repeated his conversation with Frank, word for word, including the attempted bribery. Resentment for the funeral home operator grew, and he became the butt of jokes. Someone wrote a little ditty on walls about town, including the main doors of the funeral home. Little children soon used it as a skipping song.

> *Digger Don planted trees,*
> *Farmer Bill planted peas,*
> *Funeral Frank planted none*
> *Sitting home counting money*

Carpenters made barn-board coffins, embellished with hand carved decorations. These fine pieces of carpentry comforted everyone.
Many of the dead from the old age home, and others like the Durants and Dorothy Kim, had no local family. Evy kept a meticulous record of their hand-dug graves. One day someone might be asking. Many people found comfort in visits from Al Wright.

No one made judgements about how people died. Many of the living had resisted the suicide taken by others. The living could not say why they had chosen life. Few talked about heaven and hell. Heaven was tomorrow somewhere, and most felt they had all arrived in hell. Al Wright often said that no holy book allowed one out of hell once they had entered.

April delivered nasty surprises to Bill Shadly and Stevie Hunter. One bright morning, Bill heard his truck starting and rushed out the door in time to see the vehicle pulling away from his driveway. He gave chase, in his dressing gown and slippers, but it sped away and turned north toward Owen Sound. Returning to the house, he saw Sharon, Jeff and Brandi standing together, sympathetic, but with strange half-smiles on their faces. They did not dare laugh but spent several days in a conspiracy of mirth at Bill's expense. When he finally accepted his loss, they teased Bill. Brandi painted a picture of a little red truck with a figure in a blue housecoat running after it and the exhaust emitting a puff of black smoke resembling a clenched fist. Sharon framed the picture and hung it in the kitchen.

Stevie had not been sympathetic when Bill called. He cared but had no resources to do anything about auto theft. Stevie needed to conserve his resources to support community and remain ready for actual crime. At the end of the month, Stevie had his worries taken away. Headquarters ordered him and his partner to report to Toronto to join the security force at Queen's Park. The fighting in Toronto had gotten much worse, and the government forces had taken significant casualties. Trained security officers were in short supply. The other constable, a rookie with no local family, disappeared, but Stevie refused, and Orillia fired him He reported to Evy at the town hall to volunteer.

The Council appointed Stevie Chief Constable of Centreville. His status as a sworn peace officer would add some credibility to the town's security force. Despite the fancy title, Stevie would spend most days helping at the high school, working in the barn with Brandi Shadly as his frequent helper. He often boasted to her that being an ex-civil servant made him well qualified to fork cow poop.

House searches had discovered four marijuana grow-ops, and they moved the equipment to the high school. One of the drug growers came forward to retrieve her product. She had finally agreed to help set up the hydroponics growing rooms in south-facing classrooms. She would prove to be a significant support in the effort to grow winter vegetables.

Mysteriously, the product found in the houses, including seeds, disappeared. It became common to see young people gathering in the woods west of the old rail line. When someone of self-described high morals passed on their suspicions to Stevie, the Chief Constable said he would investigate, and then went back to forking pig dung out the school door. No one raised the issue again.

Other activity also took place in the woods. In temperate climates, spring is a lean time for food. A local retiree led the search for mushrooms, fiddle heads and other plants high in vitamin content providing needed supplements and variety to the humdrum diet. Pine tea with its vitamin C became available with Tammy Weldon showing people how to make the brew. In the fall, she would add tasty, vitamin-rich rose hip tea and jam. Hunters shot a good number of wild turkey and deer, despite the keen competition from coyotes. In fact, some of these predators passed through the EAC kitchen, served up as "reprocessed turkey". These sources of protein were a godsend in a diet that lacked. It would be fall before farm animal production could meet the community's needs. The town's population of squirrels and rock doves had disappeared. No one had heard a dog bark since early winter.

***

Al Wright, weary from the stress of the April burials and his constant grief counselling, found the meetings of the CAC to be a burden. There was always a full agenda for the Council. I did not encourage him when, in May, Sharon and a group of residents interrupted a council session.

"You're an impressive bunch." Al sighed. The delegation would lengthen his meeting. "What can we do for you?"

"We have a request," One of the older men spoke up, "but we don't want to interrupt."

"Go ahead; you already did."

"We want to reopen the golf course."

"Davy, when in the name of hell would you find time to play golf?" Al Wright's references to the damned were not all confined to church, especially when tired.

"Sunday mornings."

Snickers rose from the gathering. Even Al smiled at the idea golf was preferable to his sermons.

"I'm not saying this to drum up business," the Reverend spoke in a fatherly tone, "I specialize in hard cases such as yours, and heaven has more patience than I do, but we can't spare the fuel." Wright assumed they would use the mowing equipment.

"Some diesel would be nice," the visitors laughed. "We hadn't thought of that, and a little labour at the start." There was a murmur of agreement from the delegation, but a gasp from the councillors.

"There's no spare labour and no fuel for a game." One councillor retorted.

"I think you should see if your project fits the needs of the EAC?" Warren handed Sharon a note. She loved golf and he wanted to reward her hard work with some fun. Sharon grinned broadly at Warren's suggestion.

"Thank you for hearing us." She smiled at Al. "Will you support us if we don't use any resources?"

"Can we agree to that?" Al cast Dunne a quizzical glance. Warren's oddball ideas had a way of working, and everyone nodded.

At Warren's suggestion, the self-described duffers moved the goats and sheep out to the golf course relieving the overcrowded high school barn. A parade of 40 ewes, 25 nannies with kids and lambs, walked the five kilometres to their new home. Electric fence wire powered by a salvaged charger enclosed the nine holes closest to the old clubhouse. They evicted the useless mowing equipment to rust in the weather, filling the shop with animal pens and expanded with lean-to sheds.

The animals grazed the fairway grass to an acceptable length and held things even, especially in the dry summer. Everyone involved could play one round of golf per week, with the more elderly tending animals and hand mowing the greens. Strangely, the group sported Cotswold caps or similar headgear, and men sucked on old briar pipes, even though there was little tobacco. Occasionally, someone tried a fake Scots accent and enjoyed the role of gentle farmers and golfers. These older residents looked after the lighter animals, increasing the supply of goat's milk and freeing younger people for heavier work.

The inaugural Centreville Open Golf Tournament took place in early August. A few dozen of the townsfolk played; a few hundred came to watch and picnic. They scheduled the event after combining the winter wheat and before the fall harvest. The club provided roast-lamb, potatoes and hard apple cider. Spectators contributed potluck and spread the piles of sheep and goat dung on the fairways. Players had a free drop of any ball affected by animal droppings. They held match play for the serious golfers and a "best ball" tournament for anyone else.

Sharon played in the serious competition, finishing fourth. For prizes, someone had found old three-pitch baseball shirts. Players won the number of their placing as their prize, keeping it until the next tournament.

Sharon proudly wore the bright red shirt with "Billy's Variety" on the front and a big, black number four on the back. When she arrived home that evening, a little tipsy from the cider, supported by Jean who was not much more stable, she found a sign above the door: "Number 4 is number 1" in big red letters. Brandi had been busy.

Chapter Sixteen

"Al, someone here to see you," Evy called through Al's open door. "I'm sending her in."

They ran an informal town hall. Everyone knew each other. Wright made no one cool their heels unnecessarily. Evy was not the receptionist, having her organization to run; however, she preferred her old workspace in the main office. Al worked on next Sunday's sermon, but quickly put it aside.

"Mayor Wright, how do you do? I'm Maud Dillingham," the woman extended her hand with a firm grip.

Maud was tall, *in her 40s* thought Al, with a full figure and a disarming smile. In this hungry year, she looked well fed with her full, soft looking features a contrast to the leaner, fitter, hungrier look of the local men and women. Her brown hair had a touch of grey. Deep grey eyes peered at him through oval-shaped wire-rimmed glasses. A white blouse and grey skirt made Al think of a schoolteacher. She comforted just by touching his hand. Wright had not noticed how people had all changed in appearance until he saw Maud Dillingham.

"I'm not the mayor," Al replied. "I'm chairperson of the Centreville Administrative Council. We no longer have a town." Al steered Maud to a soft chair and took his place behind Ted Johnson's rosewood desk.

"What can I do for you?"

"I'm hoping I can do something for you... uh... what do I call you?" her smile was warming.

"I'm sorry," Al blushed, "we don't get many strangers here. Al Wright chairperson of this place we call Centreville and Reverend of the United Church."

"Your native name would be Man of Many Hats," she smiled at her joke. "Can I call you Al?"

"Please do, but what do you want?" Al had travelled widely and open to people, but in this new world, he suspected strangers.

"I want to open a café," she seemed to enjoy getting to the point, "and I hoped you could help me find a location. I have supplies, and I think I can get a bit more so won't be a drain on your town but add something to it. I cook and bake well, if I say so myself."

"People don't have much cash. Why would you come here?" Al asked.

"I want to live in a safe town... been on the move ever since spring came... everywhere is dangerous or not welcoming," Maud sighed and looked tired. "I won't charge much, maybe trade for supplies, labour and a safe place to sleep. Do you have a local currency?"

"We have what we call the Centrebuck used to measure people's work contributions. So far it has only been used to ration food." The CAC had not thought of using the buck as currency.

"If people paid me in those, I would pay any help I hired that way, to keep the money flowing so to speak."

"How can you get fresh supplies?" It fascinated Wright, but he had many questions.

"I worked for the Province," she sounded cautious, but seemed to trust Al, "and they paid us big wads of cash all winter, basically for doing nothing. It helped us survive. In March, we got the boot. I saved most of my money. Prices are higher in the city, where they hand out cash, but out of town, cash seems to go further. People need more of it," a shadow crossed her face, "and a lot of bad guys want to take it. I need a safe town. I could buy supplies in Orangeville, but I just came through there, and it is dangerous."

Maud convinced Al. She would set up in the old farm store location. It had closed long ago, squeezed out by the death of the family farm, and renovated to become a restaurant with a modern kitchen. The pine tables and chairs conveyed the impression of pioneer days, but the eatery never opened. In an example of bad timing, the owner completed renovations the previous September, just before the crash, and the discouraged woman left town before Christmas.

Maud's Café opened. She never put up a sign, simply a sandwich board sitting on the walkway in front of large wooden doors. Maud's became an immediate hit. She served real coffee, a variety of teas, hot chocolate and other delights. The café offered hard cider and homemade wine. An open stage attracted the deep pool of local talent, eager to share their music. Saturday evenings became lively times at the café as people sought a diversion from the tedious daily life. The café closed at eight every night, except on Saturday it stayed open until midnight.

Maud's became the place where people could forget work and the hardship. The only negative, as Al would point out, many in the church would yawn on Sunday morning. Maud's sat in line-of-sight of the town hall, and every visit there would include a stop at the café. She was a good talker, a better listener and augmented Al's efforts as an advisor and sounding board. Everyone became her friend.

***

Maud Dillingham's trip through Orangeville stirred interest in re-establishing contact with the larger town. A few people had walked down and back, and the CAC had sent a scout down in the spring, but they found little to offer. Most of the folks who had headed that way kept going in search of jobs and a future in the city. The CAC felt it was time someone returned to explore building a stronger connection. None of the former township governments remained, but Orangeville still had a council.

Maud and Al Wright drove down in the Johnson dealership van. Maud wanted supplies for the café, and Al hoped to meet with Orangeville officials. Tammy Walden claimed a space and hoped to find much-needed medical supplies. The three squeezed into the front bench seat.

"That doesn't look encouraging." Al stared at the empty window frames of a gutted car dealership. The gaping spaces held a sinister warning. Burnt out rusted vehicles filled the sales lot.

"I heard there had been lots of trouble down here," Tammy guided the van between burnt-out cars partially blocking the highway. "Look over there." The driver glanced towards a former motel. Armed men lounged in front of the building.

"They don't look friendly." Maud shuddered. "Don't stop!"

She learned that lesson the hard way on her drive out of the city. "Keep going, fast."

Tammy gunned the engine, and they hurried towards the main part of town. Every store in the shopping plaza on the edge of town stood in various degrees of ruination.

"I wonder where the action is," Al poked his head out the window and stretched to take in more of the desolate scene. Children ran about the empty landscape, but there he saw no sign of adults.

"Where are the stores?" He called out to a group of kids between the ages of five and ten years old. The children laughed; one of the older ones stepped forward.

"You got to go down to the railway place," he said, extending his hand as if expecting payment.

"Thank you." Al smiled. The hand pushed forward, demanding or perhaps pleading.

"I don't have any money." Al reserved all money for essentials.

"Please mister," enormous, desperate eyes stared at the Reverend who could not refuse.

"Here," Al fished out an apple he had brought for a snack and tossed it to the boy. The lad caught the fruit and ran off munching furiously with the small mob of children in hungry pursuit.

"Things are in a sad state." Tammy gunned the engine.

"When I passed through here, I visited a few open stores that had almost no stock." Maud looked past Al's head. "It looks worse now."

"Why did we stop here?" Al joined Tammy on the driveway of a nursing home with Maud close behind.

"This was the old hospital," Tammy craned her neck to look up to the roof at the top of the six-story, red, brick façade. All the windows were intact, but the gardens had decayed and dust and dirt covered the asphalt.

"They moved the hospital here in the spring. It took too many people to run the high-tech one on the hill. There's only one doctor left from what I last heard. Maybe he's gone too." The trio gained reluctant admission from a burly guard at the emergency entrance.

"The doctor's busy. See Ellen over there. She runs the place." He stared.

"Hello Ellen," Tammy had worked with the nurse in the new hospital. "Things look rough here."

The women renewed their friendship, but their smiles turned to frowns. Al and Maud remained silent in the shadows of the poorly lit hallway. The Reverend contentedly drew on the dusty floor with the toe of his boot. Maud stood in the middle of the passageway, avoiding the unclean surfaces. The pair made way as a gurney pushed passed, from somewhere in the building's interior, bearing a lifeless body wrapped in a sheet. Tammy and Ellen disappeared into a back room but returned with a small plastic bag. The old acquaintances hugged before Ellen slumped into her chair.

"This is all they could spare." Tammy said as they made their way past the guard into the welcoming morning air. "Some out-of-date antibiotics and a few painkillers," Tammy gripped the bag of priceless drugs.

"It's pointless to talk to the doctor. Ellen says he's leaving town for a contract in the safe zone near Queen's Park."

Tammy wondered if she would take a good offer.

"Orangeville council ordered them not to treat out-of-town people and that leaves Centreville is on its own. Tell no one Ellen gave me these drugs."

The railway yard was a scene of frantic activity. A locomotive idled in front of the small passenger terminal. The rumbling engine fronted freight cars, two open gondola cars and a single tanker. A caboose with armed men lounging beside it completed the procession. Away from the tracks, a small crowd circulated along a row of vendor stalls. Maud headed to that promise of commerce. Al went to the station to meet those in charge. Tammy remained with the vehicle, eyeing armed men staring her way.

"Who's in charge, may I ask?" Al approached the man who appeared to be the engineer and, in Al's mind, the highest-ranking person available.

"Depends on what you're looking for." The railway man seemed friendly. "The railway honcho is over there talking to the guy who calls himself mayor of this godforsaken place. If you're crazy enough to want a ride south, see the railway man, otherwise the mayor."

Al made his way to the two men standing in the shade of the station overhang and introduced himself.

"Yeah, I heard Johnson killed himself." The mayor shook Al's hand. "Sad times these." He did not appear to be grieving. "How are things in Weyburne, as bad as here?"

Al outlined the efforts in Centerville.

The rich folks in the hills used the railway to bring in bulk supplies and paid the train boss. This allowed Orangeville to receive essential supplies and luxury goods, supporting the market on the far side of the rail yard.

Shouting and swearing erupted from down the line. Liquid gushed from a poor connection in the hose between the railway tanker and the truck. The railroad man hurried off, cursing.

"We get a little of that diesel," the spill upset the mayor. "They bring it in for themselves but give us some, and we trade it to farmers. We don't have much food."

"How many folks live here? We lost over two-thirds of ours."

"We lost more than that." The mayor sighed. "It was good though. Most of us would be dead otherwise. The commuter types from the city went back looking for work." His face clouded, "We had a big bunch die."

They shared tragic stories, but the effort did not lessen their grief. It encouraged Al that this man cared about people.

"It doesn't seem you can help us." Wright had lost hope of lessening the burden in Centreville.

"Perhaps we could pass trade goods through," the man said, "but we don't have any way of transporting stuff. Maybe the rich folks would help you out."

"I don't think so; they aren't interested." Al glanced at the heavily armed men and shook his head. The Reverend thought it might be dangerous to get involved with people who needed guns.

"If you get the chance, come up and visit. We're organized differently. Maybe we could help you with that."

"I don't think your way will do it. It sounds commie to me." Al's account of the cooperative efforts in Centreville did not impress the mayor. "Business and free enterprise built what we had and will restore it." The man sounded confident. Al quietly returned to Tammy.

"This sure is a mighty fine van." A large man armed with a rifle smirked through the open driver's window, with one hand on the door handle. Al noticed Tammy had the lock on. "Yes, it sure is a fine van." His tone threatened.

"How are you doing? Can I help you?" Al smiled.

"Who are you, buddy?" The man's mouth twisted into a snarl. "I was just negotiating the sale of this here truck with this lady. It's not your business."

Al could see Maud making her way towards them with her arms full of bags. They needed to be leaving. The aggressive man stepped back and fingered his weapon. Tammy's face turned to a look of horror. Al never lost his friendly smile. He had once been on a mission trip to Haiti and been in a few tight squeezes. The man confronting him did not match the desperation and brutality he saw in that pitiable nation.

"Tell you what," he leant against the vehicle trying to appear non-threatening, "this is my van, but if you want to ride home with us to Weyburne and protect us, you can have it in payment for your services."

Tammy's jaw almost hit the steering wheel. Her respect for Al Wright became measureless. Maud arrived and was innocently stowing her treasures through the far-side door.

"Can you come and help me retrieve a sack of flour?" Her expression became puzzled as she took in the scene on the opposite side of the vehicle. For her two friends, time had stopped. They waited for the man's response.

"Sure, that's a good deal." The man smiled relieved he did not have to use violence. Even in Orangeville, they could arrest him, perhaps send him south or off to labour in the Mono hills. "But I'll bring a couple of my buddies, just in case you think you can trick me."

"That's great, thank you." Maud mistook his answer as an offer to help with the flour.

"We'll drive over and get it." Al looked at Maud and signalled her to be quiet.

Two other mean looking men, armed with an assortment of weaponry, climbed into the back of the vehicle. They spent a nervous half hour back to Centreville. The trio in the front hoped the armed men sitting in the back would not decide to kill them. In fact, the thugs became quite talkative. By the time the van reached Centreville, Al had decided they were not killers but desperate people trying to survive.

They shook hands as if to legitimize the deal. Wright smiled at the irony of using a vehicle he did not own as payment for services that the man never rendered.

The trip had cost one van and a few dollars for Maud's supplies. They would not miss the van. They had many vehicles available, but Al lost hope he could end the town's isolation. At least for now, it was safer for Centreville to survive alone.

Chapter Seventeen

Centreville evolved into a self-sustaining village where the population laboured to produce food, with an eye to the coming winter. Grain would provide their principal food in the coming year eaten as flour or meat. Root crops, fruit and vegetables would fill the gaps, but without essential nutrients. They expected health problems without these vital foodstuffs.

A person's status as a talented gardener under the old system did not always make them suitable for growers. Many had depended upon chemicals. Still, old gardeners had an advantage. Formerly fastidious people removed slugs and bugs from plants with bare fingers, and everyone had dirt under their nails.

Enterprising people started small-scale manufacturing. One welder began salvaging steel to make heavy duty gardening implements. Most of the lightweight suburban tools wore out quickly. Wood-workers turned out maple and ash handles.

The Centrebuck became a useful local currency. The total value of the food and labour under the control of the Emergency Aid Committee limited the number of bucks in circulation. Refinements would be necessary, and they needed to set the buck's value to the Canadian Dollar. Individual transactions would decide. Canadian currency would become more important if people could purchase from outside suppliers.

The physical Centrebuck came from a promotional coupon one supermarket had used to promote Christmas turkey sales. The EAC had found bundles of the script in the store. Sharon Shadly signed each one as she issued it. To prevent counterfeiting, she used a small needle to make an almost invisible hole in the authentic notes. The bills had a colourful picture of a fat tom turkey. Sharon made the perforation where some feathers rose above "the poke's nose".

"No one," Sharon said, laughing as she explained her ruse to Bill "will think to look at the turkey's ass."

While struggling with day-to-day survival, the Centerville Administrative Council had to consider future issues. No one knew if natural gas and electricity supplies would continue, or remain free. It would not have surprised people if all services, including the phones, stopped working. Even if gasoline and diesel remained available, the committees did not have the cash to purchase replacements. After the second year's crop, they would have none. They made plans to survive in a world without outside energy resources.

The horse farmers tried to harvest some grain, but produced a dismal failure as everyone under-estimated the human labour required.

The biggest obstacle came from the rusty equipment salvaged from the back of drive sheds, woodlots or former lives as lawn ornaments. The equipment could not function properly with dull cutting blades and perished the steel. After struggle and frustration, they abandoned the effort; however, they had learned valuable lessons and reverse-engineered everything to fabricate parts by hand.

The hard work and dedication of those involved impressed the tractor boys, watching in amusement while leaning on their big flashy monsters. Several volunteered to help with the equipment over the winter. Farm-wit summed it up: "Everyone needs a hobby."

The awareness of these formidable obstacles led a few more people to leave at the end of the growing season. Most of these folks asked for a share of the summer produce. They mostly went southwest towards Windsor, where the winters would be shorter. No one headed to Toronto.

Violence had increased in the GTA accompanied by starvation. The urban governments had collapsed, and the Province handed out food rations amid scenes of chaos and bloodshed. Television reported nothing but lengthy appeals for good citizenship. Family members spread the truth during phone calls, but all the lines suddenly went dead.

Life at Sharon's parents had been hard, but they all seemed to survive. Her Dad still worked at Hydro One as a service technician earning enough cash to survive. Just days before the first anniversary of the start of the crisis, they lost touch. It devastating the Shadlys, but going to search for them was not an option. Jeff and Brandi needed their parents, and if there was to be any hope at all, it lay with the children. By the first anniversary of the collapse, the town's population had shrunk below two thousand people. If contraction of the labour supply continued, they would soon cease to be viable and would have to abandon Centerville.

September, the last month of the first year, saw developments that helped to restore confidence. One bright morning, as Maud cleared up from breakfast customers, a five-tonne diesel truck rattled up main-street from the south. On the side of the white cargo box, someone had neatly painted the words, B&B Xpress. Under that: We buy, sell and trade. Orangeville, Ontario.

Maud watched from her steps as the vehicle rattle to a dusty stop in the middle of the street. Two short men climbed from the cab.

In their 30s Maud guessed. They wore threadbare, but clean shirts and pants with new work boots. These new boots impressed Maud.

"Hi, I's Bill, and this's Bob," the driver strode right up to Maud, "we're jacks-of-all-trades," the fellow smiled as if he had made a joke. "We buys, sells, and transports."

"I'm Maud. This is my café." Standing in her apron and holding a corn broom, Maud felt like a hick. Bill grasped her hand warmly.

"We's come up from Orangeville," Bob spoke with a rather thick Newfoundland accent. Bill used a lighter version. "We has lots of stuff to sell or trade," he continued. Both men had an ingratiating charm. Maud decided she liked them.

"Come on in and tell me what you have and coffee on me." Several townsfolk followed them, excited by a vehicle from the outside world. Al Wright hurried from the town hall and joined the crowd.

"I'm Al Wright," the Reverend extended his hand. "I'm the guy set up to get blamed in this town." They sat at Maud's largest table, with the newcomers at one end, Maud beside them, and the others along the sides in a descending pecking order with Al opposite Maud and a ten-year-old boy at the foot.

Jani Coswell, Maud's lone employee, set out a pot of coffee, cream, maple sugar, and cups. Jani patted the ten-year-old on the head and slipped him an oatmeal cookie.

"We has real cane sugar for sale," Bob's opening remark coincided with him sipping maple-flavoured coffee.

"Do you have a list with prices?" Maud asked.

"If you have paper, I'll write it down." Bill took charge, but it appeared the two were equal partners. "We don't waste our time on printing out things ahead. We don't have to pay for air, so telling is cheaper." His down-home wisdom impressed Al. The Reverend wondered how he could use Bill's wit in his next sermon. Maud produced paper and a pen. Bill put down line after line of goods and prices. Opposite some, he left a question mark explaining they would negotiate a price for those salvaged items that most people still had.

"Geez gal," Bill said, "if we likes your smile, we might throw a free apple in the dozen." He winked. The flirting disarmed Maud. While Bill worked away with Maud, Bob answered questions.

"What's it like in Orangeville? How are the roads? Do you hear news from Toronto? How do you get this stuff?"

"The rail line to Mississauga's still running. A train comes up, regular like." Al had seen the end of one of these train trips.

"The railroad brings stuff for them rich folks in them hills. Most of them folks use helicopters for themselves. The heavy stuff comes by road or rail. Travellers who come up by road tells us the highway's dangerous, so the rich folks has armed guards patrol the rail line. Anyways, they hauls fuel, food, dry goods and even people and private mail back and forth." Bob checked up on Bill and took a few gulps of coffee.

"We don't knows much about the other end of the line, but they's getting things from somewhere. That's how B&B gets a lot of our stuff. It costs us a bit, but the train guys like to do business on the side. We buys diesel. I can't say where that stuff's coming from. There ain't no refineries in Toronto, but seems the rail line from Montreal's running. Maybe the refinery is in New Brunswick. I has to fish that out of the train crew."

Al Wright remembered his student days as a summer pastor at the United Church in St. Anthony. The Newfoundlanders taking the long way home telling a tale had amazed him. Bill and Bob raised fond memories.

"How does the mail delivery work?" someone asked. With no phones, many desperately wanted contact with relatives.

"It's expensive, and you takes yur chances. The post offices ain't open no more; most any place that's secure like a cop shop, or the hydro yards will hold mail. Yah goes and picks it up. Not sure if people down there knows about it. I never tried it, though I would love to get a message back home to sees how the folks is doing." He looked wistful and far away, his thoughts home in Newfoundland.

Al Wright felt his longing, thinking of his own kids east of Toronto.

Bill and Maud agreed. She took him into the back to pay up.

"Don't take that extra apple." Bob shot after them. The adults at the table snickered. Al smiled.

"I like apples." The ten-year-old boy at the end of the table innocently laughed with the adults.

No one knew how much cash Maud passed to Bill. She had priced her menu in both Centrebucks and Canadian dollars. Roger Smith paid his workers in Canadian script.

Bill delivered bags full of salt, baking powder and soda, cane sugar, refined wheat flour, cooking oil (extra virgin olive oil, no less), some cosmetic items, and other treats Maud felt worth buying. Bill presented Maud with two large stainless steel mixing bowls as a present. These were very common in the Orangeville flea market. Many of the abandoned suburban houses yielded valuable chattels.

"You're my first customer in Centerville," Bill smiled. "I knows we'll do lots of business." He winked. Maud blushed.

When is the last time someone flirted with me? She felt happier than she had in many months.

"Now don't go gettin' all soft and mushy on me," Bob laughed at Bill, "I's the single one."

Maud produced a breakfast of eggs and pork fried potatoes garnished with a dash of dried tomatoes. The men ate heartily. Bill slipped out to the truck, returning with a bottle of ketchup for his potatoes. The gifted bottle remained on the table when he left.

This started the tradition of giving them a free meal whenever they passed through. Her payment was interesting conversation, countless photos of Bill's children, and some sad and happy stories of life back home on The Rock. Bob was fatalistic about their situation.

"Back in the old fishin' days," Bob was much too young for his family to have taken part in the old industry, "before the big draggers, when a dory went out, the bye's in the boat were longin' to get back and the missus and wee ones ashore was in constant fear. Some never saw each odder agin. Bill and I's in the dory now."

Al Wright negotiated trading CAC grain for a couple of ten-inch saw blades, desperately needed for the carpentry operation. Bob said he knew how to sharpen stuff and would stop over to take care of the tools.

The two men wanted to get to Owen Sound before dark and had to move on. They did not know the condition of the highway or the folks along the way. It might be dangerous out in the "boonies" in the dark.

"Godspeed," Al said, as they climbed into the cab.

"You's a pastor," Bill looked down at the Reverend.

"How did you know?" Al thought someone must have mentioned it.

"Yur eyes, sir, yur eyes are kind." Bill gunned the truck north.

***

"They's a nice bunch," Bob stared out the right-hand window as Bill drove. "This seems like a safe place."

"Darned right," Bill replied, searching for fourth gear as the truck rolled down a slight grade out of town. He was already doing 80 past the 50 kilometres per hour sign. "I likes Maud and the Rev. They's good folks."

The two men had been friends for many years, even though they came from separate parts of Newfoundland. Bill was from St. John's while Bob hailed from St. Anthony. They met while working at a factory in Mississauga and bought adjacent houses in Orangeville. Bob had a wife and two children. Bill had never married but had a couple of offspring back home. Before the crisis, Bob sent money back to the kids and their mother. Now, with no news for many months, he did not know if they survived.

They detoured into empty downtown Dundalk. As they swung around at the major intersection to return to the highway, a man materialized from a storefront. Bob slipped the safety off the 12-gauge shotgun resting snout down beside his right leg.

"Hi buddy," Bill called in a friendly voice out his open cab window, "gots anything to buy, sell or trade?"

"Where're you from?" the lone man asked.

"Orangeville," replied Bill, nodding his head back towards the sign on the truck box. "We's traders."

"We don't have any money," the man replied, "but we sure could use some stuff. Do you have any flour, sugar, salt and oil and how about some tobacco or ammo?"

"No tobacco or ammo this time, but we's trying for the next trip. We has the rest, but how wills you pay for it?" Bill signalled Bob to be ready in case the fellow had some friends. He had seen movement inside the store.

"We have some trade stuff; saw blades, knives, tools, and we have too many guns. Are you interested in any of it?"

Bill glanced towards Bob in a signal to back him up and then opened his door and stepped down to the street. "Let's see some of it," Bill smiled at his potential customer.

The man beckoned and a young boy, perhaps ten years old, came out of the doorway carrying a shotgun. He handed it to Bill who quickly made sure it had no shells. It was an almost new pump action 12-gauge similar to the one Bob fingered in the cab. Bill handed it back to the boy. On another signal, a teenage girl appeared with a wooden box containing several brand new ten-inch saw blades, a cordless drill with a box of bits and various chisels and other hand tools.

The goods the man offered were still available in Orangeville, but Bill had seen the desperate condition of the children, dirty, dishevelled and their faces with a haunted look. The gaunt appearance of the man suggested that he was eating less to give the kids more. Bill was too soft in some things, and his heart went out to the children who were the ages of his own. He offered ten kilos of flour and one of salt, sugar and milk powder.

"We don't need milk," the man replied. "Could you perhaps give us some cooking oil instead?" Bill climbed into the back of the truck to retrieve the items. As he handed the bags to the man, he reached out and gave the boy a small bag of candies.

"Share these wit your sister." Bill thought of how close his kids had come to this desperation.

"Thank you," the boy hurried towards the girl, perhaps fearing Bill would change his mind.

"What do you need I might look for?" Bill asked.

"We have grain but are only grinding it with a baseball bat and a bowl. We could sure use something else, and some kerosene would be great. There's no electricity."

"You's should go down to Weyburne." Bill said, "They's better off than you, organized and they has electricity."

"They do?" the man exclaimed. "We thought everyone was the same as us. We lost power in the winter storms. That's when most folks left town heading to the city."

"How many is left?" Bill was curious.

"It's just us now, me and the missus and the kids. We've been surviving, but everything's running out. We have a cow, a few chickens and a garden. It isn't too bad." Bill glanced at the kids. Things were bad. Pride made these people try to hold on.

"We'll be back through here in a day or two. I thinks you should go down to Weyburne. We'll give you a ride for free if you wants to go. Just be ready when we come." Bill climbed back into the cab. "We'll stop in anyways to see how you're doing." He slipped the vehicle into gear and rolled towards the highway.

"I thought I was gonna cry," Bob said. "I sure hopes they come with us."

"If they don't," Bill said, "they won't make it through winter."

They turned up the highway, speeding among beautiful hills and forest where the roadway wound through glacial deposits.

"Maybe we should move up this way," Bob thought aloud. "We could move to Centreville."

"I'd love it, but we needs to be at the railway fer our supplies. We can't trust anyone unless we's there to guard the stuff." Conditions to the south became more dangerous the closer one got to Toronto.

"I knows," Bob sighed, "but..."

"What the hell!" Bill interrupted his friend, "Look ahead there."

Bob snapped his head up and looked down the road. An enormous pile of junk blocked the road with crude flags flying overhead. Bob eased towards the blockage, and as they closed the distance, they saw two armed men standing on platforms behind scrap vehicles that made a zigzag passage along the road. The narrow way would require slow, careful manoeuvring to pass through. He stopped short of the barrier.

"Who goes there?" one figure called out, a little too loudly. Bob and Bill looked at each other and laughed.

"Geez," Bob said, "these guys been watching bad TV."

"Get out of the truck." The second man commanded, and Bob slipped the 12-gauge under the seat.

"What're you up to?" The second guard took charge.

"We's truckers and traders." Bill responded, "We's trying to get up to the Sound to sees if there's any business. Is there anything we could buy, sell or trade with you?" Bill wanted to keep it friendly, nervous of the hunting rifles the pair cradled.

"What yah got?" The first guard asked and stepped towards the vehicle. The business end of the second man's weapon levelled on them.

"Come see," Bob left Bill to deal with the gun pointer.

"Hey Brian, they got food here and lots of stuff."

"Any ready to eat?" the gun totter asked.

"No," Bill said, focused on the snout of the weapon, "but we has flour, eggs and stuff you could cook quick. Is there anyone ahead to trade wit?"

Bill guessed they were hungry. He tried to breathe quietly, hoping the rifle's safety was on while calculating if he could grab the gun. The short men looked worse for wear, and Bill smelt booze on their breath. They might be easier to overpower with Bob and Bill stronger and sober. It didn't come to violence as hunger overpowered the guards.

"Tell you what," the boss responded. "Give us some flour, eggs and stuff as a toll. Bring whiskey and you'll always be safe."

"That cost us a lot." Bill glanced into the rearview mirror at the fast receding pile of scrap. "They's just punks, and we sure could have taken them, but not worth the risk."

"Fer sure," Bob replied. "I gots a feeling it'll cost us up the road."

By the time they had dealt with the so-called authority in the small town, they paid more goods and cash. The experience made this first trip a losing proposition. Fortunately, the weapons and ammo went undiscovered. The pair made extravagant promises to bring back goods from up the line.

As they approached the northern boundary of this robber territory, they became confused. There was only a shack near the road with a man sleeping in a chair under a porch roof. His gun leaned against the wall, and the pair did not stop; however, a sophisticated barrier surprised them around the next bend and they braked hard. The armed men did not make them feel safe.

"Get down," a tough-looking man did not smile and levelled a handgun at Bill's gut. The large men were wore camouflage and stout boots.

"Stand by the truck, hands where I can see them." The pair obeyed. They figured this man knew how to use the weapon and would not hesitate. "Who are you?" He demanded.

"We's traders from Orangeville." Bill's voice wavered. He thought gun-toting thieves inhabited this whole territory, and his heart fell at the thought of losing their business, or worse, on their first trip. "We's trying to get to the Sound to trade."

Three of the men moved to the back of the truck. Two stood weapons ready, pointed at the vehicle, as the third opened the rear roll-door. They relaxed a bit once it was obvious there were no people in the back.

"Ok back here." Someone called out. "It's cargo."

"How did you get through the punks down below?" The man with the pistol sounded sceptical. "We never see travellers. All we ever see is some of that scum testing us."

"It cost us lots," Bill spoke up, somewhat reassured that these men hated the robbers down below. "We sure wish wed known about them. We would not have come up here. I suppose yer going to take the rest."

"We're going to search the truck." The man said. "If we're satisfied, you get to go. We don't charge tolls. You might find people to do business with, in the Sound. I can't say, seldom get there myself."

The three men at the back found the weapons and ammo.

"I'm glad you didn't use that duck gun." The leader said to Bill. His tone had softened. "We can't let you take these guns along. Only the security forces and citizens up here can have guns. We know where they all are."

"We needs our guns fer protection. It's very wild everywhere." Bill was concerned. "Some were fer trading."

"We have a problem," the man responded. "I understand, but we can't let you have guns in Huron territory. You don't want to come back this way either, so I can't hold them here for you."

"Is there another route back south?" Bill had planned to swing east along the bay, maybe as far as Collingwood before heading to Orangeville.

"We have a boundary east of Thornbury on old 26 and patrols up around Maxwell with another barrier to block these thieves from getting into Beaver Valley. I wouldn't go to Collingwood. Things are bad there. You should go south by Maxwell road."

The man tried to be helpful. He realized the travellers represented land contact with other regions. Boats travelled around the lake and over to the USA, but the land routes had become dangerous. They had built the barriers to control bands of thieves, including the ones at Flesherton.

"Tell you what I am going to do, and I am inventing this, so I might get my ass kicked later," the man smiled for the first time. "I'll have Pete ride with you to guard the weapons. The folks up there can sort it out."

"Thank you," Bob extended his hand. "I's Bob and this here's Bill." The friendly Newfoundland personality poured out.

"I'm Jake, and you'll get to know Pete well. He likes to talk." All the men laughed.

Bill assumed Pete had a reputation and soon discovered he talked more than the two Newfoundlanders did. They made him an honorary Newfoundlander. Only someone from The Rock should out talk a Newfie.

Pete relayed the history of the region's struggle since the crisis and when they reached Owen Sound, they knew the locals would treat them right.

Two days of talk, trading and partying lay ahead of the Xpress crew. When they finally swung down Highway 10 from Dundalk, without the little family that had refused to move, they had a load that would make them money in Centreville and Orangeville.

They found an abandoned farm in the woods, dug a pit on a dry ridge and buried several assault rifles and ammunition. They had no customers for these, but they might come in handy. Bill scratched a crude map of the location onto the truck box.

They were back in Orangeville before dark. It had been a successful trip after all and worth the scary moments.

Except for a few times in the winter when the roads were impassable, Bill and Bob made regular twice a month trips through Centreville. Their arrival spurred more activity and signalled an end to some of the oppressive isolation of the town, becoming a shaky connection to the outside. Tammy received medical supplies, but Maud and many others relished the gossip and news as the best cargo of the Xpress.

In response to the availability of outside goods, the EAC switched the food distribution operation to the old supermarket near the centre of the town and reactivated the butcher facility and the well-equipped bakery. The shelves remained bare, but the Xpress left goods on consignment. The place became an old-time general store complete with a woman proprietor resplendent in a white, bloodstained, butcher's bib.

The Xpress created a need for Canadian dollars, and they suddenly had a purpose. The usefulness of Canadian dollars provided the impetus for some innovations. Maud became a money changer, accepting Canadian currency and the Centrebuck. The café operator had arrived in town with an unknown amount of Canadian money, and she accumulated more from Roger Smith's workers. Until the Xpress, she had had little use for cash.

The rise of the dollar shifted influence in the town towards Roger Smith. He paid in dollars and had an unlimited supply. His customers up on the hill paid generously. Some people left the EAC and the CAC to earn "real money", as their loyalties shifted towards their new benefactor. Many bought at least some of their needs directly from the Xpress and the EAC General Store using Canadian script as it appeared the economy returned to what some residents considered normal.

Young single men became a small part of those who had stopped helping the EAC. Hard summer labour tired them, and they dreamt of earning easier money. Roger Smith did not hire the lazier ones who then became potential troublemakers who killed time at Maud's whenever she would tolerate them. To prevent starvation, the Committee labelled them "cannot work" and gave them charity.

"A little welfare," Al Wright said, "is cheaper than jailing them."

The EAC controlled most of the limited food supply. To buy food, Smith's workers had to convert dollars to the Centrebuck at Maud's, strengthening her role as a banker. The EAC did not have a surplus because they limited the number of notes in circulation to the size of the food crop. Sharon refused to issue extra ones. Some counterfeits appeared, and Stevie tried to trace them back to their source, assuming someone had found a few of the old Foodland turkey coupons. Sharon referred to them as "tight-assed bucks", but only those in the know understood the joke.

The committee valued the "Turk" as equal to two kilos of wheat flour, above the average daily calorie needs of an adult doing physical labour. Members earned one for each day they worked. They valued the buck in other grains and foodstuffs, in a complicated calculation. Sharon Shadly worked out the relationships and issued the pay to each participant, and her signature on the script gave legitimate authority. People dubbed this arrangement the "buck-a-day".

One of Brandi's drawings hung above Sharon's desk. It portrayed a hand holding a pen, signing a small rectangular paper. Beneath the picture, written in bold, gothic script was the word: "Bankster".

After Brandi's drawing appeared, Sharon placed a small handwritten sign on her desk. It read, "The Buck Starts Here."

They rationed essential nutrients, especially vitamin-rich foods, based on the quantity available and the need. Those who could not work: the hurt, sick, too young, or too old, came under a special provision and the EAC set aside food. Workers surrendered bucks to buy food from the official outlet, and they removed the notes from circulation until the next harvest.

Sharon had a lot of spare turkey bucks and could add them to the flow as work days and food availability increased. Since the workforce was in decline, new ones were not in demand. A food shortage required rationing, in effect making the value of the buck fall to less than two kilos. This avoided both inflation and deflation, balancing the currency against the availability of actual food and labour resources. Considering their inexperience and attempts by a few to subvert the system, it worked well. The EAC would need years to develop a stable system.

The Xpress charged 10 Canadian dollars for a Kilo of wheat flour, setting the exchange rate between bucks and dollars at 20 to one. Even though the use of the dollar could skew things in the future, the exchange system worked well. Maud always made change in Canadian script.

Sharon had a practical understanding of mathematics, but when the exchange rate became an issue, she had asked Brent James to help. After a few hours of abstract discussion, she finally gave up and served the math teacher a nice cup of tea with an oatmeal cookie. They then spent a pleasant hour discussing Brandi's schooling and her emerging talent as an artist and writer. Samantha James had the privilege of teaching the talented Brandi. Brent lamented Brandi showed little interest in science.

The CAC's recent practice of issuing IOUs to raise Canadian dollars smacked of traditional finance. There were no taxes, with people's labour being their contribution to the functioning of the town. They needed cash to buy fuel from Roger Smith and other essentials via the Xpress. In effect, the IOUs were municipal bonds issued with a commitment of a ten percent bonus due when redeemed in five years. This last provision was necessary. Most people still thought paying interest was normal.

Al Wright embraced the process, but Warren Dunne saw grave danger in this type of debt and the interest provision and felt this would be the basis of a future disaster. Interest paid required growth to cover the increase in money, and there would be no real growth soon, if ever. Warren could not convince the majority who rightly pointed out vacant land and a shortage of labour promised growth.

Reverend Wright came from a stream of theological training that had discounted much of the Old Testament in the Christian holy book, so discounted its admonitions against usury and compound interest.

The buck-a-day system ran into resistance from another direction. Pete Woods, a farmer who had helped, thought landowners should get more than ordinary farm labourers. He felt, since he was using his land and his equipment, he should get something for his capital. No amount of arguing convinced him otherwise, even though no other landowner supported him. Pete struggled on his farm until he used all his fuel. Pete's pride did not let him admit defeat, so he suffered on his farm with his animals and family.

***

Following the B&B Xpress, another trader arrived. Bill and Warren stood on the town hall steps when the sound of horse hooves on asphalt caught their attention. A quaint, but smart-looking rig turned the corner. Two matched medium-sized black geldings stepped smartly, drawing a four-wheel wagon, longer than the standard Morrill combination and made of weathered wood, *maple*, thought Warren, with his practised eye. Two men in Mennonite wide-brimmed hats sat high on the bench seat. Four-foot spoke wheels raised them higher. The rig had no paint except on the blackened dashboard and the wheel-spokes. Stones flew from horses' hooves and the chipped the steel hoop tires and gouged the painted wood. Use had worn the harness with tan patches showing through the black polished finish. Warren noted a new hand carved whippletree, made of ash wood, a rare material these days because of the beetle.

The older man climbed down and stretched, feeling chilled and aching. Even though they experienced another unseasonably warm autumn, he had felt the chill riding in the open, even at the speed of the horses. He was in his 30s, almost two meters tall, 75 kilos and wore a black topcoat.

"Hello, brothers my name is David, David Koch and my son Jess." He extended his hand in a warm, honest grip. Bill noticed David Koch had grey eyes, projecting maturity that seemed well beyond his years.

"I'm Bill Shadly, and this is Warren Dunne, welcome to Centerville. What brings you to our town, David?"

"Centerville? We thought this was Weyburne." He seemed confused, glancing around trying to verify the location. "But most places are different these days."

"The town went broke, so we changed the name and started over." Bill amazed himself at being able to distil these months of painful events into one short sentence.

"Do you have a mayor and council? I have some greetings from our community. We are from west of here, in Wellington."

"We used to see lots of your folks here, but none over the past year." Bill tried to recall the last time he had seen a Mennonite on the town's streets. The community had become involved with the local efforts, but their presence had gradually diminished, disappearing shortly after the Jehovah-Witness congregation had left. "We have a council to run things. We are a community, but not a legal town."

"Our elders wanted us to bring greetings and to see if we could trade or sell." Koch took out an envelope and offered it to Bill, assuming the talkative man was the mayor.

"Come and see our Chairman. He's the person in charge." Bill led David Koch into the town hall.

Warren remained, looking over the rig and exchanging pleasantries with Jess still sitting on the wagon. The vehicle held several large sacks of flour, salt and cane sugar. Behind them, stout wooden baskets held several bushels of solid looking apples. The fruit was a gift, but Koch hoped to trade the rest.

Jeff Shadly arrived in search of his Dad. Warren noticed the boys were nearly the same age, both almost men. He had remarked this with Mennonite boys before but saw the Shadly lad had developed a mature, serious look. After a year of hard work and being included in serious discussions and decisions, with little time for dreaming, Jeff had matured to become a near-adult at sixteen.

Change, Warren thought, *everyone has changed so much.*

Al Wright and Bill emerged from the hall with David Koch. They had negotiated the trading of some scrap for the food items and arranged for the purchase of a real flour mill, paying with several hundred kilos of whole grain. The discussions had treated Bill to a repartee comprising biblical references and a few words of disagreement on the meaning of some scriptures. At one point, he worried divergence over some obscure ancient writing might scuttle the whole effort. It seemed it only enhanced the relationship between the two negotiators. The men had finally shaken hands. Al quipped it was easier for a camel to go through the eye of a needle than to reach a deal with traders. David Koch scratched his head in confusion over the deliberate misquote.

Bill and Jeff climbed onto the wagon to show the way to the high school. The two boys chatted amicably, with Jess explaining the horses and rig to Jeff. They unloaded the goods at the school and replaced them with about two hundred kilos of scrap iron and copper wire. Jeff gave his new acquaintance a quick tour of the facility, sharing a good laugh about the conversion of the gym into a barn. The Mennonite boy had never attended such a school but could appreciate the joke.

"Your leader is a pastor. That's good." David shook hands.

Bill pondered the look in the elder Koch's eyes and finally found the courage to ask.

"Can I ask you a personal question?"

"Go ahead, but I might not answer." David's eyes twinkled.

"I notice your eyes are calm and have a depth to them." Bill hesitated. "I would guess you are only in your 30s, but your eyes look like those of an older, more experienced man. Why is that?"

David Koch paused, considering the question as though it had never occurred to him before.

"I guess it is because we listen to our fathers".

"Thank you." The answer stunned Bill. He scanned the duo and glanced at Jeff. *What have I ever had to say to Jeff or Brandi to pass on such wisdom?* He thought. *What kind of world did we build that discounted a father's, or mother's advice?*

Bill pondered these questions far into the future. The wagon headed out. They had a long way to travel. It would be dark before the horses saw their barn.

Chapter Eighteen

Maud Dillingham sat alone at her favourite table, tucked away in the back corner of her café, taking a well-earned break. She sipped clear tea from a delicate, Royal Albert rose patterned china cup, reading a book, munching one of her poplar oil-baked muffins. Not one to brag, the results delighted her.

Her missing daughter had given her the cup. Maud cherished the warm cup's link to her girl. Jani worked in the back, washing dishes and preparing pancake mix with the clinking of dishes and the scraping of a bowl on a wooden table.

"Hello, Maud," Roger Smith strode confidently to her table. "How are you today?" Smith had always been polite, but rumour said he had a mean streak that ran deep.

"Hello, Roger, good, and you?" Maud put down her book.

She had seen little of Smith. One of his sons came to pick up his day-labourers. The Smith's early morning routine created a cash business from the men and women waiting for the ride to the estates. These workers had Canadian money and made it profitable to open early. Everyone carried personal mugs. The wittier ones called her Timmy. This reference to a lost past amused but saddened. Doughnut shops were long gone.

"Good, good," Roger had something on his mind. Maud waited him out, a trick from her government days.

"I think," he chose his words with uncharacteristic uncertainty. "A telephone would be just the thing for the café."

He surprised Maud. She had mentioned to people that she missed having phone contact with the outside. Perhaps someone had told Smith. She did not believe it possible, with cell towers and land lines dead.

It would be wonderful to talk to Mandy again. She had no word for months. Maud sipped from the warm china cup.

"Can't happen, Roger," she sighed. "All the lines are gone, and how would we pay for it?"

"I can get an air phone rigged up." Smith used the slang for cellular phones. "My friends have a tower."

"I can't afford it,"

"What if I said it would be free?"

"Nothing is free, especially now," Maud tensed. "What's the catch?"

"No catch," Smith took her hand in his. "I want to contribute to the community. I've already given diesel and lumber. This would be something extra. I wouldn't want anyone to know my doing it. Lots of folks don't like me, jealous I think."

Smith was playing the victim. It did not suit him. He was a big man, like his oldest son, well over 75 kilos, 180 centimetres, and strong and had never avoided hard work. His hair had greyed, and his hands were rough. He had the air of power and money. Maud smiled. Roger Smith was no victim.

"Would it work like a normal phone?" Maud believed he could do it.

"Yes, no long-distance charges either. My friends own what's left of a phone company." Smith sounded proud to know influential people. "They'll do it as a community service."

"I'd love to have it. I could charge a small fee. Folks would love to talk to relatives again." Maud become excited about the possibilities

"I could pay you with the fees. When can we get it in?"

"I don't want money," Smith's tone hinted at something else. "I'll send the tech guys down tomorrow. It has a little antenna on the roof and nothing more. We have one over at the pit and my house. Show him where to put it." He squeezed her hand gently and stood.

"I'll be back in a few days to see how it's working." Smith went, looking smug and roared off in his pickup truck and left Maud uneasy.

What does, I don't want money, really mean?

The next day, two fit men showed up, dressed in a black short-sleeved cotton T-shirts and black denim pants, military style.

"Are you Maud? Mr Angel sent us to hook up a phone."

"Oh, Roger Smith said he would get it done," Maud had seldom heard the name Angel, the rich man running things up in the hills.

"Ah yes, Smith," the bigger man sounded sarcastic. "Yes, we are doing it for him, I guess."

Curious, the way he said that Maud thought.

They placed the phone on the counter near the cash drawer. The two were efficient and finished in an hour. The men made a test call to someone in the hill estates.

"Here, call someone." Maud dialled Mandy. There was no answer. After a few rings, her daughter's voice was asking her to leave a message. Maud talked until she filled the memory and hung up, smiling.

"Thank you," she whispered.

That afternoon, a sign appeared in the front window: "Telephone available." She charged two Canadian dollars or one-tenth of a Turk for five minutes. At first, people were sceptical, hardly daring to ask. Once they realized it was true with no extra charges, there was a stampede.

Sharon tried to call her parents, but there was no answer. She tried every day. Most others had no luck reaching loved ones.

Maud made a few hundred dollars from the phone and sales of food and drinks to those waiting. She only charged for successful calls. Once the rush died down, she dropped the five-minute limit. The phone service became an essential focus for the people in the town. Maud hired a young boy to handle the extra business. It raised the spirits of people who had reconnected with family. Most often, no one answered, with many numbers not working at all.

Sadly, the phone led to grief as families learned tragic news about their loved ones. Al Wright had extra work comforting suffering townsfolk.

Roger Smith discreetly dropped in on Maud. Once again, he found her sitting at the corner table. Roger sat opposite Maud, accepting a coffee from Jani. Maud composed an order list.

"Going to be a busy day?"

"Yes, have to work out what I need. The Xpress is due in. It's nearly November. I want to stock up in case the winter keeps them away."

"We were lucky last winter." Roger said. "Many folks would like a track ploughed to Orangeville. Maybe I could make that pay. Only my trucks and the express go that way. Think I'll see if Al Wright wants to chip in." Smith did not sound enthusiastic. Some people thought blocked roads kept out dangerous people.

"Folks don't care about that, Roger." Maud knew of the divided opinion. Some wanted Centerville to use fuel for a snowplough. The majority opposed ploughing.

"Well, not a big deal for me. My friends fly stuff in, and bring in the big things by rail." Roger emphasized "friends."

"You sure are busy, Roger. What are they doing up there?" Maud had heard stories.

"Nothing to talk about, my dear, they are trying to live like the rest of us. Has the phone been busy?"

"It has been good. Do you want a share of my windfall?"

Smith replied, "I don't want money; however," he paused, "I would like it if you would keep me filled in on what's on people's minds."

Here it is. I knew it wouldn't be free.

"What information?" She kept calm even though it upset her.

"You don't have to do anything if you don't want to. That phone over there," Roger nodded towards the counter, "will keep functioning as long as my friends want it to." It seemed like a threat. Smith made it look like it had nothing to do with him. "We would like to know what's going on, what's on the minds of the committee leaders."

We? This whole phone thing is a setup. It occurred to Maud the people on the hill could listen to every call.

Maud did not see harm in reporting of public news.

"They don't include me in their discussions."

"They come in here often." Smith's people observed the comings and goings of the town leaders, "I am sure they talk a lot. Just let me know what you hear. You could overhear more." His voice had an edge to it.

"I don't want to spy on my friends. They've been good to me."

"I've been good to you too, Maud, what with my workers spending money, and that contraption." He nodded towards the telephone. "I don't need to be so helpful to folks." He used the word folks, but Maud understood it meant her. "The Xpress comes through because we let it. There is no sense in letting people suffer too much."

The phrase "too much" alarmed Maud. She understood that needy suffering people became loyal to the people they depended on if they did not suffer too much.

"We can easily stop those Xpress guys from getting goods or coming up the road." Smith was smiling. "See the power we have?" He paused. Maud knew losing the Xpress would probably kill her business. "So, pass on information, harmless really, and keep me happy."

He was looking at her strangely, holding her hand. Maud wondered if keeping him happy would stop at spying. She was relieved Jani was in the kitchen out of sight and hearing. Smith ran his fingers along the back of her hand but suddenly stood as if catching himself.

"Here's my phone number." He dropped a card on the table. "Call every week, and any other time if there is something you think I might want to know. If you aren't sure, pass it on anyway."

He blew her a kiss and walked out. Maud was shaking. She felt dirty yet nothing had happened. The man gave her the creeps, but she knew she had to cooperate to keep the café open. With any luck, there would be nothing special to report.

Please, please God, don't let him want more.

***

Warren Dunne had a project to keep him busy in the winter. The CAC took little time. Once the physical labour of the growing season passed, boredom became the enemy. Warren toured the gardens around town and on adjacent farms over the summer, evaluating and cataloguing the plants. He noted the best examples and gathered their mature seed.

Jean Bennett became his assistant by accident. She had worked in the central garden in the old baseball park. One day, Warren came to check the plants. Pulling weeds side by side with Jean in the beet patch, Warren explained his project. The work fascinated Jean, and she offered to help. She went to all the sites with him, picking and cataloguing seeds. By the week after Thanksgiving, they had gathered them all.

Warren stored the seed in his house to control the climate and keep them safe. They needed to sort, clean, and label each type of seed to cultivate in controlled plots. At the end of the next growing season, they would repeat the process.

Because of hybrid seeds, Warren expected most of the plants from this batch would not be suitable. He hoped, over several growing seasons they would have the best of the original genetic stock. He admonished himself for not having joined seed groups. The death of the internet and regular mail now made that impossible.

Jean had not studied biology or genetics. She had not completed high school, but the process fascinated and challenged her. Over those two months working with Warren, people noticed a change in Jean. She freed her hair from its tight bun and laughed more with a lightness to her movements.

"Jean looks happy." Sharon once remarked to Bill.

Amid the hard work and uncertainty, free of the confines of her old life Jean found happiness. She seemed like a newborn butterfly by that second October, finding a purpose beyond anything she had experienced in her previously mundane existence.

Jean hurried up to Warren's door, enjoying the fresh October air and thrilled by the beauty of the trees. The leaves had gathered in wind-whipped piles of crimson, yellow and brown. Warren had shown her hidden details in tree trunks and branches, and Jean now appreciated even a barren maple.

"Hi, Warren," she let herself in, "I have the lists ready."

"Morning, Jean." Warren looked up and laid his book on the kitchen table. "You look lovely today."

"So, do you, WD." Jean blushed; the praise felt wonderful. Jean called Warren by his initials ever since she spotted his framed name tag from the old city job, hanging on the wall. It had said "WD Dunne" in bold letters. Warren explained the city HR department had messed up his name. His real name was Warren Wallace Dunne. He enjoyed the joke so much he had the thing framed.

Secretly, it pleased Warren that Jean felt comfortable teasing him. He had not felt this light-hearted in years. Since Susan's death, Warren had become careless in his appearance and his house. When Jean began coming over to help with the seeds, he had become conscious of both, dressed more carefully and kept the house spotless. Warren looked forward to their day's work.

Their routine began by cleaning seeds and packaging them in carefully labelled containers. Over winter, they would make garden plans, designating plots for each of the packets. They formed a smooth functioning team and most times barely had to speak about the work. After two hours, they took a break.

"Here's your tea, WD." Jean made it without asking. "I made this apple cake last night." She handed him a slice and washed her's down with black coffee.

"Jean," Warren seemed nervous, "I have been thinking."

"Bad sign," she joked, "means you aren't sleeping." Warren's face was intense and earnest.

"We could get more done if you moved in here." Warren could not breathe.

Damn, why is this so hard? I feel like a teenager.

Jean kept on munching her cake and took a sip of coffee.

"Are you propositioning me, WD?" she finally said.

"I'm just asking you to live here." Warren's face burned crimson. "You would have your own room."

"There is only one room I would want here," Jean felt light-headed, "and that's your room. What took you so long to ask, you big goof?"

She realized she had to be the pushy one; he was too shy. Warren surprised her by circling the table, lifting her off the chair and kissing her deeply. They melted into each other's arms.

"I love you, Sweet Jean."

"I love you Warren Wallace Dunne." They did no more work that day.

The next day Sharon and Bill relaxed at Maud's as the two lovebirds walked in holding hands. Sharon rushed to them and hugged them both.

"Congratulations! It's about time. We have known for months." Sharon beamed and Jean and Warren glowed.

***

Al Wright picked his way up the old farm lane in the November morning sun. The frost-covered vegetation, growing along the track left a moist sheen on his pants and the tops of his black and red rubber boots. Mist from his breathing spread around his face, disappearing in the meagre warmth of the sun. No breeze stirred, but the crisp air hinted at coming cold winter winds. Grey smoke rose straight into the sky from the back chimney of the white clapboard farmhouse. Mist shrouded the farmstead, half hidden by barren maple trees. The branches wrapped around the house, icy fingers holding it in a tight grip. Al wished he had not read so much Dickens so that he could see the place as a simple farmstead. The barn stood off a short distance past the house, almost lost in the haze.

"Hello, Reverend Wright. Please come in." Janet Woods held the door open. "What brings you out here?"

"I'm sorry I haven't been out sooner," Al eased himself into the offered kitchen chair. "I wanted to see how you all were doing. Where's Pete?" The room was neat, clean and warm from the wood stove. He saw no sign of breakfast.

"He's out in the barn, scrounging up hay for the sheep," Janet sighed.

"How are you doing?" Rumour said they suffered.

"I can't lie, Reverend; we're in a fix. I can't offer you anything. We have very little." She looked beaten and had not smiled since Al arrived.

"Where are the kids?"

"They're still sleeping. You don't feel hungry lying in. We're only eating one meal a day." Signs of depression hung about the woman. It troubled Al deeply.

"I want you all to come to town. We can set you up. You won't have to worry. I've got a van at the end of the lane."

"I would like to, Reverend, but Pete won't. We already talked about it," the woman had tears in her eyes. "The kids have eaten little for two days. Pete said we should go without him, but maybe if you talk to him. He's out in the barn, just killing time."

"Get the kids ready and things you'll need right away. We can come back for the rest. Give me a few minutes with Pete, but if you haven't been eating well, we had better get going no matter what he decides."

Wright tramped towards the barn. The sound of a starter motor turning over came from the equipment shed. He let his eyes adjust to the dim interior. There was no electric light, but weak morning sunshine filtered through dusty window panes. Al could make out the shape of a tractor, a huge diesel David Brown with a cab. Pete sat in the cab, labouring the ineffectual starter. The battery died.

"PETE!" Al called several times before Pete dismounted. Peter was a big man, wearing winter bib overalls that disappeared into the standard red plaid bush jacket. The overall pant cuffs descended, farmer style, into manure stained green rubber boots with yellow covered steel toes. Pete's face had several days of beard stubble. Unkempt hair straggled out under a camouflaged hunting cap. He looked grim.

"What yah want, Rev?" Pete was from an old local family and had the distinctive accent of the country. "Damned tractor won't start. There's no fuel." Pete shrugged and spat sideways at an empty fuel container.

"I want you to come to town for the winter." Al hoped Janet was wrong. "We can fix you up nicely."

"I don't want charity," Pete glared towards Al; then his eyes fell to Wright's rubber boots.

"It isn't charity, Pete. Many people have been helping each other. You were involved. You and the family are welcome. We want to help." Al was hopeful.

"I won't leave, Reverend," he looked Al straight in the eye. Wright saw pride, courage and despair in the man's face. "I was born here; Dad was born here, his Dad built the place. I won't leave it. I can't lose it, I'll die here first," his voice trailed off. "Take Janet and the kids," Pete's voice became a whisper, and "keep 'em safe."

"I will, Pete," Al comforted, "What will you do?"

"I'm going to shoot some game. Come spring, I'll get diesel and make a crop. Send someone out to get the animals though, only hay for them and not enough." Pete was an excellent farmer. His animals were his livelihood.

"Come say goodbye to Janet and the kids." Al was eager to get them into town and fed.

Pete opened the gate. Al brought the van up to the house, bending the overgrown dead grass beneath the vehicle as he went. The sun had overcome and the frost, soaked everything.

Pete hugged and kissed each member of his tearful family. He tried to reassure them. Finally, they climbed in, leaving their father and husband standing beside the back steps. Al manoeuvred the vehicle down the lane. He looked in the mirror. Pete stared after them, his arms hanging at his sides, looking defeated.

A crew retrieved a few dozen thin ewes, left food and asked Pete to come into town when he needed more. He agreed and sent a letter to Janet.

A few weeks later, Janet pleaded for help. She had not heard from Pete. There had been a big snowstorm, so Stevie Hunter and a volunteer rode out to the Woods farm on a snowmobile. Pete sat lifeless and frozen on the seat of the David Brown. A note in his breast pocket simply said, "Janet, I'm sorry. I love you."

***

The Xpress sat outside Maud's café, looking dirty and beat-up in the dull November afternoon. Bob and Bill were on the down-leg of a trip from Owen Sound. They had hurried north the day before, wanting to get up and back fearing a storm, an overdue "Witch of November.

"Things are worse than before," Bill from the Xpress spoke between mouthfuls of coffee and pancakes. "We seen lots more empty places up north. Owen Sound is shrunk lots," Bill poured more maple syrup over his pile of cakes, "but outside of here is ugly bad."

"Why's that?" Al Wright sipped coffee, fascinated by the pair's ability to eat. Bob drew down a large hard cider and devoured a thick roast beef sandwich covered with Maud's homemade mustard and sliced dill pickle.

"Guess I's driving the rest of the way." Bill resigned himself to Bob's appreciation of anything with 'bite'. "Orangeville ain't too bad," Bill continued, "what with the railway and all. There's a few businesses, general store operations, like the Xpress with no wheels." He laughed at his wit. "But the population's way down. It's dangerous with lots of bad guys about."

Wright nodded in agreement. He was still in touch with one of the store operators. No one said "owner" anymore. Few felt they owned anything.

He knew the town had shrunk. More had left since his trip with Tammy and Maud. Orangeville staggered on, supported by the crowd in the hills.

"The railway helps them. Too bad, we don't have it here."

"Then, I wouldn't be making a living," Bill mumbled through a mouth-full. Al thought that these hard-working go-getters would have done okay.

"True," said Al, "you boys have been good for us."

"Anyway," Bill went on to more interesting things. "We met a Yankee last week, lost, but somehow got up to Orangeville with lots of news!"

Bill sluiced the last piece of pancake through a puddle of syrup. Jani slipped another pancake onto his plate.

"The good old US of A has fallen apart according to him." He forked pancake into a wide-open mouth and savoured the taste. "Lots of states have split into little countries sort of, and no one knows who's running the show in Washington. Damn Yankees are crazy if you ask me. They had a good thing going and now this." He wiped his mouth with a napkin and took a swallow of coffee.

"What about the nuclear weapons?" Wright worried about nuclear war.

"He wasn't sure who controls the nukes, but the guy said the military runs the federal government. I guess they has those too, don't know."

"One thing that happened," Bob piped in, "mobs gone wild attacked wealthy houses all over. Lots of rich folks, the ones with no escape hatch, got killed and their fancy places burnt. Plenty of them had run to South America, Montana, and places like that, and even a few to Quebec."

People listened with rapt attention as few Americans came north. It was hard to handle the problems of the existing shrunken, local population. Most people thought not having refugees was a good thing.

One wit had exclaimed, "Maybe they'll only come north after they use up all the ammunition."

Bob explained the rail system functioned along the line north of Toronto, between Montreal and Windsor but had abandoned the one going downtown. Gangs controlled the Toronto downtown. The big skyscrapers were useless to everyone, but the underground garages and malls offered hideouts. No one strayed from their territory except to fight.

The official government-controlled an area from the old city hall and law courts up to the university and Parliament buildings, surrounded by a wall of shipping containers guarded by an assortment of cops and other tough guys. They connected to the west end of town and down through the old park grounds to the island airport. Aeroplanes and helicopters still flew, but no one was sure who owned them. All this gossip came from train crews in Orangeville.

The television carried no actual news, just official announcements, threats and reruns of nonsensical entertainment from the past, totally out of touch with current reality. Sadly, many people watched these old shows, hungry for any hint of previous normality.

The Xpress chugged out of town. The first big storm cut off Centreville for several weeks until "Indian summer" opened the roads once more.

***

"Shhh!" Stevie Hunter whispered as he waved his right hand. "There's a bunch coming out of the scrub."

Three figures hid in the shadows of the bush, huddling in the cold, damp leaves and straining to see past Stevie's shoulder. Jeff Shadly hung back as Mr Banerjee, and Matt Long knelt higher. Out through the tree trunks and beyond the field, they saw a slight movement. Two female deer slowly made their way from the low swampy scrub into the remnants of the lush clover-field. The animals were unconcerned. Normally they would walk along the wind so that they could smell a predator stalking them. The hunters chose this spot on the edge of the clover patch because the breeze blew from the side, and not carry human scent into the field.

"Damn, they're females!" Stevie whispered his disappointment. The deer population had suffered from much over hunting during the previous hard winter. Hunters had made a casual agreement not to shoot females. It appeared the group's long cold wait would be a disappointment. This would be the third fruitless hunting try this week.

"Quiet!" Stevie hissed once more. He swung the rifle's scope to a point past the now grazing does. "Here comes daddy!" There was a tinge of excitement in his voice. In the late afternoon light, a tall, proud whitetail buck emerged from cover. "Six points," Stevie counted. "He's well fed."

"It's about two hundred yards." Matt tapped Stevie's shoulder. "It's your shot. I might not be good at this range."

In fact, Matt was an excellent shot but had done most of his hunting in the regulated seasons using a 12-gauge shotgun with slugs at close range. These days, everyone used rifles. Food had more importance than fun. Lower population made it less likely a stray bullet would hit anyone.

"He bred the does," Stevie rested the rifle stock on a log and brought the rifle butt firmly to his shoulder. "They are ignoring the old boy. He's more interested in the clover."

Hunter slipped the safety off. With a glance over his sights, surveying for anyone behind the target, he put his eye to the scope, exhaled and squeezed the trigger. The animal staggered a step or two before collapsing. The females disappeared into the scrub, pursuing the dying echo of the gunshot, their bright, white tails flagged high.

"Good shot," Matt stood, thankful he could relieve his cramped legs.

Shadly and Banerjee, the rookies, drew first shift carrying the carcass to town. Stevie bled and gutted it on the spot and lightened the burden. They had a good 100 kilos of venison. The animal hung from a long maple pole fed through trussed up legs. From past the Fourth Line, they had to carry it a few kilometres to the butcher shop.

Everyone anticipated bragging to the other hunting party, Willard and Steve and Gail Quinn. These three had hunted together many times in the past and led the informal competition between the hunters. The need for meat added purpose to pleasant social times.

"That's a beautiful buck." It impressed Willard.

"One shot," Matt declared. "Stevie gets the credit."

"You're empty-handed again." Stevie teased Willard as everyone helped raise the deer onto the hanging track.

"We put four turkeys into the chiller." Steve Quinn piped up. "There's a flock up on the back line in the swamp. We'll get a few more tomorrow."

"What are we going to do with the meat? There is too much for just us and not enough to give to everyone." Gail Quinn expected venison steaks but felt selfish.

"I have an idea." Mr Banerjee wiped his bloodstained hands on an old towel. Banerjee's first name was Mukta, but no one seemed to remember, so they usually called him "mister"; however, his hunting friends had nicknamed him, Banjo. "Why don't we have a community banquet like last Christmas?"

The others stared at the man, amazed at the simplicity of his perfect idea. Although they had celebrated Christian Thanksgiving, it held little meaning for non-Christians, beyond a good meal. Mukta had not found comfort in the October feast, but he loved community celebrations.

"Thanksgiving was okay, but there wasn't a lot of excitement about it." Gail said. "What do we call it?"

"Call it Bambifest?" Matt seemed serious.

"I don't think Walt's little girl would appreciate us eating Bambi." Willard said.

"Neither would my sister." Jeff tried to wipe the blood from his coat. "She doesn't even like killing worms."

"What about the Festival of the Full Moon?" Gail had moon decorations all over the farm.

"I am not big on the Christian thing," Stevie chuckled, "but that makes us sound like a bunch of Druds."

"Druids, they're called Druids, you dumb cop," Willard winked.

"Ex-cop just like you," Stevie shot back. "I smartened up."

"How about, Indian Summer Sizzle?" Mukta Banerjee searched his pockets for homemade candy.

"Banjo, that's the other Indians," Matt had a good friendship with the gas station owner. "Or is there some holiday back in India in November?"

"Not until December," the man finally located his last piece of sweet, "but it will confuse my wife's mother. I would like that." Banjo's lips curled in a mischievous smile. "I always tease her. She is so serious, and she asks me to explain why you call your native people Indians? They don't know elephants. she always says." Mukta laughed, contemplating the fun he would have at his mother-in-law's expense.

"She will say: 'Indian summer? It is too cold for a summer in India.' The man's enjoyment of his own joke was catchy, and his deepening of his accent beyond its usual faint trace raised chuckles. It reminded them half a dozen Asian families remained in their community."

"That's it then," Gail seemed satisfied. "I think we should do it right here in the parking lot and just to satisfy our resident Drud," she winked at Willard, "it will be a full moon next Thursday, let's do it then. Al Wright will be happy. It won't affect Sunday service."

"We could use another deer," Stevie checked his weapon. "Banjo, you get the next shot."

"Oh, thank you, my friend," Banerjee jumped down from his perch and brought his palms together in front of his chest. "The Raj never let me carry the guns on the hunt." He had deepened his accent to such a stereotypical level his friends could barely catch his meaning. Laughter filled the cold room. The hunting club had bonded.

The party unfolded as the organizers hoped, with almost all the residents attending. Maud set up a bar in the little garage that had hosted the store shopping carts. Even though the afternoon and night were chilly, the throng partied under the full moon until all the food and drinks were gone. It lifted spirits before the onset of winter's gloom.

Chapter Nineteen

The second winter arrived slowly as fall became longer, warmer and drier. A wild blizzard, the second of the season, hit at Christmas followed by deep cold. The winter was hard but bearable with no horrific murder-suicides, only lingering sadness over Pete Woods' death.

"That's a funny place to park the flooder," Matt Long glanced at the ice surface as he tightened his ice skates. "A gazebo would look nicer."

"It wasn't there last week." Walt Lefevre tied his skates. The Lefevre family sat beside him as Tina struggled to fit little Megan with skates.

"Hey! Gary!" Walt called to the rink-rat as he skated past. "What's up with the Zamboni?" The young man in his late teens stopped in a flurry of snow and scraping sounds. He looked unhappy.

"Hi, Mr Lefevre, it ran out of gas."

Gary, the last employee of the recreation complex, had reopened the arena and electricity for the freezing plant and lights allowed him to build an ice surface, but the disabled machine threatened to ruin the fun.

"People think it's dangerous." He glanced at the few dozen people circling the arena and the derelict rink-flooder. "It might get frozen in. We've been hand scraping, and flooding with garden hoses and ice is building up around it."

He swiped the toque from his head and mopped his brow, shifting his weight from foot to foot. Children used plastic shovels to remove excess snow and make patterns on the powdery surface.

"I'll work on it," Matt knew of barbeque tanks of propane that would get the derelict to a permanent resting spot and make Gary a lifelong friend.

With no birth control and long dreary winter, several women became pregnant. Some births took place safely during the winter using the old age home as a birthing centre. Tammy was one of the busiest people in town and expected more babies the following summer. A party marked each birth as people looked for ways to ease winter's boredom.

Social activities such as singing, music lessons, art, and carpentry became popular. Even Maud, a self-declared "weak believer", joined the women's prayer group. Al Wright explained this to Bill Shadly.

"The group is long on socializing and short on praying," extending Al's favourite saying, "Perhaps most people went to the Sermon on the Mount for the food since they didn't seem to get the message."

Several older folks who had lived long lives died alone with only a nurse or volunteer sharing their last days. The saddest episode was the death of one young boy who developed pneumonia. Tammy could not save him. He had been Brandi's schoolmate and a lively, eager participant in the town. This event, near winter's end, left a dark pall over the community as it prepared for the spring work.

***

Hard long days marked Centerville's second spring. Shortages of fuel and labour slowed planting and a wet week in May stopped tractor work.

Horses proved their worth on the soft wet ground. With a combination of locally manufactured horse-drawn tilling equipment and some newer Mennonite implements, they worked a significant acreage. Horse work needed lots of labour and suffered the shortage of human workers. Several young people learned horse farming, with Jeff Shadly one of the most eager and hardworking apprentices.

The severe lack of labour discouraged residents who hoped good people might come to Centreville, but the addition of new labour came from an unexpected source when crews worked a farm up the north county road.

"Come out of there!" A grizzled farmer from Centerville pointed his rifle towards an abandoned bungalow. The crew had noticed smoke rising from the chimney and surrounded the place. "I said, get out here!"

A hand waving a dirty white towel extended from the front door. "Come on, we won't shoot." Two frightened women and several children emerged, followed by a young man and then an older one.

"We don't have any weapons." A woman said. She sounded young but looked old, dishevelled and in need of a bath. "Can we put our arms down? We are too weak."

"Go ahead, but no funny stuff." The man pointed his rifle. "Where are you from?"

"Do you have anything to eat mister?" One child begged.

"We fled Brother Andrew's congregation." The young man said. "We really could use food. It's been days since we ate."

The farmers made lunch for the shivering refugees, distributed blankets and stoked the wood stove. Rose hip tea washed down bread and cold meat. The newcomers ate ravenously, but the rescuers denied seconds. Too much food might cause sickness.

"What happened?" One of the farm crew asked.

"It all went according to plan for the first year." The older man said. "We were snug inside during that first winter. Nuclear war was imminent and made us afraid to go out. We had remote radiation sensors and waited, attending services and trying to keep occupied."

"We had a few tiffs," one woman added, "but we got along, but became depressed when we saw no sign of a nuclear holocaust. In spring, Andrew allowed us outside but didn't plant. We believed nuclear winter would make farming impossible. Once conditions improved, after a few years, we would move out and take over; becoming the leaders of what we thought would be desperate survivors. Brother Andrew preached that the war would still happen."

"We had provided for three years. Brother Andrew quoted scripture that said it was all we would need. It was in our hearts we would meet Jesus soon after."

"The sure work of the devil did us in." The second man burst out. "We got through last winter just fine although a little grumpy, but the devil stopped our electrics." The other adults nodded. The children whimpered at the mention of the devil. Whatever evil had befallen this group, it had not shaken their beliefs.

"The pumps stopped working, and the flood ruined many supplies. It forced us to crowd together. Soon, there we argued, then fought and it got worse. People hoarded the remaining supplies. The compound split into three bunches, and even these had internal conflict." The woman spoke well. She had been a high school teacher. "Food got short. We argued about it and last week, they forced us out the door with nothing to help us survive." To the listeners, it seemed the Christian ideal of loving had disappeared from Brother Andrew's flock.

"I got them," the young man fidgeted. "I wrecked the video system and the weather stuff. Now they got to come out if they want to know what's outside."

"We found this place last night. We need help." The man pleaded.

"We'll get you to Centreville. Joe, you take them and introduce them to the Reverend."

The group became uneasy at the mention of Reverend Wright.

"We don't want some God guy telling us what to do anymore." The woman was firm. Brother Andrew's brand of unquestioning faith had led to a backlash. "God will look after us, and Jesus will be here soon."

"Al Wright will not preach. He'll fix you up, and you can stay or leave."

The refugees caused some upset in Centreville. They attempted to recruit locals to their brand of Christian belief, and it seemed the religious debate might threaten survival. A truce lasted until what believers called, "the Devil's wind", blew through Centerville in the next year.

***

The golfers held the second annual golf tournament on an improved course, with 12 holes because of the increase in the number of sheep and goats to graze the land. Once again, the tournament was a success, with fun and laughter between the hard work of haying and the fall harvest. Sharon surrendered her number four, but she looked equally good as 13. Brandi sketched golfer number 13 with a rain cloud over her and a goat trotting behind. This drawing stayed in Brandi's notebook for years.

They completed harvesting before the second anniversary of the Last Day. The CAC declare September 25th a holiday. Al Wright thought people would be more willing to move forward once reminded of the finality of the disaster. A street party took place in front of Maud's Café and attracted most residents, even those who worked for Roger Smith. The CAC sacrificed to make music, food and drink available.

In the afternoon of the 24th, Al Wright, Bill, Sharon, Warren and Jean sat in Maud's café. They spent a few hours relaxing together each week. Many times, Maud would join them. They felt comfortable with Maud and would bounce ideas off her and consider her advice. They had no suspicion that she passed their conversations on to Roger Smith. This afternoon the group sat alone.

"I wish people would stop dreaming about going back to the old days," Warren said. "There's no chance of our old life ever returning."

"People thought they had a bright future." Bill remembered his long-lost promotion. For the first time in a long time, he thought of Bob Wilson.

"We all get deluded in our youth." Al Wright said. "Some people try hard to become something, while most of us just become what we are." He paused, staring out the window. "Look at that library," he nodded at the old Carnegie style building across the street. The impressive building glowed in the yellow sunshine of this late September day. "It's full of books written by people wanting to become rich and famous. Most of their writing was self-absorbed, meaningless distraction based on personal suffering, contrived situations to present some half-baked ideological truth or merely entertain. Good distraction I guess, but you have to listen to find the real storytellers. They're all around us and not so much in books."

Wright stared off into the distance. Bill guessed Al remembered the Al Wright he had wanted to become long ago. Shadly realized none of them had achieved their dreams. They now lived a hard, brittle reality none of them had chosen in a life demanding their full effort.

"My life has become something wonderful. I think I've dreamed it." Jean flashed the warm smile that had become a part of her over the past year. "I never thought I would learn so much and feel so satisfied with life. This terrible disaster has taken me to a wonderful place."

Warren took Jean's hand and looked into the street, amazed to have found two women to love, and two who loved him, two chances at happiness. He would not have asked for the life he had travelled, the joy and pain. He was not sure the happiness was worth the pain, certainly not worth Susan's pain. Jean soothed that scar, always acknowledging his love for Susan but able to heal the pain of that loss with her genuine caring love. He looked at Jean again and decided it was worth suffering the hardship since the collapse. Warren would think back to this conversation at Maud's and remember this instant of understanding that made his life whole. He shed a tear.

"Actually," Warren lightened up and smiled, "aside from a second love, I had another bonus. Remember that neighbour of mine, the man from hell, sorry Al. The obnoxious guy left the first November."

"He probably was from Hell," Al smiled. "I've heard similar stories." Al's smile turned to a frown as he thought about the outcome for people who could not cooperate. Several of those stubborn individualists still struggled on the fringes of Centerville. Not all of those who went to work for Roger Smith qualified as uncooperative. Some led a double life working for the group as well. Only a few were hostile towards the EAC; however, there were enough to be of concern.

Maud saw the serious look on the group member's faces. She would try to find out from Sharon or Jean what was going on. Perhaps if she could give Roger something interesting, he would leave her alone. Smith had finally demanded what he wanted other than money. Maud had resisted, but he became abusive. She struggled to conceal her horror.

The celebrations, if one could call the marking of a collapse a celebration, were a success. It was hot and dry, common in late

September. People danced, sang and drank until the late hours of the night. Members of the EAC mingled with those who had gone to work for Smith. For a finale, the band played Auld Lang Syne.

Stevie had his celebrating interrupted to break up serious street fighting. The most he ever had to do previously was lock up drunks.

A few old feuds flared up. No one understood what caused the fights. The arrogance of Smith's employees, flush with money, caused resentment and envy in a few of the cooperative workers. Stevie carted off a half dozen to the lockup, and separated the two factions. The cursing and yelling back and forth between the holding cells disturbed the night.

This violence upset the leadership and reinforced the feeling the town had split into two factions. The cooperative side dominated, but the lure of money divided. One member of the CAC supported Smith. Other members held discussions outside Council meetings to avoid information getting to Smith.

****

Drunken fighting reappeared at the second annual Indian Summer Sizzle

The third winter was the hardest yet. Snow piled higher than in the previous two winters. The Xpress did not run for almost two months. They suffered major problems with electricity. Several lines around town went down with no way to fix them. They could only cut the lines and move affected families into houses that still had service. Similar problems appeared on the country roads forcing people off several farms.

The failure of the arena freezing system in this third winter added to the depression. One faction wanted to turn the ice surface into an animal barn. Gary, the rink-rat, argued passionately for keeping the place for skating, suggesting he leave the doors open to let in the freezing air. The young man's intense passion and because the surrounding subdivision offered no nearby pasture, swayed the Council.

Gary became a hero amongst the young. His little speciality gardening business in a concealed area on the edge of town also enticed many, young and old, to consider him a friend.

No one knew why they still had electricity and gas and none had paid a bill in over two years. Once, when the electricity for the whole town failed, the disruption only lasted half a day.

The power and gas functioned because it suited the needs of the wealthy families in the hills and their friends in Toronto. It would have been difficult to sever off the town and keep the estates powered up. The electricity feeders passed through Centreville, and any disconnection would have been in full view of the residents, risking a violent backlash. Roger Smith's employers realized a functioning town provided a decent source of cheap labour.

The natural gas supply had the same advantage. So far, there had been no ruptures. The elite tolerated the EAC because it helped feed the useful workforce. None of the town folks understood this in the third winter of the crisis. They were grateful for the heat and light.

One breakdown turned into a major disaster. The sewage treatment plant failed and allowed raw sewage to flow directly into the drainage system. The CAC proposed a plan to construct dams downstream to create lagoons where natural processes would make raw sewage safe. It would be a hard job and impossible without diesel oil. Given the shortage of fuel, the plan failed. On every easterly wind, a sickening stench engulfed the town.

Warren Dunne proposed a plan for composting human waste. People were much less fastidious than previously, but few wanted to handle excrement. It devastated Warren, especially since he had been doing the process for years. The majority let their waste float downstream and, "to hell with the folks down there".

Various successful progressive projects had misled Warren into believing in the majority's altruism. The crisis with the sewage showed him folks he liked and worked well with functioned in simple self-interest. The disappointment sapped Warren's enthusiasm. Only Jean's constant support kept him from quitting. He chastised himself for believing people were selfless.

Chapter Twenty

"Who're those folks?" Steve Quinn squinted through the sighting scope of his hunting rifle. He could see a group of people struggling through the distant snow. "Damn, they'll have scared the deer away."

"Let me look." Willard took the rifle from his friend. "There's men, women and children, at least two dozen. I don't see any guns." He looked up and frowned. "We haven't seen refugees from the north in over a year except those survivalists. Maybe these are from there, but the rest of that bunch must be dead."

"Let them get close," Gail Quinn watched the newcomers without a scope. "We don't want to scare them. Wait until they get too close to run away."

"They don't have guns." Steve had reclaimed the scope.

"From what the others said, this Andrew guy kept tight control of the weapons." Willard leaned against a tree to ease his aching back. It acted up on these hunting trips in the cold. He came because of Steve Quinn.

"Looks like we'll bag different turkey this time," Quinn chuckled.

"Shut up, dear." Gail poked Steve. "They're people and look like they're in awful shape."

Soon the bedraggled people passed within a hundred meters of the hunting party. "Hello there." Willard tried not to sound like an old cop. "Can we help you?"

The strangers froze in their tracks. The group wobbled as if fighting the desire to run. Their fear-filled eyes stared at the approaching armed foursome. Willard realized he looked threatening and shouldered his rifle, extending his mitt-covered hands in a friendly gesture. The strangers seemed to relax.

"Can we help you?" Willard repeated the question.

"Please," the new arrivals spoke at once, extending their arms and slumped to the snow. They had reached the limit of endurance.

"We've been walking for two days. We're desperate. The kids are… well…" He turned towards the children.

The hunting party became a rescue squad. The wind had picked up. Willard led them into the protective maple bush. Warmth and putting some water into these folks was necessary before they could complete the five-kilometre trek to Centreville.

"Jeff, get to town and find Al or your Dad. We need snowmobiles with sleighs. These folks need a ride."

Steve soon had a tin pot of snow melting beside the fire. Despite their poor condition, none of the refugees had died, and by nightfall, they had settled them all into the old age home.

Tammy discovered they mostly suffered emotional trauma. Former members of Brother Andrew's entourage, they ran for their lives after violence turned into bloodshed. As supplies ran out, and the holocaust failed to materialize, a growing number of adherents questioned Andrew's leadership. He expelled the "sinners and unfaithful devil worshipers" and declared all sinners should suffer. Many died during the fighting. Some refugees saw family members murdered.

Brother Andrew and a handful of his faithful were the only ones left in the bunker. This group saw the last of their former home while dodging bullets fired from the compound. Brother Andrew and his hardcore group still waited for the prophetic events and were capable of any atrocity. This news and tales of violence from David Koch stirred the Council to action. Security beyond the town had been a casual affair. Now, there felt a threat and organized a constabulary.

Stevie Hunter created three patrols of two people each to go out to the farms, check on the occupants, and look for squatters. People from the urban areas might finally appear even if Brother Andrew did not. The first six patrollers were fit young men and one woman, backed up by a larger group that included Bill Shadly. Stevie trained them on guns, tactics for dealing with trouble and making arrests. Patrols went out on skis or foot if there was no snow, but adopted the bicycle for use on the bare ground. In an emergency, snowmobiles or trucks would provide support.

***

Matt Long and Brenda Kovacs, on security patrol, rode up the lane of the Quinn farm, enjoying the bright April morning. The Angel estate in the hills touched Quinn's eastern line fence. They had been here several times and looked forward to tea and a chat before returning to town.

Brenda noticed the open back door and that no smoke rose from the kitchen chimney. There should be a fire in the cook stove. They leant their bikes on the garden fence.

"Stay here, Brenda, let me check this out."

Brenda un-shouldered her rifle and slipped the safety off. Matt crept towards the door and peered inside, listening.

"Hello," he called out, "anyone here? Hello? Hello?"

There was no response. Matt stepped through the door.

"Oh my God, NO!"

He staggered back out the doorway. "Brenda, stay back." He was crying. "Go get Stevie. The Quinns are dead. My God, it's horrible! Please, Brenda, go! I'll stay here. Hurry! Tell Stevie to hurry."

The desperation and pain, choking through his tears, shocked Brenda. She sped down the road. It was 20 minutes to town. Her bicycle flew along the old highway, avoiding the potholes, tears streaming from her eyes.

Matt realized he might be in danger, and the killers could still be near. He hid in the drive shed, hunkering down between Quinn's two big tractors, with his rifle in trembling hands. He slowly calmed and took a drink of water. His stomach churned, but he refused to be sick. It might attract attention, and every sound made his heart race. He could not forget the horror inside the house.

A pickup truck rushing up the lane did not reassure; however, when Stevie jumped out, Matt stumbled out of the shed and recounted the horror inside the house. Stevie went in and soon reappeared.

"They are all dead, Steve, Gail and the kids, stabbed." Stevie fought for control. "They are still warm. It must have happened just before you arrived. Keep a sharp lookout."

He would let no one in except Willard. It took Stevie most of the day to check the scene. They wrapped the bodies in bed sheets and carried the Quinns to the pickup.

Stevie found a trail leading away from the house. Matt volunteered to help him track the killers down. His fear had turned to hatred.

It was an easy track to follow. The killers had not tried to hide their path. The suspects had crawled through the culvert that took Biller's Creek beneath the highway and north to the Boyne River, and they could see the tracks where they left the stream from the road. They found three individuals at dusk, two men and a woman, in a makeshift camp just off the town line, north of the old highway. Matt and Stevie retreated to town.

Anger gripped Centerville. Stevie sent runners to find the trained constables. He and Matt sought comfort at Maud's café. The horror shook Stevie. He had investigated the Durant murder/suicide two years before. It was the only other experience in his life comparable to the butchery at the Quinn farm. He forced himself to resist the nervous exhaustion that threatened to paralyse him. The town needed him to take the lead.

People in the café gossiped and watched Stevie. Maud gave them both large hard ciders, made a phone call and sat with the men.

Every trained patroller volunteered, and Stevie chose eight deputies. Roger Smith and his two sons strode through the door.

"We're here to help, Hunter." Roger shouted. "My boys will go along."

"Roger," Stevie flared, "we have our group."

"I want you to take my boys. They will be a big help." Smith hissed.

"Roger, they aren't trained and won't know what to do." Stevie did not like Smith or his mouthy, alcoholic boys. Stevie thought they instigated trouble even though the drunken pair had not ended up in jail.

"Well, you take them!" Roger commanded. "What authority do you have?" He threatened. Smith seemed desperate to have his sons in the posse. "I've as much influence around here as you or Wright."

Stevie wanted to get the work done and did not see any sense in fighting Smith. Smith could cause trouble. It would be a long night, and they had to surprise their quarry. Stevie asked a couple of his people not to come.

Just after 11, the group of nine walked in painful silence into the darkness. A noisy vehicle would warn the suspects. Several times, Stevie scolded the Smith boys to shut up.

Chapter Twenty-One

Bill Shadly's reminiscing ended as the posse finally limped into Centerville. The three hobbled prisoners looked tired and afraid. The Smith boys, used to riding in the trucks suffered along with the prisoners. People stared in curiosity.

The early hour limited the size of the crowd; however, word spread, and a crowd gathered downtown. Someone cursed, sparking jeering and insults. Cries of "hang 'em" brought horror to the prisoners' faces. A rock flew and hit the older male captive. Stevie fixed his eye on the crowd, "Stop that! We haven't proven they are guilty. We aren't barbarians. Whoever throws something will be in a cell with them."

They put the prisoners into the holding cells, the males together and the woman by herself. The frightened captives stared at the deputies.

"Thanks, everyone, good job," Stevie yawned. He still had much to do. "Get some rest while I organize things here and write my report. When I finish it, you can read it and make sure I get it right. Willard, could you come back in an hour so I can eat and grab a bit of sleep?"

"Glad to, Stevie," Willard felt the effects of 24 sleepless hours, but he would survive a few hours sitting here. Willard shared Stevie's suffering, grieving the loss of their close friends.

"We'll stay with you," one of the Smith boys piped up, "help make sure you do things properly."

"I'll be fine, boys." Stevie ignored the insult. "You just run along and snitch to your dad."

"I think we should stay," the Smith boy persisted.

"Get going," Stevie commanded. He had no time for more stress. "We don't need you here, and frankly, I don't want you here. Get going and come back to read the report."

The younger Smiths did not have their father's fight and roared off in the pickup truck. They had missed their evening of drinking and felt rough.

Those Smiths sure know how to rub it in with that truck. Bill spotted Jeff in the crowd.

"Go tell Mom we're back and it went well," Bill yawned. "I'm having breakfast and check Stevie's report, then come home to sleep."

Jeff headed off, eager to spread the news. He fought his grief.

The exhausted deputies sat together in the café. Maud served coffee.

"Chops and eggs, men? On the house, you guys are heroes."

None of them felt like a hero. Maud scurried off to have Jani get the breakfast, and then she sat, sipping coffee, listening to the men.

"That was the worst thing I've ever done in my life," Bill Shadly said.

"Sure was tough," George muttered, "think I'll stick to farming. They can get someone else next time."

"Damn, I hope there isn't a next time," Bob exclaimed. "No more of those city thugs had better come our way."

"I say we try 'em and then hang 'em right here on the street," one of Smith's employees piped up from the crowd. "We should dump this wimpy Council and get Smith to run things."

The crowd, mostly Smith workers, murmured agreement. The onlookers should have been up at their hill jobs already.

The Smith boys up all night messed up the routine, Bill thought. *Smith's well-heeled customers won't be happy at the work interruption. Maybe they planned to have his crowd here.* Bill's temper flared.

"We all saved everyone's bacon around here," Bill shouted more than his tired body liked. "Everyone one of us is honest, just wanting to help you all out." Someone shouted aloud murmur of support for Bill. "I think you all had better think about it before wanting a one-man show."

Bill wanted to say more, but his fatigue kept him from stirring up a fight. Standing out as a Smith opponent made him nervous.

Who knew what these guys would do?

He smiled at Maude. She smiled back and winked. It was obvious the town had split into two groups. Everyone had become more vocal, especially those who saw an advantage for themselves. Bill had a lot to discuss with Al and Warren.

They ate breakfast in silence. Matt left his food untouched but consumed many cups of coffee. Willard shuffled off to the town hall. About 20 minutes later Stevie arrived.

"I can't find much from Steve and Gail's house in the stuff we collected," Stevie sounded puzzled. His use of their friends' first names increased everyone's sadness. "They ransacked the house. The killers dumped all the drawers and spilt paper everywhere. We need to backtrack and see if they hid loot along the trail. Matt, you didn't notice any yesterday, did you?" Stevie tried to recall the route.

"We only saw where they stopped to smoke," Matt tried to remember.

"Funny," muttered Stevie, "they are crying they didn't do it, saying they found them dead and grabbed the few things and took off. They say they heard a truck on the road."

"Ah, that's stupid," said a voice from the crowd. "No one was driving out that way, not even the Quinns."

There was a general muttering from the crowd. Stevie did not think it impossible, but he kept his thoughts to himself. Most people supported the speaker; however, Maud and others seemed to consider it. Maybe they were thinking the same as him; someone else could have done it. There were vehicles around the area, all connected to the hill crowd.

"Stevie, I'll come back and relieve you in a few hours, after I get some sleep." Bill spotted Jeff in the crowd and wanted to walk home with him.

"I'll do the same," Matt added, "You can rest."

***

"Jeff, I hope you never have to do anything terrible like this," Bill put an arm around his son's shoulders.

"I can guess, Dad. I sure hope I don't." Jeff was stared at the ground. "But I need to do something; we need some real money."

Bill had known for a few weeks Jeff felt depressed. At 18, he wanted to earn his way.

"What are you thinking?" Bill encouraged him to talk, happy that Jeff broke his silence. "There isn't much you aren't already doing. You have helped a lot, the past two years. You are learning horses. Is that the way to go?"

"I like horses Dad, but it doesn't pay money." Jeff sounded determined.

"I want to get on with Smith and make real dollars. I think he would hire me. Tommy works there and says it's hard, but good pay."

"I don't like the Smiths." Bill wanted to say no. Nothing good could come from the Smiths. Maybe Sharon could talk him out of it.

"I don't like them either, Dad, but they pay."

"Son, I can't forbid it. Make your own decisions. It used to be that we didn't mature until our 20s. These days it seems kids stop being kids at 13. You're an old man my boy." Bill squeezed Jeff's shoulder. "That doesn't mean I approve. Your Mom's going to give you hell."

"I know, but I have to do something."

Even though Jeff loved and respected his parents, he needed to be his own person. He did not yet think of himself as a man, but that time fast approached.

Bill filled Sharon in about Jeff's aspiration and went upstairs with Sharon lecturing Jeff behind him. He knew she would tell him to make his own decision. They already understood Jeff had to make his way, but they would always be there to help him. Jeff would need support if he went to work for Smith. Thankfully, no dreams haunted the next few hours.

***

Bill walked into the jail. Matt rested behind the desk. In the cells, the men languished in sullen and silence; the woman curled up sobbing.

"Willard sent Stevie home about noon. I just sent Willard home." Matt sat upright, looking tired. "Willard's exhausted. Stevie ordered us not to let anyone talk to the prisoners before he does his interviews."

"Sounds good, Matt. Do you want a coffee? I think Maud will let me bring a pot. Did they eat?" Bill nodded towards the cells.

"Yeah, Stevie took care of them, by the book. I hate the crud, but Stevie says we treat them right." Matt glared at the prisoners. "This scum are the real barbarians, but Stevie's in charge. I would lynch them myself. Yes, I would love another coffee."

The door burst open. Roger Smith strode in and towered over Matt, ignoring Bill.

"I'm here to talk to these killers," Smith commanded. Matt was in no mood to be bullied. He had needed to yell ever since he found the bodies.

"No, you won't," Matt shouted at Smith. "You have no authority here. I have my orders from Stevie not to let anyone talk to them."

"Look, you twerp, I'm going to get them to confess." Smith took a threatening step towards the desk. Bill quickly stepped over beside Smith. For the first time, Smith acknowledged him. "You guys think you are tough. You don't know what tough is. My friends and I don't get shoved around."

Bill guessed Smith had goons outside, ready for a fight and decided he had better defuse the situation.

"Roger, why don't you wait and talk to Stevie about it? He's the constable in charge." Bill tried to sound soothing. He hoped he and Matt might hold Smith at bay.

"You guys appointed that jerk. He has no authority." Smith glared at Bill, sizing him up.

"You're wrong, Roger. Stevie's a sworn police officer and reports to the Attorney General. He has the authority to enforce the law everywhere." Bill was not sure there still was an Attorney General in Ontario, but the argument seemed to work. Smith was even less sure of the legal status of Stevie Hunter and hesitated, his face confused in a rare expression for Roger.

"I'll have it out with Stevie," he turned, but glared at the cells and said, "You just wait, you scum. You'll be seeing me again." He strode through the doorway. Bill glimpsed Smith's boys and a couple of big men outside.

"What was that all that about?" Matt asked. "Smith took an interest in this from the get-go. He seemed to find out pretty quick about the posse."

"Maybe he was friends with the Quinns?" Bill questioned.

"Nope," Matt said, "Steve Quinn was upset about him the last time we talked, not sure why. Something happened. Maybe Steve had an issue with Smith's trucks going by the farm when they worked on the next property. That's why his name came up. Why's Smith so interested?"

Bill went for coffee. Matt occasionally glanced towards the door, as if Smith might come bursting in once more. About six o'clock Stevie returned, looking fresher.

"I stopped by Maud's," he said. "I sent some kids to round up the others and asked Maud to phone Smith and let the boys know we would go over the report. How have things been?"

Matt and Bill told him about Smith.

"Smith has sure shoved his nose into this," Stevie pondered. "He wants to run everything. Maybe he thinks this will put him in charge. It's sure not because it's the Quinns. I never once saw him and Steve talking."

Bob Spencer arrived from his farm. Soon, all but the Smith boys were present.

"Shouldn't we wait?" Spencer supported Smith.

"No, let's get it done now," Willard said. "Besides, Bob, you will pass it on to Smith. There's a majority of us here. If Smith has any complaints, Stevie can hear him out later."

Spencer did not argue, and Stevie read his summary. He detailed the crime scene at Quinn's house; what appeared to be missing and how the family died. He described the arrest at length along with the evidence at the campsite and the trek home. He included the incident where the Smith boy hit the prisoner. Spencer asked if it was a good idea to include that.

Stevie said it was better to have it up front than to have abuse charges surprise a jury.

"If the Smith kid was man enough to hit a bound prisoner," Stevie described a coward, "he should be man enough for the consequences."

Spencer lobbying for the Smiths annoyed Stevie. They all agreed to Stevie's report and added only minor facts.

The next step was to interview the prisoners. Stevie shrugged when Spencer eagerly volunteered to help.

Oh well, he thought, *Smith will find out the details, eventually. This way he can't complain.*

Stevie took the older prisoner to the interview room with Matt and Bob Spencer. There was a bit of shouting at first. Stevie and Bob's raised voices penetrated the closed door. After half an hour, Stevie led the prisoner back to the cell, extracted the other male and headed towards the interview room.

"Just tell him the truth, Jake. We know we didn't do it."

They repeated the process with the female. It took about two hours. Stevie explained the legalities.

"This was the preliminary interview. Once things go further, we'll talk to them again to see if the stories stay the same. If a prosecutor turns up, they will interview them again, as well as whoever acts for the defence."

"Why should they get any defence?" Bob Spencer sputtered. Spencer did not seem to understand accused deserved representation.

"I told you in there, Bob, we can't sweat it out of them, like you wanted."

"But we need a confession," Bob whined. "We need to lean on them."

Stevie outlined the prisoners' story. The similarity of the three stories impressed him. Willard and Matt confirmed the trio had not discussed their stories beforehand.

According to the suspects, they had walked all the way from Brampton and been on the road three days. They travelled one of the rural roads, avoiding the main highway and checkpoints, dodging armed paramilitaries originating from old criminal gangs.

Gangs controlled large territories well past Brampton. Well-guarded perimeters with street blockades protected elite strongholds, and lawlessness prevailed. Everyone avoided anyone who had a gun.

After Orangeville, they reached the Quinn farm by chance. They were walking up the concession road, intending to keep going, when they heard a vehicle up Quinn's lane. They ran into the bush. In Brampton, the only people driving were thugs or cops, both equally dangerous.

All three agreed the vehicle sounded like a good-sized diesel truck, but fear had kept the prisoners from seeing it. Once the vehicle left, they assumed the Quinn place was empty. Hoping to find food, they snuck up the fence-line to the farmstead and found the Quinn family dead, and the place ransacked. It was horrible but no worse than a few they had seen in the city. Whatever the killers wanted, it was not food. They found no guns or money but lots of food to stock up on. They took a few knives and a backpack, filled their water jugs and headed on north towards Collingwood. The woman had family there and thought it was safer.

The raid and arrests surprised them. They never hid their tracks. In Brampton, everyone would have ignored these common murders.

"I'm not sure they did it," Stevie said. "Their stories match. Except for their shoes and one of the guy's hands, there's no blood on them. We should see whoever killed Steve and Gail covered in blood."

"Now hold on," Bob Spencer exclaimed. "You can't say they're innocent. None of this proves they didn't do it."

"I never said it proved anything, Bob," Stevie was tired of Spencer's eagerness to convict these three. "The evidence shows they were there but is weak otherwise. They don't deny it, but things don't add up."

"The bit about the guns is strange," Willard added. "We all went hunting with Steve and Gail. They had a collection including a pump 12 gauge and even an illegal .303. Where are those guns?"

"The guns are something we should look for by back-tracking," Stevie said. "Tomorrow, I want a couple of you to help me search the Quinn place and along the trail these buzzards left. If we find anything, it will prove they're lying."

"I'm going to write this up and send a copy to the OPP in Toronto via the Xpress, its due tomorrow. We need some help. Just to be sure, I'll call the OPP from Maud's so that someone will expect it. Now, get going. I've got to get this to Maud before closing time."

"I'll be back at midnight," Bill said. "Maybe someone can come in about six in the morning." They worked out a schedule, and the gathering broke up. Stevie wrote his report. Centerville's police office had a working photocopier, reserved for emergencies. He figured this qualified.

Everyone stopped at Maud's for a coffee. She eagerly listened as they filled her in on the details, including Stevie's doubts. Everyone, but Bob

Spencer, agreed with Stevie. Bill headed home to sleep before his midnight shift.

***

BANG, BANG, BANG. Someone pounded on the Shadly front door just before midnight. Sharon shared tea with Bill before he left for the jail. Willard stood at the door, gasping for breath, and crying.

"Bill, Stevie's dead. The prisoners are gone."

Willard was in a sorry state, sobbing and pale. Stevie was his best friend. Willard collected a police disability pension after being hurt in an arrest. The two had a lot in common. The Quinns had been his hunting companions and good friends. Willard had lost all of them in two days.

"Sharon, I'm off," Bill called over his shoulder. "Get the rifle and lock the door! I'll be back as soon as I can."

Sharon latched the door, retrieved the .22 from the closet and slipped in a clip. She secured the back door and all the windows, turned off all the lights and sat in a chair at the top of the stairs. Jeff and Brandi slept on.

A crowed milled about in front of the town office. Matt let Bill and Willard in and bolted the door.

"Damn, this is horrible," Matt had suffered two enormous shocks in as many days.

Stevie's body lay beside the main desk. He looked peaceful but stared blankly with open eyes. There was a faint trace of blood oozing from one ear and more from the corner of his mouth.

"It looks like they hit him from behind," Willard said, "strange that he's facing the cells. Why would he let them out and get behind him?"

Bill trembled, and he took a minute to calm down, slumping into a chair. Sweat beaded on his forehead. He felt faint.

Not now, Shadly, he thought. *These guys need me, no time to pass out.*

"Maybe he trusted them too much," Bill stammered, choked up. "Stevie seemed to doubt they were guilty." Bill's head cleared. He liked Stevie but wasn't as close to him as Willard.

"That's what I figure," Matt replied.

"Seems logical," Willard stared at the body of his friend. "I did too, damn them to hell, but Stevie was a by the book cop; I can't see him opening the cell alone. We got to get going and try to find these bastards," Willard was functioning as a cop.

"You're sure he's dead?" Bill looked at Matt.

"Yes, I checked," Matt said. "He's gone."

The words sounded so final. Willard reached down and closed his friend's eyes. The three men went out the front door, to discover another 20 people had gathered, mostly men, a few women and sadly, a couple of young kids. Kids here upset Bill did not think.

"Is he dead?" Someone asked.

"Yes," said Willard, "my friend is dead, and the killers are gone. Get your guns. We'll start a search."

A pickup truck roared into the street and braked to a dramatic stop, followed by two more. Roger Smith jumped out of the first vehicle, along with black-clad toughs from the hills. Smith's sons drove the other two trucks with similar passengers leaving engines running and dust settling in the headlights.

Smith strode up the steps and into the office. The three deputies followed along with Smith's boys and two black-clad toughs. Smith stared down at the body.

"So, the big shot got killed." Smith ignored Stevie's three friends. "No skin off my nose, but we can't have these killers running about." Smith wheeled towards the door. He noticed the three deputies. "Don't just stand there bums. Let's go get them."

"My friend is dead. Our friend is dead," Smith bellowed to the crowd. "We got to avenge him... get those killers!" He sobbed and had a catch in his voice. Smith disgusted Bill.

"We should have hung 'em yesterday," a woman shouted. The crowd roared in support yelling threats and insults at the missing suspects.

"Stevie was a softy. That's why I liked him." Smith sounded sincere. "I want volunteers. We'll string that scum from a tree."

Stevie's three horrified friends hung back as the crowd filled the trucks shouting, "Get them" and "shoot the bastards".

"We got enough," shouted Smith, "thanks for coming. We are heading north and then fan out up the concessions. They were heading north towards Collingwood."

Smith slammed his driver's door and blasted the horn at a few stragglers in the way. The trucks roared off. Bill looked at Willard and Matt, dumbfounded.

"How did Smith know which direction they headed? His boys weren't there in the afternoon. Smith hasn't seen Stevie's report."

Willard forced himself to return to the office. Even though he grieved, someone competent had to document the scene. He had no camera, so he drew a diagram, detailing the location and attitude of the body. Stevie looked peaceful. The chore of letting his widow know would be his.

Stevie would not want her to see him like this. Matt covered the body with a blanket. Bill went to locate the nurse. A few people volunteered to help move the body to the cold storage at the old food store and lay Stevie beside the Quinn family.

Someone had strewn papers everywhere. Willard assumed whoever killed Stevie was looking for the key to the other cell, but that did not seem right. Both locks used the same key. Stevie kept the office neat and uncluttered. Listing of everything went quickly. At the end, Willard slumped into a chair, spent physically and emotionally. Bill took Willard over to the café. The excitement awakened Maud, and she opened the café. Several people inside, drank and chatted excitedly but fell silent when the two deputies entered. All eyes followed them to a corner table. Maud would not take their money. She poured strong coffee and set a pitcher of hard cider in the middle of their table. Unlike many people, Bill had not taken to drinking a lot of alcohol after the crisis began. He poured a large glass, downing it with generous gulps, interspersed with sips of coffee. The combination tasted terrible, but he hardly noticed.

"Willard, don't you think there's something fishy about this?" Bill whispered. "How did Smith know the three had headed to Collingwood."

"Spencer is Smith's buddy," Willard replied. "Maybe he told him."

"Could be," said Bill, "but how did Smith find out and get here so fast? It would take time to round up those punks from the hills. His boys are usually drunk by midnight. They looked sober to me. Was there a copy of Stevie's report in the office?" Bill had not thought to look.

"Never saw one, unless Stevie filed it somewhere." Willard paused. "I think Stevie would re-read it even if he had already sent it, trying to see if the evidence would convict them. He would have made that call to Toronto and brought the report over here for the Xpress."

"Stevie planned to do that first. The Xpress was due through anytime. He wanted direction from the OPP as soon as he could get it. Bill and Bob went north yesterday."

"Hey! Maud," Bill twisted in his seat. "Did Stevie make a call and leave a package for the Xpress?"

Maud hesitated a few seconds. "Nope, he never came over here. I never saw him," she sounded defensive. "Does it matter?"

Bill suddenly realized Maud always asked questions and had been doing so for a long time, almost every time he had been in the café. He had seen her in private chats with Roger Smith.

Up to this instant, he had considered Maud a friend. It unsettled Bill. She knew Stevie had questions about the prisoners' guilt. Maybe Smith heard about these doubts.

Did Maud pass the story on to Smith?

Why, Bill wondered, *would Smith even care? He took an interest in this all along.*

"Maud's chummy with Smith. Willard, I know it's hard, but can you come over to the office with me and look for the report?"

They found no trace of the paperwork, Stevie's notes or the evidence bag. It seemed strange the three would take the papers. Bill sat in Stevie's chair and leant back to look around. He noticed a spiral notebook almost hidden under the computer keyboard. He saw the word "Dailies" written in the title space, Stevie's daily report book. The last entry recorded Stevie's actions for today. The last line was: "report on Quinn murders completed and mailed to Toronto via Xpress courier." There was no mention of a phone call.

Maybe he figured it was too late, Bill thought, *and he would call later. Did he die before he took that across the street? Was Maud lying?*

Bill saw the flashing LCD message on the photocopier: "Load letter size paper". There was an unfinished job in the works. Bill retrieved a full ream of paper from Evy's office. The machine printed out a half-dozen pages of handwritten material. It was Stevie's report. Someone set the machine for three copies. This was number three.

"What happened to the other copies and the original?"

"Well," Willard's replied, "someone took them all. The diary makes it clear he took one over to send. I think Maud is lying."

"Looks like it," Bill responded, "but why?"

"We figure that out later, but we can't trust dear Maud," Willard had too many shocks and was now crashing. "I have to let Debbie know and get a few hours' sleep. Tomorrow will be a long day."

Willard locked the office behind them. He had the copy of Stevie's report tucked inside his shirt. As they walked down the steps, they saw Maud standing in the café doorway looking in their direction. By the time they crossed the street, Maud had disappeared. Bill went home to comfort Sharon. Willard headed for the Hunter home.

The next two days were the hardest any of them had ever endured. The wild posse returned in the early morning with no luck. Smith declared, "They were like ghosts but good riddance."

Everyone grieved and the town buried the Quinn family the next day. Gail and Steve had many friends, and everyone chipped in to help. The four pastors led the service and the United Church hosted a sombre wake.

The CAC swore in Willard as chief constable. He was the only in town with police experience. He knew that until the Quinn murders, Stevie had a quiet time. Most people sorted things out themselves. Stevie only intervened to keep people from hurting each other and Willard expected the same for himself. He phoned the OPP on Maud's telephone. The corporal in Toronto would try to send a constable to investigate.

"Unfortunately," he went on, "It's too busy and dangerous around the city to spare anyone and few good officers left." He did not say if that meant there were too few constables or if the majority were not good.

The next day the town buried Stevie Hunter, ex-OPP officer, police constable of Centreville, husband, father and friend. Most of the mourners were from the EAC and CAC. Roger Smith did not attend.

Maud sent refreshments to the United Church hall for the gathering after the burial and confused Bill and Willard who wondered if they had misjudged Maud. The majority had no questions. Debbie Hunter appreciated the offering and visited Maud to thank her. Those who witnessed that meeting described both women as breaking down in tears and hugging each other for comfort.

Chapter Twenty-Two

After the tragedy of early April, a routine settled over Centreville. Preparations were in full swing for spring planting. Al Wright reluctantly bought diesel fuel from Roger Smith for planting. Smith demanded a high price, but they had no choice. They bought soy bean seed from the Mennonites and planted several fields intending to make raw vegetable oil, some for food, but the bulk would fuel two medium tractors converted to run on pure oil, but other tractors had already broken down with no parts for repairs. They would soon rely on horses.

A week after they buried Stevie, Jeff came home to announce Smith had hired him and paid 20 dollars for a 12-hour day. Bill and Sharon hid their misgivings. It took about 50 dollars a day to buy enough food for a family of four. Jeff felt he was more than doing his share. Jeff would have been less enthusiastic if he had known Smith had not hired him on merit. When the Smith boys heard the Shadly kid was looking for work they were going to refuse, but it pleased Roger.

"Here's a lesson, boys," Roger told his sons. "The kid's father is an insider on the committees. I don't like him, but maybe we can draw him into supporting us. We'll need some of them when we run things and might learn from the kid. Watch who he talks to and what he says."

Early the next morning, Jeff appeared outside Maud's café. His friend Tommy waited.

"Hi Jeff, I was worried you would be late."

"I stayed up late to tell Jani." Jeff yawned.

"I'm glad to have someone my age on here," Tommy whispered. "Most are older. Just some advice, keep your mouth shut and don't be nosy."

"What do you mean?" Jeff asked. He had never had a job before.

"They have guards everywhere; they're always watching. You're a Shadly, and that's worse. Sorry didn't mean it like that, but they don't like the EAC or the Council."

Yellow school buses roared to a stop in front of Maud's café. It took four coaches for the 200 workers. On the ride up, both boys stayed silent. A man dressed in black sat at the back of the bus; the driver looked like his twin brother and kept glancing in the big interior mirror. Jeff thought the driver watched him.

The bus rattled past the Quinn farm and turned towards the hills. Jeff wondered who had tilled Quinn's fields. The EAC had moved the Quinn stock into Centerville.

The bus eased through a checkpoint laid out in a zigzag and roared to an open field a couple of concession roads over. Several men waited, holding clipboards and blueprints and divided the arrivals between them.

Jeff's bunch carried shovels and picks east along the side road. They arrived at a ditch dug into the roadbed with the debris piled on the inside towards the estates. The ditch was about five meters wide and three deep with the steep sides lined with fieldstone. It was an effective anti-vehicle barrier. The men worked on the walls and packing the berm. A 30-centimetre thick wall of rock ran through the middle of the dirt pile making it more resistant to bullets. Some of the group removed shrubs that might hide attackers from open fields beyond the barrier. Days later, when Jeff saw it again, they had ploughed and harrowed the fields.

The friendly workers kept up a light banter most of the day. Like all groups of workers, there were the smart, the hard workers, the stupid and the lazy. No one slacked too much. The supervisor threatened to fire any shirkers. Everyone wanted to be back the next day.

Jeff found the day, long and hard. When the bus dropped the group back at Maud's Jeff was dirty and tired with sore hands. He could barely close his fingers on the Canadian 20-dollar bill that made the day worth it. He went to the café and had a coffee and muffin. It was the first time he had ever eaten using his own earned money. Jeff felt grown up.

The Shadlys now had direct information about the estates from Jeff. The rich folks had lots of food and a sophisticated communication setup. Jeff helped work on the telephone relay tower that linked to Maud's and reported tight security on the only two roads into the area. On their way to work, they passed a barrier on the side-road east of Highway 10. The other was much nearer Orangeville, but Jeff only knew about it from gossip. The enclave boasted lots of vehicles and armed guards. Jeff believed no one could sneak into the controlled zone run by Mr Angel.

The other Shadlys worked hard. Bill headed the salvage effort. Sharon kept track of inventory, the work schedules and Centrebuck distribution.

Brandi tended the Shadly's home garden and helped in the community gardens and the high school barn. She grieved for Stevie Hunter. They had become close friends working in the barn and had shared wonderful conversations. Bill and Sharon knew she mourned but could only give her space and quiet comfort. Brandi had several crying episodes with Sharon. Stevie's murder highlighted the lost contact with extended family.

All this played on Brandi's heart. She had developed her way of dealing with the loss suffered during the past two and a half years by began keeping a journal after the Thanksgiving dinner when she last saw her relatives. There were now two volumes of art books full of writing and sketches. The entries detailed the Shadly's struggles and the successes and tragedies of the community. These journals also recorded her development as an artist and writer under Samantha James' patient enhancement of Brandi's natural talent.

Brandi's latest entry comprised several written pages of her memories of Stevie. This included a wonderful coloured pencil drawing of Stevie in his police uniform bracketed on one side by an image of him in the barn and on the other of him with his family at the last golf tournament. In her drawing, she depicted the family in colour and seated, with Stevie rendered in black pencil standing over them, smiling. She felt much better after she finished the picture.

The Centreville Administrative Council struggled with sewage and water. The sewage outflow polluted the small creek that drained away from town, but townsfolk only suffered putrid smell with an east wind. When the foul odour was in the wind, it mocked Warren.

The water issue unsettled everyone. The town had run out of treatment chemicals in the first winter and advised people to boil water. Few people bothered. So far, there had been no problems. Until the casings corroded through and allowed groundwater in, the supply would stay safe.

Keeping the pumps running posed a bigger problem. Fortunately, there had been five wells supplying the town. With the reduced population, the town could function on the output of only one and other wells provided spare parts. Everyone saw rust spots on the steel water tower, but no one had a solution. The CAC estimated it would be ten years before it leaked.

Almost no information came from outside the community. The television news contained insipid stories and little of anything important. They hinted at turmoil and violence, especially in the GTA with some images of victorious police leading bound prisoners into jail. No one reported outside greater Toronto. The Provincial Government ruled by decree. The time for elections had passed with no vote. Opposition politicians appeared on the news praising the Government.

***

May followed April, and the farm work reached a peak. Workers helped with the horse-powered work, but they had a large reduction in the people available and reduced the planted acreage. With no sign of the OPP investigating of the Hunter and Quinn murders, everyone had given up hope of catching the killers.

"I saw the strangest thing today," Jeff spoke between bites of his Mom's bread and scoops of goat stew.

"We were putting in fence posts on the big place near 25 Side-road," he dunked bread in a puddle of gravy to chase down a tasty bit of meat.

"I could see to the next place." He reached for another slice of whole wheat bread and looked at his Dad.

"A bunch of people worked in the orchard with armed guys guarding them. They watch us, but our guards don't have guns at the ready, and I thought I'd seen some workers before." He paused.

"That work gang had the three Quinn killers." Jeff gulped goat's milk.

Sharon and Brandi gasped, but Bill said, "I'm not surprised, Jeff. I thought it strange how the three disappeared. I think the Smiths and Angel had a lot to do with it."

"Did they break them out of jail?" Sharon sounded frightened. "Did they kill Stevie?" She had not thought of it before. Bill had suspected since the murder but did not want to alarm anyone with no proof.

"You're in danger, Jeff," Sharon decided. "You can't work there!"

"Mom," Jeff had not used that tone with her in a couple of years. "I'll be okay. I'm going to keep working, but Mom," he took her hand, "I don't want you to worry. Any sign of trouble, and I'll quit."

"Okay," Bill intervened, "Jeff, behave as if nothing has changed. Keep a sharp lookout, but don't take chances. Do what you have always done up there. Don't mention this to anyone. I'll have a chat with Willard."

It horrified Brandi that the Smiths knew the killers of her friend and mentor. She did not yet understand that Angel had made the three accused into slaves, and they had murdered no one.

Bill found Willard in the police office. The constable had arrested another drunk and was letting him sober up. He saw more drunkenness now that some had cash for commercial liquor. He found whisky bottles with some of his jail guests. Willard thought it came from the hill estates. Bill and Bob on the Xpress denied they were rumrunners.

"We would sell some if we could," Bill told him, "but no one sells us any in Orangeville. Crates of booze come off the train."

A shortage of food developed in the last week, and the committee cut off those refusing to help, reducing about a half-dozen to aggressively begging for scraps.

"What's up, Bill?" the constable still grieved the loss of his friends.

"My son's working up in the hills for Smith. He thought he saw the three escapees working up there under guard, like slaves."

"Is he sure?" Willard sat up straight.

"Yes, he had a good look at them the day we brought them in."

"I can't see us doing much about it. We can't take on the Smiths and Angel. In case you hadn't noticed, they have at least half the town depending on them and lots of guns."

"We need outside help," Bill said. "Can you get the OPP up here? Maybe the news of a slave operation and the murders will get some attention."

"I'll try calling." Willard sighed. "Let's go to the café."

"Slow down, Willard, I think Maud's part of a Smith conspiracy."

"I have my doubts about her, but it seems unlikely. She's been good to everyone, even gave food to Debbie."

"Ever notice how she is always asking questions?" Bill no longer had any doubt. They must keep her in the dark. "Every time we're there, she hovers and most times sits with committee people, even when she's busy. That's how Smith knew so many details so quickly about the Quinn's and Stevie. Maud knew everything, both times."

"Smith had the telephone hooked up, and since Stevie's murder, I have been watching. Maud talks on it a lot, and I can't figure why. She has a daughter down south but told us she couldn't get through to her. It makes me wonder why Smith had that phone installed, and how she pays for it."

"Spencer might have talked," Willard said, "at least about the killers' details. Spencer helped interrogate, but he never showed until morning."

"Just in case," Bill said, "I want Maud out of the loop."

"Okay," Willard said, "she goes up to the United Church women's group on Tuesdays. We can make the call then with only the Coswell girl there."

"Sounds like it'll work. I'll bring Jeff down. Jani likes him. He can distract her."

His role did not impress Jeff. He liked Jani, more than liked her and did not want to deceive her. On the positive, Jeff could spend time with her.

"Remember," Bill said, "don't tell her anything."

Bill and Jeff arrived first. The café was quiet on a Tuesday evening. Jani hung about the table chatting and no doubt wishing Bill would leave. Willard came in about 20 minutes later. Jani set up the phone and returned to Jeff and Bill. As the two young people chatted and flirted, Bill sauntered over to Willard and stood so that Willard was out of Jani's sight and hopefully her hearing.

"... we think the Angel family has something to do with it," Willard spoke softly, "but we don't know who is involved or if the same people killed Hunter and the family." He paused as if listening. "Okay Corporal Waterdown. Send a team soon. It's serious here." Willard hung up.

"The money's on the counter, Jani," Willard called out, heading to the door, "thanks, sweetie."

"Son, I'll just be outside for a few minutes." Bill turned to the table. "I have to talk with Willard about farm labour. Don't be late. You have an early start remember."

Bill followed Willard into the deserted street.

"What's the scoop?"

"I was talking to a Corporal Waterdown. He had the usual line about not enough labour. You heard me begging," Willard sounded frustrated. "He said he would report it to his boss but couldn't promise anything. One interesting thing though," the constable looked angry. "Waterdown said that Angel was the local, provincial representative for emergency aid. Angel's supposed to coordinate the regional distribution of food, fuel and other essentials. It is the Province keeping the Orangeville train running to ship stuff up here, some of it for us. I told him we had seen no help, and we thoughtAngel was involved in the murders. He didn't sound surprised. Angel is stealing it all."

"That explains where Smith gets his diesel and cash. It's reason to murder Stevie, but why the Quinn family?"

"I don't like talking in the open," Willard glanced around nervously. "Let's get our trusted people together tomorrow."

The men went home to a peaceful night.

"Hey, Shadly," the Smith boy's voice threatened.

Jeff waited to get onto the bus. He had slept well and felt energetic. The hour he spent with Jani had helped. Jeff frowned at Smith's scowling face.

"You got a big mouth." The Smith boy stepped towards Jeff. Shadly noticed one of the black-clad men standing beside the truck. Another stepped behind him. Neither of them matched Smith for size. Once one looked past the black uniform, few of the guards were fit or tough.

Usually, Smith arrived alone. Jeff was wary and scared and not a fighter.

The buses rolled up, and the waiting men climbed on, staring at the ground. Tommy snuck a peek as he went.

"You've been shooting your mouth off?" Smith crowded in on him. Smith's breath stank of booze. "I never thought you were bright."

He guessed they heard of Willard's call.

Oh, oh. Jeff thought. *I'm burned.*

"What the hell are you talking about?" Jeff played dumb.

"You know damn well, jerk. I'm firing you and teaching you a lesson."

Without warning, the man behind Jeff hit him hard between the shoulder blades. He staggered but did not fall. The other goon hit him in the stomach. Jeff fell onto the pavement, gasping for breath. Smith kicked him on the shoulder, ready to do more when he thought the better. He had an audience. Willard hurried from the direction of the jail, shouting.

"Watch your back, Shadly." His voice threatened, designed to intimidate the workers and Jeff. "Do nothing else stupid, or I'll settle you good." He ordered the others into the truck and roared off leaving Jeff staggering to sit on the café steps and regain his breath. Smith had broken no bones. Willard reached the café, put an arm about the boy and stared after the disappeared vehicles. Smith had linked himself to the murders.

Bill found Jeff on the back deck, drinking hot tea, with his arms wrapped tightly around his body, holding a blanket against the chilly May morning.

"What's wrong, Jeff? You didn't go to work. Are you sick?"

"They fired me, Dad, and beat on me down at the café. The younger Smith called me a big mouth. Two of them hit me, and Smith kicked me but didn't hurt me too bad, just my pride."

"Let me see," Bill removed the blanket revealing ugly red welts. He felt around with his fingers. Jeff flinched at his father's touch.

"Good thing they didn't hit your face," Bill smiled. "Jani might not like you so much." They both laughed. Jeff felt better.

"How did they know, Dad; did Jani warn them?"

"It wasn't her. She couldn't hear Willard's call or even know whom he called. Maybe it was the cop Willard was talking to or his superiors. Probably Angel can listen in on calls on Maud's phone. The Smiths assumed you were the spy. I am sorry you got caught in the middle."

Bill smiled. Sharon would be happy Jeff would no longer be in danger.

"We're getting people together to discuss what to do. Things are serious. These last few weeks have brought everything to a head."

After breakfast, Sharon headed to the school. Bill went to collect Warren and Willard. Sharon listed people they could trust. Warren and Bill headed downtown. The pair passed the café but did not go in. The place was a potential danger. Willard puzzled over Stevie's report.

"I'm convinced Stevie was right in thinking the three didn't do it. If we had tire impressions, I have a hunch whose they would be. It's water under the bridge now." Willard sounded defeated, "I talked to Jeff right after they beat on him. Does he want to press charges?"

"They didn't hurt him too bad," Bill replied. "We should do something else. Sharon and I think it's time to move on."

"Can we abandon everyone and all the hard work we've done?" Warren had invested an enormous amount of emotional energy in the past years and resisted letting it go.

"Hard work means nothing if we're dead." Bill said. "Sharon and I think it's too dangerous here, especially for us leaders. If the Smiths and Angel want the control, we would be in their way. They have proven they'll murder to get what they want. I think the writing is on the wall for the EAC. Too many now work for Smith. We can't grow enough food this year. If Smith and Angel control the food supply, they'll have everyone."

"How can we do it?" Willard wanted to leave the sadness. "I'm for it."

"Let's get the trusted families together. There might be more who want to go." Bill said.

"I'm not sure we should leave." Warren wondered if he could start over.

They decided Al Wright and two other families should be involved. They trusted Wright and valued his advice. Sharon only added two families to the list plus Shelly and her Mom. The trustees gathered at the high school under the guise of planning for the growing season. Jeff and Brandi sat out front, keeping watch.

"Is there anyone here who supports the Smiths?" Bill dove right into the issue. No one said yes. "Good," Bill felt relieved they would not have to discuss the grain crop. "Sharon and I have decided it's too dangerous in Centreville. We want to move to a safer place. Do any of you want to join us?"

"Why don't we stay and fight?" Jim Handley reflected the bravado of younger people. "I don't enjoy turning tail and running. We have friends and guns. Let's just deal with them." There was a murmur of support.

"Look at the odds," Al tried to sound calm. Talk of violence unsettled him. "Half of the town depends on Smith. About the same numbers nominally support us, but we can't be sure once the shooting starts." People murmured agreement, but all were confused and undecided.

"We don't know if the Smiths and Angel would resort to shooting," Bill interjected, "but I think they committed these murders. Jeff can tell you they aren't shy about violence. They have goons up in the hill-estates; we don't know how many, and sophisticated weapons. Their Toronto connections might reinforce them. We would lose if it came to a fight."

People named those who would be supporters, the Smith campers, and some who would wait and take the winning side.

Warren finally spoke. "I'm the last one who would want to leave. I'm a newcomer to town but have sunk deep roots over the past few years and made the effort here my whole life. When I add it up, I don't see how we could avoid a fight, and we would lose. I tried to find reasons to stay, but I have decided, at least the leaders must leave. We're in grave danger. Whenever anyone wants to take over a place, they always eliminate leaders who could oppose them no matter what their politics. Everyone here fits. Remember, Hitler first eliminated opponents inside the Nazi party."

"Why would they want to take us over? Are they ready?" Walt Lefevre asked the questions for everyone.

"Jeff," Sharon called her son into the meeting. "Tell us what you saw up there," She was now happy Jeff had taken the job with Smith but shuddered at the danger.

"Well Mom... folks, I worked there about two weeks. I saw those three killers who escaped when Stevie died being guarded and working in the gardens and orchard." People gasped.

"Tell us about the general shape of things up there." Warren wanted the others to hear firsthand.

Jeff began slowly, "I never got below 20 side road. The Smiths are only in charge down to there. I saw Roger talking with a man on the 20. He acted like Smith, but I never got close enough to hear anything. Smith shook his hand as if they were partners. I never saw Roger treat anyone as his equal, not even his kids, so I remembered that."

"What about the land itself?" Warren prompted.

"They've built a security line around the high ground down to the second line east, running up east of ten and below 89. They are working every field inside." Jeff caught his breath. He rarely talked in front of a crowd.

"How many people do they have?" Bill wanted everyone to hear it.

"I think they have about 200 guards or goons. There are about 200 town's people working there in the day. Many servants live up there. I saw a few women and kids who I think are family. It looks like the Angels have all the clan there from the grandparents on down. I never got close."

"Lisa Parker is living up there as a nanny," one woman added. "She told me they have all of their close family living there."

Bill and Sharon looked at each other with sadness. They had heard nothing of their families for many months. Their letters had remained unanswered, and the phone had not made a connection for a year. It had crossed their minds to head south to find their loved ones, but Sharon could imagine her Dad telling her not to try.

"So, they're using all the fields inside the line?" Warren tried to understand. "Do they need more land?"

"I think so," said Jeff. "It would have been better if I had more time to see. They're working Quinn fields."

"That might explain it. The Quinns' had an excellent farm right next to the perimeter." Willard saw the logic. "It would have been a natural addition. If they need additional workers, getting rid of the EAC and CAC would be in their plans. I say we get out of here and don't count on any help from outside. The OPP backstabbed us, and getting worse down there. Bill and Bob on the Xpress got an earful from the train crew. They said not to believe the TV. Dictators run the province. Many people have disappeared, maybe to jail, maybe not. Many old cops vanished, somewhere. The ones still there are not nice. A militia is involved."

"Okay, so what do we do?" Sharon wanted a decision.

"We're going," Bill said. "I hope you want to come."

They agreed the leaders should leave, and anyone who wanted to go. Everyone present trusted each other and agreed not to tell anyone else.

"Where do we go?" Warren wanted to move before spring planting.

"Dave Koch arrives tomorrow," said Bill, "I'll talk with him. I don't think living with the Mennonites would work. They have their problems."

"Good morning, Dave." Bill greeted the trader as he tied his team to the light-standard in front of the high school. The matched pair of blacks fidgeted until Dave hung feed bags on them.

"Morning Bill, haven't seen you here lately." Koch stuck out his hand.

"I am usually busy somewhere, but I need to talk with you." Bill guided Dave to one side as the efficient crew from the school unloaded the wagon, including a large bag of asparagus.

"I see you brought a treat. Ours is just coming on."

"That's why I'm alone today. Everyone is busy with planting, and I'll be sick of asparagus soon. Still, the Lord provides." Koch watched an eager volunteer carrying the treat bag into the school, munching on a sweet green stalk. "What do you want to talk about, Bill?"

"Things are seriously disrupted here, Dave," Bill glanced about as if expecting a spy. "The rich folks and their allies want to take over. We leaders are in danger and plan to leave, but don't know where to go."

Dave Koch rubbed his chin and took some time before answering.

"We've been wondering when you might run into trouble. You don't have the glue holding your bunch together as we do, and heaven knows we have enough trouble even then though no rich folks disrupted us. We have had to leave some areas, partly because of violence. We pulled back west of Highway 6 and north of eight. It has become a mite crowded, but there's plenty for everyone to do."

"What do you suggest?" Bill was open to anything reasonable.

"You don't want to join us," Koch said. "We only survive together because of our faith. The life is too different for you folks to adapt. You got to be raised to it. It has become a lot harder the past years too." Dave spat towards the horses, contemplating the fine animals, but thinking of the work they required. "I would never recommend you do that... Nothing to do with liking you or thinking less of you, but just the facts. What I think," he continued, "and our bunch has talked about this before, we believe you should go to the Beaver Valley and along the bay up there. We trade with those folks. They seem to be okay, a solid bunch. It seems they don't have any strong local enemies threatening them as you do. I would look up there and see if they want you. Beware north of here along ten. There's a nasty bunch in there around Flesherton. We detour around them."

They had already heard, from Bill and Bob on the Xpress, about the criminal bunch running things 30 kilometres north. Dave did not have any specific contacts but thought they would have a good reception. Koch did not linger. He had too much work back home.

The trusted families assembled in the late afternoon. Willard escorted Debbie Hunter into the meeting. She had not been on anyone's safe list. Willard saw Bill's surprised look and brought Debbie over.

"Debbie wants to come, Bill. I said it would be okay." Willard glanced away.

"We want to come." Debbie sounded determined. "There's nothing left for us here, except Stevie's grave. Stevie was my life. We had something special. Do you know what I mean?"

Bill looked at Sharon and knew.

Warren remarked Debbie's reference to Stevie's grave. He resolved he would find the chance to talk to her. Warren too would leave a loved one's resting place. He would never again stand on the rock bridge with Susan. Warren would not mention his longing to Debbie but could reassure her others would make similar decisions.

"Debbie, there's no problem. I'm sorry we didn't think of you. Stevie was a good friend." Bill called for order.

Bill related what Dave Koch had said. It made sense to everyone. It either was going north or down through Mennonite country. They decided to send someone north to contact the community near Georgian Bay.

"My sister lives in Kimberly in the Beaver Valley." Walt Lefevre spoke up. "I got a letter from her around Christmas. I can write a letter of introduction. She might connect us to the right people."

"We have relatives in Maxwell; we'll write a letter," another family added.

Several of the families knew people in the area and they would write letters.

"Who will make the trip?" Bill looked around the room.

"The only logical person," Al Wright piped up quickly, "is you, Bill." There was a general expression of support. When Al Wright said something, most people took it as the best idea available. Bill had no chance of refusing.

"Okay," Bill replied, "but I want to take Jeff. Two people need to go, and we haven't been camping for a while."

The laughter was genuine.

"It'll take us a day to get ready. Have those letters to me by tomorrow afternoon. We'll have to walk. The Xpress went south yesterday."

Chapter Twenty-Three

Warren, Jean, Al and the Shadly family joined Bill and Jeff in the early morning of their departure. Sharon squeezed Bill's hand and knew her son and husband walked into harm's way.

"I read the letters," Al said. "It would be best no one locally read them. They detail our plan."

"I don't expect to be stopped and searched at this end." Bill believed the Smiths did not yet worry about people fleeing. "Robbers more likely and they won't care about letters. We'll carry them inside our shirts."

"You're probably right," Warren said, "just don't take any chances."

"Hey, buddies," Sharon hugged Bill and Jeff. "Make sure you bring back a nice fat wildebeest."

"Hey, woman, we are expert hunters," Bill pumped his hand up and down as if brandishing a rifle. "If we sees 'em, we gets 'em."

"Yeah, you might find your truck," jokes helped Sharon say goodbye.

"Do you think so?" Bill used his most earnest voice. "I hope not, lover. We would have to pay for it." They exchanged a lingering kiss.

"Ugh! Break it up you two," Jeff wrapped his arms around them both.

Bill remembered a morning on their deck, so long ago when this new world started, before they knew how hard it would be.

Brandi joined the family hug, and they all cried. Those watching in silence felt their need to have this lingering goodbye. Al, Warren and Jean thought of loved ones. Jean found Warren's hand and squeezed.

Bill and Jeff hefted heavy packs and headed into a brightening May dawn. They headed west and disappeared into the gloom. They were hurrying to the old rail line before dawn broke; before unwanted eyes could follow them.

They reached the track bed in weak morning light. Last year's growth of dew soaked grass and weeds hindered. Some stars still shone from the lightening sky. Behind them, Venus ascended as the morning star with her encouraging bright steady light.

They walked easily on the smooth surface where railway ties and track had once rested and towards the Fifth Line to bypass Smith's gravel pit.

"That was hard, buddy-boy." Bill still remembered earlier times. It had been a long time since they hiked together.

"It sure was, Dad. I hope Mom and Brandi don't worry."

"Me too, Jeff, but they will. The worst that can happen, we are rejected and have to make a new plan."
Bill wore good, salvaged boots. The hard soles rolled slightly on the railway ballast lurking beneath years of weed thatch. As they passed the red-pine grove, giggling and scuffling came from the gloomy bush.

"If it isn't the Shadlys, out for a morning stroll."

Bill's heart skipped a beat, but a smiling face popped out of the trees. A female giggled deeper in the woods.

"Hi, Gary," Jeff relaxed, "what are you doing out here?" Jeff knew what Gary and whichever girl he had with him tended the herb farm and had sex. "You scared us," Jeff continued. "How's the crop?"

"Great," Gary grinned some more. Apparently, he had sampled last year's production. "Want a bit?"

"No thanks," Jeff replied, glancing at his father, "we're on a little outing. I'll catch you later. Say hi to…"

"Sally," the girl giggled, "I'll come by and see Brandi soon. Your Mom got any cookies?" The girl had enjoyed the long-gone cookie club.

"Probably," said Jeff, "check her apron pockets. I'll see you guys later."

Bill and Jeff resumed their hike. The giggling faded, leaving them accompanied by the sounds of morning bird squabbles.

"That sure startled me," Bill said.

"Sorry, I forgot about that place, Dad." Jeff said. "The sprouts are up and Gary and Sally have been hot and heavy for a few months."

"There aren't too many young people available." Bill had not had a serious conversation about sex and relationships since Jeff went to grade-eight. "It must be hard for you. We noticed Jani likes you, and you her."

"She's nice. I like her, but we don't have a future. There's no point." Jeff sounded resigned to his fate. Bill could not see Jeff's red cheeks.

"A couple of years ago, before this mess, kids like you two would be into each other big time," Bill said. "I worried about how to discuss this with you and Brandi before the collapse. Now, if something happened, we will have to accept the consequences. There are several young girls pregnant now, some with and some without a guy in the picture. Mom and

I just hope you two would think about it before taking that step, but we would be there for you no matter what happened."

"Brandi and I have talked about it. She's cool for being a younger sister." Jeff said. "Sis told me things are too sad, and she doesn't want to do anything to make more hurt. Brandi said if she liked a guy, he would probably leave or die or something. Dad, she's too deep for me. I want to hook up with Jani and to hell with the rest, but I know I shouldn't."

"The world is so screwed up; it's hard to build anything, especially family." Bill expressed the conflicts he felt.

"I don't know about the family, but sex is fun." Jeff felt comfortable talking with his dad as a friend.

"Hmm," Bill stopped and looked at his son, "so you have been doing it. I hope you know the consequences."

"We've been careful, Dad," Jeff sounded matter-of-fact. "There's a big stash of condoms in town lifted from the stores when they closed. We all have some. Sometimes they don't work, or maybe some kids wanted a baby, but they seem to be okay. We trade them like money."

It impressed Bill that young people had developed ways to make their world work. This new view of the young gave him hope.

"There'll be a need for families Jeff, but it's hard to think of having children right now. You're wise to wait and so is your sister. If the condoms are money, just don't do what your mom does to the Centrebuck to prevent counterfeits," Bill chuckled. Jeff looked puzzled. He did not know the secret of the tight ass turkeys.

"Dad, do you think we could bring Jani with us?"

"I am not sure about her family, Jeff. She's close to Maud. I don't trust Maud. She's with Roger Smith."

"I know Dad. The Coswells are pro-Smith, but Jani isn't. Maud is more of a mother to her than her own." Jeff hesitated for a long moment. "Dad, Jani, says Smith is treating Maud badly; he has some hold over her. He's forcing her to sleep with him, and makes her tell him stuff."

"What things?"

"Jani told me Maud hears stuff and passes it on to Smith. She thinks it's anything they think might be important. That's why Smith installed the phone. Jani has heard Maud talking with someone up there."

"We've suspected since the Quinn murders. Remember, we had you distract Jani so that Willard could call?"

"Jani isn't like that, Dad. She tells me everything. I want to bring her."

"I don't know if we can risk it, Jeff. She's only 16. Her folks would look for her. We need to sneak away and can barely accommodate the families who want to come. We have to take enough supplies to support us for a bit."

"I know, Dad."

They turned north on the Fifth Line, sneaking past empty houses that might not be safe and they did not know the fate of Brother Andrew's cult. Desperate survivors could be dangerous. By noon, they had passed the old garbage dump on the road to Maxwell. At midday, they found a dry clump of trees, well screened from the road, and stopped for a rest and lunch. The road had no signs of traffic but demanded caution. Beyond the little bush at the end of a swamp, an open stretch of abandoned farms ran all the way to the county line. Bill swept his binoculars over the countryside and focused on a spot to the south-west.

"See anything, Dad?"

"There's smoke from a farmhouse." He handed Jeff the glasses and pointed. A few families lived beyond the influence of Centreville. They traded with the town but stuck to themselves and seemed to survive.

"They seem like okay folks," Bill said, "but we don't know them. We shouldn't let them see us."

The two would rest and head out at dark when a quarter-moon lit the road, but they could pass unseen. Bill reckoned he and Jeff were a quarter of the way to Maxwell. If they made good progress tonight, they could get there by morning. It would have been a short drive in the truck.

Bill slept. Jeff sat up, feeling as if he should be on guard although he knew the chances of discovery were almost zero. It seemed like fun as if they were on a commando raid. Jeff decided he enjoyed being a commando. Perhaps he would get the chance.

With a sinking quarter-moon on their left shoulders, they hurried on the still smooth asphalt, pausing every 20 minutes for water. Midnight found them well into the next county. They chewed smoked beef strips as they walked. Bill froze.

"Shhh, I just saw a light up the road." They froze, straining their eyes and ears for any sign.

"There," Jeff whispered. "I saw a light moving on the rise in the road."

They retreated past a bend and considered their options.

"We passed a side road," Bill said. "Let's take it to the next road."

They turned west, soon found a road parallel to the county road. Their boots crunched on stones as they walked on rough gravel. Jeff led his Dad to the roadside. New spring grass poked through last year's thatch. Bill recognized his son's wisdom. The soft cushion of the grassy verge muffled their steps. Silently, they made their way north. The darkness oppressed and they almost fell into a creek. Someone had removed a culvert and used the fill to build a berm. Only foot traffic could pass. It reminded Jeff of the work on the estates.

A cough and a cracking twig to the east betrayed watchers. Fortunately, the pickets had not been quiet enough. The two, invisible in the dark, eased on out of earshot.

The town of Maxwell emerged from the pale light of the breaking day. Bill and Jeff took a direct line to the town through a field of knee-high grass. They walked openly, trying to appear harmless. At the intersection, an old man sat on a porch on a stuffed living room chair. The man was unshaven with long unkempt grey hair and wore dirty bib-overalls over a green, plaid shirt. Tattered, red and black rubber boots covered his feet.

"Hello mister," Bill smiled. "Is this Maxwell?"

"Sure is, sonny," the old man did not seem exceptionally friendly. "You ain't from here." The man stated the obvious.

"No, we've walked up from Weyburne looking for some folks." Jeff pulled out the letter for the family in Maxwell.

"They left. Don't know where them people are and don't care." He laid his head back in the sun and closed his eyes. Bill looked at Jeff and shrugged. Maybe they would find someone who knew these folks.

They left the man slumbering in the sunshine and moved west along old four. An hour down the road they came to a large white building labelled, "Miller's Meats". A small stake-truck sat at a loading dock. Pigs squealed in the dark recess beyond.

Two men dressed in patched overalls and old boots caked in layers of something from a farm, casually leaned against a dented truck fender. Straw hats shaded their eyes, and they casually watched Jeff and Bill.

"Are you in charge?" Bill smiled, but Centerville fears made him wary.

"Inside," one man offered the abrupt response, staring back at the strangers and not smiling. "They're out back doing the pigs." The men returned to their conversation, but kept their eyes on the newcomers.

Bill and Jeff mounted the broad, concrete stairs, crossing the equally substantial poured porch floor and through a dusty and discoloured aluminium framed doorway. They pushed through the curtain behind an empty display cooler, into a cold room that still felt cold. They had electricity available, and Bill guessed a photovoltaic system powered the meat chillers and freezer.

Their eyes adjusted to the gloom. Through another door, the killing floor smelt of a pungent mix of blood, sweat, and manure. Two skinned pig carcases hung beside them in the dim light from dirty windows, and two men lifted a dead pig onto a waiting hook. Both had seen this, many times, in Centreville, and the efficiency of the operation impressed them.

"Where would you be from?" A man extended a blood-stained left hand. Pig offal covered the man's right hand. Bill shook it, noticing the firm, friendly grip.

"Weyburne, now we call it Centreville." Bill smiled. "I am Bill Shadly, my son, Jeff."

"Meet Ed. I'm Frank, Frank Weisel. Come out front. It doesn't smell there." He laughed as he led the way.

"Damn Weyburne!" He sounded serious. "You guys handed us our asses when I played peewee hockey, still mad about it." Frank did not seem to hold a grudge.

They reached a bright, comfortable room with large, west-facing windows. Padded armchairs spread about the combination office, lounge, and meeting room that had passed its best days, and decorated with dust, cobwebs and dead flies. The comings and goings of human bums kept the seats shiny. Frank Weisel had a clean desk that supported piles of paper, the usual writing implements and a working computer.

"What can I do for you?" Frank's seemed friendly.

Bill began cautiously, "We're carrying letters for friends and family of some of our residents."

Bill paused for a moment, evaluating if he should say more. He was not sure if this was the right person to ask but decided to start somewhere.

"Some of us want to move on. It is getting dangerous down there."

Bill explained the recent events in Centreville. Frank nodded as the visitor described their fear of the town's powerful neighbours. Bill asked about delivering the letters. Weisel looked at the Maxwell letters.

"These folks in Maxwell," Frank seemed sad, "they aren't around now. The old man killed them all and himself a year ago. We had lots of those killings, but I knew these folks. I want to find one of them bankers, politicians or whoever caused this mess and kill them slowly." He paused; a dark expression crossed his face. "I don't know the others. Maybe they were newcomers. They aren't around here."

Bill looked at Jeff. His son seemed to examine the room, but Bill knew he was hurting inside. Ever since the Durants had died over two years ago, the news of any death had affected Jeff.

"We must get on if we can," Bill broke the silence. "We have a contact in Kimberly."

Frank knew her. She was active in the community and taught school.

"Everyone respects Karen Lefevre," Frank said.

"She will put you in touch with the right guys… her brother eh?" Frank was even friendlier. "Go west and take 13, north. You'll be down the hill before supper. Don't miss the turn on four though. There are toughs out that way, drunken, racist jerks who got their little kingdom. We've a barrier there and have exchanged a few pot-shots." Frank flashed anger.

"We've our share of blacks, Indians and natives here, some high up running this area. We don't have time for punks like these. Not worth our bother right now, but they better not provoke us."

Frank gripped the desk. Bill guessed the punks were more dangerous than Frank let on.

"Karen lives in the big house where the county roads split."

They waved at the men lounging by the truck. Bill noticed a rifle leaning against the cab, its butt just showing behind one man who continued to imitate an innocent bystander. Bill wondered at conditions requiring armed guards for a meat plant. He understood why Frank could be so calm and confident, having armed men at the ready. Bill suspected he had a gun hidden behind his desk.

Meeting friendly people energized Bill and Jeff. They had not reached heaven, but perhaps a safer part of the world in which they lived.

At noon they arrived at the top of the long, steep hill where the road descended into the valley and took in the spectacular view. They had passed several working farms and received a few friendly waves and long, suspicious stares. Families lived on many properties. At a small hamlet, a tourist centre before the last day, they received cool water and friendly conversation. This far inside the territory, residents believed the security force would have checked visitors.

Sixteen hours of walking had taken its toll. It was fortunate the way was downhill on asphalt. Grass and weeds covered the gravel shoulders. Feet moved on their own, one after the other, descending in an unthinking tread carrying their bodies towards Kimberly. The last few kilometres did not register. At the village, Bill's perception sharpened, searching for the house on the corner.

"Hello," the voice came from the darkness beyond a screen door that rattled in its frame as Bill knocked. "Can I help you?"

A woman confidently stepped onto the porch. She was in her 40s, Bill thought, with short brown hair, about five feet ten inches and a slight build mostly hidden by her loose, denim shirt and brown work pants, supported with a rawhide belt. Well-worn moccasins covered her feet. She looked a lot like Walt. Bill introduced himself and Jeff, producing Walt's letter.

"I'm Karen Lefevre," she said, opening the envelope. "I hoped my brother would write, but I didn't think it would arrive hand delivered."

"I think you would make the right choice, coming up here," she had read the letter. "I'll get someone to talk with you. Oh, my goodness, you must be tired!" Jeff was asleep in one of the porch chairs. "Come in and rest while I find the guy you need to talk with."

She put Bill and the almost awake Jeff into the bed in a back room. The two were fast asleep before she left. They slept profoundly with no dreams.

Bill woke first in the dark room. Faint light and subdued voices came through the partly open door. In a large living room, several people, including Karen, sat at a table, examining a map.

"Glad you had a good rest," a man stood and extended his hand. "I'm Chester Amik, an administrator in this part of the county."

"Bill Shadly," Bill took his firm, confident grip, "the rest was wonderful, thank-you."

"How's your boy?" Chester asked.

"Still asleep." Bill's eyes wandered over the rest of the group. "He's tough, but he can rest awhile longer."

"Chester's modest," Karen said. "He's the top dog for the entire valley. If we pat his head and feed him, he doesn't bite. Chester has all the land here."

"You make it sound like I own it, Karen," Chester smiled at her joke. "I keep telling you, that little orchard down by Clarksburg is yours as soon as you run off with me." Bill knew the flirting suggested a deep relationship.

"Even his name means 'beaver'," she shot back. "The river's his too."

Chester was a native Canadian, although Karen's garb looked more Ojibwe than his casual business look. Chester had a powerful build with medium length greying hair, and wore a short-sleeved business shirt and grey flannel slacks over scuffed, black leather shoes.

"Enough of that," Amik turned to Bill, "sit, have a coffee, and let's discuss what you need. I read Karen's letter so know most of it."

"We have about five families, maybe twenty people, who must get out of Weyburne. The local strongmen want to take over and want us leaders out of the way. They did some recent murders. We're in danger."

Bill impressed the group with the history of Centreville, and they understood how the powerful people nearby would make any effort doomed to failure. They explained to Bill, Huron had dangerous misfits, but they did not have power similar to the ones near Centreville. Except for the bunch near Flesherton, they had absorbed or eliminated the problem groups. Chester did not elaborate. Bill assumed Chester used force if necessary.

They served coffee and sandwiches of roast pork and chicken on whole wheat bread. The conversation went on for several hours. There were many available farms and other housing, highlighting the need for hundreds of new citizens. Bill repeated the numbers would not be that large, and they only had transportation for the twenty individuals.

"We feel we've failed." Bill was apologetic. Huron seemed well organized and successful. "We couldn't keep the majority from joining Smith. They only care about a few dollars and someone strong in charge. It's a matter of time until Smith and his buddies have most of them."

"Don't get down on yourselves." Chester patted Bill's shoulder. "We have our share of self-centred, ignorant and dim-witted, although I think the stupid are the majority. I have a couple of cousins you wouldn't believe," he winked, "but we don't have a sizeable group of rich folks who can buy their loyalty. These people see us as the best way to survive. Hopefully, we'll be strong enough and together enough to resist when the folks down your way want us too." Chester looked sad at the thought.

"They have connections in Toronto." Bill realized the actual power of Angel's group. "We couldn't resist with veggies and Centrebucks, but some wanted to fight them."

"You'll get your chance for that soon enough, I think."

"Let's hope we are better prepared before fighting starts." Karen said. "There are lots of different opinions up here. I'm not sure we could defeat an attack."

"I have a letter of passage for you." Chester wrote a document. "It gives you a passage and verifies you to anyone in Huron who challenges you. Many people might do that. Everyone is watching. Once you reached Maxwell, we knew you were here. We had trouble with some religious zealots last fall," Chester glanced at the map. "They came from your way, desperate but uncompromising and killed a couple of our folks near

Maxwell. In the end, we eliminated those interlopers." Chester seemed upset at that memory. "We have strengthened our barriers and patrols."

Bill realized the old geezer they encountered sleeping in his chair was more than he had seemed. Food was the watchword in Centreville; security was its equivalent here.

"There are four principal routes into the area from the south and east," Chester explained. "The official access roads have barriers. We blocked every side-road by removing culverts and building berms. Farmers or special patrols watch those roads. The barrier on the county road to Maxwell is the way your group should come in."

It would be a long walk home. Bill and Jeff had to hurry. The sooner the leaders left Centreville, the safer they would be. Bill went back to bed for a few more precious hours of rest. In the morning, as dawn outlined the cliff high behind the house, Karen awakened the two travellers.

"Tell Walter I'm glad he's smartening up, and I can't wait to see him," Karen put jugs of water and some sandwiches into Bill's backpack. "Be safe and come back soon. Chester has nice places in mind for you down the valley, excellent farms by the river. Just one thing, the folks who lived there killed themselves two winters ago. No local will live there. That's why they're available."

Bill and Jeff walked in the shadow of the hill on the steep climb but endured the heat in the few hours from there to the slaughterhouse. Three years ago, this walk would have almost killed them. Frank ushered them in, even friendlier than before.

"Come up through Maxwell," he mimicked Chester. "You won't sneak a sizeable group through. Trucks have to come that way, anyway. Besides, we gave those boys down there proper heck for not having the patrols out as they should have done. They won't mess up twice."

The pair faced a hard trip on hurting feet.

Chapter Twenty-Four

Bill and Jeff arrived at a locked Shadly door just after daylight. Bill knocked impatiently, grumpy with fatigue. Sharon opened the door, looking as if she had not slept.

"Why's the door locked?" he growled at Sharon.

"Bill, it's horrible. Smith has taken over the town. Warren's in jail." Sharon sobbed.

"Is everyone okay?" Bill forgot his hurts. "How's Jean? How's Al?"

"Al found Smith and a bunch of toughs occupying the town hall. Roger Smith threatened him and told him to get lost, there was no more Centreville, and Angel had dissolved the committee. Al rushed to warn everyone and found the Smith boys, with Willard Dick, arresting Warren. They had a warrant saying Warren had stolen food. He had signed an IOU for potatoes and carrots from Spencer way back in the first month of the collapse and hasn't paid for them. They say he's guilty of fraud and theft."

Bill remembered Bob Spencer had supplied the potatoes. It all added up.

"Al Wright is keeping a low profile. Willard is at the jail, watching Warren." Sharon burst into tears.

"Is Willard in with them?" Bill liked Willard, but this made him look like a traitor.

"No one's talked to him," Sharon said. "Jean's been down to see Warren. Willard treated her friendly. Jean's scared and staying here."

"Okay," Bill said, "let me get some sleep. Call the families together tonight. We have to get this thing going."

"I'll get the word out," Sharon said. "They threatened us at the school but so far nothing else. They need the EAC supplying food for now."

Jeff and Bill slept hard, but Bill woke once with a fuzzy memory of an upsetting dream. Sharon told him he had cried out in his sleep.

Everyone gathered at the school before dark.

"I want you all to know," Al Wright opened the discussion, "that Ester and I will stay to look after the congregation. Smith thinks I'm a wimp, so I'll play along."

"We're staying too," Evy spoke for her family. "I'm working at the hall for the Smiths and might be of help somehow. So far, they don't know what they're doing. The people in the hill-estates are in charge. Angel declared himself Governor and Chief Magistrate."

"Smith bragged about Maud being his most valuable asset. I heard him saying she always had good information and he owned her. He said some pretty horrible things about her to a couple of those goons in black."

"She's a tramp," Tina said. "I never liked her."

Everyone agreed that Maud would do anything to get what she wanted. Bill remembered Jeff's comments but said nothing. They had bigger problems than Maud.

"While you were away, we worked out details with only the destination undecided."

"Beaver Valley will take us, but we must get Warren out of jail."

"Perhaps we can tell Smith we'll take him away, and he won't bother him anymore." Jean said.

"Not a good idea," Al said. "Smith wants to use him to strengthen his grip, and Angel wants a show trial to scare us. If he finds out we're leaving, we'll all be in jail with Warren."

"We have to spring him." Bill said. Seeing how they operated in the valley had given him extra strength. "We need to find out if Willard's trustworthy."

"I like the guy," Walt spoke up. "If he is okay, he and Warren can just get out when we leave."

"I can't believe Willard's with them." Debbie Hunter sobbed. "The Quinn's and Stevie were Willard's best friends. He can't be with Smith."

"If he lets Warren out," Sharon said, "Willard will need to come. They'll kill him."

"He was already coming, remember?" Debbie flared.

They invented a simple plan to test Willard. Bill would visit Warren and tell him, in earshot of Willard, they were going to steal food from the grocery store for the trip. They would hide and see if the Smith forces showed up to catch them.

"They would love to charge the rest of us with theft."

They had to gather the vehicles and supplies slowly so as not to arouse suspicion. It would be a week before they could leave.

***

Bill stopped in at the Café on his way to visit Warren. There was no sign of Maud. Jani took his coffee order.

"How's Jeff? I haven't seen him in days," Jani lingered at the table.

"He's okay Jani, how are you?" Bill did not know if he should trust the girl. Jeff believed in her loyalty. "Where's Maud?"

"I'm good Mr Shadly. Maud doesn't come out much. She's upstairs in her room and only does the evening shift." Jani paused as if trying to decide if she should say more.

"No, I'm not fine!" Jani sobbed, "It's horrible."

"What's wrong? What's bothering you?" Bill flashed a reassuring look.

"Everything, Maud is upset and cries a lot; people are arguing and fighting, even my family," the girl wiped a tear. "My father and brother have guns and train with some Roger Smith militia. Dad says Smith is just what we need. I HATE HIM!"

She spat the words. Bill wondered if she hated Smith or her father.

"Come by our place after work and see Jeff. He would be happy to talk."

Bill wanted to find out more and Jeff could get details from the girl. Bill thought Jeff might get his wish but not now. Jani might get away later.

"I have to get going," he said, "go see Jeff."

Mixed emotions tormented Bill as he entered the police office. Willard sat at the desk, looking tired and depressed, leafing through some papers, listless and not paying much attention. He grinned at Bill.

"Hello Bill," Willard stood, extending his hand. Bill shook and the grip seemed genuine. "I'm glad you got back okay. What's the deal up there?"

Willard's friendliness startled Bill. He had prepared for a confrontation; Willard thought they were still friends. Bill would not betray anything.

"The jury's still out," Bill glanced towards the cell. Warren stood behind the grey-painted bars. "It's more promising with the Mennonites." Bill decided not to let Willard know anything until he trusted him.

"I thought they were hard to live with." Willard sounded like he was discussing the issue, not questioning Bill's words. "I figured we decided not to go there."

"We aren't sure it's safe the other way; they could be like Angel. Can I talk with Warren?"

"Sure, I am sorry about all this. When Smith demanded Warren's arrest, I wanted to be there to keep him safe."

"Thank you for that," Bill said and stepped towards the cell. Willard's story confused Bill.

"I can't open the door. The Smiths drop in from time to time. It wouldn't be good for them to find us friendly."

Damn it, Willard, Bill thought, *you aren't making it easy.*

"How are you, Warren?" Dunne seemed depressed. "Is there anything we can do for you?"

"Get me out." Warren smiled. "Willard is babying me, brought books and serves Maud's best."

"I'd worry about poison." Bill said. "She's in tight with Smith."

"I'm not sure about that," Warren replied. "I don't know what to believe."

"We shouldn't sell Maud short; there's more to her story." Willard said. Jani seemed to have confirm that view.

Good, thought Bill, *Willard is paying attention.*

"I had better not stay long. I don't want to meet any of the Smiths. We'll get you out. We're going about midnight tonight to take our share of the meat and cheese from the Foodland." Bill did not dare look to see if Willard had heard.

"I'll be back soon," Bill winked at Warren, "and I'll bring a lawyer." Bill had a lawyer named Remington in mind.

Willard asked about the next meeting; Bill said he would let him know. Willard and Warren chatted as the door closed behind Bill.

Bill headed through the alley behind Maud's Café and saw Roger Smith's pickup truck parked behind the place.

Damn it, he thought, *dancing with Maud is a three-step, one forward, sideways and one back. What can I believe?*

Twilight lingered well into the evening, but just after dark, Bill and three others eased into the backyard of a house opposite the grocery store. Each had followed separate routes around the town until joining. They waited silently yet staying alert. If Willard told the Smiths, there would be action near midnight. Likely, they would see a watcher turn up before then. The stars shone brightly over the darkened streets. At two in the morning, they knew Willard had not betrayed them.

***

The Sunday before departure, Al Wright entered the sanctuary through the front of the nave. As he approached the pulpit, the sanctuary doors swung open and slammed against the stoppers. A large entourage flooded into the hall. The soft music from his wife's piano faltered, before smoothly carrying on.

Wright stared at the new arrivals as he walked the few paces to the pulpit. Al laid the leather-bound folio with his sermon onto the polished wood dais. His eyes did not leave the guests.

Roger Smith led the group. The man looked nervous and uncomfortable in these unfamiliar surroundings. Burly men in black sports jackets and trousers accompanied Smith. Behind them strutted Mr Angel from the hill estates. He wore a loud powder-blue suit with a crisp white shirt and dark-blue and red tie. A beautiful woman, Angel's wife, grasped his arm. She appeared young enough to be his daughter.

The group stood at the rear of the auditorium. Angel nodded and acknowledged the people who had twisted in their seats to see the commotion. The man smiled and nodded towards the pastor as if giving the reverend permission to continue.

An un-Christian thought passed through Al's mind. Angel took his seat, followed by the rest of his party. Al Wright thought, except for Smith, the others showed deference to the man in the blue suit.

Angel believed he deserved deference and respect. He traced his family to the *Domesday Book* in England and claimed noble descent. After Smith had seized Weyburne, Angel had to appear amongst his people.

He had another reason to visit. Al Wright had led what Angel considered a pathetic attempt at self-government. Angel would do better for the residents than they could ever do for themselves. Smith claimed Al Wright was oppositional and dangerous. Angel fancied himself an outstanding leader and a man of peace, even if violence was sometimes necessary. He wanted to personally evaluate Wright and stop any opposition. Governor Angel hoped he would not need force.

Inadvertently, Wright and Angel wanted to achieve the same goal. Al decided he should try to prevent bloody conflict with their oppressors. From memory, he delivered one of his standby sermons, focusing on peace, love and forgiveness of enemies. As reinforcement, Al quoted one of his favourite scriptures. He loved the old King James language even though he knew the translation to be flawed. The pastor instinctively understood the reference to old feudal kings was appropriate. He called on the flock to turn to the "Book of Matthew", chapter 22, verse 21.

"… Then saith he unto them, Render therefore unto Caesar the things which are Caesar's; and unto God the things that are God's."

Many could imagine Wright's commanding voice to be that of Christ himself. The effect on the visitor satisfied Al. Angel burst into a broad smile, and the man glanced around at his entourage. He had taken the reverend's quotation as a personal message. Angel enjoyed the comparison to the Roman Emperor. Right then, he decided he did not need to stoop to personal negotiations with this little pastor. He had Wright's loyalty. As Al called for the closing prayer, Angel leapt to his feet.

"I want to thank the Reverend for a wonderful service." Angel's eyes swept the room for approval. "He has inspired me to redouble my efforts to be the best leader for you. I appreciate his call for peace and deference."

Angel had attended a premier private school, doing better than most in academic achievement and prided himself on his language.

"I promise you peace and prosperity under my governorship. Do not fear for your safety or provisions. I will deal severely with troublemakers, so that peaceful, loyal residents can build a new Christian order in Ontario."

He made the last statement through a big smile, yet it sounded threatening. No one in the sanctuary moved or spoke. Satisfied of his success, Angel swept out of the building without waiting for the closing prayer. His bodyguards rushed to precede him through the doorway. Wright breathed a sigh of relief. Then, overcome with a most un-Christian sarcasm, the pastor sang,

Mine eyes have seen the glory of the coming of the Lord.

Esther rushed to catch up to him on the piano. The congregation stumbled into singing the old Yankee hymn. Some caught the hidden purpose and smiled, raising their voices loudly. By the song's end, a sense of foreboding gripped Al Wright. The words of the hymn hinted at horrible deeds to come.

Al was certain someday they would surely be, "trampling out the vintage where the grapes of wrath are stored."

***

Everyone frowned when Willard entered the next planning meeting. Debbie Hunter took his hand. The others hung back.

"Just to reassure you all, Willard did not betray us last night. No one showed at the Foodland." Bill wished he had the pastor's gift of talking.

"You suspected me? Who would even think it?" Willard's voice rose. "Stevie, the Quinns were my friends. Except for Debbie and the kids, no one is sadder. I would kill those bastards, if they weren't so strong."

"Willard, we had to be sure." Bill put an arm over his shoulders. "It's too dangerous not to be sure." Bill turned to the group. "Willard told me he helped arrest Warren to make sure the goons didn't rough him up."

"What's the plan?" Willard asked, burying his resentment. "I've been out of the loop."

There were six families to move with Stevie Hunter's widow and kids coming, making the transportation problem worse. Sharon Shadly's old mini-van would tow an enclosed trailer from a bankrupt contractor. Willard's pickup would tow a double horse trailer. Stevie left an SUV when he died. It would pull a medium-sized house trailer. Finally, they had the wheelchair bus, enough vehicles to take the people, but not adequate supplies. The group agonized over this.

"Smith has a pit and service yard just north of here, on our way," Willard said.

"Yeah, so," Matt retorted. "We all know that."

"The pit only has one security guard at night," Willard ignored Matt's shortness. "He leaves his diesel three-tonne box truck there and fuel. If we could get extra stuff that far, and take the truck, we would have room."

"Good idea!" Bill responded. "We can chain a hay wagon to the bus, fill all extra space here and offload some of it to the truck. The roads are smooth. Even overloaded, we could get to the pit."

"Are you sure it's still there and there's only one guard?"

"Smith's a braggart and a loose talker. He thinks he has no opposition now that he has locked Warren up. He told one of his sons, in front of me, they only needed one guard up there. They needed the other men for more serious work. I don't know what that meant."

"Okay, let's do it." Bill said. "We go in three nights. Smith's remark about serious work meant he has something bad in mind."

It took time to decide what people should bring. Photographs and family heirloom items for sure and computers and records seemed to be valuable. Bill and Jeff's report suggested Huron had electricity. They needed three months' food for each person, adding several tonnes to the vehicles. Sharon, Debbie and Jean solved that problem. The high school held almost all the food except the perishables in the Foodland chiller.

Bill Shadly and Al Wright joined Shelly and her mom. The women sat quietly with Shelly taking notes.

"You should come with us." Bill said.

"I don't want to leave," the mother replied. "I've lived here all my life. Our family were pioneers. I'll stay."

"It'll be dangerous." Al addressed Shelly. "Angel's people are not kind or peaceful. They see someone in a chair as a burden and expendable."

Al hated to be blunt, but time was short. "Through history people like Angel and Smith disposed of anyone they saw as worthless."

Shelly sat in her wheelchair, brooding, her face full of a struggle.

"I'll stay with mom. She's my life and always here for me, especially in those years I felt useless and stupid in this chair. I won't leave her now."

Shelly's mom spoke, "Dear, go. I'll be okay on my own."

"No, Mom," the girl embraced her lifelong hero and companion. Her smile hid the tears in her eyes. "You have always been here for me. I love you too much to leave." Shelly sobbed. "Mom, there were many times, especially in high school, when I thought if my life ended the world would see no loss. I cried myself to sleep many nights once I realized I would never run, never walk in the forest, never ski or skate, never make love," Her voice cracked. "But every time I woke up to your smile and your love; each day started new. I always felt good in the mornings because of you, Mom. You brought me to the place where those feelings vanished, and I knew my life could be useful and rich. These two years here in the school have, for me, been the best."

"Even if we both die soon, I want you to know we have had a wonderful life because of you." Shelly smiled at her Mom through teary eyes. "We'll stay together."

Everyone's eyes watered, wondering if they could measure up to this young woman's love and bravery.

She turned to Al. "Pastor, can you help us? I'm scared and they will destroy the EAC. Can you find us a place to be safe and useful?"

Al Wright patted the young woman's hand. "I'll try my best my dear. You can move to the manse and live with us. There will be lots to do. My congregation needs spiritual and physical help. You would be a Godsend."

Fear threatened the reverend, fear for his parishioners, for himself and Esther. More than anything, he wanted to take this chance to reach safety, but he felt his call to serve. Taking a significant risk, Reverend DeSantos, vital in founding the EAC would stay. The two reverends worked well together, and he would ease Al Wright's burden.

Each family headed home to gather the items essential for an unknown future. Families wandered out spaced apart by a few minutes, chatting as if going home after work.

In the late evening shadows, a lone figure watched the people wandering down the street. They reported the movements, but these did not seem out of the ordinary. The hard-working EAC kept irregular hours.

The six families hardly slept for two days making many trips to the high school carrying essentials. The daytime surveillance was sporadic, with a lone watcher passing down the street from time to time. Working around the annoyance had been easy. Smith believed conspirators would only be active at night. Everyone hoped Roger thought the leaders would fight back instead of fleeing, and he would look for the wrong signs.

Bill, Sharon and the kids sat down for supper, the night before the scheduled departure, thinking this would be their last ordinary family meal for some time. It would certainly be the last time the family would eat in their Weyburne house. Two knocks, a pause, and a third knock on the back door announced Jean's arrival. Sharon thought she had finished packing up the seed collection.

"I just had to tell you," Jean began. "The television is reporting there's a group in Toronto calling itself 'The People's Liberation Movement'. It has taken absolute control and is ruling by decree."

"Who's in charge?" Bill wondered if it mattered.

"Some guy who was a cabinet minister in the old government. The rest are strangers." Jean ate. "It's more interesting. The military has taken over the federal government. Some general from the base up the river at Bidway is in charge. The Governor-General made a statement, what an idiot. We have a military dictatorship."

"When did this happen?" Sharon asked.

"The night Smith took over the town. Do you think it was part of the takeover?"

"We'll know soon enough." Bill cleared the dishes. "Let's hope they aren't strong enough to get far."

"I think they'll cause a lot of trouble before they're done. People rushed to join Angel." Sharon poured the tea. "It's good we're moving. Maybe we can avoid the worst."

***

Bill walked through the front doors of Maud's Café, trying to appear nonchalant but wanted to achieve two things. They would depart tonight. He wanted to see if Smith's forces were in town in any numbers. The Xpress was due to pass through, going north. Bill wanted to chat with the men to hear the news from the south. He wanted to make sure that the

Xpress would spend the night in Owen Sound. He did not want the refugee caravan running into them, fearing they might accidentally reveal the refugees destination.

"Coffee please, Maud." Bill watched the proprietor from his favourite table in the empty room. It surprised him to see Maud in the morning.

"Coming right up, Bill," Maud's serious look brightened for an instant when she saw Bill. She quickly frowned. "You haven't been lately. How's everything going?"

She always questions thought Bill.

"Jeff and I went hiking for a couple of days," *The best lie is as close to the truth as you could make it,* "out west, looking for turkey and deer, It was a father and son thing."

"That's nice." Maud set the mug and cream in front of Bill. She thought of her daughter Mandy, missing in the city, and how nice it would be to have a few days with her.

"You're lucky." Her eyes filled with tears, and she caught her breath. She had hoped Roger would help locate Mandy, but he had brushed her request aside, calling her a "stupid woman", and would not bother his powerful friends with silliness.

"I thought Jani did the mornings." Bill said.

"Yes, usually, but lately she's been tired and upset. I let her take the mornings off the past two days. She's having big trouble at home. Her father's a real Smithy."

Bill stared at Maud. She had turned Smith's name into a curse. Bill and Bob from the Xpress arrived and made their way to Bill's table. Maud went to make their usual egg and chops breakfast.

"What's the news?" Shadly asked.

"Lots of shenanigans down south," the newcomers eased into their chairs. "There's fighting around Toronto. The folks up here blockaded the highway at the big hill in Caledon. Plenty of guns, and tough guys there, so they say. The train has more guards and machine guns on it. Someone shot at it last time up. They say there are lots of groups fighting, but the government has thousands of fighters. It looks like they'll win, eventually." Their breakfast arrived.

"The folks up here," Bob added between bites, "have a line all around the hills and are shooting at anyone trying to come up from the city." He wiped egg from his red beard. "Folks say they's in with the government."

It encouraged Bill that the fighting to the south had Angel's attention. Maybe that was the "more important things to do" that Smith mentioned.

This might make their move easier. Bill stayed longer than planned, chatting with the Xpress boys and Maud, who had sat with her cup of tea.

Bill discovered the X-press would stay two nights up north. They worried their supply of goods via the train might stop and wanted to source merchandise reaching Owen Sound by boat.

Bill hurried home, eager to bring his reassuring news to the others. He did not hear the hoof beats of Mennonite horses arriving in town.

Chapter Twenty-Five

David Koch guided his team of matched light horses along the main street accompanied by his wife and a younger child, unaware of Angel's coup. He wanted to talk to Al Wright before going to the school. David left the rig with his wife and headed into the town hall. Several men lounged about the street, but he paid little attention to them. The town was a safe place. Only the police office was open. Willard Dick sat at the desk.

"Morning, Willard. I wanted to see Mr Wright."

"Gone," Willard responded despondently, "thrown out by the Smith crowd. You don't want to deal with them."

Willard filled Koch in on the changes. It did not surprise David, considering the conversation he had with Bill Shadly on his previous visit. His community had changed how they dealt with outsiders and now traded only at roadblocks. Towns and cities were chaotic and dangerous.

David did not mention his earlier discussion with Bill Shadly. He did not know how Willard fit in and wanted to hear Bill's decision.

Loud screaming came from the street. Willard and David rushed outside to a chaotic scene Willard thought looked like an old, wild-west movie. A man dragged Dave's wife to the ground. Several others grabbed food from the wagon and scurried away. The horses stomped and snorted, straining against their tie-down at the unsettling commotion out of their sight. A pickup truck had parked behind the wagon.

"Gimme a kiss, beautiful," the man, a goon from the hills, tried to force his lips onto Koch's wife while she struggled and screamed. Willard strode across the street and grabbed the attacker's shoulder.

"Better stop it, son," Willard's command came from his police days, "and get back into the truck."

The man released Mrs Koch and spun around on Willard, throwing a hard-right fist. The constable had retired years ago, but his training kicked in as he dodged the fist, grabbed the man's arm, and pulled, making sure the thug went down hard enough to take the wind out of him.

The man lay moaning in a foetal position, unable to catch his breath. Willard guessed Angel paid cut rate for these untrained, undisciplined thugs. The others backed off, hurling expletives. Willard wished for a sex life as interesting as these louts implied. David Koch helped his wife onto the wagon. She hugged their distraught little girl. As David climbed up, Willard looked in the back at the few remaining goods.

"Go up to the school and see Shadly," Willard fought to control his emotions, longing for the old days when they might take this punk into the back and straighten him out. "Tell Bill to load the wagon as heavy as you can take and I'll explain later."

As Koch started the team away, another small truck pulled in. Roger Smith and one of his sons strode over to Willard.

"What the hell's going on here, Dick?" Smith used Willard's name as a curse. "Who hurt my man?"

"These punks were out of line, Smith, bothering the Mennonite family, assaulting the woman and stealing." Willard stood firm in front of the belligerent larger man.

"These boys work for me, and you got no right to touch them." Roger shouted. Willard did not know if Smith hated him or the wimps. It did not look good that one went down so easily at the hand of a middle-aged, ex-cop retired on disability.

"I'm the constable here, and they've broken the law. I'm charging them." Willard looked into Smith's eyes.

"I can fix that quick," spittle flew from Smith's mouth. "You're fired!" He stepped towards Willard. "Get your stuff and get out! I run this place." He gave Willard a shove. "Harry," Smith turned towards his son, "you're the new cop, get into that office and watch that Dunne jerk."

Smith's decisive actions bewildered Willard, but the mention of Warren made him start. He would not fight Smith. The goons outnumbered him and now had leadership. This would upset the plans for tonight. He went into the office, grabbed his stuff and explained it to Warren.

"Someone will see you later," he said to Dunne.

"Don't count on it, buddy," the Smith boy said. "You ain't going to get any perks now."

Willard headed home. His hands shook as the tension overwhelmed him. His mind seethed in mix of anger, frustration and worry. In his younger days, he could put Smith into a cell, even without backup.

Willard chatted with a friend on the street, pausing to calm his jagged nerves. As they talked, he turned and glimpsed a lone figure, a layabout whom Smith paid in booze and a few dollars to do odd jobs, standing a block away, staring at them. Willard had often thrown the man into the cell to sober him up. Willard's anger turned to action.

Willard headed home, but purposely turned one street too soon and tied his shoe. The watcher clumsily rounded the corner before realizing Willard had stopped. Retreating a few steps, the man hid behind a tree. Willard circled the block at a fast pace. The drunkard tried to keep up, but his dissipated body suffered. The follower gasped for breath, watching Willard's front door. Willard went out through his back gate and down the lane, crossing Warren Dunne's unfenced yard, hopping the fence and into Shadly's house, unannounced.

"Willard, what is up? Who is watching Warren?"

"Smith just fired me." Willard's voice was matter-of-fact. He focused on the future. "They tried to rob and molest the Kochs. I intervened and decked one of Smith's punks. Smith didn't like it. His oldest kid is now the constable. David went up to the school. Did you see him?"

"Nope, I was just heading out."

"They tailed me. I left the moron out front of my place."

"There's a goof down the street here, watching. The watchers change every four hours, but don't have any radios. I guess they figure we are not a threat. Do you think they have any idea what we are up to?"

"Nope," Willard was sure, "we're lucky they are stupid."

"I think it's arrogance, and distraction. I had a chat with the Xpress boys down at the café. They said things are violent and dangerous south of here. It looks as if the hill folks are more concerned about that threat than with us. That's good news."

"Warren is still inside, and Smith's watching him." Willard worried.

"We have to spring Warren. Go out the back and to the school. I'll walk out as if nothing has happened. Two eyes out there won't be suspicious."

By late afternoon, the group at the school had loaded all the vehicles but had to wait for nightfall to leave town.

Since the watchers changed at seven and 11 o'clock, they would capture and tie up the late one. Lingering twilight would give them an hour to get moving. Timing would be critical.

"Hey, I think I have some good news." Jeff had returned from downtown. "Do you remember Tommy? I worked with him up in the hills. I just ran into him and his girlfriend, heading west out 89. They had backpacks and were in a rush. Tommy told me Angel sent all their men south of Orangeville. Smith drafted Tommy and that they would give him a gun and 50 dollars a day, but he had to go." Jeff caught his breath. "Anyway, Tommy said okay, but he had to go home first and tell his mom. He got Kelly; they are going as far west as they can get. I told him to get to the valley, but nothing more."

"I don't know why they sent the guys south," Jeff said. "I found Jani crying at the café. Her dad and brother got on one of the busses."

"This is good news." Willard smiled despite the circumstances. "Smith left his son Harry, the real drunk, as constable. Maybe he's keeping him out of harm's way or at least from screwing up down there. There won't be many of Smith's men around, mostly the drunks and bums."

At sunset, Bill called the families together.

"No matter what happens, when you get to Kimberly only wait four days for us." He looked at Sharon. "If we don't show up, go plant the crops; we'll find you. We're heading to get the watcher at the pit and then Warren. All of you… be safe." Bill did not think the four men would be in much danger.

An hour after the sun disappeared, Bill, Matt, Willard, and Jim headed out. Three circled behind observer while Bill walked openly to his house, attracting the watcher's attention. The man soon lay on the ground bound and gagged, swearing through his duct-taped mouth. They dumped him into a vacant house.

The four men walked up the rail line and the concession road to the darkness of Smith's gravel pit. The guard sat in the scale house, lights on and drunk. They tied him before he knew what had happened. The bound man sat sullenly in the corner, asking for booze. He was not front line material.

They planned to catch the Smith boy off guard and release Warren about one in the morning. The men cleaned and fuelled the three-tonne truck. Jim stayed to watch the prisoner and wait for the convoy. The three friends headed back to town, going south so that they would approach from the west. No one would expect them from that direction.

***

After the four men had left, the rest of the group hooked up trailers and the hay wagon. Sharon lay beneath the rear of the bus fastening the chain holding the hay wagon to the rear axle. A pair of feet appeared near her face. She tensed up. Al Wright's calm voice reassured her. She got out with only a slight bump to her head.

"Ouch!" she exclaimed, "I nearly used some of your professional vocabulary, Al."

"My dear, I confess using those words when in pain." They laughed. "We wanted to say goodbye, for now," Al looked at her thoughtfully, "and we have a gift and responsibility for you." He seemed so serious that Sharon laughed.

"Lighten up, Al. It can't be that bad. We'll sure miss you."

"Mom, can I go home and get some things. I thought we were going back to the house," Brandi interrupted.

"No, it's too late and too dangerous. We're behind time now." Nothing could be worth the risk.

"Mom, it's a sketchbook. It has lots of stuff in it."

"No, Brandi, you can't." Sharon knew the books were significant, but they had no time.

"Mom, I have to," Brandi sobbed.

"No, that's final! You're more valuable than the sketches. No!"

Brandi walked away, sobbing. Sharon turned back to Al.

"I have something for you to take, keep safe and use," Al picked up a large suitcase, "with no strings attached, trusting you will use it wisely."

"You got me there, Al. What are you talking about?"

"Oh, sorry," Al smiled and opened the case. "We have this money for you. It's 25,000 dollars here." Sharon was stunned and realized money might be useful, but it meant a danger and a problem for them that night.

"Al, that would be great, and we would use it for everyone for sure. I won't ask where it came from." Sharon knew Wright had kept the Centreville levy from Roger Smith. "We can't hide it. They will search us up the road."

"We thought you might run into some bandits. Esther has the solution," Al grinned. Sharon saw a joke coming. "You're going to be pregnant."

"Hey Al, I hardly know you."

Esther took Sharon, the closed case and a strange contraption that looked like a cross between a bra and a girdle into one of the old classrooms. When they returned, Sharon sported a tummy that said, "Very pregnant", covered by a maternity top with matching stretch pants.

"What are we going to name my little brother, Mom?" Jeff had heard what was going on. "You never looked that good with Brandi in you."

"You brat wait until your father gets home!" Sharon backed up her words with a punch to Jeff's shoulder. The tension needed relief. Al and Esther hugged everyone and wished good luck, and God bless.

"Al," Sharon gave the pastor another big hug, "I think you had better get all the non-whites out of town. Angel and his bunch are racist."

Al frowned, "It's too late for a few. They've been working for Smith. He drafted them into the fighting force and they went south. I'll try to convince the others to leave. Should they go to the valley?"

"Telling them that might betray us," Sharon thought. "Suggest they go north to the bay or to Mount Forest. Sharon had more on her mind."

"Al, get Shelly to destroy the records that have peoples' names on them. It doesn't matter about the names of those of us leaving, but it might put many in danger." She paused. "Al, you can't hide your involvement, be careful." She then swung into action.

"Let's go," said Sharon, "Where are Jeff and Brandi?"

"I'm here, Mom, but I don't see baby sister."

"I saw her head out around the corner of the building." Jean said.

"Damn it! She went home anyway. I have to get her."

"I'll come." Jean grabbed a heavy flashlight. Sharon carried the .22 rifle.

Brandi shut the front door of the Shadly house, wanting to get back before her mom missed her.

"What are you doing here little girl?" The voice came from the darkness behind Brandi. A hand covered her mouth, pulling her roughly back against a warm, sweaty body. "Bet you were looking for some fun, eh? All you little girls are so sexy and horny."

A set of rough lips replaced the hand on her mouth. Unshaven stubble scratched. The lips tasted of fresh whisky. Brandi squirmed and tried to fight dropping her book, but one of the attacker's arms wrapped around her pinning her arms to her sides. Another hand pawed at her breast. She tried to knee the attacker in the crotch, but he blocked her leg with his.

"I love it when they fight." The voice scared Brandi. A bright flash of light startled her and then a loud thump close to her ear. The attacker went limp and fell to the ground, visible in a circle of light.

"Are you ok, Brandi?" her mom's comforting voice calmed her.

"I... I... think so, Mom."

"Take that, you bastard!" Jean's voice accompanied the sound of the heavy flashlight hitting the man's body. The blows were hard and rapid. Light flashed into the trees and back to the ground as the blows fell. "Take that you monster, you slob. Take that, Georgie."

Jean shouted and sobbed as she repeatedly beat and kicked the attacker with vicious blows that never missed. In the intermittent light, Sharon could see his bloody face and wrapped her arms around Jean.

"Stop it, Jean! Calm down, sweetie. Brandi's ok." The violence from the usually quiet Jean mystified Sharon, especially since her well-placed blow with the rifle butt had levelled the man, perhaps killed him.

"They're all monsters. They all need to pay." Jean screamed hatred. "Georgie deserves it."

"I think his name is Harry," Sharon knew the man. "He isn't George."

Jean sobbed in Sharon's arms, but soon she calmed enough to walk back to the school. Brandi gathered her book. They left the unconscious would-be rapist oozing blood onto the front lawn.

"I'm sorry, Mom. It caused it." Brandi sobbed, both in contrition and in reaction to the attack.

Sharon said nothing. Brandi had suffered enough, and Jean needed comforting. Later, Jean told Sharon her Uncle George had sexually molested her when she was 15. Seeing the man attacking Brandi's released suppressed memories and hatred.

The episode solved a puzzle for Sharon. Before Brandi's assault, Sharon could not understand how Jean had let her worthless ex-husband James run her life; she now understood.

The convoy rolled out of the school parking lot, down the side street and turned north up the highway with everyone nervous and alert. They felt hope and sadness in hard choice of leaving friends and memories, and all carried shadows in their hearts. Sharon looked at the rear-view mirror and whispered, "God be with you, Al Wright."

She focused on the road ahead, and her thoughts turned to Bill and the dangerous work he had to do that night.

Chapter Twenty-Six

Bill, Matt and Willard crept cautiously along the main street of Weyburne. These days, few used it and no one at night. David Koch's wagon was about the only out-of-town traffic that ever used the street.

"Damn it! The café light's on!" Willard shrank deep into the shadows.

"Let's check it out. They can see the jail." They eased up to the café and only saw Maud.

"We have to neutralize her," Willard whispered. "She'll talk for sure."

"I don't want to hurt her." Maud's allegiance confused Bill.

The trio walked into the place and startled Maud.

"What do you want?" She stammered.

"You're open late," Matt snarled.

"I couldn't sleep. What are you doing up?"

"You're Roger Smith's plaything. We don't like you spying on us." Matt's accusation struck home.

"I know. You have come for Warren." Maud sobbed. "Roger said you would come, and I was to keep watch." Her words struggled through her tears. "I won't call him. They left tonight, anyway. He forced me to do everything. First, he tricked me about the phone and then threatened me. I hate him." The three men could not decide if she said the truth or a lie.

"How can we trust you?" Bill asked.

"I don't blame you and feel terrible. I think I caused Stevie's murder, but I didn't know that would happen. Most of the information I gave to Roger was not a secret. I can only promise I won't tell. He forced himself on me over and over. I hate him!" She collapsed, sobbing.

They could not take her at her word. Putting trust in the woman could mean disaster. The practical Willard found the way out. It would not matter if she lied.

"If you don't call Smith about us, he'll know you betrayed him. It would go bad for you. He isn't afraid to kill." Maud looked terrified.

"We will tie you up and gag you to make it look real. If you're lying, it will keep you from stabbing us in the back."

"I'm not lying," Maud sobbed, "but yes, tie me up and make it good."

"It will hurt." Bill said. "We have no choice."

"Hurry," Maud hopped they believed her. "The Smith boy is drunk, maybe sleeping, but he could wake up and think he needs coffee, or me. One thing I can tell you, Roger recruited many fighters for Angel and issued guns. Most of them left today for somewhere."

It sickened Bill to think repulsive Smith would force the woman to have sex with his sons. The world had become ugly. The news about the militia force confirmed Angel's forces focused on the south and not Weyburne.

They bound Maud with cord and taped her mouth. For comfort, they lay her on a rug and give her a sack of flour as a pillow. Roger Smith would expect that from people he considered weak. Bill knelt near the trussed-up woman and told her that if she ever ran, to head north to the bay. He made sure she did not know about the roadblocks and militia in case she lied. Matt tore the phone from the counter, and the trio headed to the jail.

Smith had locked the door. Smashing their way in would alert the boy who had a phone and a gun. In the confusion of Willard's firing, he had kept his office keys. The rescue squad snuck inside.

The Smith boy lounged in the Chief's chair, stinking of whisky and snoring. Bill bumped into a chair and a file tray crashed to the floor. Smith startled and fumbled for something under his desk. Willard took two quick steps and struck Smith hard on the side of the head with his service revolver. The boy thudded to the floor and twitched, eyes open.

"Did you kill him?" Matt gasped. He had seen the Quinns and Stevie's bodies but had never seen an actual killing.

"I hope not," Willard said, "but he moved. I hit him too far forward." He knelt down to find a pulse and light breathing. "He might pull through, too late to worry." Willard pulled a Glock from under, the desk.

"He would have killed us." The pistol went into Willard's belt, and he retrieved the keys.

"Got any food?" Warren asked. "He didn't feed me."

Bill ran to Maud's Café. They dragged Smith's body into the cell. Matt threw in the telephone from the café, took the truck key from Smith's jacket and locked the door. Everyone squeezed into the cab with Matt behind the wheel.

"Do we follow the others?" The engine burst into life.

"No," said Warren, "I would love the ride, but they might have GPS tracking on the truck. We need to dump it somewhere to take them in the wrong direction."

"They think we'll head to join the Mennonites," said Bill, "Let's go that way for a bit."

Warren munched a cold lamb chop and some whole wheat bread as the truck headed south. They sped west at the first side road. About eight kilometres out of town, the road ran through a grove of maple trees. They parked the truck tight against an abandoned house, out of sight from the road, and the men walked west. Matt threw the truck keys into an abandoned pasture.

In the cool, calm night, stars carpeted the clear sky. They reached the bridge where the river passed under the old highway as the eastern sky, promised sunrise. In a few hours, Smith would discover the escape and there would be pandemonium in Weyburne. They intended to walk up the streambed northwards then cut overland through the swamps towards Highway 10 and the Maxwell Road. The men found the going too hard in the muddy riverbed and cold water. They climbed the bank where a grove of willows provided a secluded spot for resting during the day. The river water tasted of decaying vegetation but slaked their thirsts. Leftovers of the food from the café took the edge off their hunger. The exhausted men slept all day in the warming sun, with no sign of pursuit.

"I wonder how everyone made out last night." Warren moved closer to Bill. He raised himself on an elbow, surveying the languid water.

"I hope they did okay. We didn't hear any gunfire. I think that the convoy got away." Bill sounded confident, but he worried. "They should have gone long before we sprang you out."

"What are we going to find in Kimberly?" Willard asked. "How will things go for us? How will we make it work?" Despite Bill and Jeff's positive report, there had been very little planning past the escape.

Bill frowned. "Chester Amik told me they had some adjacent properties for us. One has a big house and we can live in it for the first year. We'll have to plant and get farming this summer."

"A peaceful farm life sounds good to me." Matt said.

"It won't be so easy," Willard stretched. "We'll soon have to deal with these goons down here. They'll want to take that territory too. It scares me how bad things are in Toronto. I have a feeling it will come to shooting."

"I'm a man of peace," Warren looked thoughtful, "but I agree with Willard. They are thieves and murderers, and they won't stop until someone stops them. History has a way of reworking old problems."

"I wouldn't count on peace lasting. Angel and the PLM will eventually want to conquer all of Ontario." Warren frowned. "We carry our pasts like shadows, and the dictators are the biggest shadow. We must defeat them or we will have nothing."

"These Huron folks aren't shy about using force," Bill added.

"Are they just Angel reworked?" Warren worried.

"Walt was at the last service in the church when Angel had made his grand entrance," Bill continued. "He told me Angel seemed to act like Caesar, all full of himself. As far as I could tell, Amik, the leader in Huron, didn't seem like that. Walt's sister is like him, smart and helpful. I think we'll be okay. They are more democratic than us and better organized."

The men whiled away the rest of the daylight chatting about farming and gardening and fascinated Warren. These modern consumers had learned much in two years.

***

Darkness overcame the lingering late-spring dusk. The four men felt their way along a back road, navigating in the dark. They wanted to avoid houses, but they took a wrong turn and ended up approaching Riverton.

"Hold it there." The voice from the dark menaced. "Who are you?"

"We're looking for a few head of cattle got away from us." Willard sounded nonchalant. He wished he could see the man. From the whispers, he guessed there might be three men, shrouded in darkness, thirty meters up ahead to the left.

"That's a crock of shit. No one's got cattle down there."

"We were walking 'em them back to Weyburne from the Mennonites." Willard continued to try the bluff but slipped the Glock to Matt. Two of them armed would be better.

"We heard there were some killers run away from Weyburne. There's a big piece of change for them dead or alive. I bet it's you."

It seemed the Smith kid had died.

"I'll slide up the side of the road towards these guys," Matt whispered. "When you hear my voice, take off, fast and keep going and don't wait for me; I know how to get to Maxwell. I'll be fine."

Matt stepped to the left and disappeared into the darkness. Someone opened a farmhouse door. The glow silhouetted three men.

"Who are you?" Matt called from halfway towards the shadowy forms. The fugitives bolted into the night. Shots rang out behind them. The sound was from a heavy hunting rifle and a lighter gun, perhaps a .22. The distinctive sound of bullets flying past filled their ears. It had been close. Three quick shots from the Glock answered the hostile gunshots. A rifle discharged accompanied by the simultaneous sound of the Glock, then painful screams, then silence.

The fleeing men heard nothing but their own feet and tortured breathing. The trio tumbled through a snake-rail fence and collapsed on the other side. They heard no pursuit. The dog's bark broke the silence. Another shot rang out, followed by squealing from the dog, then silence. They ran, grieving Matt and reached the safety of trees and peered into the dark.

"We should go get him," Warren suggested and then moaned in pain.

"How can we do that?" Willard evaluated the odds. "Either he's okay and will catch up, or he's already dead. Nothing we can do in either case. I would guess he fired at their silhouettes… three people and three shots. Did you get hit, Warren?"

"That last shot sounded like his pistol." Willard's cold assessment of the facts upset Bill. "Matt said to keep going, so let's do it."

"I twisted my ankle," Warren gasped in pain. "I don't think I can run. You men get going."

"We aren't leaving you, Warren." Bill found his friend in the darkness. "Here, put your arm around my shoulders and we'll head to Highway 10."

The trio struggled through a thick swamp. Tree limbs snatched at them from the darkness. They wished for the ease of a roadway, but that might be dangerous. They half-carried Warren through the tangles and their heavy hearts increased the burden.

Chapter Twenty-Seven

The diesel engines alerted the barrier guards long before the vehicles came in sight. A motorcycle raced to Maxwell for reinforcements. Unexpected traffic on the road worried them. The Xpress had passed through, northbound, the day before. No one knew when the group coming from Weyburne would arrive or which route they would take, and they might be on foot. Knowing of fierce fighting south put everyone on edge.

The strengthening daylight revealed the road beyond the barrier, and a strange convoy materialized out of the morning mist. They saw several light trucks, one pulling a house trailer, a minivan towing a trailer, a three-tonne truck, and the rear brought up by a yellow school bus pulling a hay wagon. The guards laughed but held rifles ready. In a world gone crazy, nothing appeared to be as crazy as this column of misfit vehicles.

"Keep your safeties on," the barrier commander ordered. "These have to be the Weyburne refugees."

Sharon's van stopped a few meters from the barrier. She got out, hands outstretched, palms up and then held up her right hand, signalling those behind her to stay put.

"I'm Sharon Shadly. I have a letter of passage from Chester Amik." Her voice wavered, more from the fatigue of being awake for two days than fear of the armed guards.

A lone figure stepped from behind one of the rock-filled crib walls that formed the first part of a zigzag passage. The tall, middle-aged man wore hunting camouflage, a military forage cap, and a pistol on his hip.

"Please let me see it, Sharon." His sounded businesslike but friendly. Sharon pulled an envelope from a shoulder bag. He read the note.

"I'm Robert," he said, "Do you have guns with you?"

"Everyone has a rifle or shotgun or both," Sharon replied.

Robert frowned and glanced around to make sure his force stood ready. He paused as if trying to come to some decision. He had not expected to meet a well-armed group. The protocols did not cover this problem.

"Would you all please get out of your vehicles," he finally said, "and lay all of your weapons on the road?"

Sharon passed on the instruction. The armed guards watched carefully as thirty firearms appeared.

"That's impressive," Robert admitted. "I'm glad I'm not a bandit pulling a hold-up."

"There's one other person here. He's tied up in the truck." Sharon did not want these new friends to find any surprises.

"You're a strange lot. What's the story? Did you kidnap someone?"

Robert smiled, wondering at the surprises that this group gave him. Not the least, the leader was a woman eight months pregnant.

"He was a last-minute addition," Sharon replied. "We picked him up guarding the three-tonne truck we stole. He begged to come. The truck's owner would kill him."

Guards retrieved Smith's man, hung over and smelling of stale booze.

"Oh, Mom," Jeff's voice rang out from behind Sharon, "We have one extra passenger on the bus."

"WHAT?" Sharon exclaimed. "Who's that?"

"Hi, Mrs Shadly," said Jani's timid voice as she stepped from the vehicle. "Jeff helped me sneak on."

"Is there anyone else?" Robert sounded exasperated.

"I certainly hope not," Sharon replied, and turning shouted out, "IS ANYONE ELSE ON HERE I DON'T KNOW ABOUT?"

No other stowaways materialized.

They sat beside the road while guards inspected the convoy.

"Bring these folks water," Robert asked a couple of guards, "and Wolff, you get their names and ages."

He explained to Sharon; they kept a tight control on who came and went in their territory. The folks at headquarters would want to know. Robert did not explain they had only ever received a few individual refugees and never a large organized group such as the one Sharon Shadly led. He did not mention the tragic arrival of Brother Andrew.

Sharon, Jean and Debbie Hunter accompanied Robert on a detailed inspection of the vehicles. The three had been the load masters. Their well thought-out work shortened the wait. Robert told friends if he ever could go on a family trip, he wanted one of these women to pack the trunk. The refugees would be self-sufficient for several months.

"Everything's in order, but I can't let you take all these guns with you." Robert was apologetic. "Here's a list of them. Please write the owner's names beside each one. We will return them, but we want to know who has guns. If someone snaps, we want to know if it's safe to knock on a door to talk, or if we have to be more careful. In the event there's a defence call out, it's good to know who has a gun."

They matched names to each weapon. Sharon and Robert signed the list. He wrote her a receipt with the same details and signed it.

The process took over four hours. The sun hung high in the sky and the day hot. Everyone was tired, and the guards felt hungry, having missed their breakfast.

The vehicles eased through the narrow zigzag passage of the barrier with a deep trench cut at the mid-point and spanned by a timber bridge. Sharon could not see the timber support designed to be pulled out to drop the deck into the hole and make an impassable moat.

"All the best," Robert said to Sharon as they shook hands. "It is peaceful and secure, but hard work. Good luck with the baby. There's a good doctor in Meaford."

Sharon, felt guilty at the deception. The convoy disappeared towards Maxwell. Robert mused they had added good folks to the territory.

Good, he thought, *we need lots more labour.*

Robert had heard negative talk about letting new folks in, but too many had died or left. The territory was under-populated. His thoughts returned to his farm, counting the days until he could get back to the planting.

Sharon guided the small party northward and eventually Kimberly. With the stress of the past few weeks lifted, her fatigue threatened to overwhelm her. Thoughts of Bill and the others, still somewhere in hostile territory, filled her mind with grief and hope.

The convoy arrived in Kimberly with dramatic impact. The town did not have a large population, but most of the residents came out to greet the newcomers. The crowd seemed friendly, but some folks wondered when they would move on. The less friendly ones felt threatened by strangers. Newcomers might be a burden; however, this group would be self-sufficient for some time and place no strain on the valley's resources. The promise of new labour and more land in production was a big incentive to be welcoming. As a bonus, refugees would contribute to the security force, reducing the time each of the residents served.

Karen and Walt Lefevre's emotional reunion culminated in the whole town enjoying a big celebration in Karen's backyard. A hefty pig sizzled all afternoon on a spit over a bed of hot coals. Salads, the ever-present apple juice and cider, roast potatoes and many other delights appeared like magic. Karen told Sharon they loved any excuse for a party, even if it meant interrupting planting.

Musicians played everything from guitars to an indigenous drum from South America. The bug season had not fully arrived, and the crowd partied late into the gentle June night. Residents and newcomers mingled and chatted, flirted and joked. The refugees felt welcomed.

"We haven't had a family barbeque in years." Karen had dragged Walt over to sit with Sharon and the kids. "Thank you for bringing the big guy up safely. He always needed a good woman to lead him about."

Karen waved at Tina and smiled as her sister-in-law tried to keep the irrepressible Megan close to her side. Her niece and nephews brought Karen joy.

Sharon enjoyed the diversion despite the sadness of the missing men. She had miraculously become "not pregnant" between the barrier and Kimberly but dreaded the time she would meet Robert again and have to explain the ruse. The party took place on the second night after the group arrived, and the refugees squatted in front of an abandoned ski resort.

By the fourth day, hope turned to doubt and on the fifth day, despair. Jean mourned for Warren, and Sharon missed Bill. They exceeded the four days Bill requested, but everyone agreed to wait a week.

Chester Amik held a formal meeting in the Kimberley Town Hall. There were three adjacent farms available down the valley, suitable for livestock, with apple orchards, buildings and fields. Each place had a tragic story. There had been murder and suicide in two, and a family had starved to death in the other. The locals feared ghosts of the dead. None of the stories discouraged the refugees. They had seen it all in Weyburne.

During this meeting, Karen Lefevre spotted Brandi sitting to one side, madly sketching as people talked. Karen looked over Brandi's shoulder. The large piece of paper, bound into one of Brandi's books, filled with the scene of a seated crowd watching an imposing figure. Brandi's exact rendering of the intent faces and clear eyes of the audience impressed Karen. Brandi captured the confident, wise, and friendly look Chester Amik projected to everyone he met.

Karen realized Brandi was a genuine artist. At her young age, Brandi had control of her medium. The girl could use instruction in technique, but she had a keenly observant eye and precise hand. Karen stood beside Brandi for the rest of the meeting. When the formalities ended, she reached down to touch Brandi on her shoulder.

"That's a gorgeous piece of work, young lady." Karen sounded like the teacher she was. "You captured the evening and the people."

"Thank you," Brandi blushed. "I enjoy drawing. Maybe we will remember things better from the picture."

"Do you have more?" It intrigued the older woman. Brandi's words planted an idea in the teacher's mind.

"I have other books in the van." Brandi handed the half-filled art book to the woman. Karen leafed through, fascinated by each image and the notations accompanying the graphics. She paused several times, almost tearing up at the picture of the Hunter family in happiness and sorrow with the notation: "To my other Dad. Rest in Peace", scribbled in one corner. The second last image was of four figures hugging with the background half darkened and half lighted. Karen recognized the Shadly family. In the unfinished sketch, she could see the love in all the faces and a hint of grief in the self-portrait of this young girl. Karen quietly closed the book. She wrapped her arms around Brandi and squeezed tightly.

"Welcome to Beaver Valley," Karen whispered, "you will be safe here. I will make sure of that."

***

The sixth day dawned cloudy with the promise of rain. The newcomers had been planning to stay for the week, but now they were thinking they should get going. It was near the end of planting season. They would need to work hard to plant a crop.

Sharon and the kids, including Jani, had finished breakfast. They had bonded even closer during this week of waiting, and all felt the loss. It did not help their spirits to comfort Jean. She had no one to lean on. Warren had been the first genuine source of happiness and contentment in her life. Jean feared she had lost him and her tears flowed.

Sharon suffered from providing constant reassurance to her friend, her children and the other families. Despite her leading role in Centerville, the mantle of responsibility rested uneasily upon her. She had no one to comfort her. Sharon had trouble sleeping with her nights full of sad, waking dreams.

Sharon clutched a warm coffee mug and stared at the smouldering embers of their cooking fire. High in a tree, a crow called with a constant chirping of smaller birds down by the river. The kids had wandered off. In busier, happier times, she had enjoyed quiet time alone with her thoughts. Now, these weighed heavily and often no coherent thoughts came.

"Sharon is there any more coffee in that pot?" the voice was so familiar, "I am tired and thirsty."

Sharon whirled, dropping her cup and leaping into Bill's embrace, ignoring the other arrivals as she satisfied her need. Her whoops of joy stirred the entire camp. Everyone came running. Warren stood uneasily, leaning on a makeshift cane, as Jean ran from the next site. He held out his arms and hobbled to her when she skidded to an awkward stop in front of him. Their embrace was tender and quiet. Jeff and Brandi finally pried their father away from Sharon. The family hugged and cried together for a long time.

Jani stood silently apart from the throng. For the first time, she understood the decision she had made. The longing for such a feeling for herself, one that would never come from her own family, ate deep into her soul. Jani's tears mixed celebrating the safe arrival of the men with a lament at her loss. It would take all the love flowing from the Shadlys to fill her deep void. Jeff's hand extended and drew the woman he loved into the family.

Willard had no family to greet him, but Debbie Hunter and her children hugged and welcomed him. He knew how much they missed their father and husband. For the first time in a long time, Willard felt the loss of his own family in the acrimonious divorce years before. He wondered how his children and their mother were doing, but many years had passed since there had been any contact. The important issues then seemed petty now.

"Where's Matt?" Sharon asked Bill.

"Toughs near Riverton jumped us. Matt made a move at them to let us escape. There were shots fired. We don't know what happened. The last shot came from Matt's gun. We're hoping he escaped, but we don't know. We had to run to avoid the dogs." Bill could not hide his sadness.

"He told us to keep going and not wait for him. He said he knew how to get here. We can hope, but Smith had patrols out towards Dundalk. We hid in the bush for a night and spent another hiding in a farmhouse on the Second Line watching pickup trucks patrolling the highway. They gave up yesterday, and we came up through Maxwell. Warren's foot slowed us down."

It took the rest of the day to organize the group. Bill briefed Chester on everything happening in Weyburne. Chester seemed interested in how they could get more information to assess the threat. Bill suggested the Xpress boys were an excellent source of casual knowledge, and if they could communicate with Al Wright, they would get good information.

They headed down into the valley the following morning to an emotional farewell from the residents. The newcomers felt genuinely at home. It made the loss of their former lives bearable.

In the bright, warm day, Bill, Sharon, Jani, and Jeff rode together in the van. Brandi insisted on riding the hay wagon behind the school bus, sitting on top of the bags of grain. She wanted to see it all at once and the green valley spreading out around them. She made sketches with unique views of Old Baldy, the cliff high above the valley, farmsteads with wisps of smoke rising from chimneys and animals grazing in the fields.

One sketch depicted the little village of Kimberly, down the road, with the figure of a woman standing at an open gate, looking out from the paper, gazing after them.

Feeling content for the first time in many months, Brandi took out her pen and wrote in a new journal:

Life begins anew. We know not where it leads, but for now, the way is smooth, and the sky is bright.

The story continues in
**Under Shadows,
After the Last Day, Book Two**
(sample below)

Chapter One

Life begins anew. We know not where it leads, but for now, the way is smooth, and the sky is bright. The sun shines upon the valley, warming me as I sit in the open on top of the bags of seed. I am riding a hay wagon, rattling along behind a rusting yellow school bus, feeling content. I miss my Papa, Nan and Gran, hoping they are safe, and they will come this way with the rest of the family.

Our shadows, drawn sharply by the strong morning sun are chasing us, sliding over the long dew covered roadside grass. The road is running away behind me, away from my old life... our old life. What I wanted three years ago is gone. Being rich and famous has drifted out of my dreams. Now, being with my family, safe and fed are the only important things.

The view forward around the bus is blocked. It is right. We should not know the future, and I love the present rolling past me like the sides of this road, new and full of surprise and wonder. I know we must plan and struggle to survive. It is nature's way. Like tree seedlings, we start our journey, hoping and planning to reach the sky. We will struggle through the ice storms, fire, drought, and the shadows of the forest. The shadowy path will lead us to our final outcome.

My hopes, fears, dreams, desires and longings all ride high up here with me in the bright warming sun. I feel safe. I am near those I love, and I am happy.

From: "The First Days" (The Journals of Brandi Shadly Age 15, Vol. 3, p. 1)

The ride was not very long, that first morning. I remember a motorcycle passing us with Chester at the controls and Karen behind him. They waved as they passed, and before long, we slowed and then turned, with Karen and Chester guiding us, into a long, overgrown lane up towards the sun-drenched west slope of the valley. This was my first view of our future home.

From: "Conversations with Brandi Shadly" in the "Voices of the Founders" series by Erin Thomas, Mentor of Historical Ecology, Huron Ecology Institute (Kimberly Campus)

Author's note: "Voices of the Founders" series is available through re-enactment by the Truth Talker Players at the Southampton H.E.I. (Ojibwe) amphitheatre Saturday afternoons, May to October – ET

Sharon Shadly, washed in bright June sunshine, leaned against the wall where she was placing stone. It was heavy work, carefully selecting the right piece, lifting it into place, grooming the surface for a steady fit and tapping it against the angle guide. The pieces sat firmly in place, and the wall cambered inwards. Each stone sloped gently down so no rainwater would run back inside.

Almost a year had passed since they claimed this property. This was the first new building since they concentrated all the families on one farm.

Stone and timber were the best materials and did not require a factory or diesel oil, only needing human workers using simple tools and animal labour. The structure would last centuries.

The design was old and simple with two parallel dry stone courses forming a wall over two meters high. Each course of stone cambered in towards the other, beginning with a broad base and ending somewhat narrower at the top. Dirt, pounded between the two stone faces added draft proofing and strength. With Beaver Valley, the red clay from the escarpment shale provided superior filler material. They placed a course of longer header stones about every forty centimetres of height, tying the stones together. The wall was already shoulder-high. They would finish stonework within the month.

Jim Handley fashioned windows, doors and the roof with material salvaged from a house on an adjacent farm. This abandoned building, once grand and imposing, poorly constructed a decade before for a retired couple who died in despair, sat too far from the main farm operation, too close to the river in case of flooding and, with vaulted ceilings, too hard to heat.

The new structure would house three families, now living in old recreation vehicles, making room for newcomers. The compound would need the space. They expected immigrants soon, refugees from the Toronto area. The extra labour would be a help in working the farm.

Sharon removed her wide-brimmed hat and mopped her sweat-covered brow, carefully avoiding the red chaffing line. The crude straw hat took its toll on her skin. She expected some aloe plants soon and could treat the injury. Everyone suffered minor problems similar to hers.

She peered down the lane. Six figures approached. Bill was due to return from his two weeks of security service; however, he was not in this group. She could make out Warren and Willard walking with Karen Lefevre. Three were strangers.